MURDER
IN THE
MONTO

Published 2022 by Crimson
an imprint of Poolbeg Press Ltd.
123 Grange Hill, Baldoyle,
Dublin 13, Ireland
Email: poolbeg@poolbeg.com

A catalogue record for this book is available from the British Library.

ISBN 978178199-700-0

www.poolbeg.com

MURDER
IN THE
MONTO

TONY O'REILLY

POOLBEG
CRIMSON

ABOUT THE AUTHOR

Tony O'Reilly was born and raised in Dublin. He currently lives and works in Dalkey. *Murder in the Monto* is his debut novel. Tony based the main character on his grandfather who joined the British army to escape extreme poverty. Over the years he has been fascinated with 'The Monto', reputed to have been the biggest red-light district in Europe and the haunt of royalty.

ACKNOWLEDGEMENTS

The idea behind this book is based on the early years of Christopher Flinter, my grandfather. Christopher joined the British army, not out of idealism or enthusiasm for any cause, but simply as a way to escape the poverty of a Dublin tenement. However, my book is a work of fiction and my characters' involvement in events such as the sinking of the *Lusitania* is entirely fictional.

I would like to thank everybody in the Kate Nash Literary Agency for their help in bringing the book to fruition, and thank them especially for their mentoring programme. It was through the many Zoom meetings with their authors etc. that I learnt about the many stages of writing a book and bringing it to its conclusion.

My profound thanks also to my writing group, The Atrium, who read, critiqued and improved my scribbles — not forgetting Gaye Shortland, my editor, who gave it its final gloss.

A special shout-out to Justin Nash, my agent, who, fortunately for me, is an expert on all things World War I, and picked out my many errors relating to that dreadful conflict.

I would like to thank my aunts, the daughters of Christopher Flinter, and especially Neil Curran, my cousin, who pored over all of the old census records and army documents that gave me an insight into the background of my grandfather.

Last but not least, I would like to thank Bernie, my wife, who never complained when, as writers have to do, I locked myself away to write this book.

DEDICATION

I would like to dedicate this book to my grandfather,
Christopher Flinter, and to victims of all wars.

PROLOGUE

Skagway River Valley, Alaska
October 1889

It is the first snow of the year. The boy lies on his back and stares up at the snowflakes that tumble down from grey skies onto his face. He tries to count them at first, but when the number goes over twenty, he runs out of words and has to start all over again. The grass beneath his back is still soft and lush but within weeks all of the familiar rocks and shrubs that surround him will have disappeared under a thick blanket of snow. Gone too will be the sweet scent of heather and the tangy smell of tree sap. He holds out his berry-stained hand and watches as the delicate snowflakes melt into wet smears.

'*Booooooy!*'

The voice echoes around the hills, bouncing off the sheer granite cliff-face that rises above the trees, then fades into silence. The boy wonders if his father will give up and inspect the traps himself. But he shouts again, louder and angrier, the word stretching out into one long question: *Where the hell are you?*

The boy rolls over, gets to his feet and heads down the hillside towards home, wiping his hands on his trousers as he goes. In the distance their meagre holding, cut out of the forest by his father, seems tiny against the mountains behind. The log cabin is difficult to make out, dwarfed as it is on three sides by giant pine trees. To the front of the cabin is the remnants of their vegetable garden, sadly on its way back to nature after the hot summer they have just suffered. Smoke drifts up through the hole in the roof and he wonders if his father will ever get around to making a proper chimney.

As he gets nearer to the cabin the scarecrow-like figure standing in the garden turns towards him. His father is a tall, lean man with sloping shoulders and long arms that dangle at his sides. With the loss of their crop and the scarcity of game this year, he has become even thinner. Now his head looks too heavy for his body. He has a slight stoop and, when he walks any distance, he tends to take more rests. Next year, the boy thinks, I will be able to outrun him and he'll never catch me.

'Traps not goin' empty themselves, boy,' his father grunts, and turns towards the forest.

'Comin', Pa,' the boy says.

They follow the rushing stream that cuts its way through the trees in a series of small waterfalls until they come to the banks of a river. The boy's father wades into the icy water and struggles through the flow to their first pot. He reaches under the water and lifts up the hazelwood basket he calls a 'putcher', then, finding it empty, lowers it back in. The boy follows him as he makes his way downriver, examining each basket in turn. In the last basket he finds a young trout and throws it towards the bank, where the boy slaps its head off a rock and puts it into his bag. With a weary shake of his head, his father makes his way to the bank, then nods back in the direction of home.

They make their way back through the forest towards their cabin, checking each of the traps as they go. A tiny red squirrel struggles in one of them, its leg caught up in the wire loop set by his father. When it sees them coming its struggling increases and it begins to gnaw at its leg to get away. But the man gets to it first, wrings its neck and hands the still-warm body to the boy.

When they get back to the cabin all that's in the sack the boy throws on the table is the tiny trout and the squirrel.

His mother, a small, squat woman, is wrapped in a blanket and sitting beside the fire, waiting. She goes over, looks inside and shakes her head.

'Do your best, woman,' the man says and goes back outside to wash.

The meal that evening is the best they've had in days. As the woman sucks the brains from the head of the trout, the man and boy chew on the soft bones of the squirrel. Most of the vegetables in the garden outside are either shrivelled or too rotten to eat. The man had tried to hunt deer with a pointed stick, the way his wife showed him, but he was too weak for the chase and the boy too young. They don't talk any more about his decision in the spring to barter his rifle and ammunition for a wooden rocker box. The rocker box, he assured them at the time, would help in his search for gold in the river, but now it lay, abandoned, at the side of the cabin. Back then the crops were planted and were doing well and small game was plentiful. Now they face the coming winter on the edge of survival, their only hope of food his mother's tribe, the Chilkoot. But the man looks down on them and thinks of them as heathens or even worse.

Still hungry after the paltry meal, they sit around the rough wooden table in exhausted silence. The single candle casts their shadows flickering across the walls. The shutters are closed for the night. Outside the long-drawn-out cry of a wolf makes the boy move closer to his father. His father takes down the tattered Bible and begins to read aloud, his finger following the tiny writing. It's the story of David and Goliath again, one of the boy's favourites. His father's voice begins low, barely a murmur, but by the time he comes to the hacking off of the giant's head he is on his feet, making the gesture of David's sword-strike.

But his mother has not been listening and has gone over to the shutter, staring through the rifle-slit into the night. The man joins her.

'What is it?' he asks, staring out into the blackness.

'Wagon.'

Minutes pass before the man hears it himself, the sound of metal on rock as a wagon slowly makes its way towards their cabin. He blows out the candle and takes the small axe that hangs from the wall beside the door. The wagon stops outside and the only sound is the low grunting of some kind of animal. The boy's father lifts the latch on the shutter and pushes it open.

'*Who goes there?*' he shouts out into the darkness.

'*I am sent by Captain William Moore!*' a man's voice comes from the darkness. '*He has told me that you are the best man to see about getting to Bennett Lake!*'

The man's accent sounds strange to the boy's ears. The words go up and down in a funny way and some sound wrong, but he is excited to hear more about the man his father mocks. Billy Moore and his son Ben had bought some land at the mouth of the Skagway river in the hope that it would eventually grow into a great town one day, once the promised gold rush had started. The previous year his father had returned from a trek down the valley to investigate what they were up to, but he had pronounced them harmless fools.

'What's your name?' his father shouts into the darkness.

'*Anders Lindquist! My wife is Wilma and my daughter is Lilly!*'

'*Light up your lamp so's I can see you proper!*' his father shouts out.

The boy is beside himself with excitement. He goes over to the other window and pushes back the shutter to get a better look.

4

Outside stands Anders Lindquist, an oil lamp held high over his head. Behind him the boy can make out a covered wagon that looks higher than the roof of their house, pulled by four oxen. The oxen look tired and their coats glisten with lathery sweat. High up on the front seats are a woman with her arm around a young girl about his age.

His father opens the front door and steps out onto their porch.

'Those men did you no favours, friend,' the boy hears his father say, his voice sounding almost happy with the man's folly. 'Ye need mules to get up and over the pass, not that wagon.'

Anders looks back at his family and slowly lowers the lamp. The boy, although feeling sorry for them, feels a burst of pride in his father and some of his faith in him returns.

'But you can stay the night out there if ye like,' his father continues. 'There's water around the back and the wolves shouldn't trouble ye if ye keep a light goin'.'

Anders looks undecided about what to do, takes off his hat and scratches his head. The boy can't help staring at his hair which is pure white, the first white hair he has ever seen.

'I think it is better we eat first, then sleep, then talk some more in the morning,' he says, turning to his wife, who tightens her grip on her daughter.

'Ain't got much food, I'm afraid,' his father says.

'That is not a problem — we have brought a good many provisions. We can share, it is the least we can do. We can talk some more maybe.'

'Well, that's just a fine idea, Anders — can I call you Anders? Lucky thing only the boy's been fed.'

The boy wonders why his father has lied but the thought disappears after he is called out onto the porch. His father tells him to show the Lindquists where the water trough is and where they can put their wagon.

At the back of the cabin, he watches as the man unharnesses the oxen and feeds and waters them. His wife and daughter busy themselves in the back of the wagon. Although he loiters around, they seem to have no interest in talking to him so he leaves them be. When he returns to their cabin all of the evidence of their earlier meal is gone. His mother and father are sitting beside the rekindled fire, whispering to each other.

His father calls him over.

'Listen, boy, it's important to keep your mouth shut. When I tell you go to bed, just do it.'

The boy feels annoyed with his father but nods.

A little later he hears footsteps on the porch and his father ushers the Lindquist family in with a low bow. They enter the cabin but stop just inside the door, looking around them. Anders' wife moves closer to her husband and the young girl holds her hand up to her nose. They stare over at his mother who is still sitting beside the fire, paying them no heed. Other than the odd visit from some of his mother's relatives, this is the first time he can remember having callers inside the cabin and thinks that the family are probably shy.

Anders has a basket in his hand and walks over to the table with it.

'We have brought some food. Some cured bacon and beans and some corn pancakes my wife cooked today.' Anders takes out a bottle and holds it up with a smile. 'Also, some Akvavit for after.'

'That's mighty kind of you,' his father says, then turns to the boy. 'I think it's time for bed, son — you got a lot of chores need doin' in the morning.'

The boy is going to object but changes his mind, knowing he can peek down at what's going on anyway. He fetches the ladder from the corner and climbs up into their open loft. By the time he has undressed and wrapped himself up in his quilt, the table is laid out and Anders and his family are sitting closely together at one end and his father is at the other. From his position in the loft, he can't see his mother but, judging by the smell of frying bacon, she is cooking over the fire. His mouth is salivating.

His father looks up at him and shakes his finger.

'You need to get to sleep, boy — don't forget what I said about the morning. Don't have me goin' up there.'

The boy ducks back into the corner of the loft but is determined to say awake and help himself to any leftover scraps when the visitors have left. He hears his father's laugh, a rare sound, and the low voices of their visitors.

As the evening wears on he finds it hard to keep his eyes open. Anders' voice is becoming louder and at one stage he hears him singing but he can't understand any of the words. Even Mrs. Anders begins to sing and, as he listens to her high clear voice, he loses his battle to stay awake and drops off into a dreamless sleep.

The following day, it's the absence of the warmth from his parents' bodies that finally wakes him from sleep. When he peeks down from the loft, the room below is empty and everything is cleared from the table. The shutters are pushed back already and their front door stands open. Judging by the sunlight streaming through the door, the boy reckons that it's way past his chore time. A sudden movement below catches his eye. Two of the Lindquists' chickens are wandering around the room, pecking at the floorboards for any crumbs of food. The tap-tap of their beaks against the floor is a comforting sound, one that he has not heard since they killed their last hen several weeks ago. His father will be pleased with him if he traps them before they can escape so he dresses quickly and silently.

The chickens show no sign of alarm when he comes down the ladder, just wander over to the fireplace, but he will tell his father they put up a fight anyway. On his way out he closes over the front door, trapping them inside. Outside his father is making good the wooden fencing around their vegetable garden which he had let fall into disrepair, whistling as he works. Clustered together in the middle of the garden the Lindquists' oxen nuzzle each other.

His mother comes around the side of the cabin and stops when she sees him standing on the porch. She calls out to her husband who turns away from his task and waves over at his son.

'Come 'ere, boy, and lend me a hand.'

The boy makes his way over to his father and looks around for the Lindquists, but they are nowhere to be seen. He can see that their wagon is still at the back of the cabin and scattered around it are what looks like their belongings and a few more stray chickens. As he gets closer to his father, he can make out scratch-marks on his face and one of his eyes is heavily bruised and partially closed over. He is wearing a new hat, one that looks very like the one Mister Anders was wearing the night before.

By the time he reaches him, his father has put down the mallet he was using on the fence and is waiting for him, hunkering down on the ground.

'Get down here, boy. I've got some bad news.'

The boy squats down beside his father and waits. The last time his father announced he had bad news it was about his little sister, who is now with the angels. Then, he had tears in his eyes and choked on his words as he explained everything. But now he doesn't appear to be too concerned. In fact, he appears to be in a rare good humour.

'We had ourselves a bad situation in the cabin last night, son.'

'With the family?'

'Yeah. Mister Anders took to drinkin' that liquor he brought with him and you know what it says in the Bible about that. Before long he was insulting our house, your mother, just about everything I hold dear. Long and short of it, there was what you would call a brawl. But I fought them off. I sure did.'

The boy thinks about what his father has said for a while.

'What about the womenfolk?' he asks his father.

'Women? She-devils more like. Why, son, they were as mad as him. Scratchin' and bitin', but your maw took care a dem.'

'Where are they now?' the boy asks, looking around again.

'They're dead, boy, buried with your sister down in the lower field, may God be good to them. Had to put them out of their misery.'

'Like the squirrel?'

'Just like the squirrel, son. That Mister Anders was not a serious man and wouldn't have lasted anyway. But look what I got for you.'

His father reaches into his pocket and takes out a long piece of twisted cane candy. It has been a long time since the boy has seen a stick of candy — he can hardly remember the taste. This one is yellow, his favourite colour. The sun shines through it and he can see the tiny bubbles trapped inside. He reaches up for it, but his father keeps it just out of his reach.

'You can have the candy. But you have to promise that if anyone comes along in the spring, this is our secret. You'll forget all about this, can you do that?'

'Sure, Pa,' the boy says, staring at the candy.

'Good boy,' his father says and hands it to him.

The boy grabs it from his father's outstretched hand, jams the candy into his mouth and snaps a piece of it with his teeth. The explosion of sweetness in his mouth is the most flavoursome thing he has ever tasted and he closes his eyes and hugs himself.

'Things are lookin' up, boy. We have the oxen now. I can clear more of that forest and plant a proper garden for your maw. And a rifle, a good one too, a Winchester. Be shootin' deer before you know it. Yessir, we're goin' to survive just fine,' his father says, putting an arm around his shoulders.

As he squats beside his father and chews on his candy, the boy hopes that he's not dreaming. Just in case he is, he shoves more of the candy into his mouth until he almost gags. Behind him the oxen stir. First thing he's going to do is to name them. Then he's going to name all of the chickens. And every morning he'll look around for eggs and his mother will make pancakes. Before the real snow comes, he'll make the chickens a shelter at the side of the cabin. He feels the weight of his father's arm around his shoulders and closes his eyes with happiness.

CHAPTER 1

Chelsea Piers, New York City
May 1915

The dark-green Cadillac Imperial pulls up outside the entrance to Pier 54. In the back seat, William Turner sits erect, in full captain's uniform. It is the same car and driver from that dreadful night that still plays over and over in his mind. Beside him, Charley, or the man who calls himself Charley, has lit another cigarette and blows smoke out through the open window. Around them there is the usual hustle and bustle as the ship, the *Lusitania*, is preparing for an Atlantic crossing. Inside the warehouse a queue of excited people wait to be processed by the ship's personnel. Cars pull up, disgorge more passengers, and disappear back into the night. It will be several more hours before the lines are cast off.

'You swore that all you wanted from me in return for the photographs was a copy of the ship's manifest, which I have handed over to you, but now you tell me there is more?'

'Something trivial, well within your power as the captain.'

'Is your real name even Charles Moore?' Turner asks.

'Near enough.'

'If you cannot even be honest enough to give me your real name, why should I trust that the plates will be destroyed?'

Charley flicks the half-smoked cigarette out through the window and turns to face the captain.

'Well, Captain Turner, ask yourself this question: *Am I willing to take the risk?*

Turner puts his head into his hands. A humiliating scene unfolds in his mind, one that has been plaguing him for days. In it he is sitting down for breakfast with his beloved companion Mabel, in their home in Brighton. The maid brings in the morning post on a silver salver. Mabel picks up the newspaper to peruse it over her tea. Her eyes widen, her hand goes to her breast. The look of revulsion on her face cuts like a knife through his heart. Then rumours would spread. His ex-wife Alice would find out and refuse to let him visit the two boys, Percy and Norman. Cunard would get rid of him and he would surely lose his home. Everything will be taken from him if he does not comply.

'Very well,' he says with resignation. 'What is it that you require?'

'The *Lusitania* is powered by five boilers, is that not so?'

'Yes, what of it?'

'And, occasionally, one of them is deactivated. Is this correct?'

'Yes — if the company wants to cut down on costs the ship is eminently capable of cruising on four boilers. What's this about?' Turner asks, puzzled.

'On this transatlantic journey you must use only the four boilers.'

'That would slow us down — there is a war on. It would present a certain amount of danger.'

'Don't exaggerate — a few hours here or there? Remember, you will be saving money for your company — you might even get a bonus.'

Turner shakes his head. 'I fail to understand any of this.'

'You're not required to. All you have to do is carry out an inspection, pick out one of the boilers and issue a command. After all, once the ship sets sail you are in complete charge — in fact, you are God.'

'And if I do this, you will destroy all of the photographs and any copies?'

'Of course. They are of no use to me after you arrive in England.'

'But why …?'

'I have a large wager. One in which I have bet that the ship will be behind schedule. A bet that I cannot afford to lose.'

Turner feels a sudden release of tension. So, it is that simple — the whole thing has been about money. He should have known. He has heard rumours about wagers like this, sometimes hundreds of thousands of dollars at stake. He thinks quickly. The manifest is not a problem, he can say he lost the copy he had picked up at the Cunard office. Also, the maintenance of a boiler is fairly common. Even with a war raging, his ship, with the distinctive silhouette of a civilian liner, will not be targeted. Perhaps the turmoil of the last week can be put behind him after all.

'Very well. I will do as you ask,' he says.

'You've made the right decision. I bid you goodbye.' Charley leans over Turner and pushes open the door, dismissing him.

The captain, still chastened from the turn of events, steps out of the car into a light drizzle. In front of him, towering over the dockside buildings, the bulk of the ship rises, huge and squat, all its light blazing. Music from the ship's orchestra drifts through the night air. His eye moves over the upper decks, picking out his kingdom for the next several days, the bridge. His cabin is situated just aft of it. His steward will be preparing it for sea, turning down the blankets, putting fresh towels into the bathroom, checking that the drinks cabinet, for the use of special guests only, is stocked up. All he wants now is to get on board and disappear into the privacy of his cabin, have a stiff drink.

He turns as the green limousine pulls away, does a U-turn and heads back towards the city. As it accelerates past, he catches a glimpse of the figure in the back lighting another cigarette, the flame from the match illuminating a face that he hopes he will never see again.

The dark-green Cadillac pulls up outside the German Embassy and the driver is ordered to wait. He watches as the man, now carrying a briefcase, goes up the steps and disappears inside.

After more than an hour the man emerges, without the briefcase. The driver thinks nothing of this. After driving him around for more than a month he has given up trying to figure out what is going on.

The car shifts under his passenger's weight and the glass partition slides open. He is given yet another destination, this time north of the city, to the Catskills.

It will be a long drive, but he doesn't mind. The man is demanding, but a good payer. It will not be the first night that he has not made it home to his bed.

* * * *

It will be the last night, however, for the driver. His last night ever. Business has been concluded. Satisfactorily. Now it is a matter of waiting for results. Results that will rock the world.

Time for 'Charley Moore' to disappear and reappear in another guise. Dublin beckons.

Growing up in Alaska was a brutal lesson in survival, but it was worth every gruelling day. *The child is father to the man.*

CHAPTER 2

The Liberties, Dublin
Saturday, April 29th 1916

On Meath Street, Tommy Sherry is forced to use his hands to guide him through the darkness. He stumbles over a raised piece of pavement and swears to himself: those stupid rebels. Because of the fighting he has lost a week's wages in the coal yard and in the poorer quarters of Dublin the street-lighting is sporadic, at best. The more prosperous areas of the city, Grafton Street and most of the Georgian squares in the south, are, of course, back to normal, but not here. The stench from Toner's piggery drifts from a laneway on his right and he knows that he has reached his turn. On down along Engine Alley he keeps his hands on the rough brick walls, counting off the doorways as he feels his way back to his home where his wife and children are waiting — anxiously, he knows. He shouldn't have stopped to talk about the rebellion — now he's breaking the curfew for no good reason.

At last, he gets some respite. Up ahead someone has just lit up a cigarette. In the flare of the match, he can see the man is standing in the entrance to his tenement. He tries to figure out who would be outside having a smoke at this hour and goes through the various tenants, but none come to mind. He gets closer to the figure and thinks he can see the momentary glint of metal buttons as the man drags on his cigarette. Could it be a policeman, sheltering in the lee of the doorway so that he won't be caught taking a break? But Tommy can't make out the shape of the distinctive helmet. Or could it be a soldier, one of the British soldiers from the Curragh Camp or maybe one of those sent over from England? Most of them don't know their way around the streets of Dublin, so he might be lost.

If it is a soldier who has lost his way, it could be an opportunity. He could direct him towards Saint Patrick's Cathedral in return for a cigarette, or maybe two. The cigarette smoke is drifting into his face and he sniffs it, breathing it into his lungs. He's almost on top of the smoker and sees that it's neither a policeman nor a soldier, but a civilian wrapped in a heavy overcoat with the collar turned up. In order not to startle him he coughs, a polite cough that, he hopes, conveys his presence in a non-threatening manner. He's heard rumours that some of the rebels are still lurking around the backstreets of Dublin and are a bit trigger-happy after the carnage of the last week.

The man, whose face is still in shadow, turns towards him. The fact that he seems not in the least startled by Tommy's presence unsettles him. Maybe the man is not lost after all, but looking around the tenements for a bit of skirt. Dirty bastard, probably thinks he's found the red-light district — the Monto. Tommy makes to squeeze past him and into his house when the stranger speaks, at the same time clamping a hand on his shoulder, a hand with a grip so tight that he can feel it even through his heavy overcoat.

'If it isn't my old friend, Tommy Sherry.'

The voice is all too familiar. It visits him at night in nightmares as he tosses and turns in bed. Now that he is here, it is almost a relief.

'If it isn't young Christopher Flinter, all grown up!' Tommy says, forcing a smile. 'You're alive. Thank God. I heard you were dead. How are you?'

'Not dead, Tommy, I'm one of the lucky ones. Hale and hearty all the way from the Great War!' Christopher almost spits into his face. 'Home at last to pay a visit to me little brother Ned.'

Christopher drags him through the doorway and shoves him hard across the hallway. Inside it's almost pitch-black and Tommy stumbles forward, hitting his head against the banister of the stairs. A sliver of pain shoots through his stomach, adding to his misery. Was it the pig's trotters he had for lunch? Cold, wrapped up in newspaper, he had thought they were a bit too greasy. Overhead, in the small room off the landing, he can hear his youngest, Úna, screaming at the top of her lungs. The last child, they say, is the loudest — not enough milk left in the mother's breast. A little over a year old and already she's worked that out for herself. Tommy's eyes are becoming accustomed to the dark and he can make out the shape of Christopher Flinter, staring upwards towards the child's cries.

'A new lodger, Tommy? You've sublet the landing?'

'No — you know how it is, Christopher, life goes on. We had another baby, a girl, Úna. She sleeps with my wife in your old room now, so the rest of us aren't woken up all the time by her crying.'

'Does she? Because the way I remember it, Tommy, that space was paid for and it should be my brother up there. Remember my brother Ned? You were to look out for him?'

'Of course I remember Ned. Didn't he go off to join up, like yourself. To fight for all the small nations —'

The fist that slams into his mouth is like an explosion. It knocks out some of his decaying teeth and he can taste blood. The force of it propels his head backwards against the banister. His brain fills with noise and flashes of light. Surely one of the other tenants will hear the commotion and come to his rescue? But the noise is mostly in his head and the effects of the blow wear off. He opens his mouth to shout for help, but a cloth is shoved into it, almost choking him. His ears are caught in a tight grip and his head forced backwards. Christopher's face is almost touching his and he can smell his breath, a mixture of cigarette smoke and alcohol.

'*Ned was fifteen, Tommy*,' Christopher hisses.

Gripping the cloth between his thumb and forefinger, Christopher yanks it out of Tommy's mouth, taking one of the loose teeth with it. Tommy feels a sharp pain and some blood trickles down his throat, making him gag. Doubling over, he coughs to clear his throat and spits onto the floor. He leans back against the banister and holds up his hands.

'Wait, Christopher, it wasn't like that. He wanted to join up, to follow you. I couldn't do anything to stop him. He'd grown up, nearly as tall as you, a strappin' lad. And you know how headstrong he was.'

'Go on, I'm listenin'. What happened then, Tommy?'

'I begged him to stay here for another year and then, you know, drop you a line. But he had the bit between his teeth, I swear on the Holy Bible.'

'What happened next? He just toddled up to Beggar's Bush with a hop, skip and jump, joined up and lived happily ever after?'

'It wasn't like that, Christopher — I argued with him over and over — said it was too dangerous and you wouldn't like it — and then and then ...' Tommy is beginning to falter, his mind busy looking for a way out.

'Maybe he threatened you. Yes, that's it, and you a strapping coalman? Or maybe you needed that miserable space for yourself?'

Over Christopher Flinter's shoulder Tommy sees old Devenish looking out through a crack in his doorway. Devenish is a nosey bastard and, although almost blind, his hearing is sharp. He would do nothing to help him, but he might just go out the back way and run for help. It wouldn't take long to come across a British army patrol. Since the fighting in the city they've been all over the place.

'Listen, Christopher,' he mumbles through broken lips, 'Ned got down on his knees and pleaded with me, said he wouldn't be happy until he saw you … I just hadn't the heart …'

'Well, Tommy, he's not —' another punch lands, this time across the bridge of his nose, knocking his head back again, 'too fucking happy —' another blow, this time under his chin and he feels the few remaining teeth in his lower jaw push up into his gums, '*now!*'

Tommy mumbles a prayer to God through his broken mouth and begs to be released from the pain. But God is not listening. He feels a fist sinking into his stomach and his breath leaves him. He slumps onto his knees, pain shooting from his lower jaw which hangs at an unnatural angle. He tilts forward onto his face and prays silently for unconsciousness to be granted to him. But Christopher is using his boots now to stomp on his outstretched arms, concentrating on his fingers. When he tries to pull his arms in under his body, he feels a powerful kick in the side that flips him onto his back.

The face of his tormentor stares down at him.

'And do you know why he's not too happy, Tommy? Will I tell you?'

Tommy looks up and grunts for mercy through bloated lips.

'Because he's *dead*, that's why. And you're responsible for killing him, Tommy.'

'*Nooo* … mercy … please stop …'

Tommy's plea is interrupted by a cough as blood trickles down his throat. But Christopher ignores him and takes something out of his pocket. He can hear the rustle of paper.

'You were paid rent for that miserable space and more to look after Ned. Imagine my surprise as I was lyin' in my hospital bed with a Blighty wound that would send me home, happy as Larry, and then his letters caught up with me. They told a different story, Tommy. According to Ned, you wanted him out. He was desperate and had nowhere else to go — *that's* why he joined up.'

Tommy begins to cry, a whimpering sound that bubbles out from between his bloody lips. He turns on his side and curls himself up into a ball. Anything to get away from Christopher Flinter and the news about Ned's death. But his tormentor is going nowhere and sits down beside him, his back to the wall. He takes out a cigarette and lights it up.

'Battle of Loos, in September. It went on for a month. His commander was General Haig — what a fine commander, frontal attack, fought until every drop of Ned's blood was shed. Don't ask me where his body is, Tommy, nobody seems to care. He ended up in a Scottish platoon, probably because of his accent.' Christopher laughs without humour.

The pain in Tommy's jaw is excruciating. His nose is blocked with blood and bone and every time he sucks in a breath through his swollen lips a sharp pain erupts in his side. But there is hope. The fight seems to have gone out of Christopher Flinter as he sits beside him slumped against the wall, smoking. Maybe it is all over.

He hears Christopher getting to his feet and then brushing down his coat. All he can make out are his leather army boots and a part of him marvels at how clean they are. Polished and buffed to perfection. Overhead a light finally comes on and he hears his wife's long-drawn-out scream. The sound reverberates through the house.

He sees Christopher's hand reach to his waistband and take out a knife concealed there. He hears his wife scream again and then his children join in. More doors open. He closes his eyes, waiting for the blade to sink into his heart and release him from his misery.

20

CHAPTER 3

S herry's wife rushes down the stairs to be at her injured husband's side, stumbling down the final few steps. To catch her, Christopher has to drop the knife. The sudden reality of Sherry's wife in his arms and the pitiful cries of the children acts like a shock. It cuts through the fog of revenge that has taken over his mind for the past weeks. How could he leave Sherry's wife a widow and his children orphans? The door behind him is thrown open and soldiers pile into the building. The lobby is now filled with shadowy figures. Releasing the woman, he stands with his back to the wall and defends himself as best he can. The first two soldiers are no trouble, going down easily as his furious blows land in the middle of their faces.

It feels like treachery to be lashing out at men who wear uniforms like the one he wore. He has considered them his comrades, watched hundreds of them die around him, some closer than others. On those dark nights in the trenches of Flanders, as the rats grew fat on the corpses of fallen soldiers, he has shared cigarettes and food with them. Sometimes they passed creased photographs of loved ones around, some faded and soiled so much that the person was almost unrecognisable.

A Dublin Metropolitan Policeman barges through the door, an oil lantern held over his head.

'*Stand back, boys! Put those rifles away!*' he shouts at the soldiers. '*I know this troublemaker!*'

Christopher recognises the broad form of Dick Walsh.

Walsh hands the lantern to one of the soldiers, takes off his helmet and jacket and begins to roll up his sleeves. Christopher thinks about lunging for his knife which has been kicked into a corner during the struggle, but he reckons he would never reach it. As Walsh approaches him, shoulder tucked under his chin, left arm extended, he knows what will happen next. Walsh, an ex-amateur boxer with a penchant for goading people in order to beat them up, will take his time, jabbing constantly at his eyes until he can no longer see. Then he will thrust out his chest, look around him at his audience, and land a vicious uppercut that will raise him bodily off the floor. He saw it many times when he was growing up.

'Welcome home, Flinter, it's good to see you. A bit of extra flesh on your bones, I see.' Walsh advances towards him sideways, crab-like, in that familiar crouched position.

Christopher looks around for a weapon, but there is none. The only thing he can think of is his belt, a wide, brown, leather one that he unloops from around his trousers now and wraps around his right hand. Walsh stops his advance and the smile disappears from his face. The two British squaddies Christopher dropped have rejoined their comrades and formed a semicircle around the two combatants, waiting for the show.

Walsh decides to take his time and stands up to his full height, examining his opponent properly for the first time, taking in the extra

22

pounds he has put on and the hardened features. Before Christopher left to join the army, he would have taken him with a few good slaps, not even bothering to ball his fists and bloody his knuckles, but now he hesitates.

'Come on, are yeh goin' to dance with 'im or arrest 'im?' one of the soldiers, the corporal and leader of the patrol, shouts and the rest of the men laugh.

Walsh turns on them. 'Shut de fuck up — ye didn't do too well, did ye, lads?'

Christopher takes the opportunity and lashes out with his right, catching the policeman on the jaw. Walsh staggers back into the wall of soldiers who immediately throw him back into the circle. He touches his fingers to his face where the blow landed and feels a sharp pain. It's probably a dislocation, not too serious, but he is taking no more chances. He reaches down to his side and, to the jeers of the soldiers, withdraws his baton. With the familiar leather strap wrapped rightly around his hand, his confidence has returned. Watching his opponent closely, he raises the baton above his head, ready to strike. With a lightning flick he brings it down across Christopher's exposed left forearm as hard as he can and is satisfied with the solid connection.

A flash of pain shoots up Christopher's arm. In the split second that he takes his eyes off Walsh, the policeman dives at him and carries him bodily backwards until they collide with the wall. Winded, he ducks his head down as Walsh, who has dropped the baton in his excitement, is now pummelling him with his left and right hands. The blows are coming in rapidly but without much accuracy. He waits until he feels that the older man is beginning to run out of steam, then pushes himself away from the wall and back into the middle of the floor. Walsh, surprised that he is still standing, turns to look for his baton and bends to pick it up. Christopher lashes out a kick at his head with his heavy army boot and connects with the side of his jaw. Walsh staggers backwards over Tommy Sherry's extended legs and lands almost on top of Sherry's wife who begins to wail again, protecting her husband's head with her arms.

As the dazed policeman staggers to his feet, Christopher is onto him. He unwraps the belt from around his hand and loops it around the policeman's neck. Walsh, choking and gasping, puts his hands up to undo the belt, but it is too tight. He drops to his knees in front of the soldiers, his bulging, bloodshot eyes staring up at them, pleading for help.

The corporal, who has seen enough, raises his rifle and brings the stock down on Christopher's head.

CHAPTER 4

Monday
May 1st

D aniel Joyce is glad to be back at work full time. Throughout the day the apprentice has carried heavy galleys of lead type from the linotype department out to the compositors. The compositors work flat out around the giant stone benches where they assemble the pages of the newspaper. The owner, George Maybury, wants them to make up extra pages because it's the first edition of the freesheet to be published since the fighting has ended. Heads bent, green visors in position, the compositors manipulate the tiny pieces of type under the steady gaze of Mr. Maybury. Even though he is out on his feet, there is still nowhere else in the world Daniel would rather be.

In the offices of the *Irish Gazette*, every reporter is working on one story: the rebellion. He has never seen the printing works so busy. Usually the reporters, a breed apart, write their copy and are gone before the linotype operators begin to cast their words into lead. And the advertisement canvassers, seldom to be seen until payday, are more often than not out wining and dining their clients. But here they all are, shoulder to shoulder, caught up in the aftermath of the fierce fighting and dizzy with excitement.

The linotype machines make an enormous racket. Cascading brass mats hardly settle into the assembler box before the operator sends them away to be cast without even proofreading them. The brass mats offer themselves up to the mouth of the mould to be impregnated by the molten metal. No sooner has the lead line been cast when the mats are on another short journey, this time taken up by the metal hand of the elevator arm to be redistributed back into the metal magazine and await their turn to begin their journey all over again.

George Maybury hated losing money and had been leading by example, running around the printing works, encouraging the men to work harder. Advertisements which had been booked for the previous week were assembled quickly and thrown together on the metal slab. The reporters who had turned up for work were locked into their offices and told not to come out without a thousand words. *'It doesn't matter what the words are — just get me some copy!'* he yelled at them. Grown men, linotype operators, who usually came to work in shirt and tie, now looked dishevelled and were slightly shoddier versions of themselves.

Such was the emergency that Maybury cancelled all lunch breaks. In mitigation he sent up to the bakery in nearby Thomas Street and bribed the workers with bread and cakes. Peter Casey, the youngest apprentice, was given the job of traipsing down the quays and then up Christchurch Hill that morning. At the bakery he was told to go around the back and was given a wide wooden tray stacked with the bread and cakes. He held the awkward tray in front of him with the help of leather straps attached to each side and placed around his shoulders. Peter, a frail boy of fourteen, stumbled many times going back down Christchurch Hill. When he eventually arrived back at the printing house, although the loaves of bread made it in one piece, the cakes were broken and misshapen.

When Maybury wasn't castigating the compositors for not

producing pages quickly enough for the hungry printing press, he was loudly berating those scoundrels who had tried, and failed miserably, to beat the forces of the King. *'Traitors! Look what they've done to Dublin!'* he had yelled repeatedly during the day, shaking his fist up to the heavens. Sometimes he even used foul language, words that Daniel had never heard him use before. The workers tried to avoid him, scurrying here and there to keep out of his way. Even the canvassers who had sold their quota of advertisements and would usually have gone for a tipple, kept their heads down, locked away in the reading room, bent over the proofs of their advertisements, something they usually left to the lowly proof-readers.

It is all so intoxicating and, when Daniel volunteered to stay back and melt down the redundant lead type for fresh ingots for the linotype operators, Mr. Maybury had gladly assented.

Now, at the end of the day, Daniel is exhausted. He spent the latter part of the day lifting the heavy frames of type after the compositors had done their work, wheeling them down to the printing press and then lifting them up onto the flat bed of the press. He decides to go down to the smelting room early so that he can take a break in peace. After the process of smelting begins, the smell and the fumes will guarantee that he will not be disturbed.

A gaslight on the wall illuminates the dim basement where the small pot-bellied smelter is bubbling away. A load of used type comes sliding down through the hatch in the wall and lands on the floor. He shovels some into the smelter and shuts the door. He allows the type to melt, then puts in some extra antimony to help the lead harden before he begins casting the ingot bars for the linotype operators.

In the meantime, he goes to the battered couch in a corner farthest from the door, a couch that the apprentices use to sit and wait until the molten lead is ready to pour. He stretches himself out on it, getting himself as comfortable as his long legs will allow. From the couch he can keep his eye on the door to the basement in case somebody should decide to come down to see how the smelting is progressing. The latest edition of the paper has finished printing and now the sounds from upstairs are more muted. Footsteps move backwards and forwards as the different tradesmen prepare the next printing run. At some time during the lull tiredness takes over his body and, affected by the fumes from the smelter, he drifts off into a heavy sleep.

The crash of type shooting down through the hatch and landing on the concrete floor of the basement wakens him. For a brief moment, in the dimness of the basement, he can't recognise his surroundings, then the smell of the fumes from the bubbling smelter in the corner reminds him. Somebody must have come in earlier, not noticed him on the couch and switched off the gaslight on the wall inside the door. The only illumination in the room is coming from a basement window which lets in a diffuse light from the street lamps outside. But all he can see are vague shadows. He sits up, fully awake now, and panics. It's dark outside, so it must be after curfew. What will he tell his parents when he arrives home? In fact, how is he going to get out of the printing works?

Pulling himself up from the couch he makes his way over to the gas lamp and reignites it. At least now he has some light. Upstairs the presses are silent. Then he remembers what caused him to wake up: the crash of the type of the floor. Who is still here? What if it is old Maybury? He will be furious. He creeps up the wooden stairs and opens the basement door. The case room is empty, all of the metal slabs cleaned down and ready for the following morning. He walks through the silent room and on towards the press hall. At the far end of the press hall, he sees a light from one of the glass-fronted offices. Two men are standing in the supervisor's office, heads bent, talking to one another. As he gets closer, he can make out one of them: Mr. Maybury. The other is a tall man dressed in a dark suit. Unusually in the case of Mr. Maybury, the man seems to be doing all of the talking. As Daniel draws closer still, he sees the stranger reach into his pocket and hand Mr. Maybury a thick roll of money. Maybury smiles, takes it and shoves it into his inside pocket and then the two men shake hands.

Now is Daniel's chance — old Maybury looks to be in as good a humour as he's ever seen him.

As he draws nearer to the office, he recognises the man as a customer: under his jacket he is wearing a black shirt with a white collar peeking out. He is a clergyman of some sort and he has seen him once or twice before on occasional visits to Mr. Maybury.

As Daniel approaches through the line of silent presses, the clergyman is the first to hear his footsteps. His hand disappears inside of his jacket and withdraws a heavy revolver, aiming it through the glass towards him.

Daniel halts, shocked.

Maybury looks out through the glass, squinting — then, when he recognises Daniel, speaks rapidly to the stranger, who puts the revolver back inside his jacket and nods.

Daniel breathes a sigh of relief and walks on. Perhaps the man was paying Mr. Maybury for a series of advertisements, he thinks, and needed the gun for protection.

Maybury beckons Daniel towards the office.

'Daniel, I didn't realise you were still here — come, join us!' he calls out.

Maybury is smiling benignly — the first time Daniel has ever witnessed that — but the clergyman, his body still, is watching his every movement.

'What has you here at this time?' Maybury says, coming out of the office. 'I assumed you had finished up and gone. The light was out in the smelting room.'

'I fell asleep there — I don't know who turned off the light — I'm sorry, sir,' Daniel says.

'And what woke you up?' the stranger asks from the doorway.

He has a funny accent, an accent Daniel he has never heard before.

'Somebody emptied a galley of type down the chute. It landed on the floor with a crash.'

'Ah, the galley of type. Yes, I saw it on one of the compositor's desks and decided to get rid of it,' Maybury says. 'What did you do with it?'

'Nothing. It's still there on the floor. I came up to see who was still here.'

'Maybe you should sort out that type, Mr. Maybury,' the stranger suggests. 'I will see that the young man gets home.'

'Very well,' Maybury says, and heads off in the direction of the basement, leaving them alone.

'I don't need any help in getting home, sir — it's only a mile,' Daniel says to the clergyman who now stands in front of him and smiles, a wide smile that shows his perfect teeth but does not reach his eyes.

'You can call me Tom,' the clergyman says. 'All my congregation do. And I will not see a young man walking alone on the streets of Dublin when there is a curfew. It wouldn't be safe and I would never forgive myself if you were arrested or shot on sight.'

As he is speaking, he reaches out and puts his hand on Daniel's shoulder, gripping it firmly. Daniel is going to object, but the clergyman begins to direct him towards the back of the factory. The only exit there is the delivery door that leads onto the laneway behind the print shop. As they walk past the silent presses and on through the case room, Daniel can hear the sound of shovelling from the smelting room and presumes that old Mr. Maybury must be getting rid of the type. This seems odd, as he has never known the owner to do manual labour or even to visit the basement in the few years he has been employed at the printers.

They continue on through the door into the laneway and up to Temple Bar. The clergyman turns right, towards Wellington Quay, but Daniel stops.

'I go this way,' he says, pointing towards Fleet Street.

'Don't worry, I have an automobile parked on Capel Street. I can drop you home before I go back to my parish.'

Daniel hesitates. He is tempted — he has never ridden in a motorcar. But, on the other hand, there is something not quite right about the Reverend. He smiles too much, for one thing, and under the orange glow of the gas lamp, his eyes, which are cast into shadow, throw back a steady glint which is unsettling. Daniel looks around him. There are no people out at this hour, not even an army patrol. Looking towards Westmoreland Street, he can see no sign of movement, and it strikes him how odd it is that this Reverend is talking about driving around the city well after curfew. Surely he knows that they could be shot at if they encounter an army patrol? Maybe the Reverend has some special pass to attend to his religious duties, like visiting the dying?

'It is terrible what man can do to his fellow man,' the Reverend says, breaking into his thoughts. 'It has been a terrible week.'

'Aye. It will take years to rebuild the city,' Daniel says.

'But rebuild it they will, have no doubt, Daniel. Now, come along.'

Together they turn and begin to walk towards Capel Street. They make their way onto the quays and continued to walk along beside the Liffey. The tide is out and the river low, revealing masses of dark rocks and pieces of rubbish. A heavy smell of raw sewage hangs in the air and Daniel feels almost ashamed of his city, the river filthy and exposed for all to see. They turn onto Capel Street Bridge and here the Reverend stops and looks in the direction of the sea that lies somewhere beyond Sackville Street Bridge.

Further downriver Daniel can make out the lights of the gunboat that had been used to dislodge the rebels.

'What did you make of the rebellion, Daniel?' the Reverend asks him.

'Load of bloody wasters. Look what they did to Dublin, and for what?'

'But do you not think that the blood sacrifice was worth it?'

'Begging your pardon, Reverend, but I do not. Home Rule was on the way — why couldn't they wait?'

'A good observation, Daniel. I see that Mr. Maybury chooses his workers well,' the Reverend replies, putting his arm around Daniel's shoulders.

Daniel feels proud. He has impressed a customer of Mr. Maybury's and with a bit of luck the Reverend will mention it the next time he visits the printers. On top of that he is about to get a chance to ride in a motorcar. He hopes that his father will be awake to witness his arrival in a motorcar.

The Reverend has left his side and has moved behind him and now both of his hands are resting on his shoulders. They lift momentarily and Daniel feels a sudden, sharp pressure on his neck, like the stabbing pain he sometimes gets when he nicks himself shaving. But the pain intensifies. Instinctively he reaches up, but he cannot feel anything that can be causing it. His fingers feel something warm and sticky. He draws his breath in to shout out. The air, instead of entering through his mouth, rushes in through an opening which shouldn't be there. His final inhalation sounds more like a gurgle and he is being lifted up off his feet. Now he is flying through space, tumbling over and over, until he hits what must be the grey, turgid waters of the River Liffey below.

CHAPTER 5

Tuesday
May 2nd

Christopher's eyelids flicker as he struggles to open them, but even that tiny movement brings pain. He smells damp, musty earth. For a split second he thinks he is back in Ypres, in the dugout, waiting for a German attack and expecting the shrill whistle calling him to repel yet another onslaught on the trench. Then the whole disaster comes slowly back to him and he raises himself up on his side.

He is lying on a hard bed suspended from a wall by rusted chains. The wall is made from granite blocks which are stained green with what looks like algae. The room, or cell, is less than ten feet square. Across from the bed there is a wooden crate and on top of it is a solitary candle with a weak but steady flame. The floor is compacted earth that looks damp in the light of the candle.

He has lost track of time. There is no window in the cell and he has been sleeping heavily, for the first day barely conscious. He knows a couple of days have passed as someone has been leaving and taking away away uneaten plates of food — and lighting the candle.

The pain in his head forces him back down onto the bed and he has to shut his eyes. When he opens them again and looks around this time, it's without moving his head. The door opposite the bed is barely five foot in height and made from stout wood with a small horizontal hatch near the top. The walls are curved in a gentle arc. There is no window so he presumes that he is underground. At first, he reckoned the soldiers had brought him to the prison in the Royal Barracks, but from what he remembers of the barracks there were no cells underground. It's definitely not Beggar's Bush barracks. He did his basic training there and knows every square inch of it.

As his memory of the journey on Saturday night came back to him, he found it too confusing to try and identify which barracks he has ended up in. Some of the soldiers clambered into the truck after him and sat on either side. Every so often one of them lashed out with his boot, calling him a dirty deserter. One of the men flicked a lit cigarette at him but he hardly felt the burning tip that hit him full in the face and exploded in a shower of sparks. He didn't care about any of that. He knew he would now be summarily court-martialled and shot — while Tommy Sherry would still be walking around, alive. Sooner than he expected the truck came to a standstill. He recalled muffled voices coming from the front, then the truck seemed to turn around in a complete circle. Maybe they were afraid of an ambush from some stray rebels. Eventually they reached an obstacle where they had to stop and the driver spoke with somebody, then the noise as the trucked pulled into a cobbled area. The soldiers were ordered out. Hands dragged him to the back of the truck but, before he was pushed out of it, a cloth bag was pulled over his head. He was half-dragged, half-pushed across some cobblestones and into a building, through a maze of corridors and brought down at least one flight of stairs and, without removing the bag, flung into the cell, head first, where he stumbled awkwardly and crashed into the wall opposite. He must have been knocked out, but for how long? At least the soldiers had the decency to throw him onto the bed.

Miserable, hungry and cold, he waits again for the inevitable summons. Maybe they'll skip the court martial and just put him up against the wall and shoot him. On the fishing boat over from Tenby, he had read in a newspaper that General Maxwell had been appointed overall commander in Ireland. It was well known that Maxwell had been responsible for the slaughter of most of his troops by the Turks at Gallipoli and his career had been blighted. Now, no doubt, he would sort out the Irish rebellion in his own individual style and, as a deserter, Christopher would be the first to be shot.

As if on cue he hears the sound of footsteps approaching the door. He rises to his feet and brushes himself down, determined to be as presentable as possible.

But the door remains closed. Instead, the small hatch swings open and there is a pause as someone presumably surveys him. Then a tin plate with some kind of stew is thrust through. His stomach reacts to the smell and he reaches for the plate. A steaming tin cup follows and he grabs it. The hatch shuts. He sits back down on the bed. There is no cutlery, but there is a thick slice of brown bread sticking out of it. He uses the bread to scoop up the stew, shoving large chunks into his mouth as fast as he can. After he has mopped up the last of the gravy, he takes a drink from the cup — strong tea laced with sugar. He sits back on the bed and sips the sugary tea, beginning to feel some of his strength returning.

After a while the hatch opens again. He takes up the plate and the cup and hands them through, trying to catch a glimpse of his keeper, but the corridor is almost as dark as his cell.

He lies back down and drifts off to sleep, slipping into a familiar nightmare. In a relief trench somewhere near Ypres, a starlight shell has been shot into the sky and he prepares for a night attack and a call to move up to the forward trench. The inevitable bombardment begins and he feels the ground heave under his feet. A small crack appears in the earthen wall of the trench and grows larger and larger. From the depths of the crack he sees hundreds of tiny pinpricks of light: rats. They shoot out of their disturbed nest in a gush of grey, furry bodies that cascade all about him. Some of them jump straight from the wall and onto his head. He shakes it violently in an attempt to get them off, but they grasp his flesh with their tiny claws.

When he wakes from the nightmare, kicking and shouting, he finds that there had been a rat crawling over his bed. It leaps down and scurries across the floor of the cell, disappearing into a crack between two blocks of granite. The smell of the food must have drawn it out from its nest. He notices that somebody must have been in his cell while he was asleep as the old bucket to the right of the door has been changed and some loose sheets of newspaper left. The sight of the bucket doesn't bother him as when he was growing up there was a single toilet in the back yard of the tenement building with six or seven families using it.

The candle, which had been tall when he first woke up is now smaller, but not by too much, so he had been asleep for a short time. This brings him back to wondering what day it is. If he was arrested on Saturday evening, does that mean it is now Tuesday? He contemplates pinching the candle out to save it, but then realises that he has no matches to light it again.

The hatch in the door slides back and somebody peers in at him. He gets up and goes over there. This is an older person, with hooded grey-blue eyes that stare into his with an unwavering gaze, assessing him. He presumes he is an officer, or maybe a prison guard and is just about to ask what is happening when the hatch slams shut. Then he has a chilling thought: what if it's the hangman? What if Tommy

Sherry died and he's to be hanged and not shot? This fills him with more dread and he lies back on the bed, shaken. He's heard of hangings going wrong, where the man swung from the gallows, thrashing and choking after a botched job by the executioner. But at least he would be free from this miserable world of suffering and, please God, be with Ned and his mother and father. The thought of meeting up again with those who have gone before gives him some solace and he slips into a deep sleep.

The sound of the key turning in the lock rouses him from sleep. The cell door is pushed back, slamming against the wall. A soldier stands outside in the corridor. In his right hand is the familiar shape of a Webley revolver which he uses to indicate that Christopher is to get to his feet. Before he can leave the cell, he is handed a hood to put over his head and he feels certain now that he is being escorted to the hangman. So there's to be no court martial. Straight to the scaffold to be hanged secretly somewhere in the bowels of this building.

When the hood is in position, he holds out his hands to be handcuffed, but instead he is taken by the elbow and led out of his cell down a long passageway. The air feels cold and damp with that same mildew smell that had permeated his cell. Underfoot the ground is hard, but not entirely even. Occasionally he stumbles and has to reach out to the wall to stop himself from falling. After a few minutes the hand grips his elbow, pulling him to a halt.

'We're going up some stairs now,' his guard announces.

They make their way up through a narrow circular stairwell and the air around him grows warmer, the smell of must and damp falling away. When they arrive on the floor above, he can hear the sound of faraway voices and some male laughter. Down another corridor, this time hard wood, until he is told to stop. He hears the man tap a door with the revolver, metal on metal.

A voice shouts out: '*Come in!*'

The door creaks open.

Christopher is directed gently through and the door is closed after him. He steels himself for the noose to be lowered down over his head and placed around his neck, but nothing happens. He stands for a while, twisting his head around to get some sense of where he is but the room, if that's what it is, is silent except for the rustling of paper. Somebody is turning pages, then there is a low cough and finally, complete silence. He can sense being scrutinised. A chair scrapes back and footsteps approach him. The hood is gripped and lifted off his head. He blinks in the light. When his eyes adjust he sees, with relief, that he is standing in the middle of an office and not on a trapdoor.

'So, you are Corporal Flinter,' a voice states from behind his back.

Automatically he straightens and makes as if to salute.

'At ease, Flinter, this is not the army,' the speaker says and walks around, taking his place behind a large wooden desk, the surface of which is taken up with what looks like files and sheets of papers. After the man has made himself comfortable, he indicates a chair placed to one side of the desk.

Christopher sits and waits as the man continues to read, taking up a sheet here, comparing it to another, then rummaging through the papers on the desk. This gives Christopher time to study him properly. Although he is dressed in civilian clothes, he has the bearing of a military man about him. After spending two years in the British Army Christopher is able to place most soldiers in one of three categories. The first were the officers, men who were trained to lead the ordinary soldiers over the top, whistles in mouths, through bullets and bombs, their only protection their unshakable belief in King and Country. The second were the ordinary soldiers, mostly working-class men —

miners, factory workers, farmers — who had volunteered in a frenzy of patriotism in 1914 on the promise that the war would be over by Christmas and who thought it was a good chance for an adventure. The third were the smallest group, the unemployed, the poor and destitute, like himself, who had signed up before the war had even begun, for bed and board. For the most part these were the ones who learnt the ropes quickly at the front, who kept to themselves and avoided fighting alongside the new conscripts, and who, due to their longevity in the field and their talent for survival, were promoted but looked on with a certain amount of suspicion.

But the man sitting behind the desk falls into none of these categories. Perhaps he is a shell-shocked officer posted to Ireland for the duration of the war. He didn't seem to have that certain swagger of the officers he has worked under, nor the hectoring voice of the sergeant majors. Still, Christopher is wary of his own assessment and has learned in the army not to be taken in by first impressions. Sometimes it is the sergeant majors who, underneath all that piss and vinegar, are the kindest and coolest of men when you get into the heat of battle. It was the well-dressed, softly spoken officers with the clipped accents you had to look out for. They would lull you into a friendship with their effortless charm one day, and the next send you over the top on a suicidal mission without a second thought about your value as a human being.

The man wears a suit, the jacket of which is hanging up on a coatrack in the corner. His shirt is white and spotless, but undone at the neck, the white starched collar resting on the desk beside him. Christopher guesses he must be at least fifty, which is old for the army. But his physique is still lean — somebody who has seen military service but is now retired perhaps. His hair, grey at the temples, is thick and tousled and hangs down over his forehead. From what he can see of his face it is very pale, like an office-worker, but one who has not shaved in several days.

'So, corporal, what do you have to say in your defence?' he asks now, pushing his fingers through his hair.

Christopher stares into his grey-blue eyes and realises it is the man who had been looking at him through the hatch in the cell door.

The man reaches for a box on the table, takes out a cigarette, and offers the box to Christopher who hesitates but then takes one.

'Thank you, sir,' Christopher says, then tries to be as concise as he can. 'I received some letters, several weeks ago, I'm not exactly sure of the time. I was in Fazakerley Hospital, in Liverpool. I was recovering from a bullet-wound to my leg and was just about to be discharged when my post caught up with me. One of the letters stated that my brother, Edward Flinter, Ned, had been killed in action, sir. At that time, I was not aware that my brother had joined the army. I had left him in the care of somebody as our parents are dead.'

'How old was he?'

'Sixteen, almost,' Christopher answers.

'Poor little bugger,' the man says, lighting his cigarette.

He holds out the match to Christopher who notices that the man's hands are steady, the flame unwavering, and dismisses his early opinion of him being a shell-shocked officer.

'I made up my mind to pay the man a visit, the man who had agreed to take care of Ned after I left home to join up, sir.'

The man holds his hand up, picks up one of the folders and reads from it.

'A Mr. Thomas Sherry,' he reads.

'Yes, Tommy Sherry.'

'And by "pay a visit" you meant to enact some kind of vengeance for the death of your brother?'

'Yes, sir.'

'Go on.'

'That's about it, I'm afraid. I got hold of an overcoat to cover my uniform, left the hospital and made my way down to Tenby. I paid a fisherman to take me over to Waterford, then made my way up to Dublin. But I took too long with Sherry and I was caught in the act.'

'So,' the man counted off on his fingers, 'robbery, desertion, attempted murder, anything else?'

'No, sir, I thought that was enough,' Christopher replies.

The man laughs, once, a strange bark-like sound, and claps his hands together.

'I like that, corporal — "I thought that was enough" — very good.'

He stands up and begins to pace around the office.

'Now let me tell you about myself. My name is Byatt, Major Jonathan Byatt. I am in the Special Intelligence Service of Great Britain, and Ireland of course, and I am the only person standing between you and a court martial, followed by the firing squad. I am part of the British Crown forces. I am here,' he waves his arms around to indicate either the room or the building, 'among other things, to investigate certain matters pertaining to the uprising in Dublin which began on Easter Monday.'

He stops pacing and goes back to the desk to sit down. It is then Christopher notices that he has a slight limp.

'Pertaining, sir?'

Byatt looks up at Christopher to see if he is joking, and decides he is not.

'Pertaining: be appropriate, related, or applicable to. It means I want to find out how and why the rebels were hung out to dry and who was responsible.'

'I don't understand, sir,' Christopher says. 'I heard that the rebellion was a disaster.'

'That, Christopher, is what you are supposed to think,' Byatt says. He takes up a pencil and begins to tap it against the arm of his chair. 'What if I told you that without the British navy interception of an arms ship from Germany, the result of the rebellion would not have been so clear-cut? Perhaps you would be behind this desk interrogating me.'

'I doubt that, sir. Seeing as I am a British soldier,' Christopher answers.

Byatt lets out his strange barking laugh again.

'Corporal Flinter, have you no affinity … or let me put it this way … do you not have any admiration for these rebels? They are your fellow countrymen.'

'No, sir.'

'Why is that?'

'They've destroyed the city I grew up in. Nobody asked them to. Why should I admire them?'

'Do you hate them?'

'No, sir, I feel sorry for them. I don't think they realised what they were up against.'

'Oh, they realised what they were up against, believe you me. They were, on the whole, very well educated, worldly men — and women. Some very high-society women if what I have been told is true.'

Before Christopher can think of an answer, Byatt is on his feet again. He walks over to the door, pulls it open and shouts out into the corridor.

'*Bring us some food, will you, Sergeant Harrison?*'

Christopher hears '*Right away, sir!*' from somewhere outside.

Byatt closes the door, goes back behind his desk and begins to study the various pages that are littered across the top. He seems to be searching for something and is mumbling to himself in frustration.

Christopher is confused by everything that has occurred since he woke up and by the questions being put to him, but at least he is still alive.

'Can you tell me, sir — what day is it today?'

Byatt laughs. 'Tuesday.'

Sometime later, there is a knock on the door and an army sergeant comes in carrying a tray with two steaming mugs and a pile of sandwiches, finds a place for the tray on the desk, then salutes Byatt before he leaves.

The smell from the tea and the sight of the sandwiches are making Christopher's mouth water.

Byatt looks up and nods that he should help himself.

'Thank you, sir,' Christopher says, and grabs a sandwich, takes a small bite from it, then, when he thinks Byatt is not paying any attention, crams the rest of it into his mouth. He takes a second one, this time enjoying the taste of the fresh bread smothered in butter with a large chunk of ham in the middle. He is on his third when Byatt looks up.

'Do you want to go in front of a firing squad, Corporal Flinter?'

'No, sir,' Christopher answers through his full mouth. 'I would rather go back to France.'

'After you take care of Mr. Sherry?'

'No, sir, I believe now that what I did was wrong. Not about Tommy, not him. But seeing his wife and children — I hadn't really thought about them — they would have been without a father. I should have realised that.'

'From what I read in the report it will be a long time before Sherry eats solid food again. You know, a man once told me that living well is the best revenge.'

'Yes, sir.'

'Very well, Corporal Flinter — it seems to me that you have done what any red-blooded man would have done in your position, but unfortunately we cannot let you go back to France.'

'No, sir?'

'No. We, meaning the British government, have something else in mind for you. Now, as you have finished your sandwich, come with me.'

Without waiting for a reply, Byatt stands, puts on his jacket and leaves the office.

Christopher has to rush to catch up with him. Even though Byatt has a limp he has almost disappeared from view around a corner. They continue down a short corridor, through a large office with several men, both civilian and in British army uniforms, sitting behind desks. They look up and stare when Christopher enters, unshaven and dishevelled, but then go back to whatever it was they were doing. There are several windows in the office and Christopher realises where he is: Dublin Castle. He follows Byatt on through the office, down a stairwell, along another corridor, then out into the glorious fresh air.

Byatt leads him across the cobbled courtyard of the castle and into another building which looks like a stable. Inside the door he finds himself in a bright, white-tiled room. An acrid smell stings his nostrils and makes him wince. It is one he is familiar with, one that is imprinted on his brain from various field hospitals he has been in. On one side of the room there is a long, thick, wooden table, well-scrubbed, almost like a butcher's block, with a large sink at one end. Stainless-steel surgical implements of various shapes and sizes hang from hooks on the opposite wall and the sight of them makes him shiver.

He follows Byatt on through another doorway into a smaller room. This room is almost in darkness and Byatt has to light several gas lamps that are placed around the wall before he can make anything out. The room is empty except for a metal table. Under a white sheet he can see the unmistakable outlines of a body.

'I don't suppose you would be afraid of looking at a corpse, Corporal Flinter,' Byatt says, and whips back the white sheet.

The body on the table is that of a young man. He lies, naked as the day he was born. The skin on most of his body has a pale-bluish tinge. Here and there yellowed bruises stand out like small islands. His face is clean-shaven. Thankfully his eyes are closed. His mouth bears the final death grimace, one Christopher has seen so many times on the battlefield. He looks up and down the body for signs of injury but all he can see, except for the light bruising, is a thin red line around his throat.

'How did he die?' Christopher asks.

Byatt moves his hand to the top of the youth's head and puts a small amount of pressure on it. The thin red line that Christopher had noticed opens to reveal a deep gash that slices down through the skin and muscle and on through the windpipe.

'Have you ever heard of a garrotte?'

'No, sir — is it some sort of knife?'

'It was a means of execution used by the Spanish, I believe. Nowadays it is seen as old-fashioned. But the modern-day equivalent is still highly effective. Two small pieces of wood with a length of thin wire, usually piano wire, between them. Whole thing can fit in your pocket.'

'I've never seen anything like that before.'

'Few people have. A nasty way to kill somebody. It takes a certain type of person, not one you would meet every day. I believe it is still used by some American criminals, mainly of the Italian persuasion.'

'*Jesus*,' Christopher says as Byatt takes his hand off the corpse's head and, like a miracle, the deep wound closes over. All that is left is the thin, red line.

'Jesus indeed.'

'Who is this boy?'

'He was taken out of the Liffey this morning. His body had lodged into a sewer outlet just before Sackville Street Bridge. Looked for all the world like a dead animal, but when he was hauled out and cleaned up, I noticed his hands.' Byatt picks up the dead youth's right hand and turns it over, pointing.

Christopher doesn't notice anything unusual except that the tips of the fingers look stained and the nails quite short.

'I don't follow, sir,' he says.

'That stain on the fingertips is a mixture of ink and lead. It didn't take a genius to work out that he was a printer but, due to his age, some kind of trainee. There are only so many printing offices in operation in Dublin at the moment and one of them, a newspaper publisher, when contacted told the Dublin Metropolitan Police that a young apprentice, Daniel Joyce, had not turned up for work today. His parents are distraught, of course. I've sent for them to get an official identification.'

'I'm sorry to hear that. I've seen enough death to last me a lifetime, but it doesn't get any easier,' Christopher says, looking down at the pathetic body of the young man.

Byatt covers up the corpse again. 'Indeed. Anyway, let's get you a bath, I think you could do with one. Then we can go back to my office and have a chat.'

Byatt begins to turn off the gas lamps one by one, returning the young Daniel Joyce to the darkness.

CHAPTER 6

Byatt guides Christopher by the elbow as they enter the noisy courtyard. They make their way over the cobblestones and through the milling soldiers, some of whom stare curiously at the odd couple. Two plainclothes men appear at Byatt's side but he waves them away. Together they walk past the guards and through the main gates of Dublin Castle onto Corn Hill. Byatt turns right down Dame Street and Christopher follows. Mingling with people again gives him a deep sense of relief. It occurs to him that he could easily make a break for his freedom. All he has to do is turn suddenly and run in the opposite direction, past Christchurch and on into the laneways of The Liberties. Even though his own injuries are still troubling him, Byatt is in no fit shape to give chase. With a bit of luck, he can head off to … where? He has no friends, no family, no papers, and for the past two years his every need has been looked after by the British army.

'This way — I remember seeing a men's outfitters,' Byatt says and they turn up George's Street.

'Who were those two men?' Christopher asks.

'Harrison and Timmins. Bodyguards.'

'Ex-soldiers by the look of them.'

'Well spotted. That's why I don't use them often,' Byatt says.

Walking quickly through the crowd, then dodging carriages and trams as they make their way across the busy street, they end up in front of a small shop. In the window there is a collection of clothes, some new, most second-hand. Inside, the staff are preparing to close for lunch and look annoyed as they enter. Paying them no heed, Byatt walks around the store, picking out different pieces of clothing, discarding them, then picking out some more. When he is happy with the collection of clothes draped over his arm, he asks Christopher what size shoe he takes. Lifting a pair of shoes from a shelf he brings everything over to the counter and asks the older of the two shop assistants to tot up what he owes them.

'How do you know they'll fit me?' Christopher asks, flicking through the clothes on the counter, surprised to see Byatt has even included pyjamas.

'I had a very good friend who was about your size — they'll be near enough,' Byatt says and takes out his wallet.

Christopher notices that he is paying with his own cash, and not with an army chit.

Byatt points towards the dressing room at the back of the shop and says, 'Go change'.

Christopher bundles up the clothes and makes his way into the cubicle, pulling the curtain across. Inside he takes off his overcoat and uniform. Under the uniform he still has on the underwear he deserted in, grubby, the smell of his unwashed body clinging to every fibre. He takes the drawers and singlet off and wraps them in the pants of the uniform, then puts on new underwear, enjoying the feel of fresh cotton against his skin for the first time in weeks. He steps into the trousers and pulls them up to his waist, then puts on the shirt and waistcoat.

Everything is as close to his size as makes no difference. He pulls on the socks and slips his feet into the shoes — they're a good fit. After he puts on the jacket, he examines himself in the full-length mirror, the first mirror he has looked in for weeks. The eyes staring back at him look older and he notices tiny creases he has never noticed before.

'*Here!*' Byatt calls in at him and throws a collar and a necktie over the curtain.

When he steps out of the cubicle, his old clothes bundled up underneath his arm, Byatt is waiting, a hat in his hand. Byatt puts the hat on Christopher's head, adjusts it and stands back. He looks Christopher up and down, taking time to appraise his appearance then tweaks the collar of his shirt, jerks down the sleeves of the jacket and stands back to inspect him again.

'Perfect.' He takes the bundle of old clothes from Christopher and hands them to the younger assistant, with a gesture that tells him to get rid of them. The remaining new clothes are gathered together and wrapped up in brown paper and tied with twine, making a neat parcel which the assistant hands to Christopher.

Outside the shop, Byatt heads back down to Dame Street and continues towards Trinity College, walking at a fast pace despite his limp. Before they get to College Green, he turns up one of the side streets that leads to William Street. Without warning he darts down a desolate-looking laneway Christopher has never noticed before. He wonders how Byatt has become so familiar with the layout of the city in such a short space of time and hesitates.

Sensing that he is not being followed, Byatt stops and turns to him.

'When I come to a strange city my first job is to forage out a restaurant that serves my type of food!' he calls back and continues down the laneway.

They end up in front of a nondescript doorway and Byatt enters, leading them down a badly lit hallway. The clattering of utensils comes from somewhere on the floor above and the air is thick with the smell of cooking. At the end of the hallway, they emerge into a large dining room with a scattering of tables set for lunch. The room, like the hallway, is dimly lit but resembles nothing that Christopher has ever seen before. The walls are covered with gaudy wallpaper. Colourful birds vie with mythical animals against the backdrop of a jungle landscape. From the centre of the ceiling, long wide strips of what looks like silk loop down and radiate outwards, giving the room the appearance of a large, exotic tent. Spotted around the walls are stained-glass lamps behind which candles flicker and send out a gentle glow. Christopher is puzzled by such dim lighting, more appropriate for evening than the middle of the day.

A young waiter with jet-black hair and olive skin stands just inside the doorway. He smiles at Byatt, greets him by name and nods at Christopher. Even though they are the only customers, he looks around as if the dining room is full, then escorts them to a corner table. After they sit down, he hands them their two menus, lights the single candle in the centre of the table, bows, and leaves.

Christopher takes up his menu and stares at the long list of dishes, none of which he can identify.

Byatt leans over the table and whispers: 'You needn't worry, I can order for you.'

'Thank you, Major Byatt, and thank you for everything you've done for me.'

'You can call me Jonathan, I'm off duty.'

'I didn't think that a man like you would ever be off duty.'

Byatt sits back in his chair and laughs. He takes out a packet of cigarettes and offers one to Christopher, then takes one for himself. He relaxes deeper into his chair and loosens his collar. From his inside pocket he takes a hip flask, opens it and takes a long drink, grimacing as the alcohol passes down his throat.

'I won't offer you a drink, you'll need a clear head. Now, tell me, besides being thankful to me, what other thoughts are going through that head of yours?' He puts the flask away.

'To be honest, I'm surprised that we're outside of Dublin Castle without any guards. What's to stop me from walking out of here and disappearing?'

'Maybe I have a gun. Maybe I could shoot you before you reach the door.'

'You're not armed, I would've noticed.'

'Very observant, Christopher. And why do you think I brought you here?'

Christopher takes a pull from his cigarette.

'I've no idea, but I've learned that the kinder the officer, the more dangerous the mission.'

'It can't be more dangerous than standing in front of a firing squad, can it?'

Byatt lets the question hang in the air and raises his arm to attract the waiter's attention.

After he has finished ordering, Byatt turns. The mask of the gentleman officer has dropped and Christopher catches a glimpse of the real Byatt. His eyes, a grey-blue, are cool and calculating. He has witnessed that same unblinking stare from officers he has served under, empty of any emotion. He had often wondered if a certain type of man enjoys war. Or maybe they were just more capable of storing their feelings until the war was over. After all the madness, does the real person emerge again, unscathed from all the unspeakable acts they had carried out? Now, he realises, they are getting down to the real reason he is not facing a firing squad.

'Everything we discuss is confidential. If you mention it to any other person, you will be hanged for treason. No second chances.' Byatt takes another long drink from the hip flask. 'We have agents in every nook and cranny in this blighted city of yours.'

'You can trust me.'

'Of course I can, Christopher,' Byatt smiles, his mask back in position, 'because I'm a good judge of character, and, of course, you do owe me your life. Now, to business — have you ever heard of Janus, the two-faced god?'

'I left school when I was ten. The only thing I remember is that there is only one true God,' Christopher says.

'Don't let it concern you too much. Let me explain. Janus was an ancient Roman god with two faces which looked in opposite directions.'

The sound of men's voices coming up the hallway brings their conversation to a halt. Byatt sits back in his chair and pretends to study the menu. Three men enter, all wearing suits. They are greeted by the waiter who goes through the same routine. He leads the men to a table away from theirs and, after they settle down, hands them menus. Byatt waits until they have settled down to peruse their menus, then resumes in a lower tone.

'About a year ago our agent in the German Embassy in New York sent an urgent telegram. It stated that a man had delivered an envelope to the embassy. It happened to be on the same evening that the *Lusitania* set sail from New York, bound for Liverpool.'

'The liner torpedoed by the Germans?'

'The very same. Our agent managed to get a glimpse of the contents of the envelope. And what do you think was inside?'

Christopher shook his head.

'The manifest of the *Lusitania*,' Byatt says, sitting back in his chair, as if he had just revealed some deep secret. 'It listed everything, including arms and munitions that were on board the ship. Unfortunately, it also cost our agent his life.'

'But it was a civilian ship?'

'It was, but the manifest was correct. It was not a substantial amount of arms, but enough to give their attack legitimacy. Of course, at the time the existence of the arms was repudiated by our government and by the Americans. Which brings us to the reason I gave the man who delivered the envelope to the embassy his code name: Janus.'

'So, in a way, he was responsible for the sinking of the *Lusitania* and the loss of all those lives?'

'Indeed, but now it becomes more complicated, Christopher, because in a way he is doing us a favour by encouraging the Americans to join the war against Germany. And I suspect he is behind our capture of the arms ship and submarine in Kerry destined for the rebels here. Hence the codename Janus.'

'All those innocent people,' Christopher says, remembering the headlines of the sinking of the *Lusitania* and the grim photographs of the bodies floating, face up, in the Atlantic.

'It didn't work, of course, so now we believe that he will try again, but the next time by doing something even more spectacular with more loss of life. We fear that he has been gathering intelligence on …'

There is a commotion at the door and two young men enter, laughing and giggling. Both of them appear to be drunk, early in the day though it is, top hats perched lopsided on their heads. As they are being led to an empty table, Byatt nods towards one of them. For the first time since Christopher has been in his company, he seems uncomfortable and makes a show of unfolding his napkin and repositioning his cutlery. After the waiter has convinced the men to take a seat and hand over their hats, Byatt seems to relax. But then one of the young men makes his way over with the careful gait of a drunk. He sways slightly, then places his hands on their table to steady himself.

'Well, hello, Jonathan, I see you have company,' he says, looking Christopher up and down.

'Harry, this is my assistant,' Byatt says curtly.

'And a handsome assistant he is,' the young man says, giving Christopher's shoulder a squeeze.

'This is business, Harry, I'm sure you understand,' Byatt says, staring at the hand on Christopher's shoulder.

'*Oops*, I can take a hint,' Harry says, removes his hand and wanders back to his own table.

'I apologise for that,' Byatt says curtly.

They sit in silence, Christopher assessing what just happened and reassessing the man opposite him. He is about to speak when the waiter appears with two bowls of steaming soup. Byatt begins to eat rapidly, cutting off further conversation. When he has finished his soup, he pushes the bowl away and takes out his cigarettes, lights one up and blows the smoke up towards the ceiling. The other tables are now filling up, all with men, and the noise level is increasing, but still Byatt remains silent.

When Christopher finishes his soup, he says: 'Your friends are none of my business, sir.'

'Thank you so much, Christopher, that is very good of you,' Byatt says with sarcasm and stubs his cigarette out in an ashtray. 'Now, where was I?'

'Janus, the two-faced god.'

'Yes — Janus. God of duality and transitions. We have reason to believe he is now in Dublin. This is where the latest telegram came from. I suppose you've heard of the Monto?'

'Everybody's heard of the Monto.'

'Biggest red-light district in Europe if not the world and all overseen rather benignly by the Dublin Metropolitan Police. I was told it was named after Montgomery Street. I learned that Dubliners have the charming habit of shortening names and sticking an 'o' at the end. Hence "The Monto". So, at first I thought I was in luck. A single street would have been manageable to track down our man. I didn't realise it referred to a whole area.'

'What makes you think he's there?'

'There have been murders. Prostitutes.'

'Finding murdered women in the Monto wouldn't be too unusual.'

'It was the method used: some of the women were garrotted. The same method used to kill our agent in New York and, incidentally, that young boy you saw today. Also, the murdered women were all of a type. They specialised in domination. We believe they were probably murdered to protect his identity — or his ego.'

'You think it's the same person?'

'Yes, identical wounds, clean and precise, the women didn't have a chance. The only thing I cannot fathom is: why the boy?'

'But why do you think he'd stay in the Monto?'

'It's a perfect cover for him: a lax police force, thousands of people crammed into a small area, adjacent to the port of Dublin with people coming and going all the time. A nightmare for us.'

'But you said that you had spies in every nook and cranny in the Dublin — can they not find him?'

'Do you think I would not have tried that? The man is a ghost, he could be anywhere. But he's certainly not in any of the hotels or guesthouses outside of the Monto, I can guarantee you that.'

'And that's the reason I'm here?' Christopher says.

'Yes. I want you to go into the Monto and try to find out anything you can for me.'

'I'm not sure I can do that, sir. I've rarely been there, I know nothing about it.'

'*But, bloody hell, you were raised a mile or two away from it*,' Byatt hisses in frustration.

'I've passed through it in the daytime a few times — once me and my father were delivering some pig carcases to a hotel on Talbot Street and —'

'You either know it or you don't — *which is it?*' Byatt snaps.

'The Monto doesn't exist in the daytime, sir, it never did. In the daytime it's a scattering of streets with buildings that have seen better days. It comes alive at night, and I've never been there at night.'

The waiter comes back to their table with two steaming bowls of what looks to Christopher like thick, white worms submerged in a bright red sauce.

Byatt plunges his fork into the middle of them and twirls it around until he has gathered a good amount up to put into his mouth.

'Eat up, it's called pasta. It's very good,' he says to Christopher.

Christopher sticks his fork into the food and follows Byatt's example. He puts it into his mouth and finds the texture disgusting. But he is hungry and takes some more, making it more bearable by eating some bread.

Around them the restaurant is becoming more boisterous and some of the men are changing tables. Byatt looks around him and pushes a large manila envelope across the table.

'You'll need this.'

'What is it?' Christopher says, picking up the envelope.

'Identity papers. Taken off the body of a civilian caught up in the crossfire last week. You are now Joseph Andrews, a purveyor of fine wines and spirits. You'll find some money inside. I'm not sure how long it will last, but I can get you more. There's a hotel on Talbot Street I've picked out. Small, inconspicuous but respectable. The owner, I'm led to believe, is not unsympathetic to Dublin Castle. Buy yourself a small suitcase first and some toiletries — you don't want to stand out with that parcel under your arm.'

'Of course.'

'You might have a haircut also,' Byatt adds.

'How do I report back?'

'Ring the operator and give her this telephone number.' Byatt scribbles down a number in his notebook, rips out the page and hands it to Christopher.

'Is there anything else I should know?'

'This is a dangerous man. Don't, under any circumstances, try and outsmart him. If you manage to dig anything up, just get word back to me and let me take it from there.'

'I have been at the front and survived,' Christopher says, putting the piece of paper in his pocket.

'You've always fought what was put in front of you, not what's lurking behind. I repeat, don't underestimate this man. He's evaded us for over a year and left a trail of bodies behind him.'

Christopher begins to toy with his food, swirling the pasta around on his plate, then he puts the fork down.

'What's the matter now?' Byatt asks.

'What happens if I fail?'

'In that envelope you'll also find a copy of a full pardon, unsigned — for now. Either way, you'll be taken care of. I will make sure of that. Anything else?'

'It's all very fine you asking me to go into the Monto to try and find out where this man is, but how do I go about it? I'm a soldier, not a spy,' Christopher says, staring at his plate.

Byatt puts his fork down. 'I won't lie to you, Christopher,' he says, his tone softened. 'This would be a difficult mission, even for a trained agent. I wouldn't normally expect anybody to go into a situation like this without proper preparation. But, unfortunately, I have no network I can rely on. I can tell you that there is a public house in the centre of the Monto that is very popular: Phil Shanahan's. You should begin there. It's located on Montgomery Street.'

'I've never heard of it,' Christopher said.

'I believe it's a sort of no-man's land. So, though the pubs are shut until further notice, it is still operating. As usual, the police turn a blind eye on activities in the area. All kinds drink there: nationalists, soldiers, prostitutes, the high and the mighty, drunks, you name it. But that is all I can tell you. I'm sorry, you'll just have to do your best.'

'I will do my best, Major Byatt, I can promise you that. I'll begin there.'

'As to the appearance of the man, we have no idea. Based on the coroner's reports on the various murders we can surmise that from the upwards angle of the wounds, he is quite tall, and, due to the depth of the wounds, strong. Also, we are assuming that he is an American, not that that information is of much help in an area so near Dublin port. Other than that ...' Byatt holds out both arms as if in apology.

'I suppose that's something to begin with,' Christopher says.

Almost without thinking he begins to fork more of the pasta into his mouth. He has got used to the strange texture and is almost enjoying it. Something he thought a few minutes earlier was disgusting, is now acceptable. One of the things he has learned in the army is that people are adaptable. At the blast of a whistle soldiers crawl out of their trenches, stand up and march to their death. But then they repeat the same madness the following day: so even the fear of your own impending death can be adapted to.

'And you, Major Byatt, why are you taking such a risk with me in order to catch this man? You've said yourself he has been helping the British authorities in their attempt to get America to enter the war.'

'Have you not been listening to me? The man is an immoral monster and has to be stopped, *whatever my superiors say!*' Byatt stabs at the table with his finger.

'Begging your pardon, sir, but we're not that much different. I've seen and done terrible things. I've killed men in the trenches with my bare hands and I'm guessing that you have too.'

'And how are you such an expert all of a sudden … corporal?' Byatt says loudly, taking off his napkin and throwing it onto the table. He rises to his feet with such violence that his chair is knocked backwards onto the floor.

The restaurant goes silent and the rest of the diners concentrate on their food. Byatt stands unsteadily, shoulders hunched, hands made into fists at his side. His face has turned red and his breath is coming in loud rasps.

Christopher waits quietly as the passion drains from his face.

'I have underestimated you, Flinter, I will not do that again,' Byatt says, then rights his chair and sits back down at the table. He takes out the hip flask and drains the contents, then replaces the lid, smiling sadly to himself.

The drone of their fellow diners picks up again. Order has been restored.

'I shouldn't really drink so much. Letting the side down,' Byatt says, half to himself.

'War can do that,' Christopher says.

'War? I've been raised to fight for the British Empire, and before that my father and before that his father — it's in our blood. In my family we judge each other by our wars. Mine was the Second Boer War, another great victory for our empire. And better again, I got this,' he says, slapping his leg, 'a wound of honour, a Queen's South Africa Medal and a well-paid desk job. No, Christopher, it's not entirely to do with the war.'

'You've lost someone, a comrade?'

'I've lost plenty of comrades, forgotten most of them.'

'A brother?'

'A good friend, killed in the line of duty,' he says so quietly that Christopher can hardly hear him, 'in New York of all places.'

'The agent killed by Janus?'

'Howard Beasley, the agent *murdered* by Janus, in cold blood,' Byatt almost whispers.

'I'm sorry for the loss of your . . . friend,' Christopher says.

Byatt sits, slouched in his chair, nodding to himself as if reliving a memory. The noise around them has increased. The young waiter is now in full flow, walking quickly to and fro from the kitchen carrying trays laden with food and drink. His smile from earlier has disappeared and is replaced with a harried expression. As he bends low over the tables, a sheen of perspiration on his forehead is visible in the candlelight.

Christopher reaches over to console the older man, his saviour, but Byatt straightens up, pulls his arm away and calls for the bill.

CHAPTER 7

In the tiny women's snug in Phil Shanahan's pub on Montgomery Street, Nell Claffey raises her empty glass in a drunken salute. It appears over the wooden partition that separates the snug from the rest of the pub. The customers in the bar watch as the glass wavers backwards and forwards through the air. It is coming up to evening and the regulars wait in anticipation of Nell's usual rant.

'*Up the rebels! Up the republic!*' she shouts at the top of her voice before the glass disappears from view.

They hear her curse, then the sound of a table overturning and glasses crashing to the floor.

The racket brings a roar of approval from the bar. It is the usual motley crowd: dockers, men seeking a cure for their hangover, students, the odd adventurous gentleman, chancers, one or two prostitutes in for an early gin before their night's work begins and even some British soldiers.

Behind the counter, a frowning Phil Shanahan makes his way down to the snug and steps inside. Grabbing Nell under the arms, he hauls her upright and, to cheers from the bar, marches her out onto the street. He half walks, half carries her along the pavement towards Anna Macken's, the upmarket brothel just down from his pub. Hauling her up the steps, he leaves her propped beside the door and rings the bell. The door is opened by Sarah Murphy, another of Anna's strays. She stands in the doorway, all 4-foot-nothing, arms akimbo. She is a perfect miniature woman, dark curls pinned up in the style that Anna demands of the girls in her brothel. Her pretty, doll-like face doesn't quite match her pale-blue eyes that have seen too much of life in the Monto.

'She's pissed again, Sarah,' Phil says. 'Not alone that but she's shouting out "Up the rebels!" and the place full of soldiers.' He picks Nell up and carries her past Sarah and on into the parlour.

Some of the girls are already on duty, making small talk with the few potential early customers who have turned up despite the curfew and sit on the plush armchairs scattered around the room. The rest of the girls loiter in small groups, talking, waiting for trade to pick up. Anna has them well trained. The prettier girls are standing beside the bay window under the glare of the gas lamps, faces made up, hair coiffed. Phil carries on through the first parlour, past the double doors and into the more informal sitting area which is empty. In this room a large oak table is set out with food and drink in preparation for the big spenders who would begin to drift in later that night. Around the walls are padded couches, or '*chaise longues*', as Anna calls them, waiting to be occupied. On through that room and into the back kitchen which is cloudy with steam, little Sarah opening doors before him. Phil takes the usual route to Nell's tiny bedroom at the back of the brothel.

'I'll take it from here, Sarah, you can go back inside,' Phil says and pushes open the door.

Within the tiny room, the only furniture is a bed, a chair, a tiny writing table, a bookcase and a wardrobe. Phil places Nell on the chair and stands back, looking at her.

Nell opens her eyes and seems to make a sudden recovery. Grinning up at him, she reaches under her skirt and, pulling a .45 revolver from her stocking-top, aims it at his chest.

Phil grabs it from her hand.

'Don't ever point a gun unless you're going to use it, Nell Claffey — it might go off.' Phil cracks it open and empties the bullets into his hand.

'Ah Jaysus, Phil, don't give me that — you know I can handle it. How much?'

Phil examines the revolver. Probably made in Canada by the look of it, a copy of a Webley, the fancy grip a far cry from the usual guns that come across his counter. He feels the heft of it in his hand and examines the metal: good, heavy feel, the sort of gun that would hit what it was pointed at and not fall apart under sustained use. He flicks the cylinder closed and looks at her under his eyebrows.

'Would yeh not give it for the Cause, Nell?' he says. 'For all those brave men out there fighting against the odds. And you owe me a few bob for the glasses you broke.'

'Cause me hole, Phil! I had to let a big mucker from Toronto crawl all over me for that. Took most of the day. Anyway, he handed enough money over the bar for those broken glasses, so don't be puttin' on the poor mouth.'

Phil regrets bringing up the broken glasses. He looks at the revolver again, cocks the hammer and lets it back gently. He screws his left eye up and peers down the barrel, flicks open the cylinder again and spins it, then looks down the polished barrel. Probably never used. He holds it in his hand and considers it.

'You're a clever girl, Nell — how about ten bob?' he says, reaching into his pocket.

'Give it back here, I'd rather throw it into the Liffey,' she says, lunging for the gun.

'Calm down,' he says, keeping the gun out of her reach. 'You've sobered up fast, haven't you?'

'Find it hard to get drunk on the gin you serve, Shanahan. Give me a guinea or give me the gun.'

'Will you take it in drink, Nell?' Phil tries again.

'I owe Anna, Phil — give me a guinea,' Nell says, straightening up, her hand outstretched.

Phil snaps back the cylinder, puts the revolver down the waistband of his trousers and covers it with his waistcoat. He takes out a long leather wallet from his back trouser pocket and produces two ten-shilling notes, straightens them, then hands them to Nell.

'Here's a pound. And I owe you a gin,' he says.

'That'll do fine,' she says, grabbing the notes. 'By the way, I'll be in later. Connie's going up to the cattle market in Smithfield to bring a few farmers back with her, to unburden them. She'll need me to go with her to lend a hand.'

'Nell, I've told you before, less of the "up the rebel" stuff — you know the place will be full of soldiers,' Phil says, wagging his finger.

'Sure they love it, they think it's dangerous. And anyway, where did you disappear to during Easter Week, Phil?' she asks slyly, tipping her nose.

Phil Shanahan knows exactly what she is talking about and wonders how rumours get around Dublin so quickly. He had spent the week in Boland's Mills helping with the sandbagging and even took a few shots from the roof towards the river. Not that they were effective against the British gunboat that had made its way up the river to the bridge to fire at the rebel's headquarters on Sackville Street. The commander in Boland's Mills, a young man called de Valera, tall and stern, had ordered him to leave as soon as the surrender letter came. He refused at first, said he would stay on, that the pub would run without him. But de Valera had insisted, telling him that he was of more use on the outside than the inside. And from the news he was hearing now, he was glad that he did.

'We won't talk about that, Nell, will we?' Phil says, tapping the revolver hidden under his waistcoat.

'You know I'm only joking, Phil — relax, will you? Go on about your business.' She goes over to the mirror and examines her face, which looks tired and lacks any colour.

Phil Shanahan leaves Nell to her make-up and makes his way back through the kitchen and into the second parlour. Some of the clients are already making themselves comfortable in the chaise longues, plates of oysters on their laps, pretty young girls beside them. A man in evening dress who looks foreign is playing 'Pack Up Your Troubles' on the piano. Anna keeps a good house, clean and well furnished. Around the walls candles and oil lamps throw a soft, gentle light into the middle of the parlour where the well-laden table groans under the weight of all the plates of meat and fowl, and shellfish in iced dishes. She even has a large ham as the centrepiece, hot from the oven, a carving knife at the ready: things are picking up again after the fighting. His contribution, the bottles of white and red wine for the gents and bottles of gin for the women, are down at one end, glasses sparkling beside them. By the end of the night some of the bottles will be left unopened, but it could be worse.

A soft cough sounds beside him. He looks down into the tiny perfect face of Sarah Murphy, Anna Macken's good luck charm.

'How's Nell?' she asks.

'Sober.'

'That was quick.'

She stands in his way as he tries to move around her.

'I can't work her out. To be honest, Sarah, I don't know whether she's acting half the time. She came in with some Canadian soldier. She couldn't get rid of him so she starts off about the rebels. He left in a hurry, minus his revolver, back to the barracks.' Phil laughs, shaking his head and attempting to get by her again.

But Sarah has something else on her mind and stands her ground, looking up into his face. Normally her working hours are during the day, cleaning up the mess of the previous night's party. Hours spent replenishing the table, making the house presentable and threatening the strays from the night before that they should leave or be charged — again. Once, he had heard, as she was passing through the parlour she'd been picked up by some drunk as a joke. But Anna's doorman, a big Algerian called Moussa, had become involved, breaking the drunk's arm in the process. Now Sarah and Moussa are romantically linked. What an unlikely couple, he thought. Only in the Monto.

'Have you not heard?' she whispers, looking up into his face.

'Heard what? I've been working hard all day trying to make up the losses.'

'They say they're going to start executing the rebels, make an example of them.'

Looking down at her, Phil thinks that she could be a little child, even though she must be, by his calculation, in her twenties.

'They'll never do that — they're not that stupid, Sarah — don't you worry that little head of yours,' he says, and makes his way out through the growing numbers of men and women, the waft of cigarette smoke and perfume following him out into the street.

Nell stares in the mirror: she has a job on her hands to make herself presentable. Most of her mass of auburn hair has escaped from its combs. She releases the rest and pulls it back off her face. She often wonders who she resembles most, her mother or her father? Under the make-up her skin is sallow. Her brown eyes stare back at her from a strong face, not beautiful, but attractive, with high cheekbones giving her an almost foreign appearance. She picks up her hairbrush and begins to tame her unruly hair.

It had been a long day, most of it spent with the Canadian, avoiding his grabbing hands and trying to say sober. But with a bit of luck, she might be able to meet a sweet old gentleman, bring him back to Anna's and let the girls take it from there. If that went to plan, she mightn't need to keep her arrangement with Connie and wrestle with some old farmer up from the country for the cattle market in Smithfield. She doesn't know why Anna insists on them bringing her farmers when she then complains they are hard work and always want their money's worth, haggling for every copper penny.

She swears that she will take a break from it all. Maybe take herself off to that big hotel overlooking the harbour in Kingstown. She's heard the girls talking about it. Like a big birthday cake, they say, layers and layers, painted all cream with a beautiful ballroom lit by chandeliers that have electricity. After breakfast she could promenade up and down the pier until the colour comes back into her face. Or maybe just sit in the sunshine, listen to the brass band and watch the yachts in the harbour. They come from all over the world, she's been told: what endless possibilities. She hears the piano starting up, a jaunty tune popular with the soldiers. Who is she fooling? There's a war on. She dabs at her face with a make-up brush, angry, stabbing gestures that make little difference.

Another evening in the Monto lies ahead.

CHAPTER 8

Levon Mordaunt makes his way down Sackville Street and stands outside the General Post Office, now a blackened skeleton of the building that it once was. Its portico looks as if it is being propped by the six tall columns now pock-marked with bullet holes. Through the broken windows he can make out the gutted interior. Large piles of rubble from the collapsed ceilings form a smouldering mountain on the ground floor and the smell of burning still lingers in the air. Hundreds of people walk up and down the once-proud thoroughfare as if in a daze. They stop and stare through the windows of the bombed-out buildings as if trying to remember them as they used to be and not as they are now.

The thrill of witnessing the results of what was, in part, his handiwork, is intoxicating. If those rifles had landed this scene would be all so different. Never before has he been so close to such devastation. He closes his eyes and breathes in the tainted air.

'*Move along, Reverend, it's dangerous here!*' a voice calls out to him.

'Of course, officer,' he replies, tipping his hat towards the policeman standing between the columns of the wrecked Post Office.

Continuing down Sackville Street he crosses over the bridge and leaves the devastation behind him. Ahead of him the south side of the city seems almost unscathed and life is coming back to normal. He dips into a large café, one of the few still open, and orders a coffee and one of the small cream cakes that he has become fond of. He waits until the waitress leaves to get his order and opens the leather satchel hand-delivered to him that morning. The courier, a nervous employee of the Chase National Bank, had refused his invitation to stay in Dublin. Instead, he had insisted on catching the next train back to Queenstown to catch the trans-Atlantic crossing.

Inside the satchel there is a bulky envelope addressed to him, marked *Private and Confidential.* He takes a penknife from his pocket and draws it across the seal, then runs his finger under the heavy tape that binds the opening. Inside there is a thick sheaf of high-denomination American dollars. Using the table as cover, he flicks through the bundle, enjoying the smell from the banknotes that drifts up.

Sensing the approach of the waitress, he slips the notes back inside the envelope. She places the coffee and cake on the table and he thanks her, patting her hand. She smiles automatically but, when she looks into his eyes, her smile fades and she pulls her hand away.

Mordaunt reopens the envelope and takes out the message inside. Handwritten on a light-blue paper, it looks like gibberish. He takes out a pencil and begins to scribble out every eighth word, then goes back to the beginning and scribbles out every fourth word. The message reads: WILSON HOLDING FAST, UNDER PRESSURE FROM HUGHES, CONTINUE FOR NOW. He tears the letter into tiny pieces and puts them into his pocket. Woodrow Wilson. Running on a neutrality ticket against the Republican Hughes. Another six months at least before he can declare war. He did the arithmetic in his head. Six men, one in each of the ports: Liverpool, Southampton,

Portsmouth, Dover, Queenstown, Belfast, board and food plus remuneration. Then there is the man inside Dublin Castle and one in the Monto. They were cheap but it all added up. He takes out the envelope and counts the money, more closely this time. A small fortune in America, a large one in Europe.

In a better humour now, Mordaunt finishes his coffee and cake and licks the stickiness from his fingers. He looks around for the waitress who had served him, but she has gone to another section of the café and is avoiding his gaze. Some women, he thinks, really do deserve everything they get. For the briefest of moments, the blackness descends and he gets an uncontrollable urge to barge through the tables throwing everyone aside, pluck her up by her scrawny neck and squeeze. Instead, he closes his eyes and breathes slowly and evenly until the blackness dissipates and dissolves into grey. The pressure has built inside him again — he can feel it like a giant hand constricting his head. It was coming more often now and one day it will kill. But not today, he thinks, and makes plans to ease it. He counts out some money and puts it on the table, then changes his mind, scoops it up, puts it back into his pocket and stands to leave, daring anyone to approach him.

Dublin, he has found, is a perfect-sized city; everything is within walking distance. From the civilised environs of Merrion Square to the basest of squalor in the Monto is less than half an hour. In that short stroll he can witness a governess shepherding her charges towards the park for a picnic or the sorriest of women hanging onto a drunken soldier's uniform, screaming for her money. But no matter where he passes through the city, the white collar he is wearing is his passport. The good people glance at him, smile and walk on without ever really looking at him. The guilty also glance at him but then shift their gaze down and rush past.

Anglesea Street is a short walk away from the café. He makes his way around College Green and passes what used to be the Houses of Parliament Buildings, but is now the Bank of Ireland. His destination: the Dublin Stock Exchange.

Once through the now familiar entrance he is acknowledged by the uniformed concierge. He returns the salute and goes directly to Cole's office on the first floor.

Frank Cole, a heavy-set man with thin, slicked-down hair not quite covering his balding head, is behind his desk proofreading that day's stock listings. He looks up and motions Mordaunt to a chair, then goes back to his work.

The office is much the same as any broker's in New York. A place where the rich grow richer and the poor are never discussed. The enormous well-polished mahogany desk brings a gravitas to the room that is meant to impress the gullible and the uninitiated. But Mordaunt knows that all of the leather-covered volumes, or the rich panelled walls decorating the rest of the room, are there merely to deflect from what really goes on behind the façade on Anglesea Street. The stock exchange, in reality, is just a sophisticated betting shop, and, to his mind, this makes the self-important figure working behind the desk a bookmaker.

Frank Cole finishes his scrutiny of the financial listings and stands up to formally acknowledge his visitor. He holds out his hand, soft, and Mordaunt grips it in his, taking pleasure in squeezing it until Cole looks uncomfortable. He lets the stockbroker's hand go and takes up the sheet from the desk, looking it up and down. A myriad of tiny numbers covers the sheet in neat columns. At first glance they seem unintelligible, but on inspection they reveal the worth of the most important companies in the world.

Mordaunt glances at the prices of his own stock and smiles.

'Well, then, Reverend Mordaunt, you seem happy,' Cole says, taking his seat again.

'Happy today, but who knows what tomorrow will bring? The Lord giveth, the Lord taketh away.'

'Indeed, as you can tell from what remains of our once great city.'

'The city will be rebuilt one day, bigger and no doubt better than ever,' Mordaunt says, folding the sheet and slipping it into his pocket.

'That may well be, Reverend, but until then our commission, unfortunately, has dropped substantially, damn those mad rebels.'

Mordaunt takes out his wallet and rummages through it. He takes out several £20 notes and hands them across the desk to the broker.

'You are, as usual, most kind, Reverend,' Cole says, slipping the money into a drawer in his desk.

'It means a lot to me to have a first glance at the listings — our church has fingers in many pies. But you can be assured that I will take it directly to Mr. Maybury — he will have it today.'

Mordaunt bows, and takes his leave.

Outside the office he turns back towards the River Liffey, this time crossing the bridge and making his way down the quays, past the ruins of a jewellery shop and on towards the Customs House. The British navy gunboat is tied to the quay wall and scores of urchins are yelling at the sailors on board, trying to get them to toss a few coins their way. From here he turns up towards Mabbot Street and makes his way directly to the small, nondescript hotel where he passes some nights. As usual there is nobody at the reception desk and he makes his way up to his room. Before he unlocks his door, he checks that the tiny piece of paper he pushed between the door and the frame is still in position.

Inside, he takes his suitcase from under the bed, opens the lid, then takes out the false bottom. Underneath are the various telegrams he has received from the agents spotted around the British Isles. He takes them to the writing desk near the window and begins to jot down the times and dates mentioned in the seemingly innocent messages. After he has the figures in a tabulated form, he lays the sheet from the stock exchange on the desk. Running his pencil down the list of companies and their prices, he underscores here and there.

When he has finished, he sits on the bed and takes out a bottle of bourbon from the bedside locker. He pours a good measure into a glass and throws it back. The shock of the spirits hitting the back of his throat makes him squint, but then the familiar warmth spreads through his body and he dwells on the good news in the telegram. If Hughes had given up his candidacy, as he had feared, and let Wilson get on with it, the Americans would go to war tomorrow and he would be redundant.

Feeling more positive, he rises from the bed. He pours water from the chipped jug into the washbowl and plunges his head in. The shock of the cold water drives away the drowsiness from the bourbon. Putting on his jacket again, he makes his way out of the hotel and heads back towards the centre of the city. Although still early in the evening, the parade of the older women has already begun, some in small groups, others standing alone. With the influx of the British reinforcements, they are enjoying the bonus of the extra young men, hungry for the company of any kind of woman. Passing them by, he has to remind himself of the collar he wears and tips his hat when occasionally some of them bow their heads towards him. He looks at his watch. The staff in the printing works will soon be finishing for the day and he can hand over his precious list to Maybury for inclusion in the next issue of the free sheet.

The stroll up the left bank of the River Liffey is a pleasant one. With his back to Sackville Street Bridge, he can almost convince himself that the rebellion has not taken place and that he is on holiday in a European city. The sun comes out and the sudden surge of heat makes him wish that he could get rid of the heavy black jacket he has to wear, but he resists the urge.

As he approaches the entrance door to the printer's there are still stragglers emerging through the doorway. He loiters outside, leaning against the quay wall. The river is at its lowest point, the receding tidal waters fully out and revealing the flotsam and jetsam of the riverbed. He gazes at the muddy water that flows past but imagines that the young man's body is long gone, swept out into Dublin Bay. If only the boy had not fallen asleep in the basement, he would not have had to kill him, but such are the vagaries of life.

When he is satisfied that the last of the workers have left the building, he crosses the road and ducks through the doorway. Inside the empty office he lifts the counter that separates the customers from the printing works and makes his way into the machine hall. He walks between the silent printing presses and on into the case room where he knows he will find Maybury.

The owner of the printing company is sitting in the glass-fronted foreman's office, head in his hands. When he raps on the glass Maybury jumps up with a start and Mordaunt wonders if he has been asleep. He takes out the marked-up sheet from the stock exchange and waves it in the air.

'I've another job for you,' he says through the glass.

Maybury comes onto the factory floor. He looks solemn, but takes the sheet from Mordaunt's hand and walks over to one of the steel-topped work tables. Spread across the surface are the galleys of type from the stock-exchange figures of the previous edition. He looks over the sheet Mordaunt has given him, looking down at the alterations, each one to be done manually and with great patience, replacing a perfect piece of type with one more worn to make it stand out by an infinitesimal amount, for what reason he cannot understand.

'This is going to take several hours,' he says, shaking his head. 'It will need at least two compositors, and they are becoming suspicious.'

'You know you'll be well paid for your work — don't complain,' Mordaunt replies, then adds, 'You look glum — what's the matter now?'

Maybury straightens up and turns to him.

'One of my apprentices was found, drowned, this morning.'

'I'm sorry to hear that. How did that happen?'

'I was hoping that you might tell me. You were the last one to see him alive. It was young Joyce.' Maybury waits for a reaction.

'I left him by the quay wall. I was going back to my hotel and said I would drop him back to his house, but he changed his mind, as young men do. Perhaps the collar put him off.'

'I knew this boy, knew his family — he would never have strayed from his routine,' Maybury says. 'And the police are of the same view.'

Mordaunt's face becomes still. 'The police, I see. So, they are interested in the case.'

Maybury folds up the sheet of paper. 'You know, I have been thinking about our dealings and perhaps it is time we parted company.'

'Really? What about our arrangement?'

'It was an arrangement, not a contract,' Maybury says, and thrusts the list back at Mordaunt.

Mordaunt reaches out as if to take it from him but instead grabs his arm and, with a twist, forces the older man around, his arm pinned behind his back. Maybury lets out a grunt of expelled air as he is pushed against the steel working surface. The pain in his shoulder forces his mouth to open in agony but, before he can scream out, Mordaunt pushes a filthy ink-stained rag into it. Tears come into Maybury's eyes as his arm is pushed further and further up his back until he is on the verge of fainting. At the last moment Mordaunt eases the pressure slightly and pulls the cloth from the shaking man's mouth.

'We had an arrangement, Maybury,' he says, breathing into his ear. 'And it will be *I* who decides when it comes to an end.'

Maybury, in shock, nods.

'Before you have any further thoughts about reneging, just remember your wife and four children. Your eldest daughter is particularly exquisite — it would be a pity to have anything bad happen to her.'

'How dare you! What do you know of my family? I will have you arrested and imprisoned!'

'Do you think I work alone? At this moment one of my colleagues is watching your beautiful home in Blackrock … now, where is it? Ah yes, Idrone Terrace. What magnificent views it has too, right over the sea. But the front garden is very exposed and that laneway that runs behind — you really should do something about that.'

'*You bastard!*' Maybury says, tears of frustration running down his face. 'I should have trusted my instincts when you strolled in here wearing that white collar. You are no man of God!'

'Mammon, Maybury, don't forget the mammon. You were glad of it then.'

'What kind of a man of the church are you?' Maybury says, rubbing his bruised lips.

'You'll never know. Now, let's go into the office and rest that shoulder of yours. I'm afraid that you will have to do the alterations by yourself. You're right — your men would be too suspicious. Perhaps you should telephone your wife and tell her that you might be home late tonight, or early tomorrow.' He hands Maybury a slip of paper with the telephone number of his own home, along with his full address.

CHAPTER 9

A strange atmosphere hangs in the air as Christopher makes his way through the rubble-strewn streets towards the hotel Byatt mentioned. Workmen are piling up small mountains of rock from the devastated buildings. Groups of people, mostly men, congregate in front of the worst-hit structures as if waiting to see if they will collapse. Street dealers are taking advantage of the crowds and push their barrows between them, holding out random items: pieces of fruit, cheap jewellery, children's toys and brown-paper bags of home-made sweets. He walks past the burnt-out shell of a motorcar, its exposed metal blackened. A man sits smoking a cigarette on the front seat of a horse and trap and stares down at it, taking pleasure in the sight of the wreck of the new-fangled contraption once a threat to his business.

The shop with the most damage is Hopkins and Hopkins, a jeweller's he remembers passing occasionally as an over-awed teenager. The opulent window display used to change every week which meant there was always something new to stare at. A lavish display of glittering gold and silver trinkets, each one with a tiny handwritten price tag that left him slack-jawed with wonder. What manner of person could afford those prices? But the section of the display he remembers most were the pocket watches. They hung in the window from thick gold or silver chains, tokens of respectability. Standing in front of it all those years ago, he had sworn that one day he was going to buy one of those magical watches. Now his dream palace is just a pile of rubble beside which a young, nervous soldier stands guard to put off any potential looters.

Before going to the hotel, he decides to wander up to the General Post Office, where, he had read, the leaders had decided to make their stand. To his eyes it was an impossible position to defend and the people who had made the decision fell even lower in his estimation. The attack on Dublin Castle he could have understood. A powerful symbol of British power in Ireland, holding it for any length of time would have sent out a clarion call. If they had blown up the two main train stations to cut off reinforcements and concentrated all their forces on the south side of the river using the canal as an outer defence and Dublin Castle as their main headquarters, that would have made tactical sense. But the General Post Office? Overlooked by buildings to the front and rear and within easy range of the river. With the British using their artillery it should have been over in a couple of days and he reckons it was blind luck that they had held out for a week. He joins the watchers beside Nelson's Pillar for a while, listening to their hushed conversations. Most of them have no time for the rebels and are complaining about the disruption to their daily lives and the utter devastation around them. He overhears a few of the rebels' names but knows none of them, yet these men have wrecked people's lives, and for what? Some of them were probably the same pathetic toy soldiers whom a few years ago he jeered as they paraded through the city using hurley sticks for rifles.

An argument starts between two men. One, a student from Trinity College judging by his dress and his accent, calls it vandalism of the highest order. The other man is small and neat and reminds Christopher of his father. He seems to be defending the rebels as he berates the student.

'And where do you think you'll be next year when they run short of young men for the war? You'll be conscripted into the British army and end up in France, that's where!'

'You are talking rubbish — the war is nearly over,' the student answers confidently.

'That's what they said in 1914,' the small, neat man says with a laugh.

But the student insists that will never happen and Christopher leaves them arguing about the war in Europe. Turning his back on the pitiful pock-marked columns of the General Post Office, he crosses Sackville Street and begins to pick his way carefully through rubble-strewn North Earl Street. For an uncomfortable moment he wonders if his mission might be over before it begins. What if Byatt is mistaken and the hotel chosen for him is a smouldering wreck? But when he reaches the junction with Talbot Street it is as if he has arrived in a different city. One moment he's walking over mounds of rubble, then suddenly he is back in the familiar surroundings of his childhood.

The hotel is, as Byatt had said, small and inconspicuous, its entrance squeezed between two shopfronts. One of the shops sells religious paraphernalia: rosary beads, gold-embossed prayer books, leather-covered bibles and lurid pictures of suffering saints. The other is a pork butcher's — Hafner's, a German name. Scrawled across the window in white paint is the message: *OPEN SOON*. The empty metal trays in the window are covered with a layer of dust and he wonders if the family have been hounded out because of the war. He has a vague memory of his father introducing him to the owner once, in their yard. A small dark man with a moustache that spanned his face and seemed to run up to his ears. He wore a jacket, he remembered, but the underneath the jacket was a bloody apron. He had come straight from his butcher shop to complain about offal he had bought from Christopher's father. They had argued about it back and forth for a while and then his father had handed him a shilling which seemed to settle their dispute.

The hotel's name is etched into the fanlight over the door, but the glass in the fanlight is so grubby that it's difficult to make out: *The Talbot Hotel*. It has a plain door with a small cardboard sign tacked to it that says the reception is on the first floor. As Byatt had suggested, he has bought a second-hand suitcase. Inside are the rest of the clothes Byatt had bought him, some toiletries and several newspapers. For the rest of the day, he intends to study these and find out exactly what has happened during the uprising and also to catch up on news about Ireland.

Standing in front of the hotel, he realises that once he steps through the door, he is committing to being an agent for Byatt. Back in the clothing store with Byatt, he had not realised what was about to happen. He is still a member of the Crown forces but it feels underhanded, somehow, to be skulking around Dublin, pretending to be somebody he isn't. In the meantime, his brother, Ned, lies in an unmarked grave in France, still unavenged. Before he steps through the door, he crosses himself and makes a promise that when the war is over, he will attempt to find out Ned's last resting place and visit it.

A bell tinkles as he pushes open the door. The narrow hallway, illuminated by a single sad bulb that hangs from the ceiling, was obviously used by the butcher's next door. A messenger bike advertising the freshest of meat still leans against the wall, its tyres flat, a redundant lock and chain wrapped around the back wheel. A musty smell hangs in the air and the overall impression is of a hotel that has seen better days. Up the creaking stairs things are not that much different.

The reception is a simple mahogany desk. Behind it sits an elderly woman dressed in black with a pair of glasses perched across her nose. Her head is bent and she ignores him, continuing to read a newspaper which she has laid out flat across the desk. She is reading it with difficulty, her nose almost touching the newsprint, her finger following the type. When she has finished the article, she looks up, pushes a ledger towards him and tells him to write his name, address and occupation. As he is writing she begins to list off the do's and don'ts of the hotel, adding that it is a respectable establishment, that under no circumstances can he bring anybody back to his room. He looks up to say something about the curfew and his heart drops when he notices the photograph displayed prominently on the wall behind her: Matt Talbot, the most famous reformed alcoholic in Ireland and leader of the temperance movement, and he had just written that he was a salesman of alcohol.

'What if I need to stay out late at night? Can I have a key?' he asks.

'And what would you be doing out late at night? There's a curfew from half eight! Unless, of course, you intend to visit that Sodom and Gomorrah around the corner, which, by the will of the Devil is still standing.'

'Of course not,' he replies, thinking quickly, 'but my work sometimes makes it necessary to come and go at unusual hours.'

'And what would that be?' she says, turning the ledger around so that she can read his name, 'Mr. Andrews.'

Her eyes drift across the page and harden when she sees that he is salesman in fine wines and alcohol. Trusting that Byatt's information was correct about the hotel, he leans in across the desk and drops his voice to a whisper.

'You can ignore what I've written there. I'm a detective in the Dublin Metropolitan Police. But for reasons that I'm sure you would be aware of, I would prefer that not to be known.'

The word *detective* had just popped into his mind and he thinks, why not? He is as near as he ever would be to being a detective.

'I see,' she says, studying him closely. 'You seem very young to be a detective, but you also look too young to be a salesman. Sure, what do I know?'

'Yes, I am young for a detective. In the times we are living through, the older men don't like to take risks.'

'Of course, I understand,' she says. 'I believe that some of the public houses around on Montgomery Street are a hotbed of decadence and revolution.'

Christopher reaches inside his jacket pocket, takes out a notebook and ostentatiously jots down what she has said, then snaps it shut.

The woman sits back in her seat and smiles up at him.

'Thank you very much, Miss …?'

'Mrs. Daly — but Mr. Daly has passed on,' she says.

'I'm sure he would be proud of you.'

'I do my best,' she says. 'Cyril was a staunch member of the Legion of Mary and spent most of his life parading up and down those horrible streets, praying to the Lord and pointing out to the people the abominations that exist in this city. But, in the end, it all became too much for him and he succumbed to TB. That's what he got for all his trouble.'

'Hopefully, Mrs. Daly, I can help, in a small way, to carry on his good work,' Christopher says, and bows his head.

Mrs. Daly reaches into a drawer and takes out a key-ring with a single key, then clips another one onto it, handing it over to him.

'You are room number six, up another flight and towards the front of the hotel. It's one of our best rooms but I'll only charge you for a standard room. The smaller key is for the front entrance. It's not everyone who gets one, but I can see that you're a good man.'

'Thank you, Mrs. Daly. I will do my best to be as discreet as possible.' Christopher picks up his suitcase and makes his way up the narrow stairs to his room.

He unlocks the door and pushes it open. A stale smell hangs in the air, a mixture of hair oil and old cigarette smoke. The room is small and cramped, made even more miserable by the faded wallpaper. If this is one of the better ones, he can't imagine what the standard rooms are like. He puts his suitcase down, closes the door and pulls up the sash window to let some air into the room. The sounds from the street drift up and a light breeze billows out the net curtains. Now that he has a place to stay, he needs a plan of action. His time in the army has taught him to make some kind of plan, with objectives, alternative objectives and fall-backs. Already he is beginning to feel a little more in control of his situation. He takes out the notebook and a pencil and begins to write.

The Monto may have over a thousand prostitutes plying their trade, but still it isn't a huge area. After he visits the pub that Byatt has mentioned he'll go for a recce, stroll through the streets, familiarise himself with his surroundings and draw a rough map. And then what? All he knows for certain about Janus is that he is a man, possibly American. In an area such as the Monto, populated with people from all around the world, he wouldn't stand out and the odds of finding him are almost non-existent. But he has to give it a try — he owes Byatt that much.

He shuts the notebook and looks around for a place to hide it. It is the last thing he wants to be caught with in Shanahan's pub. Other than a small washbasin, the only other furniture in the room is a bed and a wardrobe. He thinks it might be too obvious but lifts the horsehair mattress anyway. The dirt underneath reassures him. It looks as if Mrs Daly, or whoever cleans for her, doesn't get upstairs too often. He widens a torn seam on the edge of the mattress and slips the notebook inside, forcing it deep into the horsehair, lets the mattress down again and smooths out the blankets.

It is early evening now, still a couple of hours left before he makes his first foray into the Monto. He decides to keep the newspapers until the following day and to take a rest. One of the most important skills he has learned in the army is to take short naps whenever the opportunity presents itself. Even under the dull thud of artillery and the sharp crackle of rifle fire he has always managed it.

On the inside of the wardrobe door there is a full-length mirror, pitted and scratched. The cuts and scrapes he received in the struggle with the soldiers are already fading but probably lent credence to his story that he was a young, active detective. And Byatt had a good eye — the suit, although second-hand, is of good quality. It is his first proper suit of clothes, he realises, and it makes him look more mature. His face, usually clean-shaven, is covered with a light stubble, but under the stubble his skin has a healthy enough appearance. His thick, dark hair, parted in the middle, could do with a wash and a cut. He would think about that tomorrow. But there is something different about the figure that stands before him. He realises he is starting to look more like his father. Not his father when he had the sickness, but the smiling man within the pages of the precious wedding album he remembers flicking through with Ned.

He undresses, hangs the suit up carefully and lies down on top of the bed. It is the first real bed he has been in for months, and he tries to drift off to sleep. But his memories of the wedding album have awakened even more memories from his past, unwelcome ones about his parents' sickness. About the priest from St Nicholas of Myra chapel who spent most of his visits berating the British, their imperial oppressors. Or the doctor who arrived to their room and didn't even bother to examine his parents, but told his father to get himself and his wife down to the sanatorium in Wicklow for the cure, that there was nothing he could do for them. These people, to a young boy, were from a different world, a world of privilege. They were the same class of Irish people who had taken it onto themselves to start a war they could never win, on behalf of the masses who had no interest in their cause.

Eventually he falls into a fitful sleep. His dreams are filled with scattered images: of his parents and Ned, of the broken city of Dublin and of the nameless shape that lurks in the shadows of the streets of the Monto.

CHAPTER 10

Faithful Place, a tiny laneway off Railway Street, is a sad collection of brown-stone two-storey houses. Located only a stone's throw from the more upmarket brothels of Montgomery Street, it is almost ignored except by a select number of gentlemen who require a more specialised service than that available in the rest of Dublin's red-light district. In the parlour of Number 3, Concepta (Connie) Noble, sits sipping a glass of fortified wine. Connie is a handsome, well-built woman in her mid-thirties. Several years previously she took the decision to stop selling her body in the local kips around the corner on Purdon Street. Working there, she foresaw her own future written in the used-up faces and bodies of her fellow prostitutes, women not much older than herself. The old saying was not far off the mark: sailors two a penny, big fat men two pound ten. Saving up every shilling she earned under the sweating bodies of drunken soldiers and sailors who hadn't enough money for the more expensive brothels, she had rented the little terraced two-storey house to facilitate the gentlemen who sought out a more exotic service.

Connie Noble had arrived in Amiens Street train station in the early stages of pregnancy, unmarried, forced by her parents to have her child away from the prying eyes of neighbours. She stood outside the bustling train station, the address of a Magdalen Laundry scrawled on a scrap of paper, folded up and held tightly in her right hand. There, she was assured by a girlfriend, she would be taken in and looked after by the nuns. Her plan was simple: have the baby, abscond from the laundry with her baby at the first opportunity, then find a job as a skivvy in one of the more affluent parts of Dublin. She imagined herself, in time, working herself up to being a parlour maid in a fine house in Merrion Square or Fitzwilliam Square. Then she would find a man who would take care of her and her child.

Originally from a townland outside Drogheda, she was a farm girl, strong, big-boned, used to working long hours on her father's farm and not afraid to get her hands dirty. But standing in the soot-filled air outside the busy train station, the clamour and confusion of the capital city overpowering her senses, she froze. Connie felt herself rooted to the spot, unable to decide what was the best thing to do: take a room in a small hotel for the night and spend some of her money, or find out where the Magdalen Laundry was, go there directly and throw herself on the nun's mercy. Crowds milled around, ignoring her. She had never seen so many uniforms, worn by loud men with strange accents, occasionally making remarks about her that she did not understand.

The lady who approached and asked if could she offer some assistance looked respectable. She was petite, like a sparrow, and had a kind smile. Connie nodded, thankful for the friendly face that beamed up at her. When the lady asked if she was feeling unwell and would she like to go for a nice cup of warm tea, Connie agreed. The woman took her hand and led her to a nearby tearoom in Talbot Street. As she sipped her tea and ate one of the small cakes that the lady had ordered for them, she began to feel better.

'My name is Dorothy Brogan, but you can call me Dotty,' the woman said between tiny sips from her cup.

Connie could never figure out why she spilled out her life story to a stranger in such a few short minutes, but the lady had that effect on her — she was a good listener. Connie told her about the impending baby and her parents and her dreams for the future.

When they had finished their tea, Dotty suggested she should go with her. Her house, she said, was nearby and Connie was looking a little pale. Connie was relieved when the woman paid for the tea and cakes. Outside, the street was full of people, mainly men, who seemed to her to be from another world: these men were, unlike the soldiers, badly dressed, small and thin with tight faces and unhealthy complexions. Scattered among them were women, most carrying baskets and staring straight ahead, anxious to get back to their homes and out of the noisy, dusty streets.

It was a substantial red-bricked house that Dotty led her to: three storeys, with a massive bay window that commanded a view of the street. It stood at the end of a terrace of similar houses that had seen better days, but Dotty's house seemed to be better kept than the rest. To Connie the house was palatial. A newly painted front door stood solidly at the top of some granite steps. Only the garden was a disappointment to Connie, a tiny patch of sparsely covered earth to the left of the steps.

Dotty, smiling benignly, opened the front door and ushered her into a wide hallway. Connie took in the high ceilings and the ornate chandelier, the beautiful plasterwork and the old paintings hung along the walls. Most of them were of pastoral scenes: men dressed in red on horseback hunting a fox, or a young lady sitting tranquilly under a tree making buttercup chains. While she stared in wonder at the paintings, Mrs. Brogan rang a bell and then directed her into one of the rooms off the hallway. The room was a little tawdrier than the hallway and the cloying smell of tobacco hung in the air.

Dotty pointed to a chair. 'Take a seat, dear. I will order some port for you. It will put some colour back into your cheeks.'

'Thank you very much, Mrs. Brogan,' Connie said, sitting down.

'Call me Dotty, all the girls do.'

A young woman knocked and entered. She smiled at Connie and stood, waiting. Dotty ordered two glasses of port and waved her away.

'And tell me, dear, why on earth did you pick the Magdalen Laundry?' Dotty asked.

'I was told the nuns would welcome me and help when I'm due. Then, after, I could look to stand on my own two feet and get a job as a maid.'

Dotty laughed. 'I am afraid you have been sold a pup as they say. The nuns will welcome you in, that much I agree. But they will take their pound of flesh. There is nothing for nothing in this world.'

Then, as they sipped their port, she described what life was like for fallen women behind the high walls of the convent: up at six, Mass, work in the laundry for twelve hours, then lights out. The only break she would get would be the birth of her child. She would then be forced to stay for three years, working in the laundry and breastfeeding her baby, after which the child would be whipped away from her and sold on to some well-off family. On and on it went until Connie finally broke down, any thought of getting a job after the birth of her child and finding a man who would protect them, gone. But Dotty had the solution: a doctor friend, very understanding, would deliver the baby when it was due, and she could get on with her life.

Connie couldn't believe her luck in finding this kind woman and threw herself onto her knees on the floor in front of her, sobbing with gratitude.

As the evening drew in, Dotty escorted her to a room in the attic and told her to get some sleep and she would talk to her the following morning. The room was tiny and directly under the eaves. It was only in the middle that she could stand up to her full height. Under the sloping ceiling there was a mattress that she had to get onto her hands and knees to reach. Still, she was so tired after her journey and the long day that she didn't mind. Lying back on the mattress, she could look through the skylight window at the stars that shone down through that small square of glass. As she drifted off to sleep the sound of music and laughter drifted up from the floors below. The lady must have other guests, she thought, before exhaustion took its toll and she fell into a deep sleep.

Over the following weeks she saw very little of Dotty. During the day the house was quiet except for a young maid who worked from dawn until night, when the lady's friends arrived in the evenings. Most of the friends, when she caught a peek of them, were men in uniform, English soldiers, loud and drunk, who sang strange songs in accents she could hardly understand, but they seemed happy. Up in her attic room she listened to the gaiety below as she ate her food, cooked by the young maid and served on a tray.

When the lady finally did visit her in her room, Connie was slightly surprised at her brusque manner — she was not at all as she remembered her. She wondered if she had done something wrong.

'How are you, Connie? Doing well up here?' Dotty asked, taking the only chair in the room.

'Everything is fine, Dotty,' Connie replied.

'You can address me as Mrs. Brogan,' she said and rummaged in her handbag. She took out a sheet of ruled paper and handed it to Connie.

'What's this, ma'am?'

'This is the bill for your board and keep.'

Connie took the sheet of paper and unfolded it. Listed down one side were the details of every meal she had eaten down to individual cups of tea, every piece of laundry that had been done for her by the young maid and every night she had spent under Mrs. Brogan's roof. Her eyes widened when she saw the total amount at the bottom of the page: forty pounds, two shillings and ten pence. A fortune. She felt her face begin to burn and instinctively she put her hand down to her stomach where her pregnancy was beginning to show.

'But I can't afford this!' she cried.

'On fripperies, no doubt. Well then, I'll have to call the police, won't I?' Mrs. Brogan replied, standing up, getting ready to leave.

'No, please, not the police! My family would be shamed,' Connie said, getting down on her knees and gripping the other woman's dress.

Mrs. Brogan seemed to stop and think for a while, then sat back down on the chair.

'Perhaps I am being a bit hard on you. How were you to know the arrangements? Very well, first things first. We will go to my friend and take care of that,' she said, looking at the bump barely showing under Connie's dress. 'It will make your bill a bit higher, but we can work something out. Now, get your coat on.'

Thus began the short, sharp descent for Connie. First stop was the back-street abortionist, an ex-nurse, who waved away all of her pleadings and covered her mouth with an unwashed cloth soaked in ether. She woke slowly and painfully but the nurse, as soon as she saw that she was awake, told her it was time to go.

As she staggered down the street, half-carried by Mrs. Brogan's maid, she could barely take in what was happening. The maid, Helen Cummins, assured her that everything was going to be fine and that she would be up and about in a week.

The week turned into two days and then, still weak from the loss of blood, Connie was standing in front of Mrs. Brogan.

'You don't seem any the worse for wear, Connie — you must come from hardy stock,' said Mrs. Brogan, walking around her, examining her like a prize cow.

'I still feel very weak, ma'am.'

'You should have thought of that before you opened your legs then, shouldn't you? Sometimes life's little pleasures turn out to be very expensive. Let me see …'

Mrs. Brogan sat down behind her desk. Mumbling to herself, she jotted down more entries into her ledger, shaking her head. Connie just wanted to lie down again in her little bed in the attic and get some rest but Mrs Brogan was taking her time and seems to be taking pleasure at her discomfort. She totted up the figures and looked up at Connie.

'Are your parents rich?'

'I beg you, please, Mrs. Brogan, don't tell my family — it will do no good. They rent a small parcel of —'

'Enough. You do realise I run a business here?'

Connie nodded.

'And you do know what kind of business?'

Connie nodded again and lowered her head.

'Well, then. The solution to all of our problems is very simple. You work for me until you have paid me back what you owe.'

'As a maid?'

'Don't be stupid. I have a maid.'

'I don't think I could do … what the other girls do,' Connie felt as if she was about to faint.

'Don't be silly, Connie, of course you can. You've done it already, and for nothing. There's very little difference. And above all, it will be a lot easier than prison.'

'Oh dear God, what have I done,' Connie moaned.

'So, you agree?'

Connie realised that she had been a young fool and had been deceived. She had made the mistake of trusting people and of seeing goodness in them that was never there. But she swore to herself that she would never make that mistake again.

Leaving her youth forever, she nodded in acceptance.

Mrs. Brogan's kip was not the cheapest in the Monto but it was far from being the most expensive. Most of the clientele were either British soldiers who got drunk and haggled mercilessly with Dotty, or the sailors who came ashore from the nearby docks to spend as little as possible in having as good a time as possible. While there were very few big spending clients, Mrs Brogan made up for this in turnover. From early evening her door was open to all comers and her bedrooms were well-used. Connie, disgusted and humiliated at first, found ways to turn her mind off. Unlike the other prostitutes, she did not drink heavily to ease her suffering, as this was what Mrs Brogan wanted. At the end of the week, after she had paid her girls, she would take out her ledger and get most of it back from the gin she supplied.

Connie was no fool and recognised what was happening. She began to save. Every penny she earned went under her mattress in the attic and then into the Trustee Savings Bank, for what, she was not too sure. But she knew that if she stayed on in Mrs. Brogan's, she would go the way of the older prostitutes, into the twilight world of the streets and into sickness and early death. She began to recognise the different types of men, the drunk, the maudlin, the cruel, the guilty, and used her knowledge to avoid the worst abusers.

One or two of her customers were different. Instead of rushing to get their money's worth, once inside the bedroom they begged to be forgiven and even insisted on being punished. At first puzzled, she soon got used to their strange behaviour as it meant less work for her. For the most part they were rich men, judging by their clothes and manners and even brought along the implements to be used. But, most importantly, they paid very well and always tipped her generously.

Eventually the day arrived when she could afford to leave the brothel and rent her own place, a small, two storey-house in need of repair. But at least it was her own and most of her special clients followed her. Dotty, incensed, made all kinds of threats against her but Connie, wise to the delicate balance that existed between madams and the police, knew that nothing would come of it.

Word of mouth meant that Connie was never short of men. Within a year she had been joined by Helen, the young maid who had been so kind to her in Mrs. Brogan's.

Sitting in the parlour of Number 3, Faithful Place, Connie prepares herself for his visit and wonders again about her newest client. Not an unattractive man, every Friday he hires her services for the entire weekend, money no object. To get a request from him during the week was most unusual.

She had suspected at first that he might be a police detective trying to trap her. But then he explained what he wanted her to do, what she was to wear when she was doing it and how to wash him from head to toe after their little play had finished. This is now his fourth week and she is wondering how she can bring an end to his visits.

She stands up and looks at her reflection in the mirror. Her face, unlike a lot of the women in the Monto, is blemish-free, but her eyes have taken on a haunted look. She thinks about ordering Helen, her maid, to pack their bags and lock up the house for a while. Then she remembers her other customers, her loyal customers, who might go elsewhere while she is away. She would be back where she started: penniless. But, she makes up her mind, there are some depravities that would never be forgiven in the confessional and she would spend eternity in hell. She is about to shout out for Helen to begin packing when the three familiar knocks sound on the hall door.

CHAPTER 11

Christopher wakes up and lies still, trying to hold on to the mishmash of memories that made up his dream. It was based around the only holiday his family had ever taken together, in the seaside town of Bray. Ned had been in a pram at the time but in the dream Christopher and his brother were walking side by side along the esplanade, both of them in uniform — which was impossible. The man who sold the cockles and mussels from the brightly painted handcart was also in the dream, shouting out at the passing crowds. Although he couldn't see them, he was aware that his parents were walking somewhere behind, laughing and talking together.

The dream had brought with it a feeling of euphoria and he tries desperately to sink back into its warm embrace, but it's useless; the harder he tries the more frustrated he becomes. He gets up off the bed cautiously and tries not to aggravate the injuries he had received in his altercation with Tommy Sherry. His body seems to have almost healed from those injuries, but the older wound in his thigh is beginning to throb. Staring out of the window at Talbot Street, he sees to his surprise that it is still quite bright outside. He looks at his watch and realises that he has been asleep for less than half an hour. But, in that brief time, he had spent several days with his parents and Ned, walking around the cliff walk or listening to the brass bands that played on the esplanade. He can remember his mother teasing out periwinkles using a small pin and shaking the flaccid piece of flesh in front of his eyes to frighten him. He savours each precious memory from the dream and tries desperately to hold onto the images and sounds of the seaside, but the more he tries to hold on to them the more they fade until there is nothing left except a few disjointed impressions and the tears that now trickle down his cheeks. The horrors of the last two years in the trenches and then the news about Ned merge together in one tearful purge. Now he has a strange, empty feeling inside that he can't explain. The anger he has been carrying around with him since he heard of Ned's death has dissipated and is replaced with a strange hollowness.

It's odd to see the change in the type of activity outside on Talbot Street. Not that much earlier the atmosphere had been much more sedate, with large families, mainly women with their children, window-shopping or visiting the few shops that were still open. Now there is a different type of person, younger, male and many in uniform all heading in one direction: towards the Monto. There is a brass oil lamp and a box of matches beside the washbasin. He lights the lamp and closes over the curtains, takes off his shirt and vest and shaves carefully, then washes himself, shivering as he splashes the cold water over his head and his body. Dripping wet, he realises that Mrs. Daly hasn't supplied a towel — he hadn't thought to buy one. After drying himself with a corner of the blanket he dresses in front of the mirror and, with one last look, leaves his room.

Mrs. Daly is sitting in the same position he left her earlier, elbows

on the table, reading glasses perched on top of her nose, her finger
still tracing across what seemed to be the same newspaper. Her head
lifts and she smiles up at him. She seems more benign than she did
earlier.

'Are you stepping out, Mr. Andrews?' she asks, holding her finger
on the newspaper in case she loses her place.

'The government's work has to be done, Mrs. Daly. Don't wait up.
I don't know what time I will be back.'

'Of course, I understand,' she says, closing over her newspaper and
getting slowly to her feet.

Judging by the stillness in the lobby and from the rooms around
him, he begins to realise that he is, in fact, the only person staying in
the hotel. Mrs. Daly is lonely and has probably been waiting for him
to come down for company.

'But I should be back before dawn,' he says.

'If you like I can prepare breakfast for you — it's not much what
with the way the deliveries are, but it is included in the price.'

'That would be nice. I bid you a good evening, Mrs. Daly,' he says
as he begins to descend the stairs.

Mention of breakfast has made him feel hungry. Outside the hotel
he turns left and makes his way towards Gardner Street. A few doors
down from the hotel he stands outside a fish and chip shop, its
window foggy with condensation. The smell of the fish and chips
frying in the hot lard and the tangy odour of vinegar is irresistible.
Inside, an Italian couple are trying to keep up with the orders. Sweat
pours down their faces as they shovel hot chips and fish onto sheets
of newspaper, fold them over and hand them out to the waiting
customers. The shouts of 'one and one' are coming at them faster
than they can manage. The man throws his metal scoop down onto
the counter, wipes his hands, and disappears into the back of the shop.

When he returns, he has a young dark-haired girl with him and he says something at her in Italian. She shouts back at him but walks obediently to the woman's side and begins to help with the cooking. When it comes to Christopher's turn, he points to the sign and asks for a large bag of chips.

Outside he opens up the newspaper and the smell of the chips smothered in salt and vinegar makes him salivate. As he strolls across Gardiner Street in the direction of the Monto, he resists the urge to eat too quickly as the long slivers of fried potato are still too hot.

When he reaches the junction with Mabbot Street, he turns left and makes his way towards Montgomery Street. He stops in the shelter of a doorway to eat his meal, observing the women, some alone, some in small groups, as they call out to the passing men. Heads come together, negotiations are undertaken, usually with a shout of laughter or encouragement from their companions. Once or twice a soldier staggers off in the direction of a laneway, propped up by a woman.

By the time he has finished his chips, the pavements around him are teeming with people. All of life is there. Soldiers, young dandies, loud-mouthed students encouraging each other with shoves and shouts over to the waiting women. Solitary businessmen, well dressed, press through the crowds, heads down, on their way to the more upmarket brothels. Any one of those could be Janus, he realises. Hard-faced children run about soliciting coppers from the women who, in their need to get rid of them, throw a few coins at them. He finds it hard to equate the hustle and bustle of the Monto with the sedate streets he had travelled through all those years ago.

He makes his way across to the entrance to Montgomery Street and turns down, almost with reluctance, to begin his search for Shanahan's pub. Pushing his way through the crowded pavements he holds his head low, half expecting to be recognised by one of the many passing soldiers. But he reminds himself that the chances are slim, as most of his company are still in France, either sitting in the muddy trenches or buried beneath the yellow-brown earth.

CHAPTER 12

Christopher has no trouble in locating the pub: it is the noisiest building on the street. The sound of men's laughter carries through the night. Instead of going in straight away, he strolls past and glances in through the window. Byatt was accurate in his description. The pub is packed, mostly with men, all types and ages. The worry of having to stand alone at the counter and exchange banter with a curious barman is put to rest. If anything, he would be doing well to catch the barman's attention. He saunters as far as the next corner, turns back and pushes through the double doors. A wall of noise and heat surrounds him. To his immediate left there is another discreet door leading into a snug. He pulls the door open, hoping to escape the hectic atmosphere, but the snug is already occupied by a soldier, his uniform undone, his face ruddy with alcohol. A young woman sits on his lap, wearing his cap. He mumbles an apology to the pair and turns to go back into the public bar. The shouts of the young woman follow him: '*Have ye no manners? Did your mother not teach yeh to knock first? I know the owner — I can get you thrown out!*'

Embarrassed, he looks around for somewhere to sit. Luckily a space appears further up the bar as two soldiers lurch away, arm in arm, towards the toilets. He shoulders his way through the crowd and holds his hand up for service. When the barman asks him impatiently what he wants to drink he realises that it has been over two years since he has been in any kind of public house. In France and Belgium, whenever his company had earned some R&R, the men had spent their time in the cafés or small bars that served local beers or cider along with food. He glances over the barman's shoulder at the bottles lined up and points towards a whiskey whose label he recognises. The barman pours out a measure and slams it down onto the counter with a glass of water. After he has paid and the barman has gone on to his next customer, he realises that he should have ordered a pint of plain porter as he could have nursed it for an hour. Now all he has in front of him is a tiny glass of spirits. He sees the barman coming his way again and drinks it quickly, wincing at the taste, then orders a pint of porter.

The noise level in the pub rises as he sips his pint. Nobody around him seems interested in conversation, not that he would get much information out of them. Without Byatt at this side, he doubts his ability to find out anything in this crowded place. Even now there could be a British agent among the red-faced drinkers watching his every move. In a funny way, his new reality is not that much different to the one he found himself in when he woke up in Dublin Castle. He is still prisoner in his own city, the only difference being he has been offered the opportunity to avoid the executioner.

A beggar has managed to slip into the pub and is standing on a table. He starts to sing a bawdy street ballad out of tune and at the top of his voice to the cheers of the drinkers. A white-aproned barman appears and pulls him down, then marches him out the door to the street.

The effects of the whiskey along with the porter has made Christopher more relaxed and he begins to pay closer attention to the conversations around him. Drunken banter, a mixture of sports and politics, but mainly, of course, the armed rebellion that has taken place not so far from where they are standing. He is surprised to hear that opinion is divided evenly, even though a large section of the city, their city, has been utterly destroyed in a such a fruitless gesture. He wonders if all of Dublin would now be in ruins if the arms shipment had not been intercepted. Under those circumstances a massive artillery bombardment would surely have been unleashed. How would all of these armchair generals have reacted then? He looks down and is surprised to see that his glass his empty, so he orders another pint.

Somebody begins to play on an old upright piano standing against the wall at the back of the pub. It is the popular music-hall song, 'A Long Way to Tipperary'. He expects everybody to join in, but the reaction is muted. He looks down towards the piano and sees one of the soldiers whose place he had taken at the bar. People have turned their backs on both him and his comrade who is propped up against the piano encouraging everyone to join in the chorus. But the chilly atmosphere in the pub has got through to them and their efforts trails off into an embarrassed silence. Christopher reaches for his glass again. The dark porter slides down his throat with ease. Now he feels a little giddy. He belches loudly and can taste the chips he had eaten earlier. He takes another mouthful of porter to get the taste from his mouth and somebody pushes against him, causing him to spill his drink. The man, well-dressed and wearing a top hat, apologises and insists on replacing the drink. The barman rushes off and comes back with another pint of porter and a whiskey. Christopher is going to object but in all the noise and confusion he gives up. The man who bought him the drinks slaps him on the shoulder and turns back to the group he is drinking with.

Christopher stares down at the two drinks on the bar in front of him. He makes his mind up that when he has finished these he will go back to the hotel, get a good night's sleep and try again the following night. But the next time he comes to Phil Shanahan's pub he will sip his drink and make it last the night. He tosses the whiskey back. This time the taste is less harsh. A fight breaks out around the piano between the two soldiers and several of the other customers. The two soldiers fight back as best they can, their backs to the wall, trading blow with blow. Every time a punch lands from either side a loud shout goes up. The alcohol takes most of the sting from the blows and the fight ends abruptly, the opponents staggering over to the bar and sharing a drink together to more cheers. Christopher also raises his glass high into the air and shouts out his approval. He feels a tug on his arm and looks around.

Staring into his face is the girl he interrupted in the snug earlier.

'*You owe me a drink!*' she shouts, to make herself heard.

'*Why's that?*' Christopher shouts back.

'*You frightened my boyfriend away!*' she answers and elbows a man who has draped his arm around her shoulder.

'*Not much of a boyfriend then, is he?*' Christopher laughs and turns his back on her.

The slap on the side of his head is not a painful one, more of a shock. When he swivels around, she is standing with her hands on her hips, daring him to do something. The people immediately around them become aware of what has happened and wait for Christopher's reaction. Red-faced, he turns back to the bar and takes a sip from his pint to loud jeers from the onlookers who feel robbed of their entertainment. The girl then turns on them, telling them to shut up and to leave her boyfriend alone, then links her arm through his. He is going to push her away but changes his mind and calls out to the barman. When the barman recognises the girl beside him, he brings over another pint for Christopher and a glass of clear spirits. She takes up the glass and drinks it back in one go, slamming it back onto the bar.

'Don't be miserable, love, get your girl another drink,' she says.

Christopher turns to the girl and looks at her closely for the first time. She is quite tall, almost as tall as he is with long, curly, auburn hair swept up in a complicated arrangement on top of her head and held together with gaily coloured hair combs. He guesses that she is probably quite pretty under the recklessly applied make-up and, when she smiles, he sees her teeth are white and even. What a shame, he thinks. What will she look like in a few years? To get rid of her he orders her another drink. When the drink arrives, she takes hold of his hand and he allows himself be dragged through the crowd towards the snug. Although he realises he shouldn't get involved with the girl and that she is probably more trouble than she is worth, the alcohol coursing through his body takes over. As they push their way through the crowd, the men wink at him and leer. He smiles back stupidly, enjoying their envy.

She leads him into the snug and shuts over the door. He makes a clumsy attempt to kiss her but she pushes him away.

'Don't think I'm like one of those girls out there on the streets,' she says, 'kissing the first man who comes along.'

Christopher is confused, then angry.

'Was I the first man to came along? What about your soldier boy?' he says.

'That was a friend, not a boyfriend,' she says, teasing him. 'What's your name anyway?'

'None of your business,' he says, turning to leave.

She grabs his arm and spins him around.

'Mine's Nell. Tell me, mystery man — what if I'd let you kiss me then, what would you have done?'

'Bought you another drink — that's the idea, isn't it?' he says with a shrug.

The slap is hard and fast and more powerful than the one she landed at the bar. Her eyes, which had been laughing till then, have changed. Her body is rigid, her arm drawn back again to strike. He blocks the blow easily and pushes her backwards onto the long seat that runs the length of the snug.

The commotion they are making brings the barman down to their end of the bar. He puts his head through the hatch.

'Nell, I warned you before. No more chances. You're barred.'

'Aw, Jaysus, Phil, we were only having a laugh, weren't we?' She turns to Christopher.

'I suppose so.' He turns back to the barman. 'I'm sorry, it won't happen again.'

'See that it doesn't. I run a respectable establishment here.' Phil withdraws his head through the hatch.

'Thanks for not getting me barred,' Nell says, sitting down.

Christopher stands there, rubbing his cheek.

'You're a strange girl,' he says. 'Why did you hit me? I'm really confused.'

He turns to leave.

Nell grabs his arm.

'Wait, don't be so touchy. What's your name?'

'Joseph Andrews.'

'Well, Joseph, to show you there're no hard feelings, I'd like to buy you a drink back.'

Nell goes over to the hatch. There's a small button there and when she presses it Christopher can hear a bell going off somewhere behind the bar.

'It's not necessary. We're even,' he says.

'I've never heard of a soldier refusing a drink before.'

'Who says I'm a soldier?'

'Instinct. Now relax and don't be so proud.'

'But I'm not a soldier. Don't be starting rumours like that — you'll get me killed.'

'If you say so, you're not a soldier — happy now?'

When the barman's head appears, she orders another round. He looks at her, then over at Christopher, assessing them, before he disappears.

Nell sits down beside him but turns away and reaches down the front of her dress. For some reason he feels disappointed. He has seen this before, in Poperinghe in Belgium, where he had gone on weekend leave. He had latched himself on to a group of Welsh soldiers who seemed to know their way around. They had ended up in a dim basement bar, almost a cave. It had half a dozen tables, each one with a candle, the only light in the place. A woman sat at one of the tables, alone, nursing a drink. When the soldiers appeared, she brightened up and joined them. During the evening, as they had become more drunk, one of the Welsh soldiers had gone back up the stairs with her to shouts from his comrades. Before he left, Christopher had seen his money disappearing into the same type of pocket in front of the woman's dress. When they had returned, the soldier wore a sheepish grin and the woman began draping herself around another soldier and they went upstairs together again. By the time his turn had come it was morning and he was too drunk to stand.

Nell draws out the purse and counts out some coins. When the barman returns, he hands out another pint of porter and a strange, stoneware bottle with a stopper for Nell. She hands him his drink and pours from the bottle into her glass.

'Ginger ale,' she says, showing him the label. 'I've reached my limit.'

'*Cheers!*' Christopher tips his glass against hers then takes a long draught from his drink.

'Easy there, soldier,' Nell teases, putting her hand on his.

Christopher grins at her and, with a show of bravado, lowers the contents of the glass in one go and slams it onto the table, then wipes the froth from his lips. His concern about his mission has disappeared and he is beginning to enjoy himself. Raucous noise drifts over the partition along with clouds of tobacco smoke. Nell's face is retreating and coming back into focus and he has to squint to see her properly. He looks up at the glass globe hanging from the ceiling and stares up at it. Reflected in its depths are what seems like hundreds of tiny people milling about. It's been a long time since he has felt this good, not since before the news about his brother in fact. The heat in the pub makes him loosen his tie.

Nell shakes her head and takes a sip of her ginger ale.

Someone barges through the front door of the pub and the sound of it crashing against the wall of the snug makes a noise like a gunshot.

Christopher laughs at the look on Nell's face.

She jumps to her feet, turns and shouts at him: '*It's a raid, you fool!*'

CHAPTER 13

The door to the snug bursts open and a nervous-looking squaddie barges in, his Lee Enfield rifle at the ready. He attempts to grab Nell by the arm but she is too quick for him and kicks out at his ankles. Christopher clumsily scrambles to his feet to intervene but the squaddie turns on him and jabs him in the chest with the butt of his rifle, forcing him back onto his seat.

A head appears in the doorway and barks out an order in a strong Scottish accent: 'Stop messin' about, laddie, and bring 'em both out here,' then disappears.

The squaddie backs into the doorway and points his rifle at them, flicking the safety catch off. Christopher gets to his feet and stands in front of Nell, holding both arms up in surrender. Outside in the bar he can hear the sound of protests from the customers and the louder commands from the officer in charge. In an instant Christopher's training takes over and the rush of adrenalin clears his mind. He takes Nell's hand and follows the squaddie who backs out of the snug, indicating with his rifle.

'Take it easy, we're comin' out,' Christopher says, his voice quiet and even.

Outside in the bar all of the men are lined up facing the wall with their arms in the air and the women are standing at the counter opposite. Christopher lets go of Nell's hand and joins the other men, some of whom are so inebriated they can't even stand up straight.

Down near the toilets the commander of the patrol, a red-faced sergeant, is shouting into the faces of the two drunken soldiers who are trying their best to stand to attention. When the tirade is over, they salute the sergeant and stagger from the pub.

Christopher reckons there are about ten soldiers in the squad and most of them look young, nervous and inexperienced. The sergeant now moves up the line of men, demanding papers. If any of the men are too slow or drunk to produce their papers promptly, he lashes them across the side of the face with his swagger stick, raising ugly welts on their faces. One of the men near Christopher has no papers on him. The sergeant drags him out, throws him down onto the floor and begins to kick him in the side. The sound of his boots hitting the man's ribs makes a sickening sound. Even the young squaddies turn away from the beating. Christopher, sensing that the man on the floor, who has a slight build, was in danger of serious injury, steps forward and stands over him, putting his arms out.

'Enough, please,' he says.

The sergeant, breathing heavily, stops the attack. He looks up and Christopher recognises that the heat of battle is already leaving the sergeant's face. Apart from the whimpering of the man on the floor there is complete silence in the pub.

The sergeant looks around at his squaddies for encouragement but they seem frightened at the casual violence of their leader. He takes a step away from the man and straightens his uniform, shoving his hand out at Christopher who hands him the forged identity papers. The sergeant looks at them and hands them back.

'*Let that be a lesson to all you rebels. Not very brave now, are you?*' he bellows down at the injured man, and moves away.

As the sergeant moves down the rest of the line of men, Christopher makes a note to thank Byatt for supplying him with the false papers.

After he has finished checking all of the men, the sergeant suddenly grabs up a stool and throws it across the pub. It hits a mirror, smashing it, and falls onto a line of spirit bottles which tumble and break on the floor. The smell of whiskey permeates the air and the sergeant draws himself up to his full height.

'*That's for the Foresters who died on Mount Street Bridge!*' he shouts, and stalks out of the pub, followed quickly by his squad.

Christopher kneels down beside the injured man on the floor. He rolls him gently onto his back, opens his shirt and runs his fingers down the man's side. People are beginning to talk and gather around them but he waves them away and calls out to the barman to bring some ice. He sits the man up. The barman comes over with some ice wrapped in a towel and Christopher holds it against the injured ribs.

'You have a couple of broken ribs,' he says. 'It's not the end of the world. Here — keep this held to your ribs.'

'*Bastards*,' Nell says, joining him.

'What was that about the Foresters?' he asks.

A man standing over them says: 'The Sherwood Foresters marched into an ambush on Mount Street Bridge. They lost a lot of young men.'

Christopher gets to his feet.

The barman comes over and claps him on the back, handing him a pint of porter.

'Quite the hero,' Nell says, takes his arm and leads him back to the snug.

'I only did what I could,' he says, taking his seat again, 'but if I were the owner of this pub, I wouldn't bother putting up any more mirrors. They'll be back.'

'Where did you learn about broken ribs?' Nell asks.

'Happened to my little brother, Ned, when he was a kid. Fell off the horse and cart we used to drive around looking for waste. I took him to the doctor and that's what he did.'

'What about your mother and father?'

Christopher took a deep swallow from his glass.

'They're dead,' he says, putting his glass down.

'At least we have something in common,' Nell says and goes over to the serving hatch. 'Let's drink to being alive.'

The pub has returned to normal and the raid is almost forgotten. The injured man sticks his head through the door of the snug and thanks him, telling him that he has paid for another a round of drinks. Christopher thanks him but then his stomach begins to react to all of the porter and whiskey he has drunk and his face feels on fire. Holding his hand to his mouth, he bolts from the snug and out through the door of the pub to the street outside. Almost immediately he throws up, the porter gushing from his mouth in one long torrent. Eyes bulging, he retches again, but not so much this time. Finally, the feeling of sickness recedes but he stays standing, hands on his knees, head bent down towards the gutter.

Nell's voice comes from behind him. 'That's a terrible waste.'

She is standing in the doorway of the pub, a cigarette in her mouth, a look of pity on her face.

He fishes out a handkerchief from his pocket and wipes his mouth. All he wants to do now is get away from the stares and jeers of the passing crowds. He spots a street vendor on the far side of the street selling food and staggers over to his stall, but all he has on display are trays of assorted shellfish. Oysters, whelks and periwinkles sit on a bed of melting ice. The fishy smell makes him gag and he barely makes it to a nearby laneway to retch again. Feeling weak, he turns his back to the wall and slides down slowly until he's sitting, his head held between his legs.

A foot taps the side of his thigh. When he looks up Nell is standing over him, arms crossed. He gets carefully to his feet. A light rain has begun to fall and he lifts his face towards the tiny drops falling from the night sky. His new suit is already ruined and he has got nowhere on his first night. The only friendly person he has met so far is a prostitute, even though she denies it. Although he feels attracted to her, it has been so long since he has conversed with anyone from the opposite sex, he would probably be attracted to any girl who had shown an interest in him. She could even be hanging around so that she can earn back the money she paid out for the drinks back in the bar. His legs feel wobbly and his feelings are confused.

'You could do with something to eat, help you sober up,' Nell says.

Christopher squints at her. 'That'd be nice — are you goin' to cook it for me?' His speech is slurred, but the worst part is that he knows it is and can do nothing about it.

'Do I look like a cook? But I can get you fed,' she says, wiping his clothes down as best she can with a handkerchief and taking hold of his arm.

Christopher allows himself to be led out onto the street. He feels better now that he is moving and puts his arm around Nell's shoulders for support. What has he got to lose? They walk down Montgomery Street together. As they move through the jostling crowds, he can feel the warmth of her body under the fabric of her dress and it brings him comfort.

He is surprised when she steers him towards one of the better-looking brown-stone houses. She goes up the steps to the imposing door and pushes it open, turns and holds up her hand for him to wait. He loiters behind the railings in front of the house, wondering if he will ever see her again. He is confused by the sense of loss he feels and wonders if it is the drink. Through the large bay window, he is able to make out a well-lit room with what looks like a party going on. He can hear the sound of laughter, clinking glasses and a piano playing.

Suddenly he feels suspicious. Why has she left him out here? He puts his hand into his inside pocket, but his wallet is still there. He pulls the collar of his jacket up and turns away to retrace his way back to his hotel.

Just then he hears a shout. Nell is standing in the doorway, a giant of a man, dark and bearded, by her side.

Relieved, he turns back and joins her at the door.

'Well, Joseph, come on in! Lucky for you Moussa's in a good mood tonight — another time he'd have you down those steps!'

The bearded giant laughs and stands back to allow him to enter.

Christopher walks through the doorway into a wide hallway.

On his right is an imposing carpeted staircase. A laughing couple come out of a room off to his left. The man, well-dressed, middle-aged and portly, has his arm around the young woman. She looks half his age and he watches them as they make their way upstairs. Nell drags him to the door the couple have just come through and stands beside him as he takes in the scene. The room is stifling from the amount of people and a blue haze of cigarette smoke hangs in the air. Men and women sit or stand around talking or rather shouting to make themselves heard. Some of the men have small plates in their hands. Reading the hunger in his eyes, Nell leads him into the room and points to a large table laden with food.

'You can help yourself or you can come with me,' she says with a mischievous smile.

115

Christopher stares, transfixed — he has never seen a feast like it. On an enormous silver tray at one end of the dining table is the biggest ham he has ever seen, its fatty skin criss-crossed with cuts. Tiny heads of cloves protrude and the whole joint is glazed. On the other end of the table sits an enormous roast of beef resting in a shallow dish. The skin, crispy brown, has been sliced through on one side and several layers of beef lie soaking up the gravy at the bottom of the dish. Between the two meat dishes the table is full of such a mouth-watering variety of delicacies it's hard to take in: lobster claws, large succulent pink prawns arranged in a circle, their beady eyes staring at each other, a long dish of smoked salmon, bowls of green lettuce, mushrooms, pickled onions, devilled eggs, slices of tomato with some kind of white cheese. The only time he has seen such a layout is in newspapers or magazines around Christmas time.

'Who owns this house?' he asks, devouring the food on the table with his eyes.

'Anna Macken — she owns and runs the place, but I told her I was bringing you here as my guest.'

The money he has left has to last him for several days.

'I can't afford any of this,' he says.

'What do you mean?'

'All of this food …. and you?'

'Of course you can't. Anna said I could take you back to my room, not upstairs,' Nell says. 'I told her you looked like a little lost boy but that I was going to look after you.'

Christopher wonders if he is caught up in a dream and reaches out for a lobster claw — but Nell slaps the back of his hand.

'I can bring us a plate later,' she says, then walks him past the food and on down a short corridor into the kitchen.

While the atmosphere in the reception rooms is boisterous and loud, down in the steaming kitchen it is frenetic. Two women wearing stained white aprons race around, stirring pots, checking the oven, cutting up even more vegetables. They continue on through the kitchen and down another short corridor. At the end of this Nell unlocks a door and ushers him inside.

It is a spartan room, clean, with little or no decoration and not what he had imagined it would be. A bookcase filled with books covers the entire wall on the left. He presumes that the room, as well as being Nell's, might have been used as a library. Against the wall opposite is a narrow wooden bed with a mismatched table beside it. On the table is a water pitcher, a small oil lamp and more books. To the right of the doorway there is a large wardrobe, its wooden panels cracked and chipped with age. The only other pieces of furniture in the room are a writing desk and chair. A fire is set in the grate, small lumps of black coal sitting on a bed of kindling. On the writing desk there is a photograph of a large family standing close together as if they are afraid that the frame cannot contain them. He walks over to it and picks it up, scanning the sepia faces. The adults are dressed in dark, almost black clothes, and the children sit in a line in front of them, all wearing some sort of peculiar petticoat.

The door closes behind him with a bang and Nell grabs the photograph from his hands and holds it to her chest.

'Is that your family?' he asks.

'Could be.' Nell shrugs, walks over to the wardrobe and puts the picture inside.

'Why the mystery?'

'I've answered your question, haven't I? They could be my family, who knows?' She begins to undo her hair.

Christopher is becoming nervous. The alcohol, which has been giving him courage and a lightness of head, is losing its effect. What is he supposed to do now? His knowledge of women is based on stories told around a paraffin lamp by soldiers who may, or may not, have been telling the truth. Certainly, the ones he told were made up, variations of the one time he took a girl out to Booterstown on a tram. That trip ended in misunderstanding and a slap across the face.

As Nell reaches behind to unbutton her dress, he turns his back to her.

'Who owns all these books?' he asks, picking one up from the bedside table and trying to make out the faded title on the spine.

'There're mine, Christopher. Now come over here and give me a hand, will you?' she says matter-of-factly.

He puts the book down and joins her. Fumbling with the delicate-looking buttons, his fingers feel thick and clumsy and it takes him a while to get them all open. Nell pulls down the sleeves then pushes the dress to the floor where it lies in a tangled heap around her. Under the dress is a flimsy white slip she begins to lift over her head. Christopher turns his attention to the bookcase, running his hands over the spines as if looking for a particular volume. Behind him he can hear Nell swearing under her breath and then the rustle of silk.

'You can look now,' she says.

When he turns around, she is standing, naked, under the glare of the single electric bulb that hangs from the ceiling. Other than the dog-eared photographs handed around between the soldiers as they waited in the trenches, he has never seen a naked woman before. In the flesh, he can see that the pictures were a bad substitution for real life. He stands in awe, taking in her long, shapely legs and the wide curve of her hips. Her white skin accentuates the dark bush of her pubic hair and deep-wine nipples that jut out from her breasts. His breathing becomes laboured and he feels an uncomfortable pressure under his trousers as he becomes erect.

'Am I the first naked woman you've even seen, Christopher?' she teases.

'Yes. No. I've seen photographs,' he whispers hoarsely.

She turns away from him, runs her fingers through her hair and shakes her head. The dark mass of auburn waves cascade around her shoulders and back. Ever so slowly she turns around, letting him take in her nakedness. When she is facing him again, she stares into his eyes. Christopher's body, with a mind of its own, moves towards her. With a gentle push of her hand she stops him and points down towards his shoes.

'I think it would be a good idea to get undressed first,' she says, and, without waiting for an answer, draws back the blankets of the bed and slides between the sheets.

In the warm glow of the coal fire they sip from a flask of brandy Nell has produced from a drawer in the bedside locker. She tells him it is her pick-me-up for when she is sad. In the darkness they swap stories about their lives and as the hours pass they make love again.

The noises from the rest of the house abate. The pianist stops playing and the many raised voices dwindle to just one or two giving slurred renditions of songs that have been played earlier. A door slams and they hear the raised voice of a man — probably Moussa the doorman, Nell explains — as he gathers up the stragglers from the dining room and from the upstairs rooms, and guides them out of the house. The silence surrounding them brings on a comfortable torpor that he has not felt in weeks. As his eyelids droop his body relaxes in Nell's arms and he falls into a deep, dreamless sleep.

CHAPTER 14

Wednesday
3rd May

When Christopher awakes there is a chill in the air. The fire has long since died down and he is sprawled across the bed. His mouth feels dry and he has a slight headache. A weak, grey light filters into the room from a skylight he hadn't noticed the night before. Nell has propped herself up on her elbows and is looking down at his nakedness. Her fingers circle around the scar on his thigh. He pulls the blankets up around his chest self-consciously.

'Did you get that in the war?'

'I did. Stupid really, a German bullet ricocheted off a rock and hit my leg and it got infected.'

'Lucky for me,' she says, snuggling in to him. 'I hope this never ends.'

With her hair spilling down over her face, he can hardly see her eyes.

'Everything comes to an end,' Christopher says, brushing her hair aside and untangling himself from her.

'Says who?' Nell says, a note of anguish in her voice.

'Says ... life, I suppose. When we were sent to the trenches first the fighting wasn't too bad. We used to shout back and forth with the Germans, jeering at each other. Sometimes they threw sausages over to us and we'd fire back some cigarettes or tea.'

'Sounds like a holiday,' Nell says.

'But it didn't last. One of the officers came down to us one night. He put a bomb into a tea caddy and threw it over to the Germans. It was never the same after that. Life changes, that's all I'm saying. You have to get used it.'

'I knew you were a soldier!' Nell jabs him in the chest.

'I was in uniform till a few weeks ago,' Christopher search for the right words, 'but now I'm doing something ... different. So, you see, things are always changing — it's the way the world is.'

'Not if it's up to us,' Nell says, sitting up.

'Don't you understand, Nell? It's never up to people like us.'

'What about you? Are you going to tell me you're off to war again and that I have to forget about you? You probably say that to all the girls.'

Christopher is becoming uncomfortable.

'I shouldn't have told you anything, Nell.'

'Tell me more about yourself, anything at all. Do you have brothers or sisters? What are your friends like?'

'My parents are both dead from TB. I had one brother, but he was killed in the war. As for my friends, I don't know. Some are married now, I suppose, or gone to America. The army was my home.'

'We're not so different then.'

Christopher nods towards the photograph in the frame.

'Who are those people?'

'Anna picked it up in a pawn shop for tuppence, said it would make me feel like I was part of a family.'

'And does it?'

'Sometimes, when I feel lonely.'

'It's hard to believe you'd be lonely in a place like this. What's Anna like?'

'She pretends to be hard, and she can be. But she adopted me from the Magdalen Laundry around the corner. She's my family now.'

'How did she manage that? Is there a Mr. Macken?'

'No, she's not married, but she says that the nuns were only too glad to let her take me. I was nine years old.'

'You must've been a handful.' Christopher smiles.

'I think Anna was their last chance to get rid of me and they jumped at the offer. I'm glad they did now — that place is nothing but a workhouse for abandoned women and children. They slave away in the laundry twelve hours a day for a pittance. What were your parents like? I never knew mine.'

'You're better off. You only realise what real loneliness is when you lose them. Suddenly you're responsible for everything, that's the real shock. After the death, that is,' Christopher says, and remembers the day when everything changed.

To one side three gravediggers smoke and chat to each other in low voices. When the coffin is taken from the hearse, they nip their cigarettes and put the stubs into their pockets for later, then bless themselves. Tommy Sherry rushes to help lower the coffins into the earth. The priest, who Christopher can see is impatient to be getting back to the city, starts the graveside prayers, his sing-song Latin rising and falling as he flicks over the pages of a well-worn prayer book. Too soon he is finished and takes a step back from the grave, gesturing towards the hole in the ground. Christopher doesn't know was to do and is confused until Tommy Sherry leads him over to the open grave, takes up a handful of earth and throws it on top of the coffins.

Christopher does the same. Tommy Sherry, puts a hand on his shoulder and squeezes it.

Around the grave there is a paltry handful of mourners. His mother's family were originally from Skibbereen in County Cork and that ruled out any of those. Of his father's family, two of the brothers were estranged so neither turned up. That left his father's sister, Carmel. The rest of the group consists of a few of his father's loyal customers, one wheelwright who hopes to get paid for a job he did on his father's horse and cart, and one or two neighbours.

Ned is now standing beside him at the edge of the grave, tears in his eyes, staring down at the wooden coffins. Without warning he turns and runs away between the gravestones towards the front gates. By the time Christopher catches up to him and leads him back to the graveside, everybody has left and the only sign that there has been a funeral is the mound of dark brown freshly dug earth with the bunch of flowers they had brought thrown carelessly on top. Christopher wonders why he'd wasted so much money on something as insubstantial and short-lived as flowers. It could have paid for the rent or for food. He hadn't planned to buy them and could almost hear his father's complaining voice coming from the coffin, berating him for having bought something as useless as that bunch of flowers.

'That sounds so sad,' Nell says when he tells her briefly about it, tracing her finger down through the sparse hair on his chest.

'I got over it,' Christopher says, lighting a cigarette and pulling on it, blowing the smoke up towards the ceiling.

'The big man!' Nell slaps his stomach.

In the grey light of morning her body has lost none of its sensuousness. As if she feels his eyes on her she grabs one of the blankets off the top of the bed and wraps it around herself like a shawl. The disappointment on his face makes her laugh.

'Then you really joined the British army because you were looking for a new family.'

'Keep it to yourself about the army, Nell. Anyway, what's wrong with joining up? They took me in when nobody else would. Fed me, dressed me and trained me to look after myself.'

Nell sits on the side of the bed and tosses his hair as if he's a child.

'Of course they did! They needed you to fight their stupid war — that's the only reason. There's nothing wrong with being in an army, but only if you're fighting for the right side.' Nell rolls away from him to reach out for the lamp on the table beside the bed.

Christopher is becoming annoyed.

'And who decides which is the right side?'

'You're Irish, aren't you? You should be fighting for Ireland.'

'I thought you said you never wanted this to end. Do you now want me to join those fools that got our city destroyed?' he says, his voice rising.

She turns on him, stabbing towards his chest with her finger.

'That's the whole point. It's not our city, is it? It's *theirs* — the English,' she says.

'Now you're confusing me, Nell. Who were those great liberators? Did you know them? No, they're just another group of men thinking that they know what's good for us, that's all. And if by some miracle they were to take over, do you think you'd be any better off? You'd still be here, working for Anna, and I'd be lucky to get a job because I was a soldier on the wrong side.'

'I do think we'd be better off. And another thing, I don't work for Anna. I'm hopin' the first thing that they'd do is to bring this rat-invested place to the ground so that women don't have to do what they do just to eat!'

Christopher, taken aback by her vehemence and confused by her reply, can only watch as she gets out of bed and begins to put her clothes on, all the while mumbling to herself.

When she is fully dressed, she leaves the room, slamming the door behind her. Without her warmth beside him in the bed, he feels cold and empty. Her room, which last night had taken on the aspect of a magical place is now just a small, shabby room in the basement of a brothel. What a fool he had been to get into a pointless argument with her. He puts on his clothes and makes the bed neatly, military-style. Then he looks around for a pencil and paper to write her a note, but can't find either and leaves the room.

The kitchen is much quieter this time with only a young girl scrubbing out pots in a large trough-like sink. When he passes through the two reception rooms the debris from the previous night lies strewn across the enormous dinner table and there is a stale smell in the air. Plates of half-eaten food have been left here and there along with empty glasses and over-full ashtrays. There is no sign of Nell and nobody else around he can ask about her. He makes his way out through the front door and into a sunny spring morning. The streets are almost deserted with just a few early morning shoppers. He looks up and down Montgomery Street, but in vain. He thinks about going back to Phil Shanahan's pub but realises that it would be closed. Now he has to face the fact that not alone has he fallen out with Nell, he has also fallen out with the only connection he had to the Monto and he's back to where he started. Stupid.

Strangely, the only person he can turn to in Dublin is Byatt.

125

Although he doesn't relish the idea, he would have to make contact with him and tell him what had happened.

What if Nell tells somebody about him? He thinks back to what he had told her but it was all a bit vague. What if Byatt decides that he is now useless to him and puts out an order to have him rearrested for desertion? But it is a chance he's going to have to take if he is to get his freedom back. He realises that now, strangely, standing at the top of the steps, his freedom seems more important to him than just twenty-four hours earlier. Why? He doesn't want to admit it to himself, but he knows the answer. Nell, the one good thing to have happened to him in a long while. He straightens his tie, brushes some of the previous night's dirt from his trousers and makes his way back to his hotel.

CHAPTER 15

Nell stomps down Montgomery Street, ignoring the greetings of Mr Cohen, the baker, who is waving to her from across the road. On she strides, mumbling to herself. It isn't until she finds herself outside Aldborough Barracks and hears the wolf whistles of the soldiers that she realises where she has ended up. Turning up Gloucester Street, she passes the Magdalen Laundry. She bends down and picks up a stone from the gully, feels its weight, and throws it as hard as she can over the wall of her former home. It lands on the tin roof of the laundry and rattles down, making a satisfying noise. Her minor act of delinquency calms her and she quickens her pace back towards Anna's. She will give Joseph a chance to apologise, then she will cook him some breakfast and see how things turn out after that.

She finds herself half walking, half running, down Montgomery Street, ignoring people's stares, her heart beating faster. She reaches the house, rushes through the silent hallway, then the parlour and back down to her little room. Outside the door to her room, she forces herself to breathe evenly. She tidies her unruly hair as best she can, then pushes open the door, her face settled in a neutral expression.

'Would you like …' she says, keeping her voice calm and level.

The room is empty. The only sign that Joseph has been there is the condition of the bed. It is made up perfectly, a soldier's bed, the top blanket drawn tightly and tucked under the mattress, the sheets folded down and perfectly aligned with the plumped-up pillow. She stands in the doorway, then goes over and sits on the bed. She can still smell Joseph's presence, the faint odour of hair oil. Surely he left a note? She looks at the bedside table and lifts up the book that lies there but there is nothing underneath. In desperation she searches the room more thoroughly, even looking under the bed in case it had somehow been blown there by a draught from the door, but all she can see is a discarded pair of stockings and lots of dust. Where is Connie when I need her advice? Although, if she had met her the previous evening and gone up to Smithfield, she would not have met Joseph.

The house around her is coming to life. Through the open door she can hear the scullery girls laughing and talking together as they clean the dirty dishes and the pots and pans from the night before. The young boy Anna uses for some chores, Seán Potts, is shouting at the girls to make way as he goes through the kitchen and on past Nell's door with a large metal bucket of ashes from last night's fires. He is going to say something to her but, seeing the expression on her face, staggers on with his load. The only other person she can think of to talk about what happened and make sense of it is Sarah, who is probably with Moussa in their converted stables at the back of the house. But she needs some fresh air to collect her thoughts

Outside, Montgomery Street is slowly getting back to normal after the end of the rebellion. Nell notices there are more horses and carriages clipping up and down and even the odd motorcar. A gang of urchins are dodging the traffic as they shovel up horse's manure from the road and put the still steaming droppings into a bucket. Anna usually throws them a few coppers at the end of the day and every Friday the children haul a full handcart of nature's fertiliser up to the Botanic Gardens for the plants and receive a shilling for their trouble. They wave up at her as she walks past on her way to Sarah and Moussa's and she waves back, remembering the days when she would have been with them. Life was less complicated back then. Lately she has been thinking a lot about her life — where she is going, if anywhere, or if she would end up stranded in the Monto?

She turns down the laneway that leads her to the back entrance of Anna's house. Reaching the gate, she puts her hand through a gap and fishes up the key hanging on a string on the other side. She lets herself into the yard. Anna has strict rules. The people who maintain her house — the scullery maids, the skivvies, the messenger boy — must never have a relationship with each other. But she had made an exception with the odd couple, and now Sarah and Moussa have their own home in the old stables in the yard. Nell marches up to their door and walks in without knocking. Moussa will be in bed after manning the door of Anna's until the early hours of the morning, she knows, but Sarah is probably up by now and she needs somebody to talk to.

Thankfully, Sarah is in the kitchen, standing on a wooden box in front of the sink doing some laundry. She steps down, drying her hands. Nell can hear the deep snores of Moussa coming from behind the curtain that cuts the bedroom off from the living area.

'What's wrong, Nell? You look like somebody's dragged you through a hedge backways,' Sarah says with a laugh.

'Oh, don't annoy me, Sarah — can't you see I'm upset?' Nell says and sits at the couple's long dining table.

'What time is it?'

'I don't know, Sarah. Morning, is that good enough?'

'I'm just asking because you look like one of Anna's girls after a hard night,' Sarah says.

'Thank you for that. First Connie stands me up, now you're picking on me.'

'Connie? That's not like her,' Sarah says, lifting a large kettle of water onto the gas stove. 'She must have met a rich gent.'

'Are you making tea?' Nell says.

'This water is for you — you can give yourself a quick wash first, you'll feel better after it, then you can have a cup of tea.'

Nell is going to object but knows her friend is right. She realises that she is still wearing last night's make-up and that her hair is a mess — no wonder the soldiers were whistling at her. She lets Sarah lead her over to the washbasin tucked into a corner of the kitchen. Before disappearing behind the curtains into the couple's sleeping area, Sarah hands her a bar of carbolic soap, a towel and a comb. She washes herself and then tries to tame her tangled hair. She can hear murmurings coming from behind the curtain: Moussa is awake.

Finishing up quickly, she shouts out: '*All done!*'

Sarah comes out from behind the curtain, followed by Moussa, who towers over her, even in stocking feet. The couple go into the kitchen and begin to take cups and plates down from a dresser. For all their oddness, Nell admires them for sticking together through all the jeers and comments they receive on some nights in Anna's. They act like an old married couple as Sarah makes the tea and Moussa shuffles around the table, fussing over the cutlery.

'Have you nothing stronger than tea?' Nell whispers to Moussa.

'For you, Nell, it will be a special tea,' Moussa says with a wink.

Moussa opens up his sailor's trunk and takes out a brown-paper bag. As soon as the teapot is on the table, he adds a spoonful of hashish and stirs the contents. No one around the table speaks until the tea is poured and Sarah comes back with some biscuits.

'Well?' Sarah says as they sip the brew.

'Can you not see? It is obvious, my little flower,' Moussa says. 'Nell brought a boy to her room last night.'

Sarah puts her cup down.

'Does Anna know?'

'She'll find out soon enough,' says Nell, who hadn't asked Anna's permission despite telling Christopher otherwise.

'He is a good-looking boy, but he cannot hold his drink,' Moussa says.

'I don't want to talk about him anymore,' Nell says. 'He's left and I don't know when or if he'll be back. Well, good riddance to him!'

'You had a row? How romantic! Isn't it, Moussa? A lover's tiff.'

'It wasn't a big row. Well, I didn't think it was anyway. But he had other ideas. Maybe it's better that he did go.' And Nell bursts into tears.

Sarah comes around the table and puts her arm around her shoulders, which is a change. Usually it is Nell comforting Sarah, sometimes after a drunken insult about her height or by some of the more lurid and insensitive comments made by Anna's customers who are clever enough not to say anything within Moussa's earshot. But now it feels good to be the one being comforted and she wonders if it's just the work of Moussa's hashish.

'I don't mind you staying here, Nell, but I have to go to work and Moussa has some errands to run for Anna. Why don't you go back to your room and get some rest? I'm sure Moussa's tea will help.'

'Maybe you're right. I could do with a few hours' sleep,' Nell says, standing up. 'No men are worth the tears, are they, Sarah?'

In answer Sarah reaches across the table and puts her tiny hand in Moussa's.

'There're some good ones out there, Nell. I'm sure you'll find one someday,' she says.

'I thought I did already, Sarah, that's the problem. Then I end up making a mess of it — just like me. Why don't you two drop around later, before the Monto gets busy again? I could do with some company.'

'Maybe we will,' Sarah says.

Nell leaves the couple at the table staring into one another's eyes and goes quietly out the door.

CHAPTER 16

The old woman seems to be in exactly the same position behind her desk as she was the day before. The only difference is that she is reading a book instead of a newspaper. As Christopher stands in front her desk, he waits to be questioned about not coming back the previous evening. He is sure that she will read the guilt in his eyes after his visit to a brothel.

But when she looks up from her book, all she says is: 'Have you lost your key, detective?'

Pushing back his shoulders, he assures her that he has not.

'Would it be possible to have access to a phone for police business, Mrs. Daly? Of course, the cost of the call can be put on my bill.'

She marks the page of the book and smiles up at him.

'I'd be happy to help the police in any way that I can. It's in there.' She points towards a door behind her.

'Thank you very much. I will pass it on to the powers that be up in Dublin Castle that you have been a great help to my investigation.'

The room he enters is the old woman's parlour. Though a fair-sized room, it smells musty and is crammed with mismatched heavy dark furniture placed around in a haphazard fashion. Worn velvet curtains block almost all of the light coming through the window and it takes him a while to take everything in. When his eyes adjust to the dimness, he can make out an enormous sideboard crammed with stuffed animals trapped under domes of glass, their beady eyes looking out at him. The walls are covered with religious paintings, mostly images of Christ suffering on the cross. The overall effect of the room is one of sadness and he wonders why somebody would surround themselves with dead animals and the dying Son of God.

He has to sidle his way between two armchairs to get to the phone which is on top of an old wooden bureau. He hesitates for a moment, wondering if he is doing the right thing, then takes out the card and dials the operator to give her the number.

Byatt answers straight away.

'It's me,' Christopher says.

'I wasn't expecting a call so soon.'

'I just wanted to call to —'

'Don't say anything more,' Byatt cuts him off. 'There've been developments. We had better meet up.'

'What's happened?'

'It's better if we talk in person and as soon as possible. Everything has changed. There's a hotel opposite the train station in Amiens Street, do you know it?'

'I do — it's at the end of Talbot Street.'

'There's a small tea-room beside it. Meet me there in half an hour.'

Christopher is about to object when he hears the click of the disconnection. He looks at his watch. Barely enough time for a wash before he meets Byatt. He makes his way back outside into the reception area and thanks Mrs. Daly before he runs up the stairs. Inside his room the bed he has not slept in looks inviting and he

134

considers lying down for a few minutes but then puts it out of his mind. He has a quick wash in the washbasin, changes his shirt and makes his way back downstairs, rushing past Mrs Daly who looks like she is getting ready to start a conversation.

On his way, he keeps replaying the image of Nell leaving the bedroom and is conflicted. One part of him, the logical part, tells him it is probably for the best and to forget her and move on and that having anything to do with a strange young woman who has grown up in a brothel is madness. But a deeper part of him is even more determined to ignore that part of her life. Passing by the street traders who are out selling their wares again, he begins feels more optimistic. The sun is even shining down the length of Talbot Street and the horse-drawn carriages seem to clip past him at a brisker pace, their heads held up, bridles sparkling in the sunlight. With a bit of luck Byatt will release him from the investigation after a few fruitless days of looking for Janus and he can meet Nell again, properly this time.

The tea-room he enters is empty except for Byatt. He is sitting in a corner facing the door, a newspaper held up in front of his face. Behind the counter a bored-looking waitress washes dishes and smiles up at Christopher when he enters.

Byatt puts the newspaper down and calls out an order for another pot of tea and some scones. Christopher joins him and is surprised by his appearance. His confidence of the previous day seems muted and he slouches in his chair, his face grey and strained-looking. A bloodstained piece of paper is stuck carelessly under his chin to cover a nick from shaving. He holds his hand up to Christopher to remain silent as the waitress puts the teapot, another cup and the scones onto the table. When she leaves and goes back behind the counter to her dishwashing, he pulls his chair closer to Christopher's and pours him a cup of tea.

'I hadn't much luck last night,' Christopher admits, between bites of his scone.

'Tell me everything.'

'I went to the hotel and got a room, as you said, then went out last night to the pub you talked about.'

'Phil Shanahan's?'

'Yes, that's the one. Crowded with people out for a good night. It was hard to get to talking to anyone. Then there was an army raid and it was impossible.'

'The raid was unfortunate, but what did you expect?'

'I don't know. I thought that it would be ... different,' Christopher says, sipping his tea.

'Did you think that a tall, shifty-eyed man would introduce himself to you?' Byatt says, his voice heavy with sarcasm.

'Not exactly.'

Christopher feels embarrassed. He didn't know what to expect from Byatt, but was hoping for at least a few kind words of encouragement for trying and maybe a second look at the plan. His dreams of an early release from his mission were quickly fading.

'People like that don't walk around advertising themselves to the world,' Byatt says. 'He could be anybody: the man standing at the bar, an office-worker, a manual labourer, even a priest for God's sake. You're going to have to go back there. Here, take this extra money.' Looking around to make sure that the waitress is not looking, he slips more notes across the table.

'What am I supposed to do now?' Christopher says, putting the notes in his pocket.

'Show your face again, become a local. Then buy the odd round of drinks, give the barman a big tip, become popular. You'd be surprised what you'd find out.'

Byatt seems nervous and keeps playing with his moustache and looking out through the window at the people passing along Amiens Street.

'Are you waiting for somebody else?' Christopher asks.

'No, why do you say that?'

'I don't know, you seem uneasy. What did you want to see me about?'

Byatt closes his eyes and put his head in his hands. When he looks up again, he leans in even closer to Christopher.

'General Maxwell has had his way. It's not been made public yet, but three of the leaders of the rebellion were executed at dawn: the main leader, Patrick Pearse — Thomas MacDonagh — and an older man, Thomas Clarke. It happened in Kilmainham Gaol after a show trial. And this is only the beginning. He's determined to teach you Irish a lesson.'

Christopher recalls the burnt-out buildings of Sackville Street and the ruins of the General Post Office. It had been one-sided and now the battle was over, so why the executions? A part of him begins to feel ashamed and petty about some of the comments he made to Nell about the destruction of the city.

'But they should've been made prisoners of war. When the enemy surrendered, we marched them back behind the lines and they were put in a camp,' he says. 'What's the difference between them and the rebels?'

'One of the main instigators, Pearse I believe, wrote a letter to his mother. In it he mentioned that they had carried out the revolt with the help of the Germans. That sealed their fate.' Byatt shakes his head in disbelief. 'Most of the leaders of the rebellion are either poets, shopkeepers or teachers. Why did they do it? I just can't understand what was going through their minds. The trial was in camera, nobody else present, but the army prosecutors were good and the bloody letter sealed it.'

'It doesn't seem right,' Christopher says, looking down at his plate, his appetite gone.

'This man, Pearse, was no fool from what I hear. Why would he do that? Unless ...' Byatt's voice trails off.

'Unless?'

'Unless he knew what he was doing and intended to make a blood sacrifice. Give the people a martyr. That's the only reason I can think of.'

'Why would he do that?'

'Crowds are fickle, they can turn on a whim. Today they complain about the inconvenience, tomorrow they'll roar about the injustice. I think the man has turned the tables on us and Maxwell has grasped defeat from the jaws of victory, the fool.'

'What do you think will happen now?'

'Now? For a start you have to be more careful. Don't mention, even in your sleep, that you are ex-army. Things are going to get tricky in Dublin over the next few days as the news gets out.'

'Should we forget about Janus?'

'*No*, we should definitely *not* forget about Janus. Remember, this is only a side-show compared to the war in Europe. Now, more than ever, we need to track him down. When these executions start, even the Monto won't be a safe hiding place for him, might even flush him out.'

'If he is there.'

'He has to be. Anyway, is there anything at all to report?'

Christopher fidgets with Byatt's newspaper, considering whether to tell him about his evening with Nell.

'I did make one contact,' he says, 'but I'm not too sure if it's a good thing or bad thing. And she's already guessed that I was in the army.'

138

Byatt sits back in his chair and studies Christopher.

'She?'

'Yes. A young woman who got me out of harm's way after the raid. I didn't realise how drunk I'd become, probably because it has been so long since I've been in a pub. She took me back to where she lives and I stayed there for the evening.'

Byatt reached out and grabs his hands. 'But that's marvellous news! I presume we are talking about a prostitute, yes?'

Christopher feels his face redden and a protective urge towards Nell. 'I didn't say that.'

'You didn't have to. A young woman picks you up in a public bar in the Monto and brings you home. Did any money change hands?'

'No. And she has a lot of books in her room.'

'So, she's a well-read prostitute,' Byatt jokes.

Christopher stands up from the table, knocking his chair backwards onto the floor.

The waitress looks over at them, then looks away again.

'Don't keep calling her that.'

Byatt smiles and gestures towards the chair.

'Pick that up, Christopher. I was only goading you. Normally, we advise against getting involved personally but, in this case, it might be of benefit to us.'

'How?' Christopher says, picking up his chair and taking his seat again.

'Because she will know the area intimately and be aware of all the comings and goings, or some of them anyway. I should have thought of that myself. Well done!'

'What should I do now? I might have messed it up. The last time I saw her she was angry with me and we left on bad terms.'

'That's the easy part. Buy her some flowers, tell her you want to get to know her, that you're sorry for whatever it was that you said or did. Then, ask her some general questions — we don't want her to get suspicious. In time you can ask her about the Monto, about the people who live there, but steer the conversation towards the prostitutes who were garrotted.'

'I'm not sure she'll even speak to me again. She's no fool — she's guessed that I was a soldier in the British army after all.'

Byatt looks off into the distance and seems to be caught up in thought.

'All good lies hold a core of truth, Christopher. I think now would be a good time to let her know about your time in the British army. Be honest, up to a point. Tell her you deserted to take revenge on your neighbour, and that you were caught by an army patrol, but that you escaped in the confusion.'

Christopher is secretly pleased that he is being sent back to make contact with Nell. Now he can justify it to himself and get over his wounded pride after she stormed out. And the money will help with his apology, because from what little he knew of Nell, she would not be the one to apologise. What had begun as a depressing meeting was now beginning to look up. He would present her with flowers, as Byatt has suggested, then ask her to walk out with him. After that he wasn't sure, but hopefully he could spend another night with her and this time get to know her better.

Byatt calls for the bill and puts some coins into the saucer left by the waitress on the table.

'You did well, Christopher. To be honest, I was taking a chance with you, but now I'm glad I did. Before I go, a word of advice. Change your gait — you still walk like you're on parade. Both sides will be suspicious of you. If you're taken in by an army patrol from another barracks, I might not be able to protect you.'

'Agreed. I'll call you if I learn anything. Will you be at the same number?'

'Yes. I'm just about to pay a visit to the newspaper office where that young boy worked. I don't think I will learn anything from it, but it's odd that Janus would have risked so much for no reason.'

'Maybe he just likes killing, have you thought of that? I've come across some men like him. Couldn't wait to get among the Germans in the trenches, hand to hand, staring right into their eyes as they brought their homemade clubs down on their heads again and again. They're a different breed.'

'We'll see. In any case, best of luck and I shall be talking to you soon, I hope. And don't forget this man is dangerous. Keep your eyes and ears open at all times.'

They stand and Byatt holds out his hand.

'Thank you for all that you've done for me, Jonathan,' Christopher says, embarrassed, shaking his hand.

CHAPTER 17

After the meeting with Christopher, Byatt leaves the café in a better humour, making his way towards the city centre. As he approaches the ruins that is Sackville Street, he can sense a subtle change in the atmosphere. Small groups of people stand around, heads bent together in subdued conversation. The news must be leaking out, he thinks. As he nears the Liffey quays, he sees a section of soldiers being openly jeered at by several young men who run away as soon the leader of the platoon calls a halt. The situation on the street is changing even faster than he has anticipated and he hopes that young Flinter is careful about what he says. Little do the people know that the three men executed that morning were only the first.

He crosses Sackville Street Bridge and turns down the south quays, pulling up his jacket collar against the stiff breeze blowing up the Liffey from the sea. The river lies to his right and is at low tide. A sulphur-tinged stink emanating from raw sewage hangs in the air. Down below a crowd of urchins search for anything of value among exposed rocks on the dried-out bank. They shout to each other as the approaching tide threatens to put an end to their search. He takes out the notebook from his pocket and consults it again, to make sure he has the right address, and carries on.

The premises of the printers where the murdered boy worked is larger than he had imagined and is, in fact, some type of newspaper. The gold-embossed sign over the door reads: 'THE IRISH GAZETTE', and in smaller type under that: 'Keeping in Touch with Irish People, Worldwide.'

When he enters through the main door the noise from printing presses is deafening. Each machine seems to have a different rhythm and the overall effect when he stands in the reception area is disconcerting. Off to one side there is a glass-fronted cubicle. The receptionist who sits inside notices him and pulls across the glass hatch. He shouts out the name Maybury and hands her in his card. She nods, closing over the hatch, and leaves the cubicle through another door that leads into the printing works.

Byatt sits down on a wooden bench that runs along the wall and waits. He thinks about his meeting with Flinter. The young man doesn't realise it, but he has done well. If he is not mistaken, the woman will be an invaluable source of information. The office girl seems to be taking her time coming back, so he takes out his notebook and writes a summary of the conversation they had together in the tea-room.

Maybury, when he eventually arrives, appears pale and strained and when they shake hands Byatt notices that the man's hand is moist with perspiration and his grip limp. It is probably down to the unfortunate death of one of his apprentices, but there is something else in the man's eyes: fear. They make their way down through the line of printing presses, the noise and the smell of ink almost disorienting. He notices that Maybury walks briskly, holding his head down, nor does he stop to acknowledge a query from one of his workers. It seems to Byatt that he just wants to be rid of him as quickly as possible.

143

Inside his office Maybury goes directly his desk, which, unlike the rest of the room, appears untidy and cluttered. He lowers himself into a swivel chair and puts on a show of straightening up the scattered papers on the desk, picks up a pen and begins to tap it on the back of his hand. Byatt, not to be rushed, takes in his surroundings. The office, even for a medium-sized printing company, is lavish. To one side of the desk there is a glass-fronted mahogany cabinet. On one of the shelves are several decanters lined up and on the shelf below a line of sparkling crystal glasses.

Maybury observes where his gaze has drifted and asks, in a cursory manner, if he would like a drink.

'No, I am on duty,' Byatt replies, sits down and takes off his hat.

'Of course,' Maybury says, holding out Byatt's card, squinting. 'Major Byatt, what can I do for you?'

'I've been seconded to Dublin Castle. Helping them with certain investigations.'

Maybury seems to go an even paler shade of grey.

'I presume you are here about our poor Daniel.'

'About his last movements, yes,' Byatt says, settling himself deeper into the chair.

'Well, there's not a lot I can add to what I already have told the police. Daniel worked in the case room, as an apprentice compositor. He left here for home a little later than usual and the next day, according to the police, his body was found in the river under suspicious circumstances, but they didn't go into details.'

'What time did he leave, approximately?'

'*Hmm*. Let me see. It would have been ten p.m. or so. He fell asleep down in the basement, poor lad — it had been a long hard day — and no-one realised he was there.'

'He headed for home, directly?'

'As far as I am aware.'

'And where is that?'

Maybury's face turns even paler and he takes a sip from a glass of water at his elbow.

'Somewhere around *em* ... Ringsend. Yes, Ringsend, I believe,' he says.

'Ringsend. Please excuse my ignorance. I am not overly familiar with Dublin. Where is that exactly in relation to here?'

'A bit downriver, just beyond the docks.'

Byatt takes out his notebook and draws a rough sketch of the river and of the spot where Daniel Joyce's body had been fished out. He hands the notebook to Maybury.

'Please. Can you indicate it for me?'

Maybury looks down at the sketch, and, almost with reluctance, puts a mark on the page and hands the notebook back to Byatt. At first Byatt thinks that he is looking at his map upside down and looks at Maybury.

'His body was found just down from Capel Street Bridge, Mr. Maybury, upriver from your premises, which indicates that he was walking in the opposite direction.'

Maybury shrugs his shoulders. 'Perhaps he was exploring the derelict buildings on the north quays. I believe a lot of the young people were poking around the ruins looking for souvenirs. There was some heavy fighting in that area during Easter Week, as you are well aware.' He takes out a silver pocket watch, opens it, frowns, and snaps it shut.

'I won't keep you much longer, Mr. Maybury. But you said that he left here after ten at night. I don't imagine he would have taken the trouble to go exploring ruins after a hard day's work? And in the dark?'

Maybury takes a sip of water, ignoring Byatt's comment.

'What time did he start that day?'

145

'I would have to look at his clock card, but usually he would start at six in the morning to light the smelter furnace and some of the other stoves around the factory to heat the premises for the first shift.'

'That means that if he started at six a.m. and finished at ten p.m., it would seem very strange that he went in the opposite direction of his home and into the city to explore. I would have thought that the only place he would have wanted to go was home to his bed. Is that not so?'

Maybury rises this time and goes to the drinks cabinet, taking out a bottle of whiskey. He pours a good measure into a glass and carries it back to his desk.

'I feel a bit of a chill coming on,' he explains to Byatt, pointing at the glass, then drinks it back in one go.

'I asked you, is that not so?' Byatt repeats.

'Who knows what goes through a young man's mind?' Maybury tries to smile.

'And there is a half past eight curfew, isn't there?'

'Yes, there is.'

'Which makes it all the more peculiar. Here you have a young lad who has been working from six o'clock in the morning until ten that night and he then decides to turn away from the direction of home rather than towards it, despite a curfew.'

Maybury loosens his tie and collar and fiddles with the empty whiskey glass before answering.

'I don't know what you want me to say, Mr. Byatt. I confess that I am at a loss for an explanation as to the poor lad's actions.'

Byatt stares into the other man's eyes. They are darting around the room, looking at everything except at him. He lets the man sweat a bit more before he begins again.

'This boy, Daniel. He was a junior?'

'An apprentice compositor, yes.'

'I would presume that he did not lock up.'

'No, I locked up the premises. As I said, the late edition had just been printed so I was here later than usual.'

'But you said earlier that you would have to check his clock card to know when he came and went.'

Maybury freezes for a moment, then the realisation of what he had actually said brings a look of relief to his face.

'I said that I would have to check when he clocked in, I said nothing about when he left.'

'My mistake, Mr. Maybury. Let me rephrase the question. Did you see him leave?'

'No, I was probably in another part of the factory, in the bindery department checking up on delivery details.'

'That's a pity,' Byatt says, and closes over his notebook.

He rises from his chair and Maybury almost jumps from his, obvious relief written on his face.

'One other thing?' Byatt says, putting on his hat.

'Yes?'

'Was there anyone else on the premises that night, a visitor?'

'No. I was the last one here. I am the key-holder along with Mr. Cahill, our printing foreman, but he was out sick.'

'You didn't notice any strangers about?'

'I'm afraid not. I checked everything before I left, made sure everything was ready for the morning, then locked up and went home.'

'I see,' Byatt says. 'You are a very conscientious owner. Most people in your position would have been long gone by ... what time must this have been? Ten? And during the curfew.'

'Yes. But we had fallen behind because of the situation in the city. We had lost a full week and we have certain commitments to other parties. It's in our contract.'

'Of course, Mr. Maybury, I understand completely. You needn't see me out. But I would like to take a stroll around the factory, to make some notes about the layout. With your permission of course.'

'Certainly. Let me show you around.'

'No, that is not necessary,' Byatt says firmly, looking Maybury in the eye. 'I'd prefer to make some observations on my own.'

Maybury looks as if he might object but instead bows and says, 'If you think it might assist … by all means.'

'Very good. I can be found in Dublin Castle if any other details spring to mind.' Byatt raises his hat and leaves.

Byatt has no real intention of making any notes but, as he leaves Maybury's office, he takes out his notebook and jots down some gibberish. Then he begins to walk down between the lines of printing presses, nodding at the printers, stopping, making another note. From the corner of his eye, he can see that Maybury is staring out through the window of his office and taking in his every move. He walks on through the presses and into the case-room area, where the young lad would have worked. The compositors are working on the next edition of the newspaper and studiously avoid his presence. He approaches an elderly man wearing a green visor, bent down over an open case of type. Byatt is impressed by the speed his fingers work, plucking tiny individual pieces of type from a wide wooden tray divided up in compartments of various sizes. He watches as the man picks up the pieces of type, one at a time, and places each one into a metal device which he holds in his left hand. When the line of type is complete the man checks it for accuracy, apparently reading the upside down and reversed words as easily as if he is reading a line of print from a book.

'Excuse me,' Byatt says, 'would you mind answering some questions? My name is Byatt, Major Byatt, from Dublin Castle.'

The man stops what he was doing and puts the metal device down carefully before turning.

'Is it about poor Daniel?'

'It is. I am investigating his death.'

'James Watts,' the old man says, wiping his hands on his apron.

'Mr. Watts,' Byatt says, holding out his hand, 'pleased to meet you.'

The old man shakes his hand.

Byatt notices the ingrained lead on his fingertips, a perfect match to those of the young man they had found in the river.

'I don't think I can be of much help. I heard he had been found in the Liffey, drowned. It was so sad, he was a lovely boy. It was most peculiar and shocked us all.'

'I am sure it did, Mr. Watts. Death is a terrible thing, especially when it takes away the young. Were you here on the day it happened?'

'Yes. Well, I was here that evening until about nine – past curfew time. Risky but we had to get the edition printed. We were all putting our shoulders to the wheel to get things back up working again, you know. The previous week had been really terrible. There was very little we could do with all the fighting.'

'And Daniel was here, I presume?'

'Yes, he was working very hard down in the cellar. Not that I saw him much.'

'Doing what exactly?'

'The typesetting machines were working flat out. They had to be kept fully loaded with the lead bars they use. It was part of Daniel's job to melt down the old type and pour new metal bars for the machines. It's a dirty job, but I did it when I was an apprentice. Everybody has to.'

'And when you left, was he still down in the cellar?'

'Yes, he was. Poor lad. Maybe the fumes made him weak in the head.'

'Fumes?'

'When the old type is melted down it gives off terrible fumes from the dross that collects on the surface.'

Byatt jots down some of what the man has said.

'By the way, when you left, was there anybody else on the premises?'

'Not in the case-room. We were all tired after a long day. There were one or two printers finishing off the edition and Mr. Maybury, of course. He was in his office with a client.'

'A client?'

'Yes. A religious gentleman, he drops in occasionally,' Watts says.

'A strange time for Mr. Maybury to be having a meeting surely?'

'For the past few weeks, the gentleman has been dropping off the galleys of type for the Irish Stock Exchange listings.'

'The past few weeks? Is that something you don't normally do here?'

'No, it's a specialised job. It's normally set outside by a typesetting company on a Monotype machine so that the type can be manipulated easily for us to make any late changes. It's then delivered here, ready to be included with the pages of the newspaper.'

'Very interesting. But why does this person deliver it to Mr. Maybury? I don't understand. Are they acquaintances?'

'They might be. Or maybe members of the same lodge, if you catch my meaning. A lot of businessmen are,' Watts says, touching the side of his nose.

'You mean they might both be Freemasons? I didn't think that a religious person would be involved in a Freemason lodge,' Byatt says.

'These are strange times, Major Byatt. Nothing is the same. I don't know where it will leave us all. And on top of that poor Daniel drowns in the Liffey.'

'I suppose you are right, Mr. Watts. Nothing will be the same after what has happened over the last week. One last question. What does this religious man look like?'

Watts stares up into the overhead light and rubs his chin.

'He's a very tall gentleman, very distinguished-looking, a full beard, the usual dark clothes. Sometimes he carried a Bible, more times not. Surely you don't think that a man of the cloth would be involved in poor Daniel's death?

'Of course not, it's just routine,' Byatt says, then adds as an afterthought: 'Is there anything about his appearance that seemed out of the ordinary?'

'Out of the ordinary? Not that I can put my finger on. The only thing I remember thinking to myself was that he didn't seem like the usual religious type, if that makes any sense.'

'In what way?' Byatt asks.

'Well, men of God usually have a certain demeanour about them, and a way of talking. A kind of holiness if you know what I mean. And are often scholarly types. This man was more, how would I put it, more vigorous. Not that being vigorous is a bad thing. When you are dealing with Mr. Maybury you do have to fight your corner.' He chuckles.

'I see. Well, thank you very much, Mr. Watts. That has been very helpful.'

'And thank you, Major Byatt. It does my heart good to see that the people in Dublin Castle are giving poor Daniel their time.'

Byatt leaves the printing factory and makes his way back towards Dublin Castle. As he approaches the metal gates, he is glad he is not wearing a uniform. A small, noisy crowd has gathered near the entrance and a man stands on a wooden box, shouting about the cold-blooded execution of the rebels that morning. The tension he has already felt in the city is being expressed more openly here and he wonders why the man is allowed to make a speech so near to the centre of power. As Byatt passes by the sentries the man is excoriating the Home Rulers, who wanted self-government but within the British Empire, as traitors and lackeys of Britain. What will he be shouting about tomorrow when more of the revolutionaries are executed?

The soldiers milling around in the upper courtyard seem on high alert, running here and there, forming into small platoons which, he presumes, are getting ready to go out and patrol the city in a show of strength. As he ducks into his building the sound of horses' hooves clattering across the cobblestones from the upper yard can be plainly heard.

He goes directly to the office he has been using since his arrival in Dublin. The two civil servants who had been assigned to him stand up when he enters and he waves them back down again. Of the two men he prefers the older one, a man called Dónal Noctor, who does his work diligently and keeps to himself. The other, William Blaney, a brash young man who spends more of his time out of the office than in, he puts down as a typical career civil servant. He has come across them throughout his life, a person who uses the system to his advantage and does as little practical work as possible, but just enough to avoid a rebuke.

As Byatt sits down, it is William Blaney who walks over to his desk, a show of enthusiasm on his face.

'Have you heard the news? They're certainly getting a dose of their own medicine now. You weren't here at the time but on Easter Monday they tried to take the Castle and were too stupid to realise there was hardly anybody here. Then they murdered Constable O'Brien — and Sir Matthew was trapped here in the Castle for hours. This will show them you can't challenge the might of Great Britain, is that not right, sir?'

Byatt tries to keep a look of disgust off his face and notices that Noctor has just kept his head down and is saying nothing.

'I heard that the three leaders had died like brave men, with honour,' he snaps.

How can someone like Blaney have that attitude towards his fellow countrymen? He was a small, compact young man, prematurely bald, who seemed to be better dressed than any of the other clerical staff. He worked mainly for the offices of the Dublin Metropolitan Police but seemed to appear everywhere in the Castle. Although he had made himself very helpful when Byatt had first arrived, it had seemed to him that he was over-inquisitive which made him suspicious — he was well aware that Dublin Castle leaked like a sieve. But he had given Blaney the benefit of the doubt, feeling his own judgment might be affected by his exhaustion after the long trip from London that included several hours on the ferry, one of the worst sea journeys he had ever taken. The more he got to know Blaney's character, the more he was convinced that he was just the kind of person who lived for gossip and not an agent for the Irish Republican Brotherhood.

Now Blaney looks crestfallen and his face reddens.

'Of course, sir, I didn't mean any disrespect. It's just that they've murdered so many of your countrymen ...'

'Not murdered, Blaney, *killed*. There's a difference.'

'Of course, forgive me.'

'I wish I had some men like that working under me,' Byatt continues and begins to open the post on his desk, leaving Blaney standing, embarrassed, in front of him.

After several awkward moments Blaney turns and leaves the office, muttering something about a letter he forgot to post.

'Noctor, you're from around here, aren't you?' Byatt asks.

'Yes, sir,' Noctor says, looking up from his desk.

'Tell me. What do you know about the *Irish Gazette?*'

'The newspaper?'

'Yes. I've not seen it in the few shops I have been in. Is it widely circulated?'

'It's sold mainly at weekends. I believe that most of the copies are sent overseas to emigrants in Great Britain and the United States. It has lots of local stories from around Ireland and business news. It keeps away from anything political or controversial.'

'I see. And its owner, Maybury. Has his name ever cropped up around the Castle?'

'Not that I'm aware of, sir. I think he's a Home Ruler, but the respectable kind. Why do you ask?'

'It's probably nothing. But the boy we took out of the Liffey worked in his printing works. I met Maybury earlier this afternoon and that's something not quite right about him. He seemed very nervous.'

'Everybody's nervous, sir.'

'I suppose you're right — it's the times we live in, isn't it? I think I will go upstairs for a bit and go over my notes before I go out for dinner. Tell Blaney when he comes back that I apologise. I was probably a bit too harsh on the young man.'

'I will, sir,' Noctor says, and goes back to his work.

CHAPTER 18

Christopher strolls past the lampposts under which, the night before, prostitutes gathered and smiled at potential customers. The night-time surge of restless people is no more and the prostitutes have disappeared from the streets. Some soldiers still remain, but in small patrols. The night-time food vendors have packed up their stalls and are long gone, the only sign of their presence the scraps of discarded food being fought over by seagulls and crows. The buskers who competed with one another, belting out songs and holding aloft their ballad sheets for sixpence, are silent.

He passes by Phil Shanahan's pub. Glancing through the glass door the only person inside is a barman shining glasses. Further up the street, he stands outside the house to which Nell had brought him. The building now seems to be completely closed up as if the occupants are away on holidays. The windows that overlook the street are shuttered on the inside and the front door, which had been left ajar the previous evening, is shut. What if there is nobody there during the day or what if Nell is elsewhere, what would he do then? The thought of having to wait around until night-time is a disappointment.

Without much hope, he makes his way up the steps, lifts the heavy brass knocker and lets it drop. The house, compared to the previous night, seems deserted. He waits for any sign of life from within but there is only silence. He tries again, this time giving several sharp raps. A woman's angry voice shouts out something to him from somewhere above his head. He stands back form the door and looks up. A middle-aged woman, still wearing a white nightdress, with her hair tied back in a tight bun, leans out of the first-floor window.

She shouts again: *'Are you deaf? I said what d'you want? We don't open until dark.'*

'I was here last night —'

'If you've lost your wallet, it's nothing to with us. And if you go to the police, you'll not get any good there — they'll tell you not to be so careless. Now go away.'

'I'm not here to cause trouble, ma'am. I was here with a girl last night, she's a friend of Anna's, the owner. Her name is Nell. I wanted to see if I can talk to her.'

'Why would she want to talk to you? Do you owe her money?'

'I don't think so.'

Christopher feels flustered. He should have thought of what he was going to say before he started the conversation and now he feels foolish.

'You don't think so? What kind of an answer is that?'

'Well, she brought me back to her room. I wasn't well. I didn't think —'

'Oh, it's you, is it? Moussa mentioned you. Wait there, I'll be down.'

She withdraws her head and the window came down with a crash.

He stands on the steps, uncomfortable with the stares of the passing people, the daytime people. Women with children look sideways up at him and the driver of a horse-drawn delivery carriage

156

shouts out something that he can't make out. A small group of black-clad nuns quicken their pace as they pass by the house of ill repute, heads bowed, the lead nun blessing herself. Christopher lifts his newly acquired hat and wonders if they are heading towards the Magdalen Laundry which he knows is somewhere nearby.

The woman who opens the door stands back in the shadows of the hallway as if the sunlight might hurt her in some way. She squints out at him, looks him up and down, then ushers him inside. The hallway he remembers stepping into the night before is a lot different now. Where he was surrounded by music and laughter, now there is total silence, except for the ticking of a tall grandfather clock that stands against one wall. The only indication as to its night-time activities is the heavy, stale smell of perfume mixed with cigar smoke.

The woman, still dressed in her nightgown, stands in front of him, her hands on her hips. She stares intently at Christopher's head and he remembers he is still wearing his hat, which he whips off.

'So, you're Nell's new beau, let's have a good look at yeh,' the woman says, lets out a laugh, shakes her head and walks into the parlour.

Christopher follows her inside and waits while she opens all of the tall shutters, pulling them apart with a crash, filling the room with light. He feels almost embarrassed with the disorder around him. Jackets are strewn across chairs, empty bottles and glasses are scattered around the floor and almost cover a table. When he had crept through earlier that morning the room was almost in darkness, but in the cruel light of day there is utter chaos.

The woman turns and laughs again, a throaty laugh that turns into a cough.

'Are you shocked?' she asks when she recovers. 'This is what you men get up to in your cups. Not a pretty sight, is it? Sit down and stop gawping.'

Christopher looks around him for a chair that isn't cluttered with abandoned clothes and picks out the only one, a stool that stands in front of an upright piano between the two windows that face out on to the street. The woman, whom he now presumes is the owner and madam, Anna Macken, goes over to the fireplace, picks up a packet of cigarettes, takes one out and lights it. She coughs after her first pull and bends over, her head almost in the fireplace. After some more coughing and clearing of her throat, she recovers and straightens up.

'The doctors say these are supposed to be good for your chest ...' she indicates the cigarette in her fingers, 'the lying bastards.'

'I heard the same,' Christopher replies.

'Well, all men are liars anyway. I'm Anna, by the way. Tell me, what's your name and what did you do to my Nell?' She sits down on an armchair after clearing it of some silk stockings and a bundled-up man's jacket.

'My name is Joseph Andrews and I did nothing to Nell,' he says. 'She ran out on me.'

'I've never seen her running from a man before — you must have hurt her.'

'I did not.'

'Then you must have got under her skin.' Anna flicks the ash from her cigarette.

'We had a bit of a disagreement, about the rebellion.'

'Well, are you for or against?'

'Against. Well, I was against. I'm not too sure anymore.'

'I'm curious — why are you unsure now and were so certain before?'

Christopher wonders if he should tell her about the raid on the pub and the executions of the leaders of the rebellion, then decides that the news would be out shortly anyway.

'They've shot some of the leaders. It doesn't seem right to me that you execute someone like that, without a trial.'

Anna stands up suddenly and begins to pace the room, her head bent in concentration.

'When did this happen?'

'Early this morning, at dawn.'

'And you're certain?'

'I'm afraid so.'

'You men, I can't believe it — things were just settling down again. Last night was our best night in weeks. Now we'll lose a lot of our customers.'

'I think they've made a mistake.'

'You don't say!' Anna answers. 'Maybe it will settle down in a while. After all, what's one or two more lives?'

'I think that they might execute more,' Christopher blurts out.

Anna turns on him. 'How would you know all this?'

Christopher's mind races. What is he supposed to say to her? Then he remembers what Byatt had advised him about partial truth.

'I'm staying in a hotel around the corner in Talbot Street. After I left here, I went back to my hotel and there were some men there having breakfast — I think they were detectives from the Dublin Metropolitan Police. I overheard them talking about it among themselves.'

Anna sits back down again and blows a stream of pale-blue smoke towards the ceiling.

'I suppose everything comes to an end,' she says, picks some loose tobacco off her lip and studies it, nodding to herself.

Christopher waits in silence for a few minutes, then says: 'Is Nell around?'

Anna looks over at him, as if she has seen him for the first time. He sees now that under the cracked and smudged make-up she still wears from the night before, she is older than he had originally thought. Some of the feistiness has left her and her face seems greyer and gaunt.

'How should I know? She comes and goes as she pleases.' She flicks the ash from her cigarette onto the floor, her mind already elsewhere.

'I thought that because she worked for you that you'd have an idea.'

'Nell? Nell doesn't work for anybody. She's a free spirit. I rescued her years back from that house of horrors on Gloucester Street, the one they call a laundry or an orphanage but it's worse than a workhouse.'

'Is that why she keeps that picture in her room?'

Anna laughs and her laughter brings on another spasm of coughing.

'Poor Nell. That's a picture that came with the frame. I bought it for her as a present. She's not even sure what her real name is — she was given her name by the nuns. They strip everything off you when you end up there. Now I'm her only family. And don't look so disgusted — it's not so bad here, unless you're religious, I suppose. There's children running around the streets of the Monto who'll die before they're Nell's age.'

Christopher feels an intense sadness when he remembers Nell's photograph of her would-be family. But then the sadness gives way to anger as he looks at the middle-aged woman who is supposed to be taking care of her, sitting in the middle of the wreckage from the night before, smoking as if nothing's the matter. Making money by using Nell. He jumps off the stool, pointing at Anna.

'Maybe she's better off taking her chances out on the streets. At least her soul would have had a better chance than staying in this den selling her body!'

Anna looks up at him in surprise, then she begins to laugh.

'Selling her body? Nell doesn't sell her body. I certainly don't sell it. I give her bed and board for escorting gentlemen back to the house.

And what do you care about her soul anyway? Would you rather her to have a clean soul and a dead body? Because that's what would happen if I threw her out onto the streets.'

Christopher is left standing, red-faced, with his finger extended, not knowing what to do.

'I apologise. I thought that ...'

'You and every other man she brings back. No, Nell's not for sale. I'm not saying she's as pure as the driven snow, but she does not sell her body. Does that make you feel better now, Christopher? That your little girlfriend might be pure and chaste?' Anna cackles with laughter again.

Embarrassed and feeling stupid, Christopher turns and leaves the room. He fumbles with the locks on the front door and eventually pulls it open. The sound of Anna's laughter follows him out onto the street. He turns and stares back at the windows. Anna is standing, her hands on her hips, still laughing. He wonders what he should do next. What would Byatt do if he were in his shoes? There is no point going back to the hotel, there is nothing for him there. Why did he tell that woman about the executions? He should learn to keep his mouth shut. He looks up the street and sees a man coming out of Shanahan's pub. It's still his best hope of finding Nell again and telling her that he had deserted the army, was caught but then escaped. But when she finds out there have been three executions, she will avoid him and treat him the way every British soldier is about to be treated — as an outcast.

Turning right onto Mabbot Street, he makes his way towards Gloucester Street, to where he had seen the nuns turn. He is curious to see the place where Nell had spent the first few years of her life. Walking past side streets full of ragged children and semi-derelict houses, he can understand how ridiculous he must have sounded to Anna Macken.

Glancing down one of the more dilapidated lanes he sees a British soldier pushing a woman down onto the ground. As he attempts to walks away from her, she grabs his leg, shouting something about money. But he ignores her and walks towards Christopher, dragging the unfortunate woman behind him. Eventually he tires of the woman, turns and kicks her solidly in the stomach, making her cry out.

'See what you made me do, luv?' he says and draws his foot back again.

'*Stop!*' Christopher shouts out, striding down towards the couple.

The soldier turns and studies the man coming towards him, but sees no threat and kicks the woman again, half-heartedly this time.

'You kin have her, matey, she was terrible,' he says, laughing.

Christopher sees that although he is not carrying a sidearm, he is older than him by a few years and muscular. He is from a Scottish regiment and wears a tam o' shanter which has shifted sideways on his head. He straightens it, patting the khaki pom-pom on top and makes to brush past Christopher who reaches out and grabs his arm, stopping him in his stride.

'Give her what you owe her,' he says.

'Listen, sonny, yeh're making a wee mistake here — yeh'd better let me go,' the soldier says and turns to face Christopher, changing his stance at the same time, his left leg forward, his right arm tensing.

The fight is quick, wordless and brutal. Christopher, already in a bad humour after his visit to Anna's and now outraged over the soldier's treatment of the defenceless woman, jabs him in the nose, a short but powerful jab that draws blood. The soldier swings out with his right but the face he was aiming at has already ducked and Christopher lands a powerful blow to his gut. The Scot realises now that he is in a real fight. He stumbles backwards to regain his balance and to reassess the situation, but it is too late. Christopher follows quickly with several blows in quick succession to his head and the soldier is now staggering backwards, trying to ward him off.

The woman, still sprawled on the ground, is the soldier's undoing. He trips backwards over her and Christopher is on him, pummelling his face as hard as he can until even the woman takes mercy on her attacker and yells at Christopher to stop. The red mist rises and he is kneeling over the bloodied face of his opponent and out of breath. As he is getting to his feet the woman is going through the soldier's pockets, takes some coins and escapes back down the laneway. Before the man can regain consciousness, Christopher rises from the ground and looks back up the laneway towards the street, but nobody has seen the confrontation. Using a handkerchief to dab the blood off his knuckles, he makes his way out of the lane.

When he has regained his breath and brushed himself down, he realises that it was a stupid and reckless act to get involved in the altercation. The sordid scene between the prostitute and the soldier must happen all the time in the Monto. He looks back down the laneway and the man is slowly getting back to his feet, searching for his tam o' shanter.

It is easy to find the Magdalen Laundry on Gloucester Street as it is the largest and best-kept building on the street. It is an imposing three-storey edifice that stretches for over a hundred yards. He walks past the railings and tries to catch a glimpse of the people inside, but all of the windows are covered with curtains. Walking further down the street he passes the entrance with its large, solid, wooden, doors. They are closed and he wonders what is going on behind them that had made Nell think she had been rescued. He decides to walk down to the bottom of Gloucester Street and circle back towards Shanahan's pub to try and get a sense of the whole Monto district.

As he makes his way through the area the buildings become

shabbier and some even seem derelict. Tired-looking women stand around in small groups and, as he goes by, they turn and smile at him, a possible customer. From what he remembers of the women working in Anna Macken's house, these seem a good deal older and more decrepit. Dressed in dark dresses and shawls, teeth missing, hair unkempt, he feels a terrible sadness for them. The grand names of the streets he passes through almost mock their existence: Mecklinburgh Street, Elliott Place, Purdon Street; one of them is even called Faithful Place. But the saddest aspect of all are the children running through the derelict tenements, oblivious to what is going on around them. Will they be the next generation or will they die, he wonders, and quickens his pace, anxious to leave all of the degradation behind him.

To banish his sad and depressing journey through the side streets and laneways of the Monto, Christopher heads over the river to the south side of the city and away from the derelict houses and teeming tenements in the Monto. He meanders up Grafton Street towards St. Stephen's Green, stopping every so often to look into shop windows and absorb the excitement of the crowds around him. The street seems to have a strange, festive atmosphere. He presumes that this is due to the fact that the rebellion is finally over and that the city is returning to normal, or this part of the city anyway. The Monto seems a million miles distant from the well-dressed middle-class citizens of Dublin, even though it is just a short stroll away. Scruffy newsboys skip through the crowds, newspapers held over their heads, shouting out the headlines about the executions. He notices that few people are buying them. Guilt or indifference, he cannot tell, but it makes him angry and he quickens his pace towards St. Stephen's Green.

But even there the aftermath of the rising is evident. Where the rebels had dug trenches in the park, workmen are now busy filling them back in. Just inside the giant metal gates a pile of rubbish from the barricades that had been set up waits to be collected. Again, the rebels had shown little knowledge of battlefield tactics as St. Stephen's Green is overlooked by the Shelbourne Hotel on one side and the men would have been sitting targets below.

He continues along the pathway and strolls deeper into the park and towards the pond. The noise from the surrounding streets lessens until it become a distant hum. He finds an empty bench in a secluded arbour and decides to sit and try and make sense of all that has happened since he arrived back in Dublin.

Looking out over the still water of the pond feels like being in a different country. In front of him ducks swim about oblivious to the turmoil that has taken place. A child walks side by side with her mother until she catches sight of the ducks. She breaks away from her mother and runs to the edge of the pond, teetering at the side of the water, pointing to the ducks and shouting. Her mother follows, grabs her into her arms, and kisses her face. The sight of the mother and the child together and all that love between them brings a sudden yearning for the past, to a time not so long ago when his parents were alive and Ned was the irritating little brother who tagged around behind him wherever he went. What wouldn't he give now to have Ned beside him on this bench? For the first time in years, it seems, he is beginning to catch a glimpse of the way back to normalcy. Was it the mother and child, or perhaps the carefree crowds of people wandering up and down Grafton Street? But the real reason, he suspects, is Nell, and, of course, Byatt. It was Byatt had saved his life, but it was Nell, in their short time together, had reawakened his soul.

He remains on the bench, taking in the fresh air and the sights and sounds of the park until the bell sounds, a warning to people that the gates would shortly be closed. How easy it would be for him to leave the park and, instead of going back to the Monto, to just take off somewhere, maybe Skibbereen, where his mother has relatives who would be glad to take him in. But would Nell come with him if he asked her? She would probably say that he was running away, like a little boy. Byatt was another matter. The man had saved him from a firing squad and trusted him to do the right thing. How easy life had been in the army compared to now. Even though there was constant danger and the chance of being killed, still army life had been predictable. He didn't have to make decisions, everything was taken care of: when to sleep, when to wake, when to fight. A middle-aged man, self-important in a parks uniform, strolls up to him and stares, rocking backwards and forwards on his heels.

'Time to go, lad, we're closing up now.'

Christopher detests his type. A little man in a big uniform, dark navy with shiny brass buttons, a sign that says 'Park Ranger' emblazoned across his breast pocket. But he gets up from the bench and follows the dwindling crowd walking towards the exit.

After he leaves through main gates of the park, he strolls to the top of Grafton Street examining his options. Should he go down to Dublin Castle and tell Byatt that he can't find Nell, hand him back his money and throw himself at his mercy? With all of the unrest in the city he might just relieve him of his mission, which was a long shot to begin with. He could bury his pride and plead with Nell to come with him, then take the next train to Cork and start his life over again with her. Or should he keep his word and go back into the Monto and continue his search? He doesn't remember being so indecisive. Was his indecision due to the fear of finding out that he had been mistaken about Nell's feelings for him? What if she had just felt sorry for him after he became so drunk and decided to bring him home, like a lost soul, more to be pitied than loved? A tram packed with passengers lumbers past. They are mostly working men, tired after a hard day's work, all, no doubt, going home. Would he ever be one of those people? Who was he fooling?

Turning his back on the park he makes his way back down Grafton Street, back across the Liffey, back towards the Monto.

CHAPTER 19

Mordaunt receives the news, initially with intense rage and then, almost immediately, calmness and acceptance. He had learned this technique from an old Chinese man he had shared a cell with in Amarillo, Texas. Still in his teens, he had been locked up for several months for nearly killing a fellow cowboy with his bare hands for no other reason than some casual remark the man had made about his appearance. It could have been about his height or his thinness, he couldn't remember exactly — it never really mattered to him in those days anyway. Confined in the smouldering cell, body bruised and bloody from beatings by the guards who took great pleasure in baiting this crazy young gringo, he learned from the old man how to tap into his fury and see it for what it was, something the Chinese man called *anatta*, or the illusion of self. He didn't fully understand what the old man was saying all of the time, but he sensed that he was on the precipice of something that could change his life.

Within several weeks he had learned to tap into his fury. Not to throw it away in one blind, senseless burst, but to stretch it out, until it took the form of a longer story. Within that longer story, he learned, anything was possible. He began to ask himself questions. Why did the guards bait him? Because he was easy to bait and it gave them the motive to drag him out of the cell and beat him up. But when he refused to be baited the tension was sucked out of the air and the guards left him alone and went on to somebody else. Over time he was able to put the anger of being locked up aside and to plan his escape. Unfortunately, it meant bribing the same hated Mexican guards with money he did not possess. But the Chinese man did, several gold sovereigns tucked away in the tresses of his hair which he kept plaited in a long pigtail — but not all of the time. He justified murdering the old man in his sleep by using the very principle his fellow cellmate had taught him: the illusion of self. It was not him that wrapped his fingers around the old man's scrawny neck, it was somebody else.

In the time it takes his informant to finish telling him everything that had occurred in the last couple of days, Mordaunt has already mapped out a plan and how to go about carrying it out. These main traits in his personality, his fury and lack of empathy, he knows, are inherited from his mother and father. The fury side he has managed to tame thanks to the Chinaman all those years ago. But the other side of his personality — his complete lack of a moral centre, as a judge once told him — he often wonders about. Now he suspects it comes from his mother's antecedents. Although his father, Eric Mordaunt, had a short fuse that erupted spectacularly, his spells of fury never lasted long and soon the cause of that fury was forgotten. In truth, he was a weak man. But his mother, a full-blooded Chilkoot Indian, was the opposite. Slow to take offence, even when some of the new homesteaders found it hard to hide their contempt of her, she ignored it and continued to wear the same stoic expression. But, occasionally, after some act of ostracism that occurred in the rapidly expanding town of Skagway, where they fetched their supplies, fate would somehow strike out at the perpetrator: a mysterious fire would occur, the water from a well that had been clean and drinkable would suddenly and without obvious cause be poisoned, or a favourite animal would go missing.

It was only years later, long after he had left Alaska and his immature fury behind him and began to earn a reputation for efficient ruthlessness and lack of morals, that he began to appreciate this trait. It coursed through his blood alongside his Scottish ancestry and was handed down from the long-lost ancestors on his mother's side, who used it to survive the brutal Alaskan winters. It was the same trait that helped his family survive that terrible winter of 1889, when the unsuspecting prospector and his family had the misfortune to visit their log cabin.

His contact in Dublin Castle, a young civil servant he had enlisted, William Blaney, stutters on and on with the excitement of his news. Mordaunt has no doubt that he is embellishing his own role in it. If they had not been sitting in full view on a bench outside Patrick's Cathedral, he would have grabbed the fool by the neck and shaken the details out of him sooner. He had settled on Blaney over the period of several weeks in which he had loitered outside Dublin Castle, taking in the comings and goings of the civil servants. William Blaney, he noted, was the only one wearing the same clothes every day. It didn't take him long to find out his circumstances. He lived in a small, artisan cottage in a side-street in Irishtown, near the Dublin docks. The cottage, which to him looked like a hut, was home to almost ten people, Blaney's parents and a rabble of siblings, all younger than the civil servant. After that it had been an easy matter to offer him a supplement to his wages.

Blaney's father, from what he could make out, either had no job or was too ill to work and his mother rarely made an appearance outside of the cottage. In a way Blaney's circumstances reminded him of himself when he was younger. Glad to get out of the cottage in the mornings, or in Mordaunt's case a wood cabin in the wilderness. But there the similarities ended. Where Mordant was focussed, Blaney's attention to detail was erratic. No matter how many times Mordaunt told Blaney to prioritise the gossip that circulated around Dublin Castle, the young man insisted on giving the same emphasis to every piece of news that occurred, most of which was of no use. He spent so much time sifting through the small unimportant details that he wondered if it would be better just to get rid of Blaney — after all, his time in Ireland was now coming to a close and, either way, he would have to get rid of him. But sometimes, on such small unimportant details, battles are lost.

'*Stop*. Who is this Byatt person and why have you not told me about him before?' he asks Blaney, suppressing the urge to squeeze the details out of him with his bare hands.

'I didn't think he was important. Major Byatt, just an old soldier sent over from London to earn his keep. Said he was going to work on certain matters that were confidential and should not concern us. Self-important has-been. It happens all the time — people come over from England, lording it over us.'

'But he has his own office and his own quarters, in the Castle. Did it not occur to you that information might have been useful to me?'

'I suppose, looking back now ...'

'Go on, tell me what you know,' Mordaunt says, afraid of losing his patience.

'Yesterday he appeared with a prisoner, a young soldier looking the worst for wear. He took him into the morgue used by the Dublin Metropolitan Police and they stayed there for half an hour or so.'

'What is there to see in the morgue?'

'The body of young man murdered several days ago is laid out there, on Byatt's orders.'

'Joyce?'

'Yes, how did you know his name?'

'Never mind. Go on.'

'I snooped around a bit. The young soldier was arrested for assault last Saturday and ended up in the cells. He was a deserter, and an Irishman. Disgusting. I thought nothing of it and expected a quick court martial and a summary execution, but then he appears with Byatt, the two almost mates.'

'And then?'

'Both of them head out into the city afterwards and that's the last we saw of the soldier.'

Mordaunt's mind works through all of the permutations he can think of, but the conundrum remains. To make matters worse the park beside the cathedral is teeming with families glad to get out of their homes after the fighting of the previous weeks and his mind is finding it hard to cope with the noise and Blaney's ramblings. He is off again, chattering on about the gossip that is circulating about Byatt.

Mordaunt turns to Blaney who is saying that Byatt is more fond of the deserter than he is of his own men.

'Wait — what did you say, before that?'

Blaney face bursts into a knowing smile. 'There's a rumour that he is partial to the company of other men.'

'Who says?'

'One of the officers in the Castle, claims he knows Byatt of old. And he eats in that funny restaurant off Dame Street, the one where all the Nancy boys hang out.'

'And do you really think that a British officer, even an ex-officer, would release a prisoner in order to satisfy his own urges?'

'I never thought too much about it. I suppose when you put it like that, probably not.'

'Not probably, you fool, definitely.'

A sly smile appears on Blaney's face. 'Then why did the quartermaster receive a request for identity papers and extra money from Byatt?'

Mordaunt fishes a ten-shilling note from his pocket and holds it out in front of Blaney who makes a grab for it. But before he can get hold of it, he whips it away. Blaney looks crestfallen.

'I want you to go over every detail you remember. Leave nothing out.'

As Blaney tells him everything that had transpired, Mordaunt is already reformulating his earlier plans. Blaney talks excitedly, boasting of how he had faced down Byatt about the execution of the rebel leaders. Mordaunt nods his head in appreciation and this encourages Blaney to go on at length about what he could do back in Dublin Castle for just a little extra money.

The park around them is still busy. Children run, trip, pull kites behind them, climb the few small trees placed around the park, while the mothers look on nervously.

'Perhaps I have underestimated you, Blaney,' Mordaunt says when the other man has finally run out of things he can boast about.

'That's not your fault, Mr. Mordaunt, people always underestimate me. How do you think I got so far in the Castle?' Blaney smiles and touches the side of his nose, an affectation that Mordaunt despises.

'I can see that now. I might have another task for you, something more difficult, but well paid if you succeed.'

'Just say the word and I'm ready,' Blaney says, puffing his chest out.

'It's a bit more complicated this time.'

'I can show you, sir, exactly what I can do,' Blaney says.

Mordaunt nods his head then looks around them at the people in the park.

'But not here, it's too crowded. Why don't we go into St Patrick's Cathedral, we'll get some privacy there.'

'Of course, good idea. I have my notebook with me. And may I say, Mr. Mordaunt, you'll not be disappointed.'

The two men rise from the bench and saunter over towards the cathedral. As they walk through the great arched doorway Blaney gives a potted history of the medieval building. They stand inside the entrance, taking in the vaulted ceilings and the stained-glass windows. The windows are illuminated by the afternoon sun that brings out the vivid reds and yellows and blues. The floor stretches out in front of them as far as the altar, small square coloured tiles laid out in geometric patterns. From the walls hang the pendants of some of the oldest Irish families, hanging limply down. The pungent smell of candles hangs in the air.

'We have nothing like this in America,' Mordaunt says, making his way further into the interior, looking around him at the decorated tombs and the polished mahogany pews. 'Is this where the nobility came?'

'These are for the ordinary folk. I believe the big families have their own pews nearer the altar.'

'It is ever so,' Mordaunt says, nodding.

Blaney is getting impatient and holds back.

'I don't have much time,' he says. 'Can we talk about your needs, Mr. Mordaunt.

'All in good time. You shouldn't worry about getting back to the office, you will be very well compensated.' Mordaunt walks on.

The two men stroll further into the cathedral. Mordaunt stops at one of the transepts, which is empty, and turns to Blaney.

'Is this for the choir?'

'It is.'

Mordaunt walks deeper into the transept until he is at the furthest end from the main body of the church and seats himself on one of the cushioned pews. He pats the cushion beside him.

'You said you have a notebook and a pen.'

Blaney takes a small, leather-covered notebook and a fountain pen out of his inside pocket. He opens the notebook onto a blank page, takes the top off his pen and waits.

'That is a beautiful pen — may I see it?' Mordaunt asks.

'Of course, but it's nothing special,' Blaney says and hands him the pen.

Mordaunt takes the pen and examines it closely, working the small lever at the side which sends a squirt of ink down the nip and drips down the front of Blaney's shirt.

'I'm so sorry,' he says. 'How clumsy of me!'

Blaney looks down in disbelief at the spreading blue stain. As he looks up to complain, Mordaunt plunges the pen into his left eye as far as he can, at the same time covering his mouth. His face is frozen in shock and he struggles, tears of blood running down his face, but he is no match for Mordaunt's strength. With a final, violent push with the heel of his hand his attacker hammers the pen all the way into Blaney's brain until barely an inch of it sticks out of the eye socket. Blaney lets out a final breath, almost a sigh, and slumps forward in the pew, his head resting on the cushioned rail.

Mordaunt wipes his bloody hands in Blaney's jacket, takes the ten-shilling note from his pocket he had given him earlier and adjusts the dead man's head away from the body of the cathedral until the pen is no longer visible to any casual observer.

He gets up from the pew and makes his way down the transept, turning once to look back. Blaney's pose is perfect: a young man taking a nap after a hard day's work in the office.

CHAPTER 20

Back in the Monto, Christopher's first port of call is Phil Shanahan's pub. It is now evening but still too early for the night-time people to be seen parading through the streets. He walks through the doors and steps into an almost empty bar with a sprinkling of men, mostly workers, sitting along the counter. The same barman who had been giving out to Nell the previous evening nods over to him. He pushes opens the door into the tiny snug, half expecting to see Nell sitting there. Inside there are two elderly women sipping glasses of ale and swapping gossip. They look up at him and he mumbles an apology. They cackle with laughter and want to know if they are too old for him.

Red-faced, he takes a place at the bar and calls for a pint of porter.

'Have you any food?' he asks the barman when he arrives back with his drink.

'You're in the wrong place for that,' he says with a wink, 'but wait around — Nell might take you up to Anna Macken's for a bit of food — and maybe something else as well.'

The barman turns to the other men at the bar, laughing at his own joke. Christopher's arm shoots out and grabs a hold of the barman's apron, pulling him almost bodily across the bar. As he is about to draw back his fist to strike the barman in the face, he feels an enormous hand enveloping his fist from behind and squeezing it. Christopher pushes the barman away and swivels to face his assailant. It's Phil Shanahan. He tries to jerk his hand free, but it is locked in a grip of steel. Phil, a tall and well-built man with a red face and a drooping moustache, stares down into his eyes. Christopher tries to take a swing with his left, but Phil draws his face back and catches his other hand.

Christopher is now powerless.

The customers sitting along the counter sipping their drinks turn towards them.

One of them speaks up. 'Leave him be, Phil, he was doing no harm. Johnny was out of order, as usual.'

'What did you say, Johnny?' Phil, says to the red-faced barman, who is straightening his tie.

'Nothing, Phil. He was looking for food. He was here last night with Nell, so I just suggested that he might go back up to Anna's if he needed some food, that's all.'

Phil shakes his head. 'Are you telling the truth, Johnny? Because, if you are, I'm going to teach this man not to be too free with his hands in my establishment.'

The barman looks down and mumbles something.

'*What's that, Johnny, I can't hear you?*' Phil shouts.

'I said I might have said something else,' the barman admits, 'but it was only a joke.'

'I thought so. Now, why don't you apologise to the young man?' Phil looks down into Christopher's face, putting more pressure on his hands. 'And why don't you apologise for losing your temper and laying your hands on my barman?'

Christopher can feel the bones of his fingers being squeezed together and thinks that they are about to snap. He nods in submission and Phil releases both his hands.

'No hard feelings?' Johnny says, and thrusts his hand over the bar towards Christopher.

'No hard feelings. Just don't mention Nell like that again,' Christopher says, and carefully shakes the man's hand.

'Now that was easy, wasn't it?' Phil says. 'And you, sir, can come into the back and I'll drum up some food for yeh. My name is Phil Shanahan, same as over the door, owner of this wonderful establishment. How about a fry? That's about all I can manage.'

'That's very kind of you,' Christopher says, rubbing life back into his hands. 'I'm Joseph Andrews.'

Phil leads the way to a wooden flap set into the counter and lifts it up for Christopher to go through. There is a door marked *PRIVATE* behind the bar and he follows the bar owner inside. A line of beer kegs run down the length of a dark hallway and at the end of the hallway another door leads into a parlour. Phil Shanahan waves his hand towards one of the chairs set around a dining table and continues on through into what Christopher presumes is the kitchen. Outside the light is fading. Through the single window he can make out a small enclosed yard with more beer kegs piled up against a wall. A ginger cat stares in at him from the top of the one of the kegs.

The parlour looks like a bachelor's quarters and is cluttered with odd pieces of well-used furniture, its walls covered with a mixture of religious paintings and framed photographs. Curious, he gets up from the table and examines the photographs more closely. Some are unremarkable, posed family photographs, most of them outside a cottage somewhere in the countryside. Then there are photographs of men, some in uniform, others in civilian clothes. In one photograph a column of men march, with what looks like ancient rifles slung over their shoulders, their embarrassed gaze staring into the camera. If they weren't armed with rifles, they carried pitchforks or hurling sticks.

'Proud men of the Irish Volunteers, Joseph, ready to fight for the freedom of Ireland,' Phil says from behind him.

Christopher turns. Inches away from his face is the black muzzle of a Webley revolver similar to the one he had bartered away in Birmingham for a few pounds. The hammer is drawn back and he can make out the tips of the lead bullets resting in the chamber. It's a big revolver, but in Phil Shanahan's ham-like hand it looks like a toy. He puts his hands up slowly, his eyes fixed on the mouth of the gun barrel.

Phil flicks the revolver, motioning him back to dining-room table.

After Christopher sits down, hands still raised, the bar owner takes another of the chairs and sits facing him, the gun still pointing directly at his head.

'So, Joseph … if that's year real name. I'm curious, why is there a British soldier creeping around the Monto spying on us?'

The extent of Shanahan's knowledge shocks Christopher. He is well aware of what damage the gun would do to him at this range. It would lift the back of his skull off and splatter it over the wall. He stares into the eyes of Phil Shanahan, assessing if he has the nerve to shoot a man while looking him in the eyes and decides that he has. He remembers Byatt's advice again: stay as close to the truth as possible.

'I'm spying on nobody,' he replies with what he hopes is offence.

'Don't try my patience. You have the bearing of an army man if ever I saw one. Soldiers usually wear uniforms around here. We mightn't like it, but at least we know who they are. I could shoot you as a spy where you sit, after what happened this morning.'

'You're right. I was in the army but I deserted,' Christopher admits.

'That's a handy excuse to have when you have a gun pointed at your face,' Phis says, waving the barrel of the revolver from side to side.

'If you don't believe, why don't you shoot me?' Christopher says. 'That's a Webley Mark 5 with a .45 calibre bullet. I used to have one. Not only will it make a mess of your parlour, it will also bring half the bar back here.'

'You're pretty cheeky considering you're so close to death's door.'

'I've been living close to death's door for almost two years. I'd almost like to find out what's on the other side,' Christopher replies, trying to keep the tremor from his voice.

'Let's say I believe you — tell me, what made you desert?'

'A personal matter.'

'Was it a woman? Nell will be disappointed. I think she took a shine to you. She popped in earlier, says she was looking for money I owed her, but it wasn't money she was lookin' for.'

'It wasn't a woman.'

'Why don't you just come out and tell me, lad? Then I can be the judge of your story. And, by the way, the men in the bar won't bat an eyelid if they hear a shot coming from back here, not after what the British army did in Kilmainham Gaol this morning.'

'Alright, I'll tell you. I trusted a man with looking after my younger brother. He broke his word and my brother died because of him. Now he's lying in a field somewhere in Flanders. I deserted so that I could come home and take the man's life for my brother's.'

'And did you? Kill him?'

'Nearly. I just beat him up badly. He had a wife and children. I'd forgotten about them. I wasn't going to leave those children without a father, same as me. In any case, I was caught in the act by an army patrol and brought to Dublin Castle. But I managed to get away.'

Phil lowers the gun but keeps it in his hand.

'You were better off not killing him, Joseph. It would have ruined the rest of your life. Keep your hatred for someone who deserves it. And, by the way, your story seems to match what one of our spies in the Castle reported about a badly beaten young soldier being taken in. I'm presuming that was you, although I don't know how you escaped out of there. We could use a man like you. You can lower your hands now.'

Even though the gun is lowered and he is out of immediate danger, Christopher feels deflated.

'What did Nell tell you about me?' he asks.

Phil lets out a laugh and slaps his thigh.

'Jesus, boy, you should see your face. I'll have to tell the lads. Didn't blink when I poked a big fucking gun into your nose, but what a look of pain now!'

'It's all in your mind. Nell means nothing to me,' Christopher snaps.

'That's a pity. Underneath all that muck on her face she's got a good heart.'

'Good with everyone, do you mean?'

'Don't be a fool. She makes a living out of the soldiers, but not the way you think. And she does drink a lot, I will attest to that, but who wouldn't to survive around here?'

'She lives in a brothel.'

'Anna lets her live there — it doesn't mean she works there,' Phil says, losing his patience. 'Do you want her roaming the streets of the Monto, or worse the laneways with the kips who'll put her to work until she ends up like those two biddies in the snug?'

'No, I don't,' Christopher admits.

'Listen, around here Anna Macken's brothel is as good as it gets. You don't have to walk too far to visit some of the other kips full of overworked girls just up from the country. Worse than animals, those madams.'

'Do you really believe she's better off living in a brothel?'

'Around here, yes. So, you can stop that heart of yours bleedin' all over my floor.'

Phil rises from the chair, tucks the revolver inside his belt and goes back into the kitchen. Christopher hears the whoosh of a gas cooker and soon the smell of frying pours through the door and into the parlour. Phil makes several trips in and out of the kitchen, setting the table with plates and cutlery. Christopher, recovering from the shock of being held at gunpoint, realises that he can use this opportunity to try and get some local knowledge from Phil. But the pub owner is no fool, and he thinks of ways of approaching the questions without making him suspicious. Phil comes back in carrying an enormous blackened frying pan full of still-sizzling sausages, rashers, black pudding, kidneys and what looks like slices of liver. Floating in a shallow pool of grease in the middle of the offal are two eggs frying away. He tips most of the food onto Christopher's plate and keeps just an egg and some liver for himself, then joins him at the table.

'Eat up, lad, you've lost too much weight in your search for revenge,' he says with a laugh.

Christopher attacks his meal, barely giving it time to cool down. Halfway through, Phil leaves and comes back with a loaf of white bread and cuts thick slices off it. He notices that Phil hasn't eaten that much himself and has barely toyed with the egg. The parlour is almost in darkness and Phil gets up again and lights some oil lamps. He takes out a pipe from his waistcoat pocket and lights it up, puffing contentedly on it and blowing rings that float upwards and disappear into the shadow then dissipate around the room. By the time Christopher has finished his food they are surrounded by a cloud of blue, fragrant smoke.

'That was good, thank you very much,' Christopher says, patting his stomach.

'It was nothing, I'm glad you liked it. I enjoy watching a young man with a hearty appetite,' Phil says, leaning further back in his chair.

'Have you been in the Monto long?' Christopher asks.

'Too long. I'm a proud Tipperary man, but my soul is trapped in Dublin now, I'm afraid.'

'But if you don't like it here, why not go back home?'

'I never said I didn't like it here. It has everything I need, quietness during the day so that I can get some sleep and excitement at night. Maybe a bit too much at times. And anyway, Tipperary is not for me anymore. I don't think the parish priest would take kindly to a man who owned a public house in the middle of the Monto — the largest den of inequity in Europe, they say.'

Christopher rises up from the table, walks over to the photographs on the wall again and begins to study them.

'Maybe the priest is right. I saw what the women working on the street go through. I believe some even lose their lives,' he says absently.

'It would be the same anywhere. That's what happens when you mix men, women and drink in a cramped neighbourhood. Sometimes things get out of hand. A soldier refuses to pay or occasionally a gentleman. The woman fights back and that's the end of it.'

'Sounds horrible.'

'It is. I've interfered a few times and had my windows broken for it.'

'But what about murder?' Christopher asks, still studying the photographs.

There is silence for several seconds and Christopher thinks that he has been too inquisitive for Phil's liking, but then he hears the knocking of a pipe against a plate and realises that Phil was just cleaning it out.

'Ah, there have been a few of those but nobody likes to talk about it. They say it brings bad luck.'

'A terrible way to die: alone, scared, afraid to meet your Maker after living a life of sin.'

'In the Monto we're all afraid of that,' Phil answers, gets up from the chair and disappears into the kitchen, leaving Christopher no wiser now than when he had started.

He curses his own ineptitude. He struggles with how to bring the conversation back to the murders again and decides to take a chance before Phil returns to work. The background noise from the bar had been increasing and now there was a steady hum of voices.

Phil comes back out of the kitchen and begins to stack the things on the table.

'Nell told me that some unfortunate women had been strangled, probably by the same man,' Christopher says.

'Ay. Strangled is a kind word for what they went through. That was strange right enough. People think we've another Jack the Ripper on our hands. But they're a superstitious lot around here.' He carries the things into the kitchen. '*And do you know where most of them were found?*' he shouts out to Christopher. '*Tyrone Street, and Faithful Place — it's the area where they provide the more specialised services. Imagine that, meeting your end in a place called Faithful!*'

'*Did they catch the murderer?*' Christopher calls out.

'No chance,' says Phil, coming back and sitting at the table again. 'Nobody has time to worry about the likes of those poor women. Most of them are carted off to Glasnevin Cemetery and put into a pauper's grave. The priest won't even say a prayer over them, says they go straight to hell.'

Christopher joins him at the table. 'How could anyone get away with murdering women in such a busy area? It's hard to understand.'

Phil shrugs, takes the pipe from his waistcoat pocket again and puts it onto the table, then takes out a packet of tobacco and a small penknife.

Christopher watches with impatience as the man carefully pares off some tobacco and rolls it in between the palms of his hand before stuffing it into his pipe and lighting it.

'I like a couple of pipes at the start of an evening, before the crowds, it helps me relax,' he says, blowing smoke rings up towards the ceiling again.

Christopher can hear the background din from the pub becoming increasingly louder. Shanahan will be going back inside soon and his chance to uncover more information about the murdered women will be gone. But the pub owner is no fool and he lets him smoke away in the hope that he will drift back to the subject.

Without warning, Phil starts to speak again. 'People have their theories.'

'About what?' Christopher says.

'About the murdered women.'

'And what do they say?'

'Most of them are bunkum. As I said, some think that Jack the Ripper has moved from London and is now plying his murderous trade here.' Phil chuckles.

'That happened nearly twenty years ago.'

'That's what I told them. Old Jack, I said to them, is well gone by now. Probably in America.'

'What do *you* think?'

Phil tips another lighted match to his dying pipe. Christopher can see there is not much time left.

'Well, if I were to take a guess, I would have to say that the man is mad, but cunning. How else could he have got away with it for this long without anybody catching sight nor sound of him? I would also hazard a guess that he is a powerful man, maybe in the government or high up in the army, during the daytime anyway. Most of the men who visit those women go there to be humiliated for some reason that's beyond me. Put that all together and you have a very formidable person.'

'Everybody makes mistakes — in time,' Christopher says.

'Well,' Phil says, tapping his pipe into an ashtray, 'nobody's found any, yet.'

Grunting, the bar owner gets up from the chair and stretches.

'Time for work,' he says. 'You can stay here for a while if you'd like. I'm sure Nell will be in sooner or later and I'd prefer if you weren't hanging around the bar.'

Christopher feels disappointed. He has learned nothing useful. Phil over to a coat rack and picks a spotless, white apron, wrapping it around himself carefully. He goes over to a drawer and takes out some gramophone discs, putting them on the table.

'Here, you can listen to these while you're waiting,' he says, then goes towards the door.

Before he leaves, he turns to Christopher.

'People say he uses the tunnels to get away, but nobody will go down to prove it,' he says, chuckling.

'What tunnels?'

'All of this area is reclaimed land. Some of the houses were built on top of granite culverts that were put in in case of flooding. Some tunnels, they say, lead down to the docks. They also say Prince Albert used them to go in and out of the flash houses when he was visiting, but I don't think His Majesty would have risked getting the pox in the Monto.'

'Flash houses?'

'The more upmarket brothels like Anna Macken's,' Phil says, opening the door. 'Anyway, it's just a rumour, like all the rest of them. You can take your pick.'

CHAPTER 21

Moussa is flopped down in the only chair in the room, his long legs stretching out across the floor, making the tiny living quarters seem even smaller than they are. Sarah slaps his thigh, a sharp signal that makes him draw his legs back in and at the same time sit up straight. It is a familiar scene and one that Nell never tires of witnessing: Anna's diminutive helper exercising control over her giant Algerian boyfriend. On the bed, sitting on an old newspaper, is a cluster of what looks like shrivelled brown crab apples on a long stem. Moussa picks one of the pieces off the stem, holds it up to show the girls, then puts it into his mouth and chews with a look of great contentment on his face.

'Disgusting,' Sarah says, and slaps him on the thigh again.

'What are they?' Nell asks.

'These,' Moussa says, taking a moist stone from his mouth and holding it up for everyone to see, 'are the foods of the gods: *dates*.'

'In for a penny, in for a pound,' Nell says, plucks one of the dates off the stem and examines it. It is soft to the touch and sticky. Closing her eyes, she puts it into her mouth and bites down on it carefully.

The flesh, when her teeth break through the skin, is overly sweet and she finds it repulsive, but she smiles, and spits the stone out onto her hand.

'Have another,' Moussa says.

'No, one is enough, thank you,' she says.

Moussa seems relieved when she refuses and takes another one for himself. He sits back on his chair and closes his eyes.

'He's been doing that all day. Says it reminds him of home,' Sarah says and, this time, puts her hand gently on the giant's thigh.

'Where did he get them?' Nell asks, prodding the dates with her finger.

'There's a Spanish ship in. He went down to the docks and bumped into one of the crew. And wouldn't you know his luck, he was a fellow Algerian. He spent most of this morning on board drinking strong coffee and eating dates in return for a list of the all the best whorehouses in the Monto.'

'Not this one.' Moussa opens his eyes. 'I would never give Anna's name out to sailors. Too much trouble. Get drunk, use knives, no good for me.'

Sarah moves her hand up to his face and caresses his beard. Nobody knows how old the Algerian is, but intertwined through his black, wavy beard are strands of grey. Nell guesses that he is at least in his forties which makes him almost twice Sarah's age, but nobody comments on the difference. They are just two more exotic creatures thrown together in the night-time world of the Monto and people just accept them for what they are: a couple. She watches them with envy, two lovers adrift in their own world.

Sarah catches her looking at them.

'And what about your mystery man, has he not shown up?'

'No. And I don't really care,' Nell says, her face reddening, something that never happens to her. She looks away to hide her blushes.

'Anna took me aside, told me not to disturb you, that you're a bit down,' Sarah says.

'Oh, she did, did she?'

'What did you think was so special about this one?' Sarah says and punches Nell playfully in the side. 'Tell me all?'

'Nothing to tell. I brought a man back to my room. He was too drunk to let loose in the Monto, would've ended up in the gutter without his wallet. What could I do?'

'You could have put him in a cab,' Sarah says. 'You've done that before.'

'Come on, *mes petites*, I saw this person as he came in,' Moussa says and takes up another date. 'Good-looking boy, what is the mystery?'

'Good-looking boy stays overnight in Nell's room,' Sarah says with a smile. 'What did Anna think?'

'She's been taken in by him as well. He came back this afternoon looking for me, but he went away again — who knows if he'll be back.' Nell stands up and begins to walk around the tiny space, looking at the books, the photographs on the wall, remembering every detail of what had passed.

'What are you going to do about it?'

'I don't know, Sarah. We had an argument, I walked out on him. He thought the rebels were fools. How could I put up with somebody like that?'

'You and your hot head, Nell! Maybe he's right, maybe they were fools and now that all this fighting is over, we can get back to normal. Sometimes you have to see the other person's point of view. Do you want to stay a spinster for the rest of your life?'

'Who says I'm even interested in getting married?' Nell turns, eyes flashing. 'And what about you two, living in sin?'

A hurt expression crosses Sarah's face and Nell is ashamed of what she has said.

'I didn't mean that — I'm stupid,' she says to them.

'That's all right. What is it you say in French, Moussa — you know, when you want to say forget about it, that everything is all right?'

'Oubliez ça — ça va!' Moussa answers and flutters his hand.

'I'll need to learn French now, Nell.' Sarah glances at Moussa.

'Why?' Nell asks.

'Because … Nell, there's something I want to tell you but you must keep it a secret for the moment. Promise?'

'I promise.'

'Nell, Moussa is taking me to Algeria, when we have saved enough money. He wants to buy a little house for us on the coast. He says that we can live well for a while on the money he has saved, then he will go back to sea, or even fish.'

Nell stares, not knowing how to how to react. 'That sounds very romantic, Sarah,' she says then. 'Have you told Anna?'

'No, not yet,' Sarah says, looking down at the floor. 'That's going to be the hardest part.'

Moussa leans forward and puts one enormous arm around the child-like shoulders of Sarah and pulls her towards him. For such a big man he is very gentle. He places a kiss on her cheek and runs his fingers through her hair.

Nell looks at the two of them, staring into each other's eyes, oblivious to her presence.

'Why is the whole world changing? I don't understand,' she says. 'One minute life is so simple: I do my work for Anna, have a bit of fun, read my books. Suddenly there's a bloody war in Dublin, you two are talking about leaving, Connie is probably gone off with a rich farmer and I've just met somebody I can't understand.'

'It must be love so,' Sarah says, laughing. 'Maybe you can come away with us, you and your new boyfriend. We can sit on the beach and let the men fish all day long.'

'What if he gets tired of looking for me — doesn't come back?'

'He'll be back. He confronted Anna, didn't he? Not many people would do that, even for a sweetheart,' Sarah says and helps herself to one of the last dates.

'But I can't wait around for him — I'll have to meet up with Connie to go up to Smithfield Market as usual to bring some farmers back here. Anna will be as mad as hell if I don't, especially as Connie didn't turn up yesterday. What do I do now?'

'Just go around and tell Connie you can't go — she's well able to latch on to a farmer by herself,' Sarah says, clapping her hands together with excitement. 'Then you can just happen to be in Phil Shanahan's this evening. Your young man is bound to show up — it's the last place left for him to look. And leave off the war paint.'

'But what about Anna? She'll be expecting Connie and me back with a couple of customers!'

'You have Anna wrapped around your little finger — she won't mind.'

'Yes, Nell, Anna is very fond of you,' Moussa says, wrapping up the stones from the dates into the newspaper and getting off the bed. 'Now is time for work.' He holds his hand out for Sarah and with little effort helps her to her feet.

'I never thought that I'd see the day when I was giving advice to Nell Claffey,' Sarah says.

'I hope I don't rue taking your advice, Sarah. I'll slip out and make my way around to Connie's. It's only fair to tell her, that's if she's there.'

✳ ✳ ✳ ✳

Nell's mood begins to lift as she makes her way to Connie's house. After her row with Joseph and then returning to find him gone, she remembers that strange, empty feeling inside. Was that what being in love was like? Was Sarah right? She had been content with her life until she met him, but now, somehow, something had changed. If she were to be honest, it wasn't anything that Sarah had said that made her think she might be in love, it was just being in the odd-looking couple's presence and witnessing the effect they had on each other in unguarded moments.

She thinks about the bond that exists between Sarah and Moussa, a bond that she has never quite understood before. Two unlikely people who have come together in the madness that is the Monto and are now a true couple, besotted with one another. They had triumphed, why couldn't she? She begins to walk faster, almost skipping now, and smiling at anybody who catches her eye. Even the squalor of Faithful Place when she reaches it does not dampen her spirts. She knocks on Connie's door, hopping from one foot to the other in her eagerness to tell her the news.

The sound of the knocker reverberates down the hall as she waits for Connie's shout telling her to hold on, that she's not deaf. But the house remains silent. She tries again, knocking harder, in case Connie is in the backyard using the toilet. After a few minutes she opens the letterbox and peers up the hall. There is no sign of Connie or her girl, Helen. She is not unduly worried as Connie sometimes can have an early client, usually a married man who can't visit her in the evening because of a watchful wife.

Down the street there are a few urchins playing around a lamppost. They have tied a rope around the top and are using it as a swing. She goes down to them and holds up a halfpenny.

'This is for anybody who can tell me where Connie is,' she says to the children.

'*I seen her a few days ago!*' a boy shouts out.

'What about today? Did any of you see her today?'

'*No, missus!*' their voices chorus together.

'Are you sure? Were you here all day?'

'*Yes, missus! Since this morning!*'

'Here!' she says, and throws the halfpenny towards them, causing a stampede of skinny bodies as they jostle with each other on the ground.

In a way it makes her task easier. She can tell Anna that she could not find Connie and that she would not be able to go up to Smithfield Market without the older woman. She knows that Anna wouldn't expect her to.

She turns and heads back to Phil Shanahan's and can feel the nervousness of meeting up with Joseph again making her stomach tighten. They will both be sober. Will it be different? What will they talk about? She takes the long way back to Montgomery Street and on the way up Talbot Street sees a small crowd of people surrounding a newsboy. He is finding it hard keeping up with the demand and by the time she reaches him all of his newspapers are sold.

'What's happening?' she asks him as he counts through his coppers. He points at the sandwich board that leans against a shop window.

'THREE LEADERS OF REBELLION EXECUTED,' the main headline reads, and under this: 'PEARSE, CLARKE, AND MACDONAGH.'

So, Phil Shanahan had been mistaken. Another momentous event, and all in the space of a week. She is shocked by the news, then angry. She overheard Phil saying that Clarke was an older man, a shopkeeper, and that they would probably let him go back to his shop. As she heads back to Shanahan's the atmosphere in the streets is muted. People go about their business as usual, the women with their shopping baskets, the men gathered in small groups here and there, but something has changed. She thinks about going back to Anna's — she always goes to Anna when something has happened. The woman always seems to know what to say. But she changes her mind and goes straight to the pub instead.

The atmosphere inside the pub is no different to the streets. Customers stand around or sit, nursing their drinks, talking in hushed tones. She opens the door to the snug but it's empty. Phil is behind the bar serving a customer and another barman is washing glasses and putting them in a row for the expected evening rush. She ignores their glances and even turns down the offer of a drink from a well-dressed older man. From the corner of her eye she can see Phil waving over at her and ignores him for as long as she can as she is certain that he wants her to leave.

'Nell, did you not see me waving at you?' Phil says from behind her.

She turns, acting surprised. 'I didn't, Phil.'

'Have you heard the news?'

'I have. They must be mad — what are they thinking?'

Phil leans in closer to her. 'I might need more of the 'you-know-whats'. This is going to get dirty.'

'Maybe it'll blow over — they've executed the leaders now, so maybe …'

Phil stands back.

'You've changed your tune all of sudden. What's happened to 'Up the Republic'? It wouldn't be anything to do with that young man you were with last night, would it?'

'I don't know what you're talking about. He was in the Monto for a good time, like the rest of them. Probably won't see him again.' Nell turns to go.

'Don't lie, Nell — I've never seen you so jumpy.'

Nell whirls on him. 'What are you, a priest all of sudden?'

'That's more like the Nell I know. But before you storm out,' he bends towards her and whispers, 'I have your young man out the back.' Phil nods over at the door marked *PRIVATE*.

For a dreadful moment Nell thinks that Joseph is captured, locked up in the back of the pub and under guard with the very gun that she handed over to Phil the previous day.

'You do know he was in the British army?' Phil says.

'Of course I knew, I could tell almost from the moment I laid eyes on him. But did you have to lock him up, Phil?'

'Lock him up?' Phil stands back and laughs out so loudly that most of the bar turn to see what's going on. 'Lock him up, she says. I didn't lock him up. Maybe my cooking didn't agree with him, but the last time I saw him he was alive and belching quite loudly after a big fry-up. He's in the back room. He came looking for you earlier. I had to make sure he was the one escaped from the Castle.'

A wave of relief flows through Nell; the world about her has shifted.

'What did he tell you about the army?' she asks.

'He told me he had deserted to come back to Dublin to take care of a family matter. That's quite a journey to make. Then to get captured and beaten up by your former comrades.'

'Well, I suppose after all he's gone through, I should go in, shouldn't I?' Nell says.

'I wouldn't like to hold you back, but go gently with him, he's had a bad few days.' Phil lifts the flap of the counter, nodding at the door into the back of the pub.

Nell rushes behind the counter and over to the door. Before she goes in, she pats her hair and straightens her dress, then pushes through. Standing in the dark corridor she hears the sound of music drifting up from somewhere deeper inside the private residence. She creeps down the hall and comes to a half-open door.

Peering through the gap, she sees Joseph standing in front of the gramophone, his head almost buried inside the mouth of its cone-shaped horn. She pushes open the door silently and studies him, amused by his boyish fascination as he stares into the dark mouth of the horn as if trying to catch a glimpse of the singer inside.

Her recollections of him from the previous night are borne out. Under the light of the gas lamp on the wall she can still see the same uncertainty on his face, as if he is waiting for something unpleasant to happen to him.

The quality of the singer's voice coming from the gramophone is not very good and he is mouthing the words of the song to himself and tapping his foot on the floor.

Nell is surprised that Phil Shanahan even has that particular record in his collection. 'It's a Long Way to Tipperary' is commonly thought of as a popular British army marching song and she imagines that Phil plays it to himself when there is nobody around.

'You won't find John McCormack hiding in there,' Nell announces loudly.

Christopher looks up quickly, hitting the side of the gramophone. The needle jumps off the record and a loud scratching noise sounds as it lands on the rotating turntable. He stares over at her, panic on his face, then tries to forcibly stop the turntable from turning around with his hands, but only makes matters worse. Nell walks over to the phonograph, pushes him gently to one side, then plucks the arm up and places it back onto the cradle.

'Phil won't thank you for breaking his precious Victrola,' she says, turning to face him.

Christopher put up both arms in surrender.

'Don't tell him. He shoved a gun into my face earlier.'

'He's harmless underneath it all, and when I threaten to tell everybody in the bar that he has that recording hidden away back here you'll be forgiven.'

'Coming to my rescue again.' Christopher bows.

'Somebody has to. And I saw you tapping your foot to it too, so there's a pair of you in it.'

'It's a catchy tune, what's wrong with that?'

'It's John McCormack's song and he's a Home Ruler, didn't you know?'

'You don't give up, do you?' Christopher says, and, walking over to the table, picks up his hat.

Nell panics. Only five minutes together and she is already preaching. A part of her wants to go over and put her arms around him and beg him not to go, but another part wants him to agree with everything she believes in and, if he doesn't, well, that's an end to it.

Before he even puts his hat on, she is beside him. She can't remember deciding to move towards him, it was just a natural thing for her to do. He puts his hat back on the table and takes her in his arms, kissing her mouth and then her forehead. She nestles her head under his chin and can hear his heart beating in his chest.

'You came back,' she says.

'Of course I did.'

'Why?'

'For more punishment, it seems.'

'I can be hard to put up with sometimes, I admit to that, Joseph. But I'm not ashamed of that. Anna brought me up not to bow down to nobody.'

'Even the nuns?'

'Especially the nuns. Every time I walk past that laundry, it sends a shiver down my back.'

Christopher lifts her chin up and stares at her.

'Anna's a wise woman — she saw through me anyway.'

'Did she say anything to you about me?' Nell asks, again feeling the red heat of embarrassment creeping up from the bottom of her neck.

'Nothing to be ashamed of,' Christopher says with a smile.

'That's mighty kind of you,' Nell says in mock anger and pushes him away from her.

The door to the parlour is pushed open and Phil Shanahan stands in the entrance, a grey, ashen look on his face. He raises the towel he uses to polish the glasses in the bar and mops his brow with it then walks over to one of the armchairs beside the fireplace and sits down.

'What's wrong, Phil?' Nell asks.

Phil's body seems to have shrunk inwards. He pushes his fingers through his hair and shakes his head.

'I can't believe it — the fools are going to execute more of the rebel leaders — it's not over.'

'No!' Nell shouts out. 'Who told you?'

'A squaddie drinking in the bar, says he knows somebody in Kilmainham Gaol. Most of the soldiers think it's madness, but that bastard Maxwell's not going to change his mind. He's another Cromwell, mark my words.'

Christopher looks from one of them to the other.

'What do you think will happen now?' he asks.

'It's going to get dirty now,' Phil says, 'but this time the ordinary people will be on our side and not all of the rebels surrendered.'

'Do you think there're enough of them out there to continue the struggle?' Nell says.

'Of course there are. MacNeill called a stop to the rebellion, but then changed his mind. But before he did lots of men had already stood down. What do you think they're going to do now?'

'I can't believe the Castle is being so stupid,' Christopher says.

'You've changed your tune,' Nell says.

'No, I haven't. I still think it was a lost cause and I've seen enough of those in Flanders to last a lifetime. But whoever made the decision to begin executing the leaders to make an example of them is making a big mistake.'

'You're damn right,' Phil says. 'We'll be on one side of them and the Germans will be on the other — we'll get them in a pincer movement.'

'Mr. Shanahan, with all due respect, you don't know what you're talking about. The British army will never let that happen, it's not in their nature. You don't realise the amount of men and equipment they have, and they will use every last bit of it.'

'But we gave them a bloody nose, few though we were,' Phil says.

'Bloody noses are for children. Most of the soldiers over here are untried. If they decide to send over their veterans, what happened on Easter Sunday will seem like a picnic.'

'And you would just surrender?' Nell snaps, taking a step away from him.

'Calm down, Nell, I didn't say that. What I meant was that I wouldn't have started in the first place — it was suicide —'

'So says you who went to fight and then deserted!'

Phil Shanahan stands between them and holds up his arms.

'Will you two stop it?' he says. 'You're like children! You won't solve anything by falling out with each other, will you?'

Then he turns to Christopher.

'I know you were a soldier and you're looking at this with a soldier's eyes. But it's not all about tactics. It's about winning the heart of a nation.'

Then he turns to Nell.

'And you, Nell, you should know better. Before last week you were treating this like a game, but it's not a game anymore. We're all going to have to stick together. Now, what I suggest we do is to hold our council, wait and see. Maybe the squaddie is wrong. In the meantime, I've a pub to run.'

Nell and Christopher bow their heads and nod in agreement. A grandfather clock in the corner strikes the hour of seven o'clock and the little light that makes its way through the net curtains hanging limply across the solitary window is beginning to fade. The hum of voices coming from the bar have become noticeably muted with the latest news.

Phil takes Nell's right hand, then Christopher's, then puts them together. Their fingers, stiff at first, close around each other's. Phil stands back, nods approvingly, then leaves them standing in the shadows together and makes his way back to the bar.

CHAPTER 22

Tired and drained after a long day, Byatt makes his way wearily across the yard, waving his two bodyguards away with his cane, and strolls out onto Dame Street. The main gates to Dublin Castle are now kept closed and a platoon of soldiers stands outside, rifles at the ready. Disillusioned by what the military had got up to in Kilmainham Gaol that morning, he is looking forward to a quiet meal and a bottle of wine. He turns down Dame Street towards the restaurant and tries to put the mess that his government is making to the back of his mind. The atmosphere, even in this better-off part of Dublin, is palpable but again he is glad he's not in uniform. It's early evening but the Olympia Theatre has closed its doors early because of the curfew.

Taking the turn down the laneway to the restaurant, he wonders how Christopher Flinter is getting on. In his experience, sometimes it is the last throw of the dice that can win the game. That thought raises his spirts as he enters the restaurant and makes his way down the now familiar corridor. When he enters the dining room, he is dismayed. Instead of the usual crowd, he sees that tonight it is almost deserted.

A dread silence hangs in the air and the only sounds are of a low conversation from a couple in one of the corners.

He is on the verge of leaving and going back to the Castle when a waiter he has never seen before approaches, leads him to a table and hands him the menu, then disappears into the kitchen. He is disappointed with the lack of other diners around him as he had wanted to try and lose himself in the noise and laughter to take his mind off things. He would not even mind bumping into Harry and his noisy companions again, just to try and lift the dread he feels tonight. The effects of the executions, it seems, have even made their way here.

Another customer comes in and stands hesitantly in the doorway with the waiter. He has never seen him before and feels sorry for him as he looks almost embarrassed. Probably a husband from the suburbs, a middling civil servant, with a wife and family tucked away at home but with urges he cannot control. He mumbles something into the waiter's ear and he is led to a nearby table. The man sits and accepts the menu handed to him and asks for an aperitif: it's the first time he has heard that request since he has arrived in Dublin and he becomes curious. Obviously, the man has some sophistication and he reassesses him as he studies his own menu. Perhaps he is a well-travelled soldier, like himself. Dublin is now full of military personnel, and more arriving each day. He feels a certain amount of pity for the man, possibly dragged from a training barracks somewhere in the English countryside and told that he is not being sent sailing east to take part in the glorious war to end all wars, but is in fact ordered in the opposite direction, to that strange troublesome little island just off the west coast: Ireland.

But why waste time on dwelling on the problems of others? He has enough of his own at the moment. He takes out a notebook and begins to jot down names and places at random: Janus of course,

Flinter, Maybury, Joyce, Blaney, Noctor, the Dublin stock exchange, the Monto, the River Liffey, Dublin Castle, Phil Shanahan's Pub. He leaves his own personal bodyguards, Harrison and Timmons, off the list as he can vouch for these two soldiers, both regulars and both professional, like himself. He has lived with, eaten with, fought with that type of man throughout his life. He stares at the scribbles on the notebook and begins to cross out everything that he deems extraneous. Now he is left with Janus, Joyce, Maybury, the Monto. Maybury, he has no doubt, is hiding a secret. But it could be anything from his guilt at the death of his apprentice to being a tacit supporter of the rebellion. He recalls his conversation with the old typesetter. What if the man purporting to be a man of the cloth, was, in fact, Janus? Why would he be delivering type to a printer? He scribbles a note down to remind him to drop in on Mr. Maybury again, or better still, to go to young Joyce's funeral and use that as an excuse to question him further.

He writes the word 'garrotted' down at the top of a fresh page and underneath it he puts the names of Joyce and the last prostitute found murdered by that method, a woman named Margaret Heffernan. He then adds some other question marks representing other possible victims found in the Monto, but not fully assigned to Janus. Looking back over the police files for a period of four months, several bodies had already been buried before he arrived in Dublin and some of the testimony was either evasive or suspect. His main cause of concern was not how or who, but why? Prostitutes would be a useful source of information, especially in a hotbed like the Monto where visiting officers and soldiers, no doubt inebriated, would boast about their exploits. Or had the prostitutes been used in some deviant fashion by Janus and he was disposing of them? But Joyce, a young apprentice, what information would he have that marked him out as a danger?

Or was he on the wrong track altogether — was he just chasing a phantom through his own mind because of what happened in New York? Worse still, perhaps Janus was dropping false clues for him to find but which led nowhere.

Losing patience, he scribbles over all he has written and puts his notebook back into his pocket. Dublin city, he feels, is about to become a very unfriendly place in the following days. He has no doubt that the executions will continue and that Maxwell will turn victory into defeat by losing the populace. How that will affect his own situation he does not know yet, but he suspects that he will be called back to London.

A waiter approaches his table, carrying a tray with a bottle of wine and two glasses.

'I'm afraid there must be some kind of mistake,' he waves waiter away, 'I didn't order that.'

'It's from that gentleman over there,' the waiter says and puts the bottle and two glasses on the table.

Byatt looks over at the man who has sent the wine, the same man who had entered after him and he isn't all that surprised. The man is obviously a lonely soul looking for some company. But has he the time or the inclination to help him and become that island of safety the man so obviously desires? Then he remembers himself in similar situations in other cities: Calcutta, Cairo. He remembers the dangerous situations he had to put himself in to meet somebody, anybody, for a discreet encounter. The waiter is filling up one of the glasses, but diplomatically poises the mouth of the bottle over the other. Byatt hesitates, then nods once and the deed is done. When the waiter has finished pouring the second glass the man takes the seat opposite him and looks hugely relieved.

Byatt extends his hand across the table.

'Jonathan Byatt,' he says as the other man shakes it.

'Adam Craddock, at your service, very glad to meet you,' the man almost whispers.

'You are safe here, Adam, no need to whisper,' Byatt says and lifts his glass, taking a sip.

'I am so relieved. I cannot tell you what it's like to arrive in a strange city, especially one that is in such an uproar.'

Byatt studies the man across the table from him. He has learned to be careful about such approaches as sometimes they are traps set by the police to dig out degeneracy and to punish it. But Adam Craddock is either a marvellous actor or is just what he says he is. Sitting across quite a small table, still he bends forward slightly in that manner Byatt knows so well, a ploy to make himself inconspicuous. He is clean-shaven and his skin is smooth and boyish-looking. His eyes, a dark-brown colour, along with his sallow complexion, give him a slightly exotic appearance. Byatt reassesses his first guess and instead places him somewhere in an expatriate community overseas, possibly FILTH — Failed In London, Trying Hong Kong — type of a situation, except he has ended up in Dublin.

'I've been in worst places. Once you know where not to go you should be alright. Where are you staying at the moment?'

'I've taken a room in the Shelbourne Hotel until such time as I can find suitable lodgings,' Adam says. 'It's quite passable.'

'No wonder you look shell-shocked — weren't the army using the hotel to take pot shots into Stephen's Green?'

'They certainly were. I had to move out of my room for several days.'

'Well, you can rest assured that it's all over now,' Byatt says and pats the back of the other man's hand.

'Are you certain? There still seems to be an ugly atmosphere around and about.'

'More like disgruntlement. It should all blow over when the executions are finished.'

'You seem to be very well up on the situation — are you connected in some way?'

'Let's just I have the pleasure of knowing my way around Dublin Castle,' Byatt says, and takes another, deeper sip of the wine.

'That's so gratifying to hear,' Craddock says.

'Don't worry, Adam, you'll be safe. Now, drink up and we can order. It's not a very complex menu. In fact, I've tasted most of the dishes and can advise if you like?'

Adam smiles at him. 'That would be great … Major Byatt.'

In the time it takes him to fully take in the final two words it is too late. He can feel his tongue going slack in his mouth and the activity in the restaurant has slowed down. The most appalling thing is that he can still think clearly. His hands fall into his lap and he can feel his body begin to tilt to one side. Craddock leans across the table and stops him from tilting over onto the floor.

'Don't worry, Byatt, I would never let you fall,' Craddock whispers, his face a picture of innocence, his smile wide and charming.

Byatt wants to ask him what was in the wine but what comes out is: '*Whaaa d wine?*'

'A simple concoction added to your wine, the ingredients gleaned from an old Chinese practitioner in San Francisco. It won't kill you, just make you seem very drunk — but don't worry, you'll be aware of everything that is happening to you'.

'*Jaaaan,*' Byatt mumbles, feeling now that the numbness has seeped down to the top of his legs and is sinking further and further downwards.

'Yes, Janus. The two-faced god of duality, transitions, and also doorways and passages which you will soon see is very apt.' He laughed. 'But, as we will be becoming better acquainted later, you can call me Levon.'

Levon Mordaunt leans back in his chair and glances around the dining room. The lone waiter is busy serving other tables. From time to time, he looks in the direction of the two men to see if they are ready to order. Mordaunt leans in closer to Byatt and smiles.

'Now, Agent Byatt, I'm afraid this is going to be a one-sided conversation until the drug takes effect, but I can tell you what is going to happen. We will sit here for several minutes. Then I'll become alarmed and call the waiter over. At that stage you will be already drooling from the corner of your mouth and unable to stand. The waiter will then give me a hand to get you out of here and will wait with you while I fetch my carriage which is parked nearby. And no, there will not be any fuss from him — he will not want to draw attention to this type of establishment, will he?'

Byatt accepts that he will be dead soon — he is a soldier and has lived with that reality for most of his life. But there is a small part of him that admires the ruthlessness and cunning of Levon Mordaunt. Through blurred eyes, he tries to focus on the man across the table from him. He still wears a wide smile and is seemingly talking as if discussing something light-hearted with a friend. If he is much over thirty years old, he would be surprised. Where has all that ruthlessness and barbarity sprung from? What was he doing dressed as a clergyman going to and from Maybury's printing company and most of all, why kill the young man Joyce, and all of the unfortunate women? So many questions that will be left unanswered before his imminent death. His legs flop to one side.

'Nearly there, Jonathan.' Janus leans over and pats him on the knee.

As he feels the rest of his body lose control and he tilts forward onto the table, Janus has his arm in the air, waving it dramatically, calling out *'Waiter, waiter!'* in an alarmed voice.

As Mordaunt had foreseen, the alarmed waiter rushes over and, without examining Byatt closely, suggests they take him outside to the fresh air as quickly as possible. Mordaunt, his face a picture of concern and panic, agrees, takes Byatt's cane, then both men pick him up and stumble with their dead-weight burden towards the exit and on into the laneway.

They prop him up, seated against the wall, and Mordaunt leaves his line of vision.

He can feel the roughness of the stone cutting through his jacket as he slides sideways. On his back on the ground, he tries to catch the attention of the waiter, blinking and pleading with his eyes, but the waiter ignores him. And then the final ignominy: he is looking up into the waiter's face as he, glancing around furtively, goes through his pockets and takes out his wallet. He rifles through it and extracts all of the notes, then puts it back. As he is putting the wallet back into his jacket, he notices the gold fob chain of his watch, a present from his beloved Howard, and this too disappears into the waiter's pocket. Byatt hears the sound of a carriage approaching and the whinnying of a horse.

Then Mordaunt is standing over him again.

'I will take it from here,' he says to the waiter, handing him some money.

The relieved waiter nods and leaves them.

'That was all too easy, Jonathan, unlike my time with your friend Howard in New York,' Mordaunt whispers into his ear as he wrestles him up from the ground and into the carriage. 'Yes, he put up quite a fight. What a mess! All of that struggle, even as the wire sliced through his fingers, and then his windpipe, and then his artery. Fought so much that he ruined my favourite suit.'

Byatt, staring up at the roof, tries to shut his eyes and blot out the presence of Mordaunt and the death of his dear friend, but cannot even manage that. Tears of sadness and frustration pour down his cheeks and onto the carriage floor. Mordaunt is finding it hard to get him completely into the carriage as his legs are getting in the way. There is a momentary pause, then he can feel himself being manhandled and turned onto his stomach, his legs bent backwards. His cane is thrown in beside him, the door is slammed and the carriage tilts under Mordaunt's weight. Byatt hears a whip and the carriage moves, rocking gently at first until, he guesses, they have reached the street, then it accelerates and the movement becomes more pronounced. Occasionally he can hear the crack of the whip as his captor encourages the horse onwards.

All too soon the carriage slows down. There is the sound of a gate opening and the carriage is in motion again, the horse's hooves clattering across what must be cobblestones. From the distance he can hear the gates being closed over and then the sound of a bolt being driven home, making a sound like a gunshot. The door of the carriage is wrenched open and his arm is grabbed roughly and his sleeve pulled up. He feels a sharp jab. An icy coldness creeps slowly and inexorably up into his brain and, this time, he falls into blackness.

CHAPTER 23

C hristopher stands on the pavement outside Shanahan's with Nell and is not sure what to do next. Two years in the army has taught him everything about self-reliance and survival and made him into a proficient soldier. He has seen men being killed and others receive horrible injuries and he has also inflicted his share of pain. But now, back in what is called civilisation, he is at a loss as to how to behave. It is a cool evening and Nell stands with her arms wrapped around herself. The gas lamps are being lit but it is still too early for the crowds. A few soldiers walk past them into the bar but they seem uncomfortable and there is none of the usual swagger. He thinks back to one or two of the girls he courted a lifetime ago. Most of the time they had just gone to the Volta Electric Theatre on Mary Street to sit in the dark and watch moving pictures. Usually they were westerns or comedies, American-made films with simple plots. Sometimes European films were shown, French or Italian. The audience just booed at these more serious and complicated films and shouted for the proprietor, a young, bespectacled man, to put on the comedies instead. But Nell doesn't seem the type of woman who would enjoy sitting in the dark. It was Nell who made the first move.

'Well, what'll we do now?' she asks him.

In desperation he thinks of asking her back to his hotel, but then remembers the sentinel behind the desk, Mrs. Daly, and knows that he would be thrown out of the hotel if he attempts to bring somebody like Nell there. Although she is wearing very little make-up, the clothes she is wearing, a colourful dress with a low-cut front and a short, velvet-type jacket, would make Mr. Daly, the deceased former owner of the hotel and husband to Mrs. Daly, turn in his grave.

'Would you like to go to the Volta? There might be a comedy film on,' he asks lamely.

Nell looks at him and her eyes widen. 'The Volta, and get fleas? You must be joking. Besides, you've forgotten – it closed at eight because of the curfew. Come on, let's go back to Anna's and I'll introduce you to my friends.'

She takes him by the hand and they walk up the street together towards Anna's house, but instead of leading him to the front door, they pass it by and turns down an alleyway that runs down the side of the house, then another, and stop outside tall wooden gates. Christopher calculates that it is the back entrance to Anna's house and probably the old access to the stables when the houses were first built. It was hard to believe that the Monto, the most notorious red-light district in Europe, was once an area favoured by the gentry. She puts her hand through a gap in the gate and fishes around, then withdraws a large key that hangs at the end of a string and uses it to open the gate. When they step through, they are standing in a long yard, cluttered with old, discarded furniture and mostly overgrown with thistles. Nearer the back of the house there is an area which is passably clean and criss-crossed with clothes lines drooping down with white linen sheets and towels that sway gently in the breeze.

On one side of the yard there is a low redbrick building, probably a stable and coachman's house, that runs down almost the whole length of the garden. At the farthest end of the coach house an orange glow shines through one tiny window. Nell walks up to the wooden door and knocks. Christopher notices a head appearing in the window, almost filling it, and hears voices from inside before the door is finally opened.

Taking up most of the doorway is one of the largest men he has ever seen, a monstrous dark shadow staring out at them, backlit by the light coming from inside the building. Even in the semi-darkness he can see that he has a heavy beard and his hair is thick and wavy and stands out from his head. It's Anna's doorman. Behind him he can hear a girl singing at the top of her voice — one of the popular bawdy ballads. She interrupts her singing and shouts at the giant not to be standing there like a statue and let them in before they freeze. The man moves to one side and waves them inside. The girl is standing in front of a large, stone sink up to her elbows in suds, washing clothes. While the man was one of the tallest and hairiest he has ever seen, the young woman, or girl, or child he cannot be quite certain, was one of the smallest and neatest. To enable her to comfortably reach the sink, she is standing on a wooden crate, as she rubs the sodden clothes up and down a washboard in time to her song. He stands in awe, surprised and fascinated by his surroundings.

The room they are in is long and narrow. At one end there is a compact kitchen and at the other a curtained-off section that, he presumes, is the bedroom. But the living area between the bedroom and the kitchen is by far the most unusual room he has ever been in. Several low, mismatched tables are placed randomly around it. Placed on the tables are the only form of illumination, oil lamps covered with orange-and-red shades that throw out an ochre-tinted light. The flooring, underneath the many scattered embroidered rugs, is the original flagstone

212

of the stables that has been scrubbed clean. Cloth tapestries illustrated with colourful landscapes and scenes of crowded market places hang on the whitewashed walls and add to the strange and exotic nature of the room. The smell of cooking and spices hangs in the air.

Nell walks past him and makes straight for the kitchen. A large earthenware pot with a conical lid is simmering gently on a massive cooking range, tiny wisps of steam escaping through a hole in the lid.

'Smells wonderful — what've you made?' she asks the giant.

'Lamb tagine, but I had to use real plums and not the dried ones and also a different spice.' He shrugs and joins her at the stove, lifting the lid to show her the result of his efforts.

She puts her nose over it and sniffs. 'Delicious!'

The smell reaches across the room to Christopher. It reminds him of the foreign smells drifting through the air in the restaurant where he had the meal with Byatt. The memory of his meal with Byatt makes him wonder if he is sitting down to his dinner around now, alone, or if he has company, another young recruit, like himself.

Nell turns away from the stove.

'This is Joseph, by the way.' She's trying to sound off-hand but not quite covering up her nervousness.

Moussa bows his head, while Sarah turns from the sink and examines their new guest.

'Pleased to meet you at last,' she says shyly.

Now that he can see her features properly, he realises that she is older than he had first thought, possibly in her twenties.

'The pleasure is all mine,' Christopher says, the greeting often used by the officers in Flanders when they introduced themselves to each other.

Nell and Sarah look at one another and burst out laughing. Sarah dries her hands on her apron, steps down off the box and walks over to him, reaching out her hand.

'No, Joseph, the pleasure is all mine,' she says and curtsies and the two girls begin laughing again.

This time Moussa joins in and his laughter rumbles up from his stomach and fills the room. Christopher is annoyed at first, but their laughter, he then realises, is not meant to make fun of him and soon he is laughing along with them.

Moussa stirs the contents of the pot with a large wooden spoon, then scoops up some of the sauce and tastes it, smacking his lips.

'It is ready, Sarah, time to eat,' he announces, replacing the lid. He goes to pull out a long, wooden kitchen table that has been pushed against the wall.

'Don't be so ignorant, Moussa,' the tiny girl-woman says. 'There's enough for us all.'

Moussa looks up. 'I mean no offence, Sarah. I was talking to our guests also, of course,' he says and looks pained.

Sarah walks over to a wooden dresser and begins to take down bowls and plates, placing them around the table. Even the mismatched bowls look foreign and exotic, with bright shades of reds, blues, and yellows criss-crossed with complicated patterns and symbols. She puts a vase of flowers in the middle of the table, then some candlesticks. When she has finished laying it out it reminds Christopher of the cover illustration of a book he had read when he was a child — in it there was a story about a magic lamp and a giant genie — a bit like Moussa — there to do the lamp-holder's bidding — oh, yes, *Aladdin*. The bowls and the plates, which in an ordinary house would look out of place, go with the interior decoration of the home that these two seemingly mismatched people have made together.

Nell and Sarah immediately sit down beside each other and Christopher takes a stool at the far end of the table. Moussa makes his way back with cooking pot and has to stoop underneath the wooden beams that cross the room. He puts the pot in the centre of the table before whipping back the lid and letting the full aroma escape in a cloud of steam.

'*Voila!*' he says, then returns to the kitchen and, using a towel to protect his hands, takes out a metal tray from the oven which he leaves on top of the stove to cool. Using the tips of his fingers, he prises up what looks like flattened disks of bread which he puts onto a large serving dish. He reaches into a dresser and takes out a large bottle of wine, puts everything on a tray, then joins them at the table, his great bulk resting precariously on one of the small stools.

'You look surprised,' Nell says to Christopher. 'What's the matter?'

'I guess he is wondering to himself what a grown man is doing in a kitchen, that it is woman's work. Is this not so?' Moussa laughs, plunges a metal ladle into the stew and stirs the contents around before he ladles it out.

'My mother would not let my father into the kitchen at home,' Christopher admits. 'That was her domain and she guarded it against everybody.'

'What about the army?' Nell says. 'The cooks there must have all been men.'

'I wouldn't call them real cooks,' Christopher says, and stares hungrily at the heaped food that the smiling Moussa has ladled on his plate.

'I learnt to cook on a ship when I was a boy,' Moussa says. 'I can cook stews, bake breads and cakes. I even make the sweet baclava so beloved of all Algerian men, but not here.'

Christopher takes up a spoonful of the stew and tastes it.

'You should open a restaurant,' he says, and plunges his spoon in again.

'That's what I told him,' Sarah says, then adds, 'I didn't realise you were in the army.'

Nell looks up at Christopher, then across at Sarah.

'It's a long story for another time,' Christopher says, and notices that Moussa, who had been pouring out the wine, has stopped smiling and is staring at him, a puzzled look on his face.

'This is good wine, from Oran, Algeria,' Moussa then says. 'From vineyards planted by the French. They try to keep the best of the wine for themselves and leave the vinegar for us. I was given a case of it several months ago by a French sailor I rescued from the attentions of several soldiers. This is the last magnum, the best.'

Christopher is humbled by the generosity of his host.

'I didn't think you made wine in Algeria,' he says, then sips the wine which is strong and smooth to the taste.

'The French planted vines when their own vineyards got the disease. Soon we were making more wine than them. It is about the only good thing they brought with them.'

'You have the French and we have the British,' Nell says, and holds up her glass. *'Death to all of them!'*

Moussa looks uncomfortable. He takes a sip of wine and shakes his head with sadness. 'After the French came to Algeria slavery and piracy stopped, Nell. Nothing in this world is ever simple. In the Quran it tells us to fight only in self-defence, but how do you fight men who have made your country a better place? You see, it is not so simple.'

Nell is about to answer him when Sarah interrupts.

'Moussa reads the Quran every day. It's like their Bible.'

'Doesn't the Bible say an eye for an eye?' Nell persists.

A silence descends on the table and the only sound is of the clinking cutlery.

'I met some men in the army who had fought in India, Moussa, where there are a lot of Muslims,' Christopher says to break the tension. 'I didn't know Muslims were allowed to drink wine.'

'Would it not show disrespect to Allah if I did not drink the fruits of my Muslim brothers' labour?' Moussa winks at him.

'Men! There's always an excuse,' Sarah says to Nell. 'And I expect he'll be asking me to go into the harem with his other wives when we go back?'

Moussa puts up both of his arms in protest.

'That is not true, Sarah — you will be my only and most beloved bride.'

The mood around the table lightens and the meal continues as before, but without any more talk of war or death. Although there is only one bottle of wine between the four of them, it's a magnum and seems endless. Moussa tells them about some of the voyages he has been on as a sailor. He tells them about the Suez Canal, a man-made waterway big enough to take great ships, that connects the Mediterranean to the Indian Ocean. Then he tries to convey to them the majesty of the Great Pyramids in Egypt and about his trip on a filthy camel that took an exception to his excessive size and would not move. His voice is deep and rich and he takes great delight in imitating the various people he has met over the last number of years — from the Chinese sailors he came across in the city of Marseilles, with their tiny ponytails and their propensity to gamble, to the nomads he came across in North Africa, blue dye rubbed into their skin, most of them as tall as himself.

'How did you end up in Dublin?' Christopher asks when there is a lull in the conversation.

'I found Anna's on my first night ashore from my ship. I could not believe my luck. All of the other sailors who had been ashore had told me not to waste my money in the Monto, that it was too tough, and to save it for Southampton, our next port. But I had to get onto dry land for at least one night before the ship sailed. I was in the front parlour, waiting, when a fight broke out in the hallway. It was nothing, just two men who wanted the same woman. I separated them and it was over. Anna was very grateful. She offered me a job straight away. She said that she would buy me a uniform and I could stand outside the door. But I refused. I said that I was leaving Ireland the following day.'

'Anna doesn't take no for an answer.' Nell grins at Christopher.

'Anna is a bad woman. She said that she had no hard feelings, which I did not understand, and that I could help myself to the food and the drinks if I liked and to pick out a woman. After three weeks at sea, I could not refuse. It was the best night. I ate and I drank very much, too much. I was so happy I fell asleep.'

'Anna might have helped a little with one of her powders — she said she didn't, but I still wonder,' Nell says.

'In the morning I woke up in this very room with a bad pain in my head. *Ahhhh!* Moussa exclaims dramatically, pulling at his thick hair. 'My ship has sailed. It is not the morning, it is the afternoon — I am ruined!'

'What did you do then?' Christopher asks.

'My friend, it says in the Quran: "*Do not lose hope, or be sad.*" An angel appeared before me!' He looks across the table at Sarah who bows her head. 'She brought me water and food and put it beside my bed — then she left. And when she left, my friend, a light left with her. I forgot about my ship, I forgot about everything.'

'And now he's taking her away,' Nell says.

'No, Nell, not taking — she is coming back to Oran with me. Dublin is not a good place anymore. We go back, we buy a small house near the sea, we let the sun into our bones.'

'Tell us about Oran,' Christopher says.

'It is beautiful,' Moussa says. 'All the buildings are white and shine in the sun. But in the casbah the alleys are narrow and stay cool. There is a great harbour, ships coming and going all day. Around the harbour the French build their mansions, like Anna's house but grander, with palm trees in front to give them shade.'

'If it's so beautiful, why did you leave?' Christopher asks.

'I was young. I did not realise what I had around me. I wanted to see the world before I settled down, and to earn some money for my mother and father. I got a job on a ship as a cabin boy and took many trips. But over the years I was never able to save money. I spent it all when we reached port. Then the war started and I had no choice.'

'But you must have seen some beautiful cities?' Christopher asks.

Moussa agrees and tells them more stories about his journeys around the Mediterranean. He is relating a story about his trip to Rome when there is a loud knock on the door. He takes out his pocket watch, throws his eyes to heaven.

'It is Anna, I wager, wanting me to stand guard over the front door.'

He rises from the table to answer the knock.

Christopher can hear a mumbled conversation between him and somebody he is unable to see as the giant almost fills the doorway. It goes on for a few minutes before he stands aside and lets the caller in.

It is Anna Macken in all of her working regalia. Gone is the barely awake woman Christopher had met earlier that day. Now she is back in all her glory: a long green-velvet dress, face made up to perfection, hair pinned up in an elaborate style and smoking a cigarette through a long holder.

As she steps through the door, they, as one, stand up from the table, but she waves them back.

'Just here for Moussa, continue on with what you're doing,' she says, and then to Christopher, 'I see you found our Nell.'

'Yes, ma'am, thank you,' Christopher says.

'At least that's some good news. Thanks to the executions, it's like a morgue in the house.'

'Do you really need Moussa, Anna?' Nell says. 'We're having such a good time. Maybe you could join us?'

'You can have him when I'm finished with him, young lady,' Anna says. 'Connie's neighbour has just called to say there were shouts coming from the house and there's no answer from the door. I need Moussa to go around and see what the problem is. If he finds her drunk or with one of her peculiar customers, I'll having words to say to her. I need some of those farmers she promised.'

'Maybe she's on her way back from Smithfield Market and got held up,' Nell says.

'The mart's been over hours — if she's bringing them back now, they'll be of no use to me, they'll have spent the few shillings they've made already.'

'She's never let you down before, Anna,' says Nell. 'I'll go around with Moussa and Sarah. If there's no sign of her inside, he can help Sarah through the small scullery window in the back — she might be still drunk.'

Anna thinks for a moment.

'That sounds like a good idea. Sorry to break up the party, but with all this trouble in the air I'd like to know why she didn't show up.'

She turns to leave, but then changes her mind.

'Nell, do you think Connie's mixed up with any of this business?'

'What business, Anna?'

'I'm not such an old fool, Nell. I know what goes on in Phil Shanahan's pub, above and below the counter. Does she have anything to do with that?'

'Connie is a working girl — she has no time for that kind of thing,' Nell says.

Happy with her answer, Anna waves at them and leaves.

Moussa goes behind the curtain at the far end of the room and returns wearing a jacket.

'It will not take long, Joseph — you can remain here and we can have some coffee when we return — it is not that far,' he says.

'Yes, please stay — it's been so nice to have our first guests,' Sarah says, joining Moussa.

Christopher has never seen a couple so at ease with other. He realises that it is the most content he has been in a long time and doesn't want the evening to end.

'Joseph can come with us if you like, Moussa — he can keep me company,' Nell says.

'*Perfect!*' Moussa booms. 'We can then come back and I will serve you all cake and coffee.'

CHAPTER 24

Byatt begins to recover consciousness again, this time in small stages, each more wretched than the last. He tries to claw his way back into the comfort of oblivion, but his approaching awareness is unstoppable. Although there is little physical pain, the realisation that he has failed and faces certain death, and that Mordaunt will remain free, is more painful than any physical torture he can think of.

Earlier — exactly when he has no idea — the drug began to wear off. Then he had dared hope that he could best his kidnapper. All he needed was enough strength to unsheathe the sword from his cane, which Mordaunt had overlooked and was on the floor beside him. The fury he felt after Mordaunt had mentioned his lover's name was like a burning hot ingot of steel at his core and he used it to make one final effort. But it was not to be. Just as he was recovering on the floor of the filthy basement kitchen and could feel life coming back into his fingers, he had felt another sharp jab in his arm and Mordaunt's face began to waver and then fade into nothingness.

Now his mouth tastes sour and his body feels unnaturally constricted. As he becomes more aware of his new surroundings, he feels the tightness that encircles his chest is making it difficult for him to breathe. The more he struggles the more difficult it becomes and when he comes fully to his senses, he realises he is lying on his back on a table, expertly trussed up: Mordaunt left nothing to chance. The more he struggles to free himself the more his bindings tighten, making matters worse. He forces himself to remain calm and to breathe more slowly.

Thankfully he can turn his head from side to side. From his limited perspective he can make out a vaulted brick ceiling directly overhead. For a fleeting second, he is caught up in the illusion that he is somehow back in London, trapped on the floor of the underground railway, and that the arrival of the next train is imminent. But the more he drifts back to reality, he discounts that as ridiculous, probably the effect of the drugs Mordaunt has given him.

Fully conscious now, he takes several, slow, careful breaths to calm his beating heart and to take stock of his surroundings. If there is going to be another chance to get his hands on Mordaunt, he needs be able to think clearly. The air around him is damp and musty so he assumes that he is underground, possibly another room off the kitchen where he had begun to gain consciousness the first time. Mordaunt, who, on first impression had seemed like a fairly weak specimen, was obviously a good actor as it would have taken a great degree of strength to carry his deadweight. A flickering light casts shadows across the ceiling and he surmises that there is some source of illumination on the floor. He is glad that he is on a table as he can hear a steady drip of water onto the ground somewhere off to his left and the skittering of rats all around him,

When his mind has settled down somewhat, he begins to review the overall situation. The man who drugged him in the restaurant, Mordaunt, is the man he has been looking for the past year, the man whose codename is Janus. But how did Mordaunt discover who he was, and why is he keeping him alive? He has been in Dublin now for less than a fortnight and only a handful of people know of his existence. The two bodyguards assigned to him are old guard, career soldiers. Flinter he rules out straight away. Could it have been Maybury? Highly unlikely, there was something not quite right about the man, but not in his wildest dreams could he imagine him, a steady and successful businessman, commit treason. The restaurant maybe? It certainly was a possibility.

Dublin was, perhaps, part of the problem. In London he could visit any of the discreet bars and eating places known to his kind scattered among the boroughs around Whitehall without meeting anybody from his circle. But Dublin was a small city. To the best of his knowledge the restaurant was one of the very few places where men could meet without being arrested. But that still didn't make sense. How could the man have known he frequented there, then planned a chance meeting and have the foresight to carry out the abduction? Someone in the service must have betrayed him, it was the only answer. That left Dublin Castle. He was warned before he left London that it was riven with infighting and intrigue. He had made very few friends there, not that he had tried. But who had betrayed him and why? The first name that jumped into his mind was Blaney, the junior clerk — he would bet his life on it. Which brought him back to Christopher Flinter. Was Blaney aware that he had been enlisted by him to track Janus? Definitely not — it had all happened too fast and there was no paperwork in existence. But he would have been aware that there was a British army prisoner in the cells on charges of desertion who suddenly, for no apparent reason, was released. Then it all comes together: this is why he is being kept alive — it has all to do with the whereabouts of Christopher Flinter. Mordaunt doesn't know where the young Irishman is and that threatens him.

Over the noise of the dripping water and the scrambling of the rats he hears the faint sound of approaching footsteps. Judging by the time it takes for the person to reach him, he works out that he is not in a basement or a subbasement, but in a tunnel of some sort. Possibly an abandoned railway-tunnel, but where? He hears a match strike behind him and a cloud of smoke drifts past his line of sight. Mordaunt is taking his time and seems in no rush to interrogate him. Byatt begins to concoct a cover story just in case that he is mistaken about his abductor. Perhaps he is just a minion and not Janus himself. As if his mind has been read a voice comes from somewhere behind his head.

'Major Jonathan S. Byatt, late of His Majesty's army, newly seconded to the Secret Services, alias Room 40, alias 40 OB. His mission? Tell me, Major, what are you doing in Dublin?'

The sound and power of the voice now echoing off the ceilings and walls bears not a trace of the man who had picked him up at the restaurant. He knows, with certainty, that he is going to die in this tunnel and that the voice is probably the last he will ever hear. He is surprised at his own detachment of his imminent death and laughs out loudly at the absurdity of his last resting place, somewhere under the streets of Dublin. When he had joined the army, he had assumed, naively, that it would be in a hastily dug grave in some far-flung region of the British empire, the Punjab or possibly Africa and that his end would be by a bullet, fast and clean.

'You're amused?' Mordaunt says, his voice echoing upwards and into the ceiling above.

'I was just thinking of the different ways I thought I was going to die,' Byatt replies, 'but I never thought it was going to be at the hands of a madman in a tunnel somewhere in Dublin.'

He hears the hiss of a cigarette as it hits a pool of water and then

Mordaunt's pale face appears in his vision. Other than the physical resemblance to the man who he had met the previous evening, the face in front of him now is radically different. Beside the absence of the obsequious smile, gone also is the air of meekness and affected guilt that he had exuded. In its place there is a vacuum, an indifference, as if he, Mordaunt, is studying a specimen from the lower orders. He seems taller, too, due to the fact that his body, or what he could make of it, was erect, shoulders slightly thrown back.

'I can assure you that for all the different ways that you think you can die, you will come up short,' Janus says and begins to take off his clothes.

Byatt watches with fascination as he takes off his jacket and shirt, folds them carefully, then disappears from view. For the first time since he has awoken, he feels genuine, animal fear. A shiver runs down the length of his body and he closes his eyes tightly. The last time he prayed was at Howard's funeral, and that was more of a rant against God. Now he prays for a quick release. When he opens his eyes again Mordaunt has come back into view and is completely naked. His body, out of the clothes, is heavily muscled and scarred with what looks like old whip-marks. In his left hand he has a hammer which he holds up to make sure that Byatt can see it.

'Going to do a bit of woodwork, old chap?' Byatt asks, forcing a tone of nonchalance into his voice. 'I could never trust a carpenter who uses a hammer. I thought that a mallet was always preferable when dealing with wood.'

Mordaunt smiles and disappears from view. When he reappears, he is carrying a carpenter's drill in his hand.

'You could have a point,' he says, turning the drill-head around and admiring the new, shiny metal bit clamped in its jaws.

Byatt shuts his eyes, waiting for this new nightmare to begin. He feels the tip of the drill resting on his left knee and then a slight pressure. The sharp, intense pain that erupts from his leg makes him clench his teeth in agony, but it is the sound of the steel bit drilling through bone that brings out the screams. He is no stranger to suffering and had thought that he could hold out for longer, but the sheer horror of what is taking place exposes his animal instincts. The screams have no effect on his tormentor and he continues drilling until the bit has travelled through the bone and on through cartilage, erupting through the skin at the back of his knee. Mordaunt turns the drill in the opposite direction and slowly begins to extract it from his leg. As soon as the bit is removed from the wound blood spurts out onto the surface of the table and then onto the floor. Byatt's screams echo off the walls as he feels the bit touching his other knee and he is vaguely aware of the frenzied screeches of the rats about to feast on his blood.

Just before he loses consciousness, Mordaunt stops and slaps his face.

'Listen, I already know why you are here in Ireland. You are looking into why I am helping the Germans. But you are also conflicted. What country does not want the might of America behind them in their time of need?'

'Who told you I was in Dublin?' Byatt says through clenched teeth.

Mordaunt walks back into view again and stares down at him, examining him as if he is some insect inside an inspection jar.

'I suppose it doesn't matter one way or another, now. It was one of your compatriots, in Whitehall. Then Blaney, your trusty clerk, confirmed it.'

'Someone in Whitehall. I don't believe you.'

'Unlike you, he valued the information I supplied about the German arms shipment to the Irish rebels. Paid for it too.'

Byatt is shocked, but in a twisted way it makes perfect sense.

'But which side are you on?'

Mordaunt disappears again and comes back dragging a chair. He sits down beside the table.

'It's a brave new world out there, Byatt. Your problem is that you look at life through a narrow gaze. If I tell you all about it, will you promise to tell me who you sent to find me?'

Byatt nods. All he needs is a little more time to put off the coming agony.

'Good. Are you a religious man?'

'No,' Byatt answers.

'That makes it easy to skip Adam and Eve and get straight to the point. Man evolved over thousands of years, our brains getting bigger, our intelligence growing, but not fast enough to avoid killing each other over what is just blind patriotism. But now we are evolving beyond all that, Byatt, or some of us are. It's the dawn of a new civilisation. The new rulers will not be men elected on a whim by people who know nothing and care less — they will be the great leaders of industries, people who —'

'Spare me your dreary sermon and get on with it,' Byatt snaps. 'Why don't you just tell me who you're loyal to? America?'

'I am American, that's true, but I don't follow the flag blindly. I prefer to call myself a globalist. My chessboard is the world, whereas yours is infinitely more limited. The shipment of arms to the Irish rebels, for instance. I did receive a certain amount of payment, but that had nothing to do with it. I need your country to be still in the war, not bogged down in Ireland fighting on another front.'

'So, you are telling me that you are a man without a country, without a home, a mercenary whose only motivation is greed.'

'For now, I follow the men who made America what it is today, men who know what's good for their country. Real Americans.'

Byatt lifts his head up as far as it will go and turns to Mordaunt, spitting into his face.

'And no doubt you're well paid for it, paid treble in fact, if you're being paid by the Americans, the Germans and us. So why make up these elaborate excuses and try and lecture me about evolution? You're not American, you're a nothing — you're a traitor who believes in nothing, an empty shell who sells his soul to the highest bidder. Tell you what, I'll double whatever you are being paid.'

Mordaunt wipes the spittle from his face. He is still smiling but Byatt can see that there is no humour in his eyes. They are dull, like those of dead fish, and seem to be turned inwards towards some dark, terrible place.

'We've seen your handiwork, it's the handiwork of a craven coward. Why did you have to kill all of those innocent people on the *Lusitania*? And why that innocent boy, what did he ever do to you? And what about those unfortunate women you saw fit to kill? I was told that they all had one thing in common, that they offered a special service to weak men who hadn't got the balls —'

'*Shut up*,' Mordaunt says, standing up. 'I'm tired of this. Stop talking. Now, what's the name of the person you sent after me and where is he?'

'I'll never tell you. Why should I? You're an imposter, a fake. The man is the opposite to everything that you stand for. He has a purpose, and honour, and he's not doing it for money, unlike you. Look at you, you can't even fuck properly, you have to be punished first. *Please. miss, can you whip me some more!*'

'*Stop it!*' Mordaunt roars.

'Why should I? It's true. You're a psychopath, you murder people from behind, you're afraid to look your victims in the eyes. You've no honour, you're contemptible. My only regret is that I won't be around when you meet your end, as you will, and I hope it's a slow and —'

Mordaunt's fingers are around his throat, squeezing it with incredible strength. His face is livid, his eyes filled with pure rage. Byatt can smell the sweat from him. His loss of control is now total. Gone is any semblance of the mastermind who could control the destiny of countries. Now he is a feral animal, blinded by one thought: *to kill.*

'*I'll show you!*' he shouts, saliva dripping from his mouth. '*I'll show you who's afraid to stare into the eyes of a dying man!*'

Byatt feels himself drifting into unconsciousness. His head is jerked upwards and then he feels the wire being looped around his throat. It eats into the flesh around his neck, deeper and deeper, until it reaches a place from where there is no coming back. Mordaunt is bent over him, staring into his eyes to witness the life ebbing away.

Just before Byatt takes his final breath, he smiles up at his killer and manages to mouth the words: '*You lose.*'

Mordaunt staggers back from the table, cursing when he realises what he's done. Byatt had riled him on purpose, he can see that now and, what was worse, he had underestimated him. Now he has no way of knowing the identity of the person coming after him. It would have taken another half hour, at most, to get the information from Byatt, but now it's time to cut his losses. He picks up one of the lanterns off the ground and holds it over Byatt's face. Though grey and lifeless the smile is unmistakable. In anger he catches the table in both hands and tips it over, sending it crashing to the ground. It makes no difference to Byatt, he is beyond pain, but the simple act rids him of some of his frustration.

It is well past midnight and in the abandoned tunnels that criss-cross under the streets of the district he now calls his home, he has several hours to clean up the mess. Not that too many people wander down here anymore, even in the daytime. But occasionally he has heard the echoing voices of workmen carried through the tunnels. He picks up the pickaxe he has brought and in the flickering lights of the lantern, he digs out the last resting place of Major Jonathan Byatt, late of His Majesty's Secret Service.

When he has gone down far enough in the rocky soil, he drags Byatts body and throws it into the hole, shovels in the loose dirt and pats down the earth, scattering the excess further away. The bloodied table he puts against the wall, an abandoned piece of furniture that nobody will question. He stands in the middle of the tunnel, looking around him, but there is little evidence of what had occurred. He takes the canister of water he has brought with him and holds it over his head, letting the cold stream of water wash the dirt and blood from his body. The act of cleansing his body has been a ritual for most of his life. The purifying effects of the water not alone washes his body, but also his soul. Now, absolved of his sins, he goes back to the chair where he had left his clothes, dries himself off as best he can with a handkerchief and dresses carefully, making sure that no blood gets onto his white collar. After he has finished dressing, he looks around him one more time, then, one by one, douses the lanterns and makes his way back down the tunnel.

CHAPTER 25

C hristopher and Nell stand outside the little terraced house in Faithful Place as Moussa and Sarah try to gain access from the rear. Nell is subdued and stands with her arms folded, waiting for the couple to appear at the front door to let them in, and yet, at the same time, seems to be dreading it. Christopher has witnessed that same dread in his fellow-soldiers in the trenches, waiting for the sound of the whistle. He wonders at her change of mood, then remembers the recent murders in the Monto. Nell, for all of her bravado, is concerned, he realises. He puts his arm around her shoulders and draws her to him. Some of the older children from the neighbourhood, still out playing on the streets, start to jeer at them. Christopher is about to let out a shout at them when he hears the sound of a bolt being drawn back and the front door opens. Sarah is standing in the hallway, holding a candle. As soon as they step through the door Christopher gets a faint odour hanging in the air. Nell is calling out Connie's name and he puts his hand on her shoulder.

'I think you should stay here, Nell — me and Moussa will look around,' he says, glancing at Moussa.

'Good idea, my friend,' Moussa answers, sensing something in Christopher's tone.

Nell takes Sarah by the shoulder and they go into the tiny sitting room where Connie sometimes entertains her guests before bringing them upstairs.

Christopher closes the door and whispers to Moussa: 'Can you smell it?'

'Is it gas? The taps of the cooker had been left on and there was a lamp left on a nearby table, but, by the grace of God, the meter must have run out of money almost immediately,' he says, shrugging his shoulders.

'No, it's something else.'

Moussa sniffs the air again.

'You are right, my friend, something sweet, like the medina on a hot, sunny day. Do you know what it is?'

'It's chloroform. I recognise it from the hospitals at the front. I'm going to go upstairs to look through the rooms — wait here.'

'What if the assassin is still up there, do you not want me to come with you?'

'My guess is he's long gone. Anyway, we've made enough noise to frighten anyone away — it's better if you stay here with the girls.'

'Very well, my friend, I will stand guard,' he says and hands him the candle. 'Take this.'

Christopher takes the creaking wooden stairs one step at a time, holding the candle out in front of him. The candlelight flickers across the wallpaper, a vividly coloured pattern made up of birds of paradise intermingled with palm leaves. After every few steps he stops and listens, then continues on. He comes to a turn in the stairs and looks back at Moussa who is staring up at him and regrets not taking the big man up on his offer. He takes the final three steps to the short landing which has doors leading off each side.

The first room is a bathroom, dominated by a large claw-foot bathtub which sits in the middle of the floor. He moves the candle over it. The inside of the bath, painted white, is streaked with stains of what looks liked dried blood. He goes back out onto the landing again and listens. The silence is oppressive and seems to suck the life out of the air. He wants to turn back and join the others but can't. It is the same silence he remembers hanging over the house when his parents were laid out.

Before he continues, he stoops down and holds the candle closer to the floor. A line of dark droplets on the carpet lead from the bathroom up the corridor, disappearing into the darkness beyond the candle's light. He walks slowly following the trail of blood which stops outside a room on his left. He taps on it and listens but there is no sound from within. The handle turns freely and he gives the door a slight push, allowing it to swing inwards.

Standing in the open doorway there is no mistaking the smell that is emerging from the room. Before he enters, he takes out a handkerchief and holds it up to his nose, then steps inside. Holding the candle higher over his head he makes out the corpse of the woman lying full-length on the bed, her hands crossed over her chest. For a moment the light flickers in such a way across her features that he almost believes that she is alive, if it wasn't for the bluebottle walking over her face. Instinctively he bends over the body and shoos it away.

The woman, Connie he presumes, is fully clothed. She is wearing a heavy dress with a ruffled collar. On first inspection he can see no obvious injuries. It appears that she died from natural causes. Maybe she had unexpectedly had a miscarriage — it wouldn't be uncommon in her line of work. She left the gas on when she suddenly felt it coming on and had made it to the bathroom and then back to the bed. If he looks in the bedside drawer, he will probably find a bottle of chloroform.

He puts the candlestick onto the bedside table and searches through the drawers, but doesn't find anything that could contain the chloroform. He leans over her body to see if she dropped it somewhere on the bed. Her hair, which has become undone, is covering one side of her face. He brushes it away to get a proper look at her features but in that unnatural rocking movement of her head his hopes are dashed: Janus has been at work here.

Christopher takes up the candle again and walks around the room searching for any clues as to what happened. He pulls back the heavy curtains and tries the window but it is locked. In one of the furthest corners the light from his candle is caught by something that glistens in the darkness. He makes his way over to examine it. On the floor he finds a wide circle of shards from a broken mirror. The empty wooden full-length frame is pushed back into a corner. What he thinks is a rope lies across the shards like a dark snake. He bends down to examine it more closely and can make out the coiled leather strips of a scourge. Other than the presence of the whip, the rest of the room appears like an ordinary bedroom.

He tries to picture the scene of the murder and imagines Janus creeping up behind Connie and putting the wire around her throat, then pulling the two handles together with all of his strength. The pair then possibly crashed into the mirror, breaking it. If that was the case the floor should have been covered with Connie's blood, but he can see none. He nearly jumps when he hears the tap on the bedroom door. When he swivels around, he can make out the large figure of Moussa looming in the doorway.

'This is not good, my friend,' Moussa says, stepping inside.

'Poor woman,' Christopher says, and holds up the candle.

'Is it another one?' Moussa asks.

'I'm afraid it is.'

'The Devil walks among us,' Moussa says and bows his head.

'I can't understand why there is never anything in the newspapers about these types of killings.'

'This is the Monto, my friend, and what happens in the Monto stays in the Monto. Nobody wants to destroy the dream.'

'The Monto is not a dream, it's a nightmare. What are we going to tell the girls?'

Moussa steps around him and gets closer to the bed. He puts his hand on Connie's pale forehead and rocks it gently. He whispers something to himself and folds the blanket over her body.

'We tell them the truth, they are not children,' he says.

Christopher holds the candle up again and examines the room more closely.

'Something is wrong, Moussa.'

'What is wrong, my friend?'

'Where's all of the blood? There's none on the bed and just a little on her dress. The monster must have killed her here in the bedroom then walked down to the bathroom and washed himself. The bathtub is heavily stained.'

Moussa points to the wardrobe and Christopher nods. The big Algerian takes the revolver out of his belt and approaches the wardrobe. For such a large man his movements are sure and silent. He reaches out for the small, metal key sticking out of the lock and turns it and pulls it open. The body of a young woman topples out onto the floor and the bottom of the wardrobe is full of blood-stained towels.

Moussa points. 'There is your blood.'

Christopher has seen enough and leaves the room, followed by Moussa who has the presence of mind to lock it and take the key. As he makes his way down the stairs, he can hear Sarah and Nell talking in low tones, as if they already know what he had found. But as he steps back into the hallway, he can hear that they are just talking about him and Moussa, just girls' tittle-tattle to each other. When he enters the sitting room, he finds them sitting opposite each other, knees touching, a guilty look on both their faces.

He takes a deep breath.

'We found Connie and her girl, upstairs in the bedroom.'

'Is she drunk?' Nell asks, but he can see by the look in her eyes that she fears the worst.

'No, not drunk,' he says. 'I'm very sorry, Nell, but they've been murdered. Whoever did it left the gas on in hope that there would be an explosion and a fire to cover it up.'

Nell lets out a shrill scream and makes a rush to the door, but Moussa is standing there, immovable. She tries to push him out of the way but hasn't got the strength. Sarah goes over to her and puts her arm around her waist. She has the most composure of all of them.

She turns to Christopher. 'Moussa can stay here and watch over Connie. I'll take Nell back to the house and tell Anna what's happened. She knows some of the higher-ups in the Dublin Metropolitan Police — she can sort everything out.'

'What do you want me to do?' Christopher asks.

'You can come with us and tell Anna what you found up there,' Sarah says, and leads the sobbing Nell through the hall and out into the night.

They make their way down Montgomery Street. A light rain, almost a mist, is falling. The streets of the Monto, although not deserted, are a lot less crowded than Christopher remembers from the night before. He looks at his watch: almost one o'clock in the morning. His immediate instinct is to get to a phone and ring Byatt to tell him what has happened. But Byatt is probably in bed by this time and if not his staff certainly are. He will have to wait until later in the morning.

Although he does not want to leave Nell he needs to sleep. Then he will meet up with Byatt and they can discuss the death of the poor women, no doubt at the hands of Janus.

They walk up to Anna Macken's house in a slow procession. Through the bay window that looks into the front room, Christopher can see that it is quieter than the night before, just a few of the girls standing around talking to one another.

Anna herself is standing in the doorway of the house vetting the few callers. When she spots Sarah's arm supporting Nell, she waves them inside and ushers them down the hallway towards a room to the rear. Before they enter, she calls out to one of the girls in the front parlour and asks her to send in a bottle of whiskey and some glasses, then closes over the door.

Sarah leads Nell over to a couch and gets her to lie down.

'What's happened?' Anna asks.

'Joseph found Connie's body,' Sarah says.

'Dear Jesus,' Anna Macken says, crosses herself and sits down on a chair.

One of the girls knocks and comes in with a tray with the whiskey and glasses and places it on a side table before leaving. Nobody moves until finally Christopher goes over and pours whiskey into the glasses and takes one over to Nell. She shakes her head, but he insists. Nell takes a sip and closes her eyes.

Anna joins them and puts her hand on Nell's forehead.

Nell opens her eyes.

'Connie's dead, and her girl, by that monster.'

'What kind of a devil would do that?' Anna says to Christopher, shaking her head.

'A clever one. The door was bolted on the inside. He even had time wash away the blood. If it wasn't that the gas ran out almost

238

immediately there would have been an explosion and nobody would be the wiser.'

'He must have escaped through the back door?'

'That was locked as well,' Sarah says.

Anna shakes her head.

'It's hard to think properly, it's been a long day,' Christopher says. 'I'm going to go back to my hotel for a few hours' sleep. Will you be all right, Nell?'

Nell nods and begins to cry again.

'Get some rest and come back in the morning,' Anna says. 'I'll make some calls. Sarah, take Nell to her room and stay with her.'

CHAPTER 26

As rapidly as he can, Christopher makes his way back to his hotel. He lets himself in and creeps up the stairs to the reception area. Mrs. Daly's newspaper is still stretched across the desk, her spectacles left to one side. An oil lamp burns on a low flame on the desk and he wonders has it been left out for him. He cups his hand over the lamp and blows it out, then goes into the back room, making as little noise as possible. He takes out the slip of paper Byatt gave him and dials the operator, giving her the number. There is an unusually long delay and he wonders if his connection has dropped but then a sleepy voice asks him for his name. The voice, he is disappointed to hear, is not that of Byatt. But it is an English accent and he wonders if one of Byatt's bodyguards has answered.

'I need to speak to Major Byatt. It's urgent,' he whispers.

'I said, who's calling?'

Christopher hadn't planned for this. Should he give his name or a false name? Or would his name mean anything anyway? He looks at his watch: almost two o'clock. Whoever is on the other end of the phone must be billeted in Dublin Castle so he presumes it is one of the bodyguards and so has a reasonable amount of information.

'It's Christopher Flinter. I work for Major Byatt,' he says finally.

'I remember you. I'm Harrison, the one that brought you a sandwich. What the hell's going on, Flinter?'

Christopher recalls the tall good-natured sergeant who had brought him the sandwich in what seems like an age ago. 'I'm sorry, I can't say.'

He hears a curt 'Wait' and then silence and footsteps walking away. The man returns to the phone after five minutes.

'I've checked. Everybody thought that he was with you. He's not been seen since he left for dinner. This place is in an uproar. We need him back here, it's not safe in the city and he shouldn't be out alone.'

He feels a chill, as if somebody had just opened a door. He considers telling the sergeant everything, but then changes his mind. It could all be a misunderstanding.

'Maybe he's outside, on the streets, trying to find out what's happening,' he mumbles.

'We're all in a curfew here. He should have been back by half past eight or, if not, he should have called in. When did you see him last?'

Christopher has to think. When was it? So much had happened since they had spoken — was it only yesterday that they had met up?

'Yesterday, on Talbot Street. We had tea and talked for a while. He said he was going to question the owner of the printing company where the dead boy, Daniel Joyce, worked.'

'I know all that. He came back here for a while but went out again in the evening. Said he was going for something to eat.'

Christopher knows where Byatt would have gone for dinner. He remembers the young man who had come over to their table and wonders if Byatt has made up with him, or met somebody else.

'Thank you, I'll try again later in the morning. Maybe he just met someone he knew and decided to stay out,' he says lamely.

'He's a soldier first, he should know better,' the sergeant answers stiffly and hangs up.

Christopher flops down onto a small settee. He's tired and he can't think properly but he has to make sense of what has been happening. After finding the body of the dead girl earlier, was he being overly suspicious? After all, Byatt was an old soldier and could handle himself. There has to be another explanation. But he needs to sleep. Perhaps he would see things differently after a few hours in bed.

Upstairs he can hardly manage take his clothes off, he is so tired, and he throws them loosely over a chair. The insipid light from the gas lamps on the street outside barely manages to make its way into the room through the stained net curtains but it is enough to keep him awake. He pulls over the heavier curtains tightly together, leaving the room in darkness. But sleep doesn't come as quickly as he hoped. He wants desperately to clear his mind, suspecting that if he falls asleep thinking about the murdered Connie and her maid, the terrible discovery will follow him and become a part of some gigantic nightmare. Instead, he thinks of the two new friends he has made, Moussa and Sarah, and their dream of leaving for Algeria and spending time beside the sea, away from everything: the fighting, the executions, the senseless murders of the prostitutes. As his mind drifts off, he dreams that he is lying on a sandy beach under a clear blue sky with gentle waves washing over his feet. Somewhere behind him he hears footsteps approaching and a long, dark shadow falls over him.

CHAPTER 27

It is a bright morning and the locomotive pulls slowly out of Blackrock railway station, gradually picking up speed on its way to Dublin city centre. George Maybury is engrossed in a daily newspaper, scanning the advertisements to see if any of them are suitable for his own publication and jotting down the names of potential future clients. Then he feels a presence beside him. Almost immediately he senses who it is. He puts his notebook down and stares out of the window. Dublin Bay is stretched out on his right, a green-and-white marbled expanse of water that he has been gazing out on for over twenty years. The bay is busier than usual. Ships that had been anchored off shore since the beginning of the rebellion were now steaming towards Dublin Port or Dun Laoghaire Harbour, their funnels billowing black clouds of smoke into the air. He stares resolutely out of the window, hoping against hope that he is mistaken.

'How is your family, Maybury?' Mordaunt asks.

'Do you really care, sir?'

'Of course I care, Maybury. We have more business to attend to and it is only correct to ask about your health,' Mordaunt says quietly.

Maybury, who has been an acute businessman for over thirty years, can sense a change of tone in Mordaunt's voice. It is a tiny shift, but a shift none the less. The interview with the policeman has kept him awake most of the night and he is feeling angry on top of the exhaustion from all the extra hours he has had to put in at the printing works. When he turns to face Mordaunt, he is surprised by his appearance. Gone is the beard, which he had always suspected was a fake, and gone too is the white collar of a churchman. Mordaunt is wearing a suit which looks crumpled and a white shirt with no tie. His eyes have lost some of the power which had made him such a formidable figure.

'Why should I be prepared to do any more business with you after the way you treated me?' Maybury whispers.

'You never complained when I gave you the money, did you? This next transaction will be our last.'

'You've said that before.'

'This time it is certain. I have all of the information I need written here,' Mordaunt says, patting his pocket. 'Just one more lot of alterations and that's it — you will never see me again.'

'But the next issue of the *Gazette* won't be printed for another week.'

'I am talking about this issue, the latest.'

Maybury looks around him to see if anyone in the carriage is paying them any attention but his fellow-travellers seem caught up in their own worlds.

'As you well know, this week's edition has already been printed. I am going into the office now to organise the deliveries.'

'Then I must press upon you the importance of reprinting the issue, with my new alterations.'

'Impossible. I would have to destroy twenty thousand copies, not to mention bringing in the extra staff for a new shift,' Maybury says.

'Surely you can just reprint the stock exchange figures and replace the pages?'

'It's not that easy. It would take almost as much time unfolding the issue, taking out the pages and inserting the new pages.'

'I will make it worth your while,' Mordaunt says and slips a thick envelope from his pocket.

He passes the envelope over to Maybury who, against his better judgement, opens it and peeks inside: a tightly packed bundle of bank notes, new by the look and smell of them. He opens the envelope further to make out the denomination of the notes and tries to keep the look of avarice from his face. If he is not mistaken there is ample money in the envelope to defray all of his costs and also leave him a healthy margin. The advertisements in the latest issue are thin on the ground. Also, he remembers, all of the type for the newspaper pages are still locked up in their metal printing forms, awaiting to be disassembled by the apprentices in the case room, so there would be no overhead there. The only cost, in reality, would be that of the newsprint which is nominal, but he isn't going to explain any of that to Mordaunt.

'Out of the question, I would be ruined,' he says, closing the envelope.

'Have you not forgotten our previous conversations,' Mordaunt hisses, an angry spark appearing in his eyes.

'I believe you were bluffing, Reverend Mordaunt, or should I say *Mister* Mordaunt,' Maybury says and holds out the envelope. 'You can take this back.'

'Are you sure you are willing to risk it?'

'I don't have to. I sent my family away this morning. By now they are halfway to their destination, many miles away from Dublin and out of harm's way.'

Mordaunt looks at the envelope, then reaches into his inside pocket, taking out another one and thrusting it at Maybury. Maybury calculates that it must hold almost the same amount as the first and tries to hide the triumph that he feels surging inside him. He is lying about his family; they are still at home. He knows he is taking a risk, but feels the game of poker has switched in his favour. A part of him wants to make Mordaunt squirm some more but it would not do to push him over the edge. He is still a formidable man and it is impossible to predict what he would do if he lost control. He reaches out and takes both envelopes and puts them into his pocket.

'Very well, I will do as you ask. But it is not for the money.'

'Really? And what is it for — your professional integrity?'

'No, sir, it is not. I am doing it because of Daniel Joyce. This travesty has gone on long enough. Another detective came to my premises yesterday making enquiries and I just want you out of my life.'

He expects Mordaunt to be surprised, or at the very least show some concern, but there is no reaction.

'Would that have been a Major Byatt by any chance?'

Maybury nods.

'Poor Daniel, a terrible tragedy. But I can assure you here and now that you will get no more visits from the police.' Mordaunt sits back in his seat and closes his eyes.

The train arrives at Westland Row station just as the Angelus rings out from a nearby church. Under the wide, glass canopy of the train station, the sound of the noonday bells are amplified and Maybury looks on it as a sign from above.

Both men hurry down the stairs, each anxious to be rid of the other. The beggar outside the station, who knows Maybury by sight, holds out his hand for alms. Usually Maybury would slip him a penny, but today he brushes past ignoring him. Mordaunt calls a hansom cab and gives the driver the address of Maybury's company, telling him there would be an extra shilling in it for him if they arrived there before half past nine. The cab driver pulls the horses' heads around and at the same time whips their flanks. The cab makes a tight circle and soon they are heading in the direction of Sackville Street Bridge at a fast clip.

Maybury strides through the entrance followed by Mordaunt and, without greeting his receptionist, goes straight onto the factory floor. Standing on the steps of his office he pulls on the bell rope and keeps ringing the bell until the workers have gathered around in a semicircle. With the latest edition already printed they are expecting another speech about the rough times they are going through and the need to redouble their efforts, or worse, layoffs. Instead, he seems almost relaxed. Holding up his hands, he smiles at them and asks for quiet. His smile, seldom seen, only brings a look of anxiety to the workers' faces.

'I have an announcement to make,' Maybury begins. 'It does mean some extra work to be done, but you will be well paid, overtime rates plus time off in lieu to spend with your families. We need to reprint this week's issue along with some alterations which I will personally supervise.'

A murmur rises from the workers, but Maybury can tell it's not a negative one. One or two faces are glum, but they're the usual troublemakers.

He continues. 'First things first. Please do not break down the old pages of type. I will supply you with a page plan this afternoon which will tell you which pages can be reprinted straight away. Secondly, the remaining pages, the stock exchange pages, will be the last to be printed. And last but by no means least, the advertising canvassers will need to get back to their clients to tell them that there will be a delay. You will be given extra expenses for the more difficult ones and can wine them and dine them if necessary.'

A scattering of laughs come up from the canvassers who are standing together at the back of the crowd. All in all, Maybury is happy with the way things are going. The one dark cloud hanging over everything is his complete loss as to what is going on and he doesn't trust mysteries. He had presumed it was some sort of financial skulduggery tied up with the American stock exchange, but now he is not sure. Why was it necessary to make extra alterations at this time and why does Mordaunt seem to have lost some of his confidence? But he sticks to his maxim: what you do not know should not overly concern you.

He claps his hands together and shoos the men away, then turns back into his office. Mordaunt has a copy of the newspaper in front of him and is marking a large number of alterations from a notebook, his head bent in total concentration on the tiny sets of figures.

'There, you see, Maybury, it was not that difficult, was it?' he says without looking up at the owner.

'The one good thing to come out of this, sir, is that I will be very glad to see the back of you,' Maybury replies, goes back behind his desk and takes down some ledgers to work on.

Mordaunt ignores the insult and continues on with his work.

CHAPTER 28

Christopher wakes up from a fitful sleep and looks at his watch. It is early afternoon and he is disappointed that he has slept so long. A stray ray of light cuts like a knife through the dimness of the room and lands on his face. Without it he would have probably slept on until the evening and he is grateful that the sun has found a chink in the curtains. He rises out of bed and has a quick wash in the washbasin, promising himself a bath later in the public baths across the river. He dresses, making himself look as presentable as possible for the ever-present Mrs. Daly who is undoubtedly taking note of his unusual sleeping habits.

Down in the reception area the old woman is sitting, straight-backed, and seems to be waiting for him. As soon as he appears, she holds up a copy of a newspaper and stabs her finger at it. The headline almost covers the top half of the newspaper and has only one word: EXECUTED. He tries to work out what his reaction should be. After all, he is supposed to be a member of the DMP and, as such, working for the Crown. On the other hand, the executions seem to have brought about a latent hostility in most of the people he has encountered.

Then his eyes fall on the small red lamp that illuminates a print of Jesus Christ who is exposing his bleeding heart. He remembers the same print on the walls of most of his neighbours when he was growing up in the Liberties. He blesses himself.

'May God have mercy on their souls,' he says with solemnity.

Mrs. Daly immediately blesses herself and sighs.

'I was not one to hold any love of what happened on Easter Monday, but those men were all God-fearing Christians. It is not right that they should have been put up against a wall and shot,' she says.

'No doubt it was done to quell any more dissenting voices,' Christopher says.

'But the news is that they've shot another three more, and one is a brother of Patrick Pearse. Think what their poor mother is going through now. No, it is not right, Mr. Andrews, and I do not care if you are a policeman — it is not right.'

'I am in agreement with you, Mrs. Daly — those men should have been tried in a civil court of law and, as an officer of the law, that is my honest opinion.'

Mrs. Daly smiles sadly. 'I can see that you're a decent young man,' she says.

'I try to be, with the help of the Good Lord,' he says and nods towards the picture on the wall behind her.

'*Amen.*'

'By the way, Mrs. Daly, is there any chance that I can use your phone again? I will pay, obviously.'

'Of course you can, Mr. Andrews, you know where it is. And don't you dare talk about paying for it.'

Christopher nods, goes into the parlour and closes the door behind him. He dials the operator and gives Byatt's number, hoping that he has returned to Dublin Castle while he has been asleep. While he waits for the connection to go through, he listens to the whirs and clicks coming through the earpiece and tries to figure out what he will do if Byatt hasn't turned up.

'Yes, who is it?'

It is Harrison's voice, a stroke of luck.

'Christopher Flinter again, sergeant — can I speak to Major Byatt?'

There is a long pause and Christopher can hear the faraway sound of marching soldiers and loud voices shouting out instructions.

'I'm afraid not — he has still not come back,' Harrison answers in a gruff, authoritative voice, then more gently, 'We're very concerned.'

'I'm sorry to hear that … perhaps we're being too pessimistic?'

'Perhaps. But the body of one of the civil service clerks working here in Dublin Castle was discovered last night in St. Patrick's Cathedral, murdered. Would you have come across a Mr. Blaney?'

'No, I haven't, sergeant. But I must go now,' he says and hangs up before he can be asked any more questions.

Christopher flops down onto a chair. Now he has to face his new reality: Janus has somehow found out about Jonathan Byatt and the man who saved his life could now be in captivity, or dead. A torrent of questions floods into his mind. How did Janus find out? How had he managed to capture Byatt, a professional soldier and spy, an intelligent man who had known his way around Dublin and knew where not to stray? But the most important question of all: had Byatt revealed to Janus the understanding between them and had he revealed his identity, or even the name of the hotel he was staying in? He thought back to his last meeting with Byatt, but nothing in their conversation gave him any clue as to what happened. The one thing he was sure about was that when Byatt left the café he seemed in good humour, so at that moment he did not suspect anything amiss.

Sitting alone in the back parlour and wondering what to do next, it suddenly occurs to him that if Byatt was murdered, it would mean that he is now a free man. The sergeant made no mention of him having to come back to Dublin Castle and hand himself in and the situation in Dublin is now so fraught that he would be at the bottom of a long list of priorities for the authorities. The thought of freedom brings a brief moment of happiness, followed by a feeling of guilt. It was Byatt who had spared his life and without him he would probably by now be buried in a pauper's grave somewhere in Mount Jerome cemetery. Could he spend the rest of his life not knowing what happened to Byatt? The least he owed him was to find out for definite if he was being held prisoner or if Janus had murdered him as he had murdered all of those other victims.

But there were very few lines of enquiry he could follow. If Blaney was mixed up in it, that was now a dead end. He thought over his last conversation with Byatt. He had said he was going to visit the printing company where Daniel Joyce worked. Was it a coincidence? Byatt goes to try and find out if there was a link between the young printer and Janus and then he himself disappears. It was a tenuous link, but the only link he had to follow. But how could he even begin to question a respectable businessman when he himself was, in fact, a deserter in the eyes of the Crown?

He hears a polite cough outside the door and realises that he has been sitting in the parlour for nearly half an hour. Mrs. Daly sticks her head around the door and when she sees that he is off the telephone, comes into the room.

'Excuse me, Mrs. Daly, I was just thinking about an investigation I am on. Thank you very much for the use of your phone,' he says, getting up from the armchair. 'I'd better be on my way.'

* * * *

The Monto feels almost deserted. People shuffle along Montgomery Street, their heads to the ground, minding their own business. Even the weather seems to have turned its back on the city. The temperature, which had been rising steadily promising an early summer, had taken a step backwards and now it is cold. Smoke once more pours from the chimneypots. A dense, grey cloud of smog already hangs low in the sky and there is a sense of a loss of space. Christopher makes his way to Anna Macken's to see how Nell is after the shock of losing her friend.

When he arrives at Anna's house the front door is partially open. Inside he can tell that no housework has been done. In the front parlour cups and glasses are still scattered around on tables and along the mantelpiece. In the back room most of the food from the night before remains uneaten on the long table. He passes through the kitchen and it is clean, but there is no activity. As he moves on through the short hallway he begins to doubt if Nell is even in her room. He knocks at the door and is relieved to hear movement from inside. When she opens the door, he is shocked by her appearance. Her hair is down around her shoulders, almost hiding her face which is pale and exhausted. Her once sparkling eyes are red from crying and she is wearing a shapeless nightdress that hangs almost to the floor. She stands back and lets him in, closing the door behind him.

'How are you?' he asks.

'Sad.'

'Of course you are,' he says, putting his hands on her shoulders.

'You were right about one thing. Everything is changing and there's nothing I can do about it,' she says, looking into his eyes. 'Can you make it all just stop?'

'Stop change? No, you can't stop what you've no control over — you just have to make the best of it that you can.'

'Anna says it was like a morgue here last night. What's tonight going to be like?'

Looking over her shoulder he sees a battered brown-leather suitcase lying open on the bed. Strewn around it are various articles of clothing and one or two books. His stomach gets that same tight feeling he got before rising out of the trenches and facing the unknown.

Nell follows his gaze to the bed.

'I've packed that suitcase and unpacked it a few times in the past hour. Moussa is insisting Sarah go with him to Algeria. He says he feels that the city is about to erupt and that there is more trouble on the way. There's a Spanish ship down the docks which will be leaving tomorrow. They've asked me to go with them.'

'You're not going to leave, are you?'

The idea of losing both Byatt and Nell, the two most important people in his life, terrifies him.

'I don't know any more. I don't think Anna can stay in business much longer and I've lost my friend to a monster. Not to mention what's going on in Dublin.'

'But I thought that we had ...'

'That we had an agreement? Just because we spent a night together?'

'I didn't mean that. But what about Anna? I thought she was like family to you. Does she know that you're all leaving her?'

Nell put her hands to her face. 'Why do you think I've packed and unpacked so many times?'

Christopher sits down on the bed and stares at the floor.

'But, listen,' she takes his hands in hers, 'you could come with us to Algeria. Moussa says there's plenty of work there because of the war.'

'I'm done with wars, Nell.'

'That's the best thing, Joseph — the war hasn't reached there —

it's peaceful and warm and there's plenty of work. We could move in with Moussa and Sarah at first — he's going to buy a small house. Then we could save up and buy our own if we had to.'

'And what's Anna going to say?'

'It wouldn't be forever. I'm sure that after I've talked to her about it, she will give us her blessing. Things are going to get worse in Dublin before they get better and I don't think the Monto will ever be the same again. Too much has happened over Easter and it's not finished with yet.'

Christopher is being carried on by her enthusiasm until he remembers Byatt. He pictures him limping ahead of him down Dame Street on the way to buy him his clothes and remembers the meal they had together. He could be dead already but, then again, he could be imprisoned somewhere in Dublin, Janus as his gaoler. If he left now, he knew he would never be free of that constant question: was Byatt alive or dead? He would have to be sure.

'I can't do it,' he says finally, shaking his head.

'But why not?' Nell says, squeezing his hands. 'You've nobody left in Dublin and you can't go back into the army. What else are you going to do?'

'There is somebody.'

'Who? It's not another girl, is it?' Nell says, her pale face suddenly growing red.

'No, not a woman, it's a man I owe my life to. He's disappeared and I have to find him. If I leave now, I'll regret it for the rest of my life.'

'I don't understand — how do you owe him your life? Was he in the war with you?'

'You'd better sit down, Nell — it's a complicated story. I'd better start by telling you my real name: it's Christopher Flinter.'

Nell sits on the bed, her face changing from anger to bewilderment as Christopher tells her about the letter he received about his young brother's death, of his escape from hospital and his journey back to Ireland to avenge Ned. But most of all he tells her about Byatt, the man who rescued him from the firing squad.

When he is finished Nell takes hold of hand.

'I'll ask Moussa to help you — he knows Dublin better than any of us. He takes things in, he knows people: policemen, soldiers, some of the toffs.'

'What makes you think that he'd help me?'

'It's worth a try, isn't it? What good can *you* do? You've been away from Dublin for two years. You didn't even know your way around the Monto when I met you.'

'I don't know, Nell — can I trust him?'

'Of course you can. Didn't you hear what Sarah told us? He prays a lot, every day. In any case he won't be doing it for you, he'll be doing it for Sarah who'll do it for me.'

'Are you sure?'

'Yes, if I promise that we'll go away with them.'

CHAPTER 29

Sitting opposite Moussa now he can see that he is a different person to the one he met the night before, more business-like. The table is cleared of all of the colourful dishes, even the tablecloth. Some of the paintings — Moussa called them batiks — have been taken down from the walls and are folded up on the chair. Three large wooden tea chests lie open in the middle of the room filled with odds and ends wrapped up in newspaper. Everything that made the room seem homely has disappeared into the chests, even the blanket that separated the bedroom from the living quarters. Now the room is almost back to the way it was: a stable. Sarah sits beside Moussa, looking up into his face, her tiny hand on his arm. Nell sits beside Christopher in almost the same pose as Sarah, the two women almost acting as seconds in a boxing ring, except both of them are wanting the same outcome.

'Explain to me again, my friend Joseph, or should I say Christopher, why you want to find this man? How do you know that he can be found? As you can see,' Moussa opens his arm to take in the half-dismantled room, 'I am very busy now. I have a lot to do before we leave.'

'If you want me to leave,' Sarah says with firmness, 'I'm not going anywhere without Nell.'

'My heart, we are going around in circles. You will not leave without Nell, she will not leave without Christopher, Christopher will not leave until he finds this man, but he will not tell me anything about him. How can I help if I do not know what is going on? It is inconsiderate.'

'I can't leave because I owe this man my life, Moussa.'

'Now we are back to this again. Nell tells me that you deserted the army and have just arrived back in Dublin.'

'That's true. I was taken and held in Dublin Castle. I should have been executed, but this man set me free.'

'This does not make sense. If you desert an army during war, you are shot. How could this man let you go? You told Nell that you escaped. I am sorry, you will have to tell me more.'

All eyes turn on Christopher who puts his hands up.

'I admit I lied, but I had to. If I had been found out, especially after the executions, I would have been branded a spy and shot.'

Moussa runs his fingers through his beard. 'This is true, but you have to tell us more, you have to trust us.'

Christopher, again, goes through everything that has happened to him since he arrived back in Dublin. Moussa, to his credit, does not interrupt him once — he just sits, nodding his head.

When he is finished Moussa gets up and goes over to one of the chests, rummaging about inside. He comes back to the table with a bottle and four tiny glasses and pours a colourless liquid into them but tells them not to drink it yet. Then he goes over to the sink and fills a jug with water. Christopher sniffs the air, trying to identify the odour coming from the glasses: aniseed. Moussa pours water into the glasses and the liquid turns cloudy. He picks up one of the glasses and hands it to Sarah, then one to Nell before taking one himself.

'This is the finest pastis from Marseilles. I have been keeping that bottle with me for the last two years, but now I want to share it with my friends and toast our future.'

They touch glasses together and take a sip from them. Christopher's eyes water as the stringent taste trickles down his throat. It reminds him of medicine he had taken as a child.

'But can you help me?' he asks.

'I will do my best,' Moussa answers.

'Where do you think we should start?'

'I am advising you against it, my friend, but if you are insisting, it is as you have told me yourself. The first thing we must do is to visit this newspaper — everything comes from there, you have said. It is the last place that you know for certain Major Byatt paid a visit to. It is also where that young boy worked, the boy who died by the hands of the man who killed our dear Connie. I think that it is time for Detective Flinter to go on duty and make an official visit to the newspaper.'

'Me, a detective? What if I'm caught?'

'In all of this,' Moussa says and waves his arm around to take in the city, 'nobody will question you, trust me. Also, I think I can persuade Philip Shanahan to loan us a firearm, just in case I am mistaken. But before we do anything, maybe a quick visit to the public baths would be in order. It is on the way and you will feel so much better. You can bath and I can go and have my beard shaved and get some of my locks cut off.'

Christopher's face reddens.

'Moussa is right. You have to look the part, Christopher. I can brush down your suit and make you look presentable. But you really do need a good soak in a bath,' Nell says, smiling.

✳ ✳ ✳ ✳

The Iveagh Public Baths, located on the edge the Liberties are exactly as he remembers them. The cold rectangle of water is full of thrashing bodies and noisy shouts that reverberate around the walls. A heavy chemical smell lingers in the air from the disinfectant in the water. Most of the swimmers in the pool are children, confined to the shallow end by a rope that goes from one side of the pool to the other. Beyond the rope, in the deep end, several men swim sedately backwards and forwards. The pool is lined on either side by wooden dressing rooms and overlooking it all is a spectators' balcony. He pays his entrance fee at the hatch into the men's inner bathing area, the first time he has ever been in the inner sanctum. Hanging up his clothes in the locker, he realises that he could be using the same locker as his father, who bathed here once a week.

After taking a hot bath, he decides to go back into the public swimming pool. The last time he was there was with Ned. His parents were alive then and it was his responsibility to keep an eye on his younger brother. But they needn't have worried. Ned just held onto the bar in the corner of the shallow end of the pool and would never let go. He glances over to the spot, half-expecting to see Ned hanging on for dear life and pleading with him to take him home but all he sees are the thrashing limbs of another generation of children. Why did Ned finally let the bar go and join the army? The answer was plain: it was to see his older brother again. What loneliness he must have felt every night sleeping, alone, in Tommy Sherry's little room. To banish the picture of his younger brother from his mind, he dives into the deep end of the pool and lets the tepid water wash over him.

The same attendant, older and slower, limps out of the office and blows his whistle for the end of the hour, but Christopher is not ready to leave. He dives to the bottom of the deep end, closes his eyes and holds his breath. The pressure builds up on his ears. He stares up towards the filtered light, watching the bubbles floating upwards from his mouth, bubbles of mercury that twist and change as they rise. How hard would it be to just stay down here? He lets more of his breath escape until he has no more left to give. His lungs begin to burn and he closes his eyes and concentrates on not breathing. He pictures Ned, his skinny white body disappearing into the dressing room, laughing, delighted to be out of the water. Then he sees his parents sitting around their kitchen table, waiting for him and Ned. It must be Friday, he thinks. In front of them are four hot parcels of fish and chips from Burdocks on Werburgh Street. Him and Ned join their parents at the table as his mother opens up the newspaper to uncover the once-a-week treat. The smell of salt and vinegar and hot batter fills the kitchen. He reaches out, but before he can touch the meal the burning sensation in his lungs finally sears through his brain. He kicks up from the bottom, letting the air out from his burning lungs as he rises, breaking the surface and gulping in the chlorine-tainted air.

When he breaks the surface, he discovers that he is alone in the pool. The attendant stares down at him and shakes his head in exasperation.

In the cramped cubicle of the dressing room he sits for a while, still shaking. But after his recollections of Ned and how he wasn't around for him, he feels a new determination: he is not going to let any harm come to Byatt if he can help it — at least this is in his power.

He dresses quickly and goes outside to meet up with Moussa who has gone looking for a barber for a shave and a haircut. He emerges into the cold air, shivering after the warmth of the pool, and looks around, but Moussa is nowhere to be seen. He takes out a cigarette and places it into his mouth. Before he can light it himself, a hand appears in front of his face with a flaring match. He looks up into a face he does not recognise. For a split second he thinks that Janus has second-guessed him and he steps back, but then he hears the booming laugh he has come to know: it is Moussa after his visit to the barber, his hair shorn and his beard shaved off.

'You look shocked, my friend!' Moussa laughs, delighted to have caught Christopher out.

For some strange reason Moussa without the beard and with short hair looks older than Moussa with the beard and wild mane. Running across his clean-shaven face, from the corner of his mouth up to his ear there is a pale scar. His long, wavy hair is now a no-nonsense short back and sides and, along with the suit, lends him an air of authority. Christopher now puts his age more in his late forties. What had seemed like a far-fetched plan now seems more plausible. With someone like Moussa behind him, he can do anything.

'You look … different.'

'It is still me, my friend,' Moussa says and puts an arm around Christopher's shoulders.

Christopher and Moussa make their way up Patrick's Street and on towards the archway of Christ Church Cathedral. On his left is his old home, the Liberties. He knows and loves every road and laneway, every building. But after the eerie vision of his family and the almost near-death at the bottom of the pool, he feels that he has finally left that part of his life behind him and is ready to move on. If Tommy Sherry had offered him the whole top floor of the tenement now, he could not have taken it. Nell, he suspects, is somehow responsible for this change. She has drawn him away from his past in some subtle way and is offering him a new future. Onwards up the hill, on past the new red-brick buildings put up by Edward Cecil Guinness for the poorest of families. His family had been eligible for one of the apartments and everything could have been so different. But his father, a proud man, would not apply for it.

They approach the junction of Thomas Street and Christchurch, the exact place where Christopher had started out in the past on his way to the Smithfield Animal Market. Always early morning, sometimes in the dark, with a freezing wind whipping up from the Liffey so cold it numbed his fingers. In his pocket, wrapped up in a handkerchief, a few shillings to pick out the piglets his father would eventually raise and slaughter. Moussa stares up with wonder as they walk under the stone arch that links Christ Church cathedral with the synod hall.

As they make their way down Winetavern Street towards the Liffey, Christopher stops and studies the page he ripped out of a Thom's Directory of Dublin. The only publishing company on the quays, he tells Moussa, is the *Irish Gazette*, so that must be the one Byatt had visited. They decide that Christopher will have to do all of the talking, while Moussa can stand back and leave his jacket hanging open to reveal the firearm that Philip Shanahan has loaned him. If all comes to the worst, Christopher says, we can just use that to threaten him. Now that they are about to carry out the plan Christopher has become more nervous and when they finally stand outside the steps leading up to the front door of the printing company — which is a more imposing enterprise than he had thought — he hesitates.

Moussa takes his arm and walks him past the building.

'You will fail, Christopher — you are too nervous. A policeman would never act like that. Wait.'

Moussa leads him down an alleyway along the side of the building.

When they are out of sight from passers-by, Moussa takes out a silver cigarette case and opens it. Inside there are several cigarettes, all hand-rolled judging by their crumpled appearance. He takes one out and puts it between his lips.

'Watch what I do,' he says, then lights the cigarette and takes a deep pull, holds the smoke in, then lets it out in one long breath. The smoke from the cigarette has a sweet, sickly smell. He hands it to Christopher and nods. 'This is hashish — it will make you more serene,' he says with a wink.

Christopher has heard stories about hashish but has never tried it. He takes the hand-rolled cigarette from Moussa and follows his example, dragging in a deep breath. He holds it for a while and releases it. Within a few minutes it seems to slow his mind down and lessen his nervousness. His friend encourages him to take another drag which he does, holding it for a longer time before letting it out with a cough. He finishes the cigarette and throws it onto the ground.

'Now, we can go,' Moussa says and leads them back down the alleyway.

This time Christopher marches up the steps and on into the office. A receptionist sits behind a desk, typing. She looks up and her eyes rest on Moussa who stands in the doorway, almost filling it.

'Can I help you, gentlemen? We're about to close,' she says, patting her hair.

'Dublin Metropolitan Police. We would like to talk to the proprietor,' Christopher says.

'Mr. Maybury?'

'Yes.'

'Very well, but he is a very busy man today and I cannot imagine how another visit will help. But I suppose it's all for the good if it solves the mystery of our poor Daniel. Please take a seat.'

She disappears through a doorway into the printing works beyond.

The sound of the printing presses fill the tiny reception area and Christopher catches a glimpse of a cavernous building filled with noise and activity.

After a few minutes a grey-haired, middle-aged man dressed in a suit comes through the door. Under the jacket of his suit Christopher can see that he is wearing a dark apron.

'George Maybury, how may I help you?' he says, wiping his hands on the apron.

Christopher takes out a notebook from his pocket, opens it and holds it on his knee, his pencil poised over a page.

'I am Detective Flinter, this is my colleague Detective Smith. We are following up on a missing colleague, Major Byatt. We believe that this was the last known address he visited before returning to Dublin Castle yesterday.'

'Byatt? Yes, he was here, but then he left and that is all I have to say about it,' Maybury says, looking from Christopher to Moussa.

'Major Byatt was investigating the murder of Daniel Joyce,' Christopher continues, 'and then he himself disappears. You can guess why we're here.'

'Murder? He never mentioned murder to me. He did say that the body was found in unusual circumstances, but I presumed that it was something to do with where the body was located. The Liffey is a tidal river after all. I wish had pointed that out to him.'

'Then he never mentioned that it was a murder investigation?'

'Are you implying that I had something to do with it?' Maybury laughs nervously.

'No, sir. But we have to examine every avenue.'

'Of course, but as I say he came in yesterday, asked some questions and left and that is about the size of it. Now if you will excuse me, I have to put a newspaper to bed.'

Maybury walks to the door.

Christopher is at a loss. He looks at Moussa who shrugs his shoulders.

'Mr. Maybury!' Christopher says. 'Did you know that young

Daniel's throat was severed right through to the bone?'

The receptionist, who had been pretending not to be listening, looks up and puts her hand to her face.

Maybury stops and turns slowly.

'No, sir, I was not aware of that.'

'Yes. And did you know that the same method was used on several women in the Monto district?' Christopher continues.

'Oh dear God, the man is the very devil himself!' Maybury blurts out and flops down onto the side of the receptionist's desk with his head in his hands.

Moussa looks over at Christopher and nods.

'Who exactly is this devil, Mr. Maybury?' Christopher presses him.

Maybury looks up at him. 'The Reverend Mordaunt!' He almost spits out the name. 'He threatened my family. I didn't believe him. Dear God, I have to go and protect them.'

He stands up suddenly.

'You'll be more of a help to them if you tell us everything, Mr. Maybury,' Christopher says.

'I promise I will help. But you must excuse me, I have to ring home and warn them — follow me,' he says and rushes back into the printing works.

Christopher and Moussa try to keep up with Maybury as he rushes past the thundering printing presses and the curious looks of the printers.

Maybury enters a glass-fronted office and, by the time they reach him, he is talking to his wife, demanding that she leave the house at once. When he puts the phone down, he seems to be more relieved and flops into the seat behind his desk.

'This Mordaunt, what do you know about him?' Christopher asks.

'Almost nothing, if I am to be honest.'

'Was he American?'

'I'm not quite sure — sometimes, when he got excited, he had the trace of an American accent. But he was a very good customer, one of the best, paid on time, didn't quibble with the invoice.'

'What address did you send the invoice to?' Christopher asks, taking out his notebook again.

'I never did. I handed him a pro forma invoice personally and he paid there and then.'

'Pro forma — what does that mean?'

'It's an invoice we send in advance to show what we have done. It's rarely paid until the official invoice is sent.'

'And you've never sent an official invoice?' Christopher said, disheartened.

'No, we have an invoice on file but it is just a copy of the pro-forma one.'

'Tell me anything you can about him.'

'Mordaunt presented himself, oh, towards the end of last year. Our dealings began by him wanting to take some advertising with us.'

'What sort of advertising?'

'General religious advertising, selling Bibles, prayer books, that sort of thing. He was a prompt payer, so we were glad to have him as a customer.'

'And that's all he ever did?'

'It was, at first,' Maybury says.

'And then?'

'He is a very persuasive man. He began to take an interest in the workings of the newspaper, from the typesetting, the layout, the printing, the delivery, everything. Said he enjoyed the details, found them fascinating. Wanted to learn all about it. He said that one day he would like to set up a religious publication. But then, of course, things changed.'

'How do you mean?' Christopher asks.

'One of the contracts we have is with the Irish Stock Exchange. He began to take a special interest in that and delivered the copy to our typesetters. It is a specialist job and is done in a separate company.'

'That sounds like odd behaviour.'

'It seems so now, but you've never met this man. I tried to get rid of him at the time, it was more trouble than it was worth, but then he said that he did not want to inconvenience me and could pay me a fee, to treat him as an indentured apprentice. Stupidly, I agreed. Obviously, I regret it now.'

Christopher looks across the desk at the grey-haired man. He sits slumped in his chair, playing with the strings of his apron. Perhaps it was the shock of finding out that his apprentice, Daniel Joyce, was murdered, but there is something wrong. Maybury is an intelligent man. Would he not have figured out that a detective from Dublin Castle does not follow up on a drowning, however unusual it was?

'Do you want to tell us anything more? What does he look like?'

'Tall, bearded, dark, in clerical garb — but that won't help you now. Last time I saw him he was clean-shaven and in ordinary clothes.'

'And you didn't think that suspicious?'

Maybury keeps his eyes on the desk and shakes his head.

'We find, Mr. Maybury, that it is better to be honest in these matters. If we capture this man, who's to say that he won't implicate you, and that makes you an accessory.'

'I know nothing of his whereabouts, and I do not wish to know. I have been a businessman in this city for over thirty years — a jury of my peers would never take his word over mine!' Maybury hits the desk with his hand.

'But you have to look at it from the Dublin Metropolitan Police's point of view, Mr. Maybury. A young boy is murdered and the detective in charge of the case goes missing shortly afterwards. And now you've given us to believe that the potential suspect has been threatening your family?'

'*Oh dear God!*' Maybury cries.

'If you tell us the whole truth about your dealings with this Mordaunt, we will mention in our report that you cooperated fully with us.'

Maybury looks from one to the other of them and signals Moussa to close over the door.

'I will tell you all that I know but, as I cannot fathom what this is all about, I'm not sure that it will even help you.'

'Let us be the judge of that,' Christopher says.

'Very well,' Maybury says with a sigh. 'In the very early days he took out advertisements for Bibles, prayer books etc. Within the advertisements he had various quotations from the Bible with their Biblical references. As a churchgoing man I knew almost from the beginning that the references were incorrect. I pointed that out to him and he thanked me profusely, said he was useless with numbers, always had been. He even left it up to me to make the corrections. Sometime after that he became interested in the stock exchange price listings. He said that his church had investments and pensions and that he was interested in how they were doing and that it would be an advantage to get an early glimpse of the figures.'

'And the stock exchange prices, they appear within the newspaper?'

'Yes, every issue. Prices change constantly. It's a lucrative contract for us — without it we could not survive.'

Christopher feels that he is getting nowhere. What would Byatt do if he were in his position?

'Does that mean that Mordaunt was here every day?'

'Only on days coming up to publication.'

'When did you last see him?'

Maybury bows his head, his answer mumbled.

'Earlier today, on the train on the way into my office, he appeared beside me. As I said, clean-shaven and dressed in ordinary clothes. I told him that I never wanted to see him again, but he promised that it would be his last time. '

'What did he want?'

'He wanted to scrap the paper we had just printed and to print another edition. I told him it was out of the question, but he promised that he would cover all of the costs. At that point I was just tired of him, I wanted him out of my life, and, reluctantly, I agreed. He waited until we had the first copies off the press then gathered up an armful and left. He didn't even wait around for the main bulk.'

Moussa tipped Christopher on the shoulder and pointed towards the door to the office. He excused himself to Maybury and they stepped outside into the clamour of the printing presses. Moussa bent his head down to Christopher and shouted in his hear.

'Ask him for a copy of the newspaper.'

'Why?'

'Whatever this man is up to is contained within the pages of the newspaper. If we can fathom what this mystery is all about, then, maybe, we can use that to flush this demon from his lair.'

'Should we not go the police and tell them what we know?'

'*Bah!* They will not believe a deserter from the army. You will be locked up and then it is all over. No, we have to try ourselves.'

Christopher knows that Moussa is talking sense. If he appeared at Dublin Castle, without Byatt's help, he would be locked up and then handed over to the army. He nods to Moussa and both of the men go back inside the office.

'Mr. Maybury, would it be possible to examine a printed copy of the newspaper?'

'Of course. If you will excuse me, I will fetch one from the bindery department,' he says and seems glad to leave the office.

'What if we don't find anything?' Christopher says.

'Then you will have done your best,' Moussa whispers, 'and now it is time to think about your future, and of course Nell's. We can be on that ship tomorrow night and out of this nightmare.'

'I suppose you're right,' Christopher admits.

Maybury comes back into the office and places a copy of the newspaper onto his desk. Christopher and Moussa stand over it, not knowing exactly what they are looking for.

'What pages are the stock exchange figures on?' Christopher asks.

'Towards the back, you can't miss them.'

Christopher flicks over the pages. Most of the stories are about the aftermath of the rebellion interspersed with advertisements about everything from men's hair-grooming products to the sale of farmlands and even the sale of tickets to America promising a safe and quick voyage to the new world. The content was different to any of the newspapers he remembered as a youth.

Maybury caught him staring at some of the advertisements.

'Our newspaper is very popular with Irish people who have emigrated to America. They like to hear news from the old country, but they also like to be kept informed on the more practical aspects of coming back home and what the conditions are like in the country. Some of those emigrants left when they were children, at the time of the Great Famine.'

'I see,' Christopher says.

Moussa is looking over his shoulder as he opens out the newspaper on to the stock-exchange listings pages. The pages are crammed with the smallest type Christopher has ever seen, all laid out into columns that go from the top of the page to the bottom. Hundreds of companies are listed, each one with a long line of figures after them, none of which make any sense to him.

'I can't even begin to understand these figures,' Christopher says, pointing to the page.

'There are not too many people who can. All I can say is that Mordaunt just wanted certain numbers brought out more in a slightly different typeface.'

'Different?'

'Yes, we had to use slightly older, worn type from our cases here. You'd hardly notice, unless you were looking out for it.'

'Why would he do something like that? It doesn't make sense.'

'I gave up trying to make sense of it months ago,' Maybury says. 'Here, use this.'

After searching around in a drawer in his desk, he hands Christopher a magnifying glass. Stooping over the pages he is just able to make out that among the crisply rendered numerals that fill the pages, some of them are not quite as sharp as others. But they are scattered all over the page with no discernible pattern and mean absolutely nothing to him. Giving up, he hands the glass to Moussa who bends his head down and begins to peruse the page. After several minutes of seemingly fruitless searching, he feels Moussa's leg tipping his. Christopher stares down at the section of the page his friend is examining but can see nothing amiss. He feels his leg being tipped again, harder this time, and Moussa picks up the newspaper, hands Maybury back the magnifying glass and indicates that they should leave.

'Whatever it is, Mr Maybury, it is beyond me,' Christopher says. 'We'll take it back to Dublin Castle and examine it more closely'.

'I would hazard a guess that it is beyond most people. Possibly some sort of financial fraud that is taking place in America and perpetrated by the so-called Reverend Mordaunt. Who's to know?'

'If, on an off-chance, he shows up again, can you detain him as long as possible and send a boy around to the Castle?'

'Of course, detective,' Maybury says, a relieved look on his face.

Outside the printing office Moussa puts his arm around Christopher's shoulders.

'You have done well, my friend, but now it is time to accept the truth. You have done all that any man could be expected to do. It is obvious that your Major Byatt found out what was going on and has paid for it with his life. Now it is time to take care of your own life. And, of course, Nell's.'

'How are you so certain he's dead?' Christopher says.

'Because of the information contained in the newspaper. Trust me, if this man Mordaunt, or Janus, or whatever you would like to call him, has captured your friend, he is already dead, I am sad to say.'

'I can't believe he would kill an officer in the army and risk calling down the wrath of the British. The Monto will be turned upside-down — all that for some kind of fraud with meaningless figures in a newspaper?'

'Those were not meaningless figures, my friend. As somebody who has spent his life working on ships at sea, they are all too familiar.'

Moussa opens up the newspaper on the stock-exchange pages, folding it down.

'Here —' He points to the first set of figures at the top of the page, figures that were slightly more worn than others. 'This is a measurement of latitude. And this,' he moves his finger down, 'a measurement of longitude. They are coordinates. This goes on down the pages, there are a lot of them.'

Christopher stares at the figures. 'Ships?'

'Yes.'

'What does it mean?'

'From the figures I recognise, I can say with an amount of certainty that they are located somewhere in the Atlantic.'

'But whose ships?' Christopher asks himself.

'That I do not know for certain, but would guess French or American or possibly English or all three. But there is another set of figures, even more important.'

'What are they?'

'They are the dates that go with the locations.'

'Byatt was right all along. Janus is sending information to the Germans. We'll have to halt the delivery of those newspapers, Moussa. It's the only way we can be sure to stop him.'

'You forget one thing, my friend. This devil has outsmarted us, he must have been suspicious and taken some copies so that he could post them himself. Perhaps he already has. Believe me, Christopher, it is too late for your friend. Come away with us tomorrow. In two weeks, we can be Algeria, sitting on the beach, looking up into the sun and all of this will be a bad memory.'

'But I have to find out what happened to Byatt,' Christopher insists. 'You can go, you've done more than enough to help me. Now it's up to me.'

The look on Moussa's face is one of frustrated anger, then acceptance. But he lays his hands gently on Christopher's shoulders.

'I truly advise against it, but if that is what you want, so be it,' he says with sad resignation.

CHAPTER 30

'This is all very hurtful to me, girls.'

Anna Macken strides up and down past the suitcases and the large travel trunk that now take up most of the floor space in Moussa's living quarters. She pulls on her cigarette, flicking the ash onto the floor, shaking her head and mumbling angrily to herself. Every time she passes the trunk her dress makes a swishing sound, as if annoyed by its presence. Sarah and Nell sit on the bed, heads bent in embarrassment. The room is almost back to what it had been before Moussa moved in: a forgotten outbuilding that was of no use to Anna.

She stands in front of the bed with her hands on her hips.

'All I've done for you two!' she says for the fourth or fifth time.

Nell looks up at her, fearful but defiant.

'We know that, Anna, but we've never been wanting in doing the hard work. We've paid our way.'

'At least I gave you a job — who else in this bloody city would have hired you. Look at the pair of you!' Anna's laugh is shrill and humourless.

Sarah reaches out and squeezes Nell's hand. Anna begins her striding again, staring at the bare walls, going over to the kitchen and examining the still-draining pots and pans on the draining board.

'And to think I set Moussa up in here,' Anna says, turning to Sarah. 'I let that man move into this place because you took a shine to him — now you repay me by running away with him?'

Sarah stands up from the bed and faces Anna, her head barely coming to the older woman's shoulders.

'And I thank you, but both Moussa and me never let you down. We've earned every farthing you paid us and now it's time to leave. Look around you, your place is finished. The soldiers are kept in the barracks at night, most of the businessmen are staying out of the city. There's not enough men left to keep the lights on, Anna.'

Anna laughs out loud again, a forced laugh.

'So, little Miss High and Mighty is telling me that the Monto is finished. The Monto, in existence for twice as long as she has been on this earth. The Monto, where royalty came to dip their knobs? But listen, I've seen worse than this. Don't forget — three years ago during Jim Larkin's big lockdown, we nearly went out of business. But we pulled through in the end.'

Sarah reaches out and takes Anna's hand.

'This is different, Anna, and you know it. How many more rebels are going to be executed? It could be going on for weeks, and each time the streets will be filled with rioters and the last thing on people's minds will be a visit to the Monto.'

Anna finally stops her pacing and flops down onto the bed. Her head drops to her chest and she looks old and beaten all of a sudden.

'You have to get out of Montgomery Street yourself, Anna. Sell it. Buy a new house out in Kingstown and retire. Something evil is happening here. You weren't there in poor Connie's house.'

Anna looks up at her tiny face.

'My girls, all grown up. Maybe you're right, maybe I should get out.

But what can I do, an old bag like me? No. I'll stay here in the Monto and fight on, it's all I know.'

The sound of the back gate slamming shut makes the three women jump. They hear footsteps coming up the yard, approaching the stables. The door bursts open but it is only Christopher and Moussa standing in the doorway.

Sarah's hands fly to her face and she tries to suppress a laugh. Moussa, self-conscious with his new appearance, throws his hands up into the air.

'It is what I had to do, Sarah, but it will grow again,' he says.

'You look like one of those big farmers from Cork. Just up to do business in Smithfield Market and wearing their Sunday best. What do you think, Sarah?' Nell then turns her gaze on Christopher. 'And you all fresh and clean.'

The two men stand, like children.

'Did you find out anything?' Nell asks.

'Moussa did most of the finding out. Now we know what the man is up to. We're not altogether sure why, but we have a good idea.'

Anna stands up, brushing down her dress.

'Is the world going mad? Why did you cut all your hair off, Moussa? And why are you looking so prim and proper, young man?'

'It's a long story, Mrs. Macken,' Christopher says.

'I don't want to hear any long stories, they bore me,' Anne says, standing tall. 'And I don't give you my blessing. I don't believe in doing that unless I'm certain, and I can't find it in me for now. But as for you, Moussa, I will pay you all that I owe you and you, Sarah — it's the least I can do.'

She turns to Nell.

'Nell, you've been more like a daughter to me. I will see you right, don't you worry.'

'Mrs. Macken, we think we know who is responsible for Connie's death,' Christopher blurts out.

'Connie knew the risks she was taking. It's not natural to practise such things on a man. It was bound to happen someday,' Anna says.

'But with all due respect, Mrs. Macken, you don't understand. It's the same man who's killed all those other girls, and he's kidnapped my friend and I have to find out why and if he's still alive.'

Anna holds up her hand to stop him talking.

'Poor Connie, may God be good to her. But I could have told you what he was up to if you'd only asked me. It's about money, it always is in the end.'

'It has to be more than that, Anna,' Christopher says.

'Don't complicate things. When you strip all the nonsense away it will be about money, believe me.'

Moussa puts his arm protectively around Sarah. 'You may be right, Mrs. Macken. But I agree with Christopher. I do not think that it is all about money.'

Anna shrugs. 'If that's true, he is all the more dangerous. You say you know where to find this man?'

'There's a rumour he's been using the tunnels,' Christopher says.

'The tunnels, you say?'

'Yes.'

'There's a story that the Crown Prince used the tunnels in order to dip his royal wick,' Anna laughs, 'but it's been a long time since I've heard mention of them. Some reach right down as far as the docks, they say. But they haven't been used in years. Nothing but rats down there.'

Nell puts her head in her hands. 'Those poor girls!'

Christopher looks around again at the stripped-down room. A beautiful mahogany seaman's chest lies open near the bed which is now visible as the curtain dividing it from the rest of the room has been removed. It has the deep sheen of something that has been treasured for years and an elaborate 'M' is inlaid into the side.

'Nell, he's murdered his last girl, I give you my word,' Christopher says.

'Are you really going down there?' She takes hold of his arm.

'Yes, I have to.'

'We are going together,' Moussa says, slapping the revolver in his waistband.

'You're going nowhere without me,' Sarah says, her hands on her hips.

'But, my dearest, it is too dangerous,' Moussa pleads.

'Nor without me.' Nell stands beside her tiny friend.

Anna throws up her hands into the air.

'I think you're all mad. Wait until tomorrow and let the police take care of it.'

'Anna, do you really think the police will care a damn? He's killed a few whores, so what?' Christopher says.

'But you can tell them about your friend, the Englishman.'

'Who's going to believe a deserter? They might even arrest me for his murder. Byatt could be still alive and tied up somewhere down in those tunnels.'

'Or he might be dead,' Anna says.

'If he is, I want to see his body,' Christopher says.

Anna sighs.

'Men, look where you've led us. Alright, Christopher, and you too, Moussa, you go on this fool's errand if you want to prove something to yourselves. But leave the girls behind and that's final.'

Sarah rushes to Moussa's side, clings to his arm and begins to cry. The big Algerian puts his arm around her shoulders.

'She is right, dearest, where we are going is dangerous and is not a place for women. What if you were injured, how would I forgive myself?'

Anna walks over, puts her arm around Sarah and leads her gently away from her lover.

'You two be on your way. I'll look after the girls until you come back,' she says.

CHAPTER 31

Moussa rolls his head around in a circle, the sound of clicking bones filling the empty silence. Christopher stares at the door the girls have just disappeared through, doubts already beginning to creep into his mind about his course of action. What had seemed a straight-forward plan now seems like the outpouring of a teenager and he thinks again on Anna's advice about the police. Moussa takes out the revolver, flicks open the barrel and checks that each chamber is loaded. His demeanour has changed. The constant smile has gone and now he is all business.

'We'd better make a move before the girls decide to revolt,' Christopher says without conviction.

'Yes,' Moussa replies and puts the revolver down the waistband of his trousers.

'I think I know where we can find out more about the tunnels,' Christopher says, making for the door.

'Where might that be?'

'Phil Shanahan's pub. If he doesn't know how to get down there, some of his customers might. He might even give me the loan of a revolver. Two is better than one.'

Moussa reaches out and puts a hand on his shoulder.

'Stop, Christopher. We do not need him. It is obvious how we get into them.'

'How?'

'Think about it. Connie's house. All the doors were locked from the inside, all the windows bolted,' Moussa says.

Christopher realises that he is right and it makes him feel even more inadequate. He nods in agreement and leaves without waiting for Moussa to follow. Outside the crowds are still thin, small groups of mostly men standing around, heads bent, talking. The few women around are mainly housewives dipping in and out of shops as if expecting a shortage. The city was in a state of high excitement after the first executions, but it had mainly burned out by the evening. Now with the second, the mood has become worse. How many more men would be executed? He wished he had Byatt beside him now, for his level-headedness and his experience.

'Are you sure you want to go ahead with this, Christopher?' Moussa says when he catches up to him.

'Of course. We are agreed, aren't we?'

'I have been thinking, Christopher. Perhaps it would be better if we let the police take care of it. I am sure the girls would be happier with that. It is less dangerous.'

'It's too late to turn back.'

By now they are halfway to Faithful Place. Light is leaving the sky and the dark silhouettes of the surroundings buildings seem to chip away at Christopher's conviction. Destitute families stand huddled in the doorways of their tenements taking some comfort in the gas lamps that have just been lit. There are no children playing on the streets and the few prostitutes who are out walking the streets all wear the same look of indifference. A horse and cart rumbles past, the shrunken man on the seat whipping the horse harder to get them home and off the streets.

The nearer they get to Connie's house the harder it becomes for Christopher. The very idea of going back into that house of death and on down into the underworld of Dublin in search of Byatt scares him. Even when he had faced possible death on the battlefields of Belgium, it had been with a naïve optimism. When he was determined to return to Ireland with the risk of facing a firing squad, he had still never been afraid, knowing that it had been his decision alone. But now, he realises, he has more to lose. It is not just about himself anymore, it is also about Nell.

Walking even more slowly now, they turn into the squalid reality of Faithful Place. It has only been a few hours since Chris left there, but the horror of the discovery of Connie's body comes back to him. An old woman stands in a doorway at the top of some steps, sweeping dust out into the streets, not minding or caring where it ends up. Moussa's plan of leaving Ireland and everything that has been happening is beginning to take hold.

Just when he is about to call a halt to their mission, he spots Byatt limping away further down the street. He shouts out his name and runs after him. The man turns but limps faster and rounds a corner. As Christopher sprints after him he almost stumbles upon the man who is standing his ground, both fists up and ready to fight with his pursuer. In reality the man looks nothing like Byatt and Christopher mumbles an apology before turning back towards Connie's house.

Moussa is outside the door, smoking one of his cigarettes.

'I thought you had gained some sense and were running back to Nell,' he says and hands the cigarette to Christopher who turns it down.

'I admit I was just about to. I saw that man and mistook him for my friend — it wasn't. But it reminded me of why I'm here.'

'And why is that?'

'Because Byatt treated me like a person and not just a nameless soldier. He's a decent man and time is not on his side. I'm certain that he would do the same for me.'

'So be it, Christopher,' Moussa says and throws the stub of the cigarette onto the ground.

CHAPTER 32

Anna Macken leads the two girls in a sad procession across the yard, back through the main house and up to her private quarters. She takes out a key which hangs from a sturdy necklace around her neck and opens the door to her private domain. The room, rarely visited by anyone except her personal maid, is on the first floor and affords Anna a view of the comings and goings of her clientele. From here she can count the number of visitors and relay a message down to Moussa to diplomatically turn people away. Sometimes private horse-drawn cabs pull up, disgorging special guests: politicians, high-ranking policemen, businessmen or even army officers, usually accompanied with a bodyguard, and these Anna sees to herself, escorting them directly into the sitting room at the rear.

The room is wide, the width of the building and, like in the rooms downstairs, the ceiling is quite high. Anna must have been smoking a lot that morning as there is still a strong smell of cigarette smoke. The two large windows which overlook Montgomery Street give a view over the rooftops of most of the city. To the left are the Dublin mountains, the dark and moody line of hills almost indistinct in the growing darkness. Straight ahead Nell can see the figure of Admiral Nelson, standing astride the column in the middle of Sackville Street. When she has taken in the panorama of the city, she turns back to look at the room. Not for the first time, she thinks that for such a rich woman as Anna, it is very plain. The only sign of opulence is a faded chaise longue that has seen better days and a dressing table cluttered with tiny bottles and phials. Along one wall there is a line of mismatched wardrobes and along another, a large chest of drawers cluttered with photographs beside which is a bookcase, which is odd, as Nell has never seen Anna reading a book. A Japanese paper screen hides Anna's bed in one corner.

Anna waves them onto the chaise longue while she takes a seat beside a bureau, her workspace which is covered by sheaves of paper and a large open ledger. She takes up a bell and her young maid, Jenny, comes into the room, a nervous look on her face when she sees the two girls sitting as if waiting to be scolded.

'Bring us some tea, Jenny, like a good girl, and maybe some biscuits,' Anne says.

When the door closes over, she looks from Sarah to Nell.

'Well, this is a queer to-do,' she says.

'I'm sorry if I've let you down, Anna,' Nell replies.

'You don't surprise me, Nell. You were always mull-headed,' Anna says, but smiles, then turns her gaze on the other girl, 'but you, Sarah, you *have* surprised me.'

Sarah bows her head and refuses to look at Anna in the eye.

'But I blame Moussa for your actions — so, Sarah, I hold you no ill will.'

'Thank you, Anna,' Sarah says quietly.

Anna falls silent, eyes downcast, lost in thought.

286

Some minutes later, Jenny comes in and puts a tray down on the low table in front of the chaise longue. As well as the teapot, cups and a plate of biscuits, there is a glass of clear liquid which she gives to Anna before leaving and closing the door after her. Nell can smell the gin from where she is sitting and waits for the lecture. But Anna is taking her time and while Sarah pours their tea, she sips her gin and stares out of the window, flicking her fingernail off her glass to the ticking of the wall clock. She stops suddenly, stands up and faces the two girls.

'I've made a decision,' she announces.

She takes a packet of cigarettes from the bureau and takes one out, lighting it. She begins to pace up and down the room as if forming her thoughts. With her back to the girls, she stares out of the window.

'Sarah, I'll deal with you first. You believe you have found a good man in Moussa. So be it. I will pay both of you what I owe you and a small extra. I wish you both well and I release you from your duties. But, for what it's worth, you should remember that Moussa is the first man who has ever paid any attention to you. I'm not sure that that's a good enough reason for you to follow him overseas, but so be it.'

'Thank you, Anna,' Sarah says.

'But what do I know? I'm still an old maid,' Anna says, turning and smiling down at her.

She walks over to the bureau and takes out a metal cash box. The key for the box is on the same necklace as her door key. The contents of the box are hidden from the girls as she sits with her back to them and they exchange a knowing smile. Nell can hear Anna murmuring to herself as she calculates how much she owes Sarah and Moussa. She counts as puts some notes to one side. When she turns, she has the notes folded in her hand. She hands them to Sarah who slips them in the pocket of her dress.

'I think you'll find I've been more than generous, but you've been a good worker. You've never let me down or shirked any duties I've given you and you've always had a smile on your face. Now leave us, I need to talk to Nell, alone.'

Sarah, glad to be out of the room, jumps up off the chaise longue and leaves.

Anna stubs out her cigarette and takes her seat beside Nell. She stares at the young woman, then reaches out and brushes a stray hair that has escaped from under Nell's hairband. Nell draws back slightly, embarrassed.

'Now, why would you mind me touching your hair, Nell? Was it not me who fed you, washed you and looked after you, put a roof over your head, let you lead your life the way you wanted to?'

'I'm sorry, Anna, I'm just a bit nervous after everything that's happened. I didn't mean to be ungrateful.'

'Not to worry, I know the answer anyway, Nell. The reason you're pulling away from me is that you're being drawn towards somebody else. It happens all the time. Children will drift free from their parents, it's only natural.' Anna reaches out and tries to take hold of Nell's hand.

'But you're not my mother, Anna, are you?' Nell says and rises from the chair, feeling uncomfortable at the older woman's unfamiliar tenderness.

'That's where you're wrong, Nell,' Anna says.

'Do you mean that you're like a mother to me and I should be glad of you? If so, sure wasn't I always here for you? I've brought enough money into this —'

'*Stop it, Nell!*' says Anna, raising her hand. 'What I mean is that I'm your natural mother. I'm the woman who carried you around inside of me for nine months.'

Nell puts her hands up to her ears and shakes her head. She hurries towards the door, needing to get away from Anna who she thinks has lost her mind. But before she reaches the door, Anna grips her arm and spins her around.

'And as for you working here, anybody could have done what you did, and done it better. You always had a quick tongue in your head and you drove more customers away from here than you brought in. Why do you think I put up with it, Nell? And why do you think I never let you join the girls?'

Anna puts her hands on Nell's shoulders but Nell pushes her away.

'You're just a sad old woman. I know why you're doing this, Anna. You don't want me to go away with Christopher. You just want me to stay here for the rest of my life. To look after you.'

Anna lets out a sharp laugh.

'Not bloody likely, young lady. I'll hire a nurse to do that. No doubt you'll convince some priest to marry you and expect to live happily ever after somewhere in Africa where you can laze in the sun all day and cuddle up to your soldier all night. Is that what you think?'

'You mean you won't try and stop me going off with Christopher?'

'Sit down, Nell. Just hear me out and I'll tell you everything. Maybe then you'll understand. *Please.*'

Nell's head is spinning. Everything is happening too fast and she is confused. She flops down onto the chaise longue and huddles into its corner.

Anna stands in front of her, a frail version of the woman she has looked up to for as long as she can remember. She looks at her more closely, trying to see if she is telling the truth, looking for some resemblance to herself, but seeing none.

Anna sits down beside her again.

'I did take you out of the Magdalen Laundry, that part is true. But it was me who put you there in the first place. They'd promised me that you'd be looked after. You were such a tiny thing. But I couldn't keep you. I'd bought this place with money my parents gave me to leave Kingstown. They were ashamed of me, you see, and ashamed of your father.'

'What was wrong with my father — was he poor?'

'Money wasn't the problem, Nell … he was … a foreigner.'

'A foreigner? From where?'

'North Africa.'

'Like Moussa?'

'Yes, like Moussa. But Morocco.'

'What became of him?'

'He did what most young men do at the first sign of trouble, ran back home, scared of being tied down for the rest of his life. And then you came along. I couldn't keep you, that was out of the question. But I was able to buy somewhere cheap in the Monto, near the laundry, and I hardened up and started my business. First as a gentleman's lodgings, then, well, you know the rest. Over the years I found out that those nuns were just using children like you as slave labour, and I made up my mind to get you out of there. It took years, but I did it. Now you know everything.'

Nell paces the room trying to pick holes in the story, but it all seems to fall into place: why Anna never put pressure on her to work on the 1st floor, gave her own room. Maybe, in the back of her mind, she has felt it all along. Maybe it even explains why Anna went to such lengths to ensure Moussa would stay around — he must have reminded her of her lost love.

Anna lights up another cigarette. The air in the room is blue with her cigarette smoke and Nell is beginning to feel suffocated. She turns to Anna, struggling to come to terms with what she has said.

'Why tell all this now? Do you imagine it will keep me here?'

Anna shakes her head. 'You don't see, do you, Nell? Someday you're going to want to have a family of your own. You'll have to tell him then about your background – your father. He might react badly.'

'That's a terrible to thing to say!'

'Nell, you don't know that for sure but you know now why I will always take care of you. But you can't put your trust in this Algeria notion.'

'On the contrary! It sounds to me that's exactly where I should go! To where my father came from!'

'Grow up, Nell! This is the Monto, it's not a real place. You can't trust anybody. Everyone's just struggling for survival. Listen to me. Phil Shanahan isn't a barman, is he? He's a gunman. Moussa wasn't stranded here, he jumped ship. He hadn't a penny to his name and no doubt he's going to go through Sarah's money. And your friend, Connie — how do you think Connie bought her house and has a maid — what did you think she really got up to around there? And I can guarantee you that there's more to your young man than meets the eye.'

'*What if you're wrong, this time?*' Nell hisses. 'What if he's decent man who came back home to do what he thought was the right thing?'

'It'd be a first, Nell.'

'At least Sarah is just Sarah.'

'She is, more's the pity. How long do you think Moussa will be around after the money runs out? But love is blind and she's made her own mind up. My concern is you, not her.' Anna takes her hands, squeezing them. '*Please believe me.*'

CHAPTER 33

T hey had closed over the door to Connie's house earlier, but it is only on a flimsy latch. Without any difficulty Moussa puts his shoulder to it and after one or two shoves the latch gives under the pressure. Christopher enters the dark hallway and takes up the lamp they had left on a table near the front door. He adjusts the wick until it is a steady glow. The sound of the forceful entry brings some people out onto the street and they shuffle around Moussa who is standing, waiting outside. But when Christopher returns to the doorway with the lamp in his hand and stares out at them, they disperse back to their own homes. He holds the lamp over his head, beckons Moussa inside and closes the door after him.

'Where do we start?' Moussa whispers.

'I noticed a coal chute on the street outside so there must be a basement. I'll try the back of the house and work my way towards the front — you search around here.'

He makes his way down the hallway and on into the dining room. A large oak table set for a meal takes up almost half of the floor space. The light from the lamp picks out the plates and cutlery for a meal that will never happen. He continues on through the dining room and into a tiny kitchen, holding the lamp aloft to illuminate every corner. Beside the soot-blackened range there is a wooden door, but when Christopher pulls it open it is just a tiny scullery. Across from the kitchen he comes across another likely room, a storage room, which Connie seems to have used as a place to keep some older furniture. He moves all of the heavier pieces away from the wall but still there is no access to the basement. As a last resort he checks the small yard at the rear of the house but after finding no sign of a doorway returns to the house, wondering if the coal chute he had seen earlier belonged to Connie's neighbours.

Disheartened, he makes his way back through the house to join Moussa who is waiting beside the front door. As he is making his way up the hallway, he notices what could be a small doorway in the shadows. It is half-hidden behind a heavy mahogany console table placed in the recess under the stairs. He lowers the lamp to get a better look and can make out that the door is slightly ajar. Janus must have escaped through it but forgotten to shut it completely after him.

He asks for Moussa's help and they slide the table out from the recess. Moussa takes out his revolver and stands back as Christopher pulls open the door. With the help of the lamp, he can make out a steep stairway, almost a ladder, disappearing down into the basement. A cold draft comes up out of the darkness, bringing with it a smell of damp and mould.

'I'll go down first with the lamp, you cover me from up here,' Christopher says, and Moussa nods.

Holding the lamp over his head, Christopher makes his way carefully down the rough wooden steps. When he reaches the stone floor of the basement, he turns a full circle, throwing the light into every corner. Connie must never have thrown anything away. Most of the floor is taken up with discarded pieces of broken furniture, some covered with old sheets. He almost trips over an old bicycle lying on its side. When he is satisfied that the basement is empty, he whispers up to Moussa to follow him down. The wooden stairs shake under the Algerian's weight and he has to stop once when one of the treads makes a loud, cracking noise.

'I thought that it was going to collapse,' Moussa says when he stands beside Christopher.

'Can you feel that draught?' Christopher asks, turning his face in its direction.

'What a stink! It smells of the sea and dead fish,' Moussa says.

'That makes sense — the tunnels are supposed to run down to the river.'

The draught feels chilly on his face and he follows it across the basement to a mound of coal piled up against the wall. To one side of the coal, in the furthest and darkest corner, a curtain made from sackcloth hangs down. From time to time, it billows out slightly and the smell increases in intensity. Christopher points to the curtain and Moussa takes out the revolver and aims it at the curtain as Christopher jerks it back.

Behind the curtain they find what they have been looking for, a rectangle of blackness that leads them into the forgotten catacombs of Dublin. Christopher holds the lamp out in front of him and stoops down through the doorway and into some sort of tunnel. He holds the lamp to his left and then to his right but the light from it is too weak to probe the darkness and the tunnel disappears in either direction. The arched roof overhead is made from brick and at its highest point allows him to stand up easily enough, but Moussa, who follows him into the tunnel, has to stoop slightly.

'I think we are under the street now,' Moussa whispers.

'Look at the floor of the tunnel — it seems to be rising slightly

294

upwards to the right. So, if we go in the opposite direction, downwards, we should eventually come to the docks. The question is, which way?' Christopher says, and without waiting for a reply turns to his left.

As they make their way down the tunnel, skittering noise catches his attention. Just at the limit of the circle of light from the lamp, small, furry shapes scamper away into the darkness. Rats. He can feel Moussa tense up beside him and he puts his hand on his arm to steady him. The rats hold no fear for Christopher as he lived with them for nearly two years in the trenches, bigger ones, well fed on the flesh of fallen soldiers. He lowers the wick on the lamp until it is just a weak glow and indicates to Moussa that they should now be as quiet as possible.

They feel their way along the tunnel, their fingers touching the dank walls for guidance. Now and then, inset into the walls, they can make out the darker shapes of doorways leading off to other basements. Old pieces of furniture and general rubbish lie strewn around these doorways and force them into the middle of the tunnel. It becomes slightly wider the further they progress and on one side there is now a walkway of flagstones under which they can hear the sound of flowing water.

'It's a culvert, probably covering a stream leading down to the Liffey,' Christopher whispers.

The tunnel begins to veer to the right and as they make their way tentatively around the curve Christopher can make out a light of some sort in the distance. He puts his hand out to stop Moussa and points, then lowers the wick of the lamp all the way until it is extinguished. Immediately they are plunged into total darkness with only the pinprick of light in the distance to guide them on. Without the lamp to keep them at bay the rats have become braver and Christopher can feel them scampering over his feet. The smell is now almost overpowering and the overall effect is one of disorientation.

'Do you think that it is him?' Moussa whispers out of the darkness.

'It could be. We have to move more carefully. I'll put my hand on the wall to guide me — you can hold on to my jacket, but keep that revolver ready.'

As they make their way slowly towards the light, it grows in definition. Now Christopher can make out that it is a lantern with a single candle flickering inside. It rests on top of a simple wooden table that seems to float in the darkness. It is impossible to see much beyond the table as the flame from the candle is too weak to carry very far down the tunnel. As they draw nearer, he can make out the darker shadow of a door in the wall. He stops and whispers to Moussa.

'You stay here and cover me, I'll try to get nearer — there's something on the table.'

Pressing himself up against the wall he approaches almost to the edge of the pool of light cast by the candle. The top of the table is in plain view now and lying diagonally across it he can make out the shape of Byatt's distinctive walking stick. The sound of scraping comes from the doorway and he pulls further back away from the light. A man emerges through the doorway and into the candlelight, pulls out a stool from under the table and sits down. He picks up the walking stick from the table and holds it out in front of him, studying it. It has to be Janus.

Christopher realises that he has been holding his breath and lets it out in one long silent stream. He backs away further up the tunnel as quietly as possible to locate Moussa. When he arrives at where he had reckoned his friend would be, he whispers his name. A finger tips him lightly on the face and he jumps.

'It's him, Moussa, it has to be. He has Byatt's walking stick,' he whispers.

'Then, let us go and capture the fiend,' Moussa whispers back.

'Very well, but we have to be careful he doesn't get away through the doorway behind him. Are you ready with the revolver or do you want me to take it?'

'No, I could even hit him from here.'

Moussa tiptoes down the tunnel towards the table with Christopher close behind. The man seems to be engrossed in the walking stick, examining the ivory handle. They are only a short distance away when he twists the handle and extracts a long, steel sword.

Moussa rushes the last few metres forward and stands in front of the table, the gun extended in front of him, the hammer cocked back. Christopher, close behind, is relieved that Moussa seems to know enough about firearms to be prepared.

'Greetings, Moussa,' Mordaunt says, unfazed by the revolver which is inches from his head.

Christopher's jubilation turns to confusion as Moussa turns the revolver towards him, shrugging his shoulders apologetically.

Mordaunt stands up from the table and looks down the blade of the sword at Chris.

'I'd wager that this is the finest Toledo steel,' he says, and swishes it several times through the air.

'Well done, Moussa, you'll be an even richer man now,' he says.

He walks around the table, the sword held in front of him, and waves the tip inches away from Christopher's eyes.

'So, you are Major Byatt's secret weapon. You've caused me a lot of trouble and money.'

'Where is Byatt?' Christopher demands.

'That's his grave, over there,' he answers, pointing the sword towards a patch of fresh earth.

Enraged, Christopher makes a lunge at Byatt's killer. But Mordaunt is faster, takes a step backwards and halts him in his tracks with the point of the sword. Smiling, he traces it up from his stomach until it is at his shoulder, then, with deliberate slowness, sinks the tip into the shoulder, forcing it through the flesh and the muscle and on past the bone, ignoring the screams that reverberate around the tunnel.

CHAPTER 34

Blood pours from the wound in Christopher's shoulder through his fingers and drips onto the floor of the tunnel. After the initial shock of the injury the pain is reduced to a dull throb. Moussa is standing to one side of the table, the revolver held loosely in his hand, his eyes looking everywhere except in Christopher's direction.

Christopher looks up at his attacker who is sitting at the table and is shuffling through his wallet, examining his identity papers.

The only hope is Moussa, who had looked away when the blade had sunk in.

'*Why, Moussa?*' he asks desperately, trying to get the Algerian to look at him.

Moussa avoids his eyes and shrugs.

'Anna is a very clever woman, my friend,' he answers. 'She told us that at the end of it all, it is really about money. And she was right.'

'You see, unlike you, Moussa is a survivor,' says Mordaunt. 'True survivors thrive on adversity. You can put them into the hottest desert or the coldest of plains and they will claw sustenance from whatever source.'

'What about Sarah, Moussa, was that all a lie?'

Moussa shuffles his feet and bends his head, but still refuses to look at him.

'Perhaps I was wrong, Mr. Flinter!' Mordaunt jeers. 'Perhaps there is a bit of the survivor hiding in you somewhere.'

'I've been to war, everybody wants to survive.'

Mordaunt makes a steeple of his fingers. He looks like a teacher trying to communicate with a slow pupil.

'Obviously everybody wants to survive, that's a given, but it is the degree to which they go about it that separates some from the rest. How desperate are they? What depths will they plunge to?'

'Is that true, Moussa? You've betrayed me for more money — what will Sarah think of that?'

'She will never know, my friend, for who will tell her?'

Mordaunt slams his hand against the desk and the noise reverberates down the tunnel.

'Enough of this! Moussa is not for turning. You and Byatt have already inconvenienced me and cost me a lot of money. I could still be trading my secrets, but now, unfortunately, it is all at an end, just as your life is. Moussa, hand me the revolver.' He holds out his hand.

Moussa hesitates, finally looks at Christopher, his eyes a picture of sadness. He hands the revolver over to Mordaunt, who examines it.

'Take it back, Moussa!' Christopher says. 'Can't you see he's got to get rid of you too? He's not going to take a chance and leave either of us alive!'

'Bravo, Mr. Flinter, we should have met earlier!' Mordaunt says, turns, and trains the revolver on Moussa.

A single shot rings out, sounding like an explosion in the confines of the tunnel. The bullet hits Moussa over his left eye, carries on through his head, and erupts out of the back of his skull taking with it mass of bone, flesh and gore. For a split second there is a surprised look on his face. With comic slowness he drops down to his knees, tilts forward and ends up face down in the dirt.

'You should have kept your advice to yourself, Christopher — he could have had an extra few days. It's a pity.'

'*You bastard!*'

'If only I had been,' Mordaunt says, looking down at Moussa's lifeless body, 'but I had parents, I can assure you.'

CHAPTER 35

An hour before

Sarah and Moussa's door is open and Sarah is singing in her high-pitched childlike voice. When Nell steps inside, her friend is too busy to notice her. She has unpacked one of the tea chests and the contents are laid out across the floor. For a split second Nell is flooded with relief: Sarah has changed her mind. But then she sees that her friend is just refolding clothes, mainly Moussa's, and putting them back into the chest properly.

'You're definitely going?' Nell says.

Sarah, startled, puts a hand to her chest.

'Of course, that's what we agreed. You're coming too, aren't you, with Christopher?'

Nell takes a seat at the table and begins to fidget with her hair.

'I had a talk with Anna …'

Sarah continues to fold a dress that Nell recognises, her Sunday best.

'And what did Anna have to say? Did she say we're mad?'

'The usual. To be careful with Christopher, that he might not be all he says he is.'

'And you believed her?'

'It's a long story, Sarah. But you know how she is — protective.'

Sarah puts the dress carefully into the box, puts a layer of newspaper over it and takes a seat at the table. She reaches out and takes Nell's hand in hers.

'She means well, Nell, but she thinks of the business above anything else. I hope she didn't put you off?'

'Not completely, but she made me think. What do I really know about Christopher?' Nell pauses. 'And what do you really know about Moussa?'

Sarah slaps the table with her hand, making Nell jump.

'I knew it! She just wanted to put Moussa down, behind my back! The old bag is going to —'

'Stop! It wasn't like that. She just warned me, she didn't say I couldn't go. But what if, and I know it's something you don't want to think about, what if you land in Algeria and find out that Moussa isn't all you've thought? What would you do?'

'I trust Moussa. And you should trust Christopher. If you don't trust people you'll be stuck here for the rest of your life. Do you want that? Rebels fighting in the city, war rations, not to mention what's going to happen after more rebels have been shot — there's sure to be rioting in the streets. And, mark my words, the Legion of Mary will have this place shut down.'

'Maybe you're right, Sarah, but it's one thing to be in trouble in your own country, but what happens if you're hundreds of miles away in a foreign country where you don't even understand the language?'

'Nothing's going to happen. Moussa's saved enough money, and with what Anna gave me we'll be alright. For years, according to Moussa.'

Nell puts her hand over Sarah's.

'Are you sure? Anna told me he doesn't earn that much, Sarah. How could he have saved? You've seen the amount of stuff he buys down the docks, the hashish, the wine and that weird food — that couldn't come cheap.'

Nell can see that she's getting through to her friend and feels guilty. She has dampened her mood and made her restless.

Sarah gets up from the table and disappears behind the hanging curtains at the end of the room. When she comes back, she is pulling Moussa's chest across the stone floor, bent over double with the effort. When she has it in the middle of the room, she points to it.

'This is everything else he owns in the world, Nell, and this is the key.' She holds up a tiny key. 'I'm going to open it now, before he comes back. If I can't find money in there, you and Anna are right, he's been fooling me. But if there is, before God, I will never speak to you again.'

Before Nell can stop her, Sarah already has the lid up and is rummaging through the contents of the chest. She is just about to tell her to stop when Sarah's expressions changes in rapid succession: triumph, hope, then puzzlement.

She looks over at Nell.

'I've found his savings, but there's so much of it.' She shakes her head, confused.

Nell joins her and looks down into the chest. In the base of it there is a tin ration box. The lid is off and stacked inside is a fortune in bank notes. Sarah picks up a bundle and pulls out one of the strange-looking notes.

'What is it?' Nell asks.

'It's a twenty-dollar American note,' Sarah says.

'Where would he get so much money?' Nell asks.

'I don't know, Nell. He's never talked about money to me. He said he had some saved, but nothing like this.'

'I don't like this, Sarah — there's something wrong. Why would he have lied to you?' Nell reaches over and picks up another of the bundles: English five-pound notes. She throws the bundle back into the chest as if it's contaminated.

'Maybe he wants to surprise me,' Sarah says with little conviction.

'That's rubbish, Sarah, and you know it. He has more money in here than Anna would pull into the business in a year. Where did he get it, and what did he do to get it?'

Sarah is on her knees, almost in tears, as she shakes her head in disbelief at the damning evidence in front of her.

'I don't know what's happening, Nell. I thought I knew everything about him. Was everything he said a lie? I feel such a fool.'

Nell rests her hand on her friend's head.

'Don't feel bad, Sarah — he's fooled everyone. You, me, Anna and Christopher … My God, we need to warn Christopher that there's something strange going on.'

Nell reaches down into the chest and pulls out a handful of notes.

'I'm going down to the tunnels after them,' she said, and stuffs the notes into her pocket.

'I'm going too,' Sarah says.

'Good. Bring a lamp, meet me outside Connie's house. I have to pay a visit to Phil Shanahan. And don't let me down.'

'I'll be there, I promise.'

CHAPTER 36

Nell barges through the door of Shanahan's and looks around for Phil. The only customers are a scattering of die-hard regulars sitting at the bar nursing their drinks. She marches up through the bar and, ignoring the shouts of the only barman, lifts the counter and goes straight through the door to Phil's private quarters. John McCormack's voice drifts up the hallway. The song is 'The Minstrel Boy', one of Phil's favourites and one he plays only when there are no soldiers around or when he is too drunk to care.

'*Phil, it's Nell!*' she shouts and walks into Phil's parlour without knocking.

Phil is slumped back in an armchair, looking the worst for wear. There is an open bottle of whiskey by his feet and he is staring up at the ceiling, his eyes wide and unblinking. She thinks that he might be dead. His normally clean-shaven face has a dark shadow of stubble and his shirt is open. She has never seen him without a tie or a waistcoat. His hair, usually swept to one side and slicked into place by copious amounts of pomade, sticks up in unruly clumps. His moustache, the ends always waxed and twisted upwards into fine points, droops down on either side of his mouth but she can see by the quivering hair that he is not dead.

'*Wake up, Phil! I need to talk to you!*' Nell shouts and slaps his face.

'Jaysus, Nell, go easy … why'd you do that?' Phil splutters awake.

Nell picks up the half-full whiskey bottle and rushes into the kitchen. The sink is full of dirty dishes and she pours the whiskey over them, shaking every last drop out. When she goes back inside Phil is still in the armchair, brushing his hair back with his fingers, then buttoning up his shirt.

'I came here to buy back the gun I sold you.'

'Oh you did, did yeh? What are you up to?'

'It's a long story. Just sell me the gun and be quick about it! Here!' she says, and throws the notes onto his lap.

'There's over fifty pounds here, Nell — where did you get it and what do you want with a gun anyway?'

'I just need that gun back, Phil. When I'm finished I'll return it to you.'

'Unused?'

'Are you goin' to give me the gun or not? Here, give me back the money, I'll go down to the barracks and find someone who'll sell me one,' Nell says, holding out her hand.

'Don't be getting upset. I'll not give you any gun, Nell. You don't know how to use it. You'll probably blow your boyfriend's head off by mistake.'

'*Then give me the damn money back!*' Nell shouts at him.

'Hold your temper. I said I'm not giving you the gun, but I didn't say I wouldn't help you.'

'What do you mean?'

'If Anna finds out that I let you out of here with a loaded gun she'd have me shot. I'm goin' with you,' Phil says, and disappears into the kitchen. When he returns, he's carrying the gun wrapped up in a cloth. He unwraps the cloth and takes the gun out. He sticks it inside his belt, puts on his jacket and closes it over, smoothing it down.

'Come on,' he says, leading the way. 'Now tell me what's going on.'

Sarah is as good as her word and is waiting outside Connie's house, pacing up and down, her face creased with worry. She has a brass carriage lamp in her hand already lit and passers-by are giving her strange looks. She is surprised when she sees Phil.

'Hello, Mr Shanahan, I didn't realise you were comin',' she says.

'I didn't know either, Sarah. I believe you're having boyfriend trouble.'

Sarah lowers her head and nods. Phil tries the front door and it's unlocked. Taking out the gun, he motions the two girls to stay outside, then enters himself. The lamp in the hallway is turned down low but over his shoulder Nell can make out that the door under the stairs is ajar.

'Where's Connie?' Phil turns and whispers to her.

Nell points upstairs and Phil blesses himself and murmurs a prayer. She joins him in the hallway but avoids looking towards the stairs. Already she is beginning to regret being responsible for the discovery of the money in Moussa's chest.

Sarah joins them, closing over the front door behind her. The noise from the street outside is shut out and they are standing in that strange silence of a house where death has paid a visit. The only sound is coming from Connie's most prized possession, the grandfather clock in the parlour. The ticking noise is slowing down and erratic. Nell realises that the last person to wind the clock must have been Connie as she never let anyone else near it. She even remembers the day it was delivered. It arrived on the back of a horse and cart and the anxious look on Connie's face as the two men manoeuvred it into the house made her laugh. The memories of her friend, now lying up on her bed, dead, brings back her determination.

'Are you sure you want to go through with this?' Phil whispers.

In the orange glow of the lamp Nell realises that even he is scared.

'I want to get to the bottom of this, Phil, one way or the other,' she says, and reaches out for Sarah's hand, 'for Connie's sake.'

'So be it,' Phil says.

He takes the lamp from Sarah, pushes the revolver into his belt and leads the way down the basement stairs cautiously, stopping at the bottom. With the help of the light from Sarah's lantern, he spots the opening into the tunnel with the curtain pulled away from it. He waits for the two girls to join him.

'From now on, keep as quiet as you can,' he whispers, pointing to the entrance.

Inside the pitch-black tunnel Nell and Sarah reach for each other's hands and follow close behind Phil, who holds the carriage lamp over his head. The deeper they go into the tunnel the more fetid the air becomes. Occasionally Phil stops and lowers the lamp to frighten away the rats who are becoming ever more curious about the visitors to their world. Phil stops and holds up his arm.

'Quiet, can you hear that?' he whispers to Nell.

Nell leans forward and closes her eyes. To her left she can hear running water but nothing else. Then, very faintly she hears a voice crying out, then nothing.

'That sounded like Christopher,' she whispers to Phil, and grabs his arm.

'It could be just a stray shout coming from one of the buildings overhead,' Phil whispers.

The sound of a shot echoes down the tunnel, reverberating over and over as it travels past and around them.

Sarah cries out: '*Moussa!*'

Nell clamps her hand over her friend's mouth.

'*Shhhh, it could be anybody,*' she hisses.

As the echoes die away Phil takes out his revolver and proceeds down the tunnel. They come around a curve and can hear the sound of voices in the distance. Phil walks faster, their footsteps covered by whoever is talking. Nell's heart jumps when she recognises the sound of Christopher's voice. They approach another curve. Phil, who is ahead of them, holds up his hand to halt and extinguishes the carriage lamp. They proceed in the darkness in complete silence until they are around the curve.

Ten yards away a disembodied scene, reminiscent of a theatre stage, is illuminated by a single candle and floats in the darkness. A man who Nell doesn't recognise stands looking down at Christopher who is slumped against the wall, almost invisible in the gloom. Beside the table on which the lantern rests, the motionless body of Moussa lies, face down.

CHAPTER 37

'By the way, I'd like to introduce myself. My name is Mordaunt, Levon Mordaunt. I think it only right that you know your executioner's name.'

'What kind of a monster can kill so many people?'

Mordaunt trains the gun onto Christopher again, his hand unwavering.

'So preacheth the deserter just back from the slaughterhouse that is Europe,' he says, pulling back the hammer of the revolver.

'But why did you have to kill those women — and the boy — what had they got to do with your plans?'

Mordaunt takes out his watch and flicks it open, then snaps it shut again.

'We have time. Firstly, the boy was unfortunate. He might have overheard too much. I couldn't take any chances. As for the women? You wouldn't understand. Let's just say they saw me at my most vulnerable and I couldn't let them live.'

Christopher's arm is throbbing and he is beginning to feel faint but still Mordaunt hasn't pulled the trigger and he needs to keep him talking if he has any hope of survival.

'I've seen men doing some terrible things to each other,' he says, 'but they had a reason. What you did —'

'*What I did?* Let me tell you about real survival. My father worked a miserable piece of land in Alaska that could barely sustain us. One autumn we were on the brink of starvation when a young family happened by. The husband was foolish for bringing them into danger. It was the wrong time of the year and he had brought the wrong kind of equipment. They were doomed. But my father had the courage to put them out of their misery so we could survive. They would have died anyway. You see, Christopher, all of this,' he points at Moussa's body and over towards Byatt's last resting place, 'means nothing to me.'

Mordaunt walks around the table in order to get nearer to Christopher. His arm extends, pointing the revolver at his head. Christopher closes his eyes, whispers a short prayer and readies himself for the inevitable. He hears the click of the hammer being drawn back and can picture the cylinder revolving. The final thoughts of regret flash through his mind, intermingling with each other — his parents, his brother Ned and lastly, Nell.

Nell sees the man's arm straighten and point and recognises the shape of a gun in his hand. As he continues talking an ominous click sounds and she realises that he is about to shoot Christopher.

Without thinking she snatches the gun from Phil. Holding it in her two hands she walks towards the man and points it. She can hear Phil hissing at her to stop, to give him the gun back, but she ignores him. She can see Christopher, eyes closed, waiting. She stops and pulls the hammer back, taking aim at the man's head and remembers what a young soldier had once told her: keep calm, aim, hold your breath, fire. She squeezes the trigger. The gun recoils and knocks her backwards and she just about manages to stay on her feet. Her eyes close from the explosion and flash of the shot and when she opens them the man lies sprawled on his back across Christopher's legs. She goes into shock when she sees that one side of his face has disappeared and a horrendous wound exposes his jaw bone and broken teeth.

When the echoes of the shot eventually die down it is like a signal and everything seems to happen at once. Phil takes the gun from her trembling hand and puts it back into his belt. Sarah runs over to Moussa's body and shakes it, as if trying to wake him up, even though it's evident from his wound that he will never wake up again. When she is relieved of the weight of the gun, Nell stumbles over to Christopher, half expecting to find him on the verge of death or, worse, dead. Bending down over him she sees that most of the blood on his jacket is from the man she has shot. He opens his eyes and smiles up at her.

'Good shot, now can you give me a hand?' he says, and tries to push Mordaunt's body off his legs.

'Who is he?' Nell asks, as she helps him roll the body away.

'He told me his name was Mordaunt, but as to who he is I don't know, Nell. I've never come across evil before, but I think we've all touched it tonight.'

Nell reaches out and tries to help him to his feet but he winces and lets out a loud groan. Fresh blood, she can now see, is pouring from a wound in his shoulder. Phil comes over and helps her to her feet, then kneels down beside Christopher and examines the wound.

'He'll live,' he said, 'but we'll have to strap it up nice and tight. Go over to Sarah, Nell, I think she might need you.'

Sarah is on her knees beside Moussa's body, cradling his bloody head in her lap, moaning. As Phil takes Christopher's jacket off to get a good look at his wound, Nell picks up the extinguished carriage lamp from the ground and lights it up from the candle in the lantern. She walks over to her friend and puts her hand on her shoulder. Sarah's dress is a bloody mess and her hands are stained red with Moussa's blood. Nell tries to get her to stand up but she shakes her away.

'Leave me be with him,' she says.

Phil has Christopher on his feet and is struggling with his weight on him. He manages to get him over to the chair. His shirt is open and reveals an ugly gash in his shoulder. The wound, with the exertion of getting to his feet, is pumping even more blood and Phil is wiping it away as best he can. Christopher's face has lost all of its colour and his eyelids are drooping.

'Here, let me,' Nell says, and gently pushes Phil away.

Christopher's eyes open and he smiles as Nell pulls up her dress and begins to rip apart her white slip into long strips. She bunches up one of the strips and holds it tightly against the wound, stemming the flow of blood. When she is satisfied that the bleeding has eased, she wraps a make-shift bandage around his shoulder and ties it off as best she can. Her hair has fallen down around her face and Christopher brushes it away.

'I promise I'll buy you a new dress,' he says, smiling.

'You can buy her whatever you want after we get out of here,' Phil says. 'You've lost a lot of blood. It's too late for these two, but at least we can save you. Can you walk?'

'I think so,' Christopher says. 'Here, help me to my feet.'

Together, Phil and Nell help him to his feet and he stands unsteadily between the two. Nell turns to her friend, still grieving over Moussa's body.

'Sarah, we have to get Christopher back to Anna's and get a doctor to look at him. We can go to the police and tell them what's happened after. They'll come and bring Moussa out.'

Sarah nods and gently lets Moussa's head back onto the ground. She straightens out his soiled jacket and brushes off some loose dirt with her hand, then lays his arms across his chest. Rising unsteadily, she takes the carriage lamp from Nell. With one last look at Moussa, she turns and makes her way back down the tunnel, lighting the way forward for the others.

CHAPTER 38

Sunday
7th May

The female voices that drag him out of sleep become louder and louder. As they ascend the stairs their muffled conversation rises steadily in volume. Now they are standing outside his door arguing in that genteel manner of women that he could never understand. One of the voices belongs to Mrs. Daly. She has been nursing him through his fever for days and has also assumed the role of shielding him from any callers. The other voice belongs to Nell, who is refusing to back down.

Back and forth they trade barbed niceties until he can stand it no longer and shouts out: '*It's all right, Mrs. Daly, she works at Dublin Castle!*'

The voices stop immediately and he can hear the slow tread of Mrs Daly as she goes back down the stairs, defeated.

Nell knocks on the door and steps inside before he can pull up the blankets to cover himself. The nightshirt he is wearing used to belong to Mrs. Daly's husband and has been repaired and patched beyond recognition. Nell looks at it and shakes her head, laughing. She walks over to the window and pulls the curtains back, allowing the light to pour into the room, then opens the window. The bells from St. Mary's

Pro-Cathedral ring out for early Mass and compete with the voice of the newspaper boy on the street outside shouting out the latest headlines.

'This room smells like a hospital,' she says as she walks around it, opening the door to the wardrobe and examining the contents.

'You can blame the doctor for that,' Christopher says. 'The bandage he wrapped around my shoulder was soaked in something.'

'Doctor?' Nell says. 'That wasn't a doctor, that was a vet. What kind of a doctor would pay a house visit to the Monto?'

'Are you serious?'

'Yes, I am.'

'I suppose I should've known when I saw the size of the syringe,' Christopher says, rubbing his hip.

'How do you feel?' Nell says and sits on the side of the bed.

'Still a bit weak, but I'll live.'

'He had to knock you out for a while — you were raving. I'd say it was probably a horse tranquiliser.' Nell takes his hand.

'Not too much bad language, I hope.'

'You were going on about somebody called Tommy Sherry. I left him at it — I couldn't bear to watch him stitch your shoulder up.'

'How's Sarah?'

'Confused and sad,' Nell says with disdain and drops his hand. 'You men have to destroy everything.'

Christopher pulls himself up into a sitting position.

'Moussa was fooled by an expert, Nell, don't be too hard on him. I think he really wanted to go away with Sarah. But I had to spoil it by trying to get to the bottom of Byatt's disappearance. Then he did the only thing he could think of: he handed me over to Janus. But near the end, in his own way, I think he regretted what he was doing and tried to warn me.'

Nell gets up from the bed and goes over to the window. The bells have stopped ringing and the newspaper boy is shouting out the headline: '*French soldiers fail in Verdun!*'

Christopher raises himself out of the bed gingerly, relying heavily on his left arm, and shuffles over to her.

'No more executions?' he says. 'That's hopeful, isn't it?'

'There was one more on Friday — McBride. But the rumour in Phil Shanahan's pub is that there'll be more,' Nell says sadly.

'What happened after the vet knocked me out?'

'Phil rang the number you gave him and told them where the bodies were, but he didn't give his name. They were all taken over to Dublin Castle. The British are using the castle yard as a make-shift morgue now.'

'What about Byatt?'

'Him too, they dug him up. The reason I'm here is to do with Byatt — Phil Shanahan's downstairs, he wants to talk to you — that woman wouldn't let him come up with me. So you'll have to talk outside the hotel.'

'He wants to see me?'

'He does. Why don't you splash some water over yourself and I'll help you get into your clothes?'

With fumbles and curses Christopher pulls the nightshirt over his head. His right shoulder is wrapped in a bandage but there is no trace of blood. He washes himself as best he can and Nell takes out a new shirt from the wardrobe and helps him into it, buttoning his collar and looping a tie around his neck. Mrs. Daly has cleaned and repaired the jacket of his only suit, the suit that Byatt had bought him. The slit where Mordaunt had stabbed him has been stitched and the bloodstains are hard to see. He checks his wallet and there are still a few pound notes left of the money Byatt had given him.

Nell straightens his tie and stands back to look at him.

'Not perfect, but it'll do,' she says, hands him his hat and leads him out of the room.

When they arrive downstairs, Phil Shanahan is sitting in the reception area under the suspicious gaze of Mrs. Daly. When the old woman sees Christopher, she blesses herself and comes around the desk. A long set of rosary beads hangs from her hands. She thrusts them into his pocket and goes back behind the desk.

'They were my husband's,' she says shyly, 'and they brought him great comfort.'

'Thank you very much, Mrs. Daly. And thank you for all you've done for me.' Christopher bows his head.

'Don't mention it, Detective Andrews, it's the least I could have done under the circumstances.'

Out of the corner of his eye Christopher is aware that Phil Shanahan is trying to suppress a smile and Nell has turned away and is studying a picture on the wall.

'I'd better be getting on now — I have to go with these people and make a report out,' Christopher says, and puts his hat on.

'Of course, I understand,' Mrs. Daly says.

Outside the hotel Phil Shanahan offers him a cigarette but he refuses. It feels too good to be out of his stuffy room and breathing in the fresh, morning air. All of the shops on Talbot Street are closed and the only sign of life are a few stragglers on their way up to the Pro-Cathedral to attend Mass. But the sun is out and he turns his face towards it to soak in its heat and banish the memory of the last few weeks. Phil flicks his unfinished cigarette into the gutter.

'They're burying your Mr. Byatt today,' he says to Christopher, then spits on the ground, 'or should I say getting rid of him. Apparently, he's an embarrassment to His Majesty's government.'

'How do you know?'

'One of our agents in the Castle, a typist,' Phil says and hands him an envelope. 'And she found this.'

'What's this?' Christopher says, opening the envelope.

'A copy of your pardon, already signed by Byatt. It was in his desk drawer. He was a British soldier, but a good man, and that's all I have to say on it.'

Christopher stares down at his name on the envelope and under that Byatt's confident signature, his eyes watering. He refolds the pardon and puts it back into the envelope.

'Now you know my real name.'

'It didn't take a genius to find out your real identity, Christopher. We were able to make inquiries about you. A Mr. Sherry was only too glad to tell us all about you.'

'Why didn't you say anything?'

'Luckily for you most of our leaders are locked up. So I used my own common sense. Now I'm glad I did.'

'Poor Byatt. All he ever did was his duty and his only reward is to be treated like a criminal.'

'Why so, lad?'

'Because he was in love with a man, and soldiers like that are not allowed to be heroes.'

Phil shook his head. 'Clever bastards, the British, taking him out at noon on Sunday when the streets are empty — everybody at Mass or at home preparing dinner.'

'Where are they taking him?'

'The British military cemetery up in Grangegorman.'

Christopher knows the cemetery. It is a featureless flat piece of land near the Phoenix Park located on the edge of Dublin. It is used mainly to bury the common British soldier and not an officer like

Byatt who died in the course of duty. He recalls his conversation with Byatt about Janus: the two-faced god, selling secrets to both sides. Somebody on the British side obviously wants Byatt out of the way and forgotten. There were also political reasons why they wouldn't want to give Byatt his due. Mordaunt had ostensibly been trying to pull America into the war — had the British been willing to allow him to operate even at the expense of all those slaughtered women? But he never would forget Byatt. How could he forget the man who was responsible for his freedom and his life?

He looks at his watch.

'I'm going to take a stroll up to the Dublin Castle — do you two want to come?'

'Not likely, they know my mug up there,' Phil says, 'and they're still trigger happy. I'm not sure you should go either.'

'I'll go with you,' Nell says. 'How could I resist a man who's taking me to a funeral? And besides, I wouldn't like you to faint. We can take a stroll up Dame Street, two lovers out for a walk on Sunday.'

Phil laughs loudly and Christopher feels his race reddening. It's the first time he has seen Nell without her night-time make-up and she looks younger, her face more open. She is wearing a mustard-coloured dress to her ankles and a short green jacket that comes to her waist. She takes his uninjured arm, puts it around her waist and walks him up and down the pavement in front of Phil, the skirt swishing around her ankles, her head held high. Her hair is caught up under a straw bonnet decorated with dried flowers around the rim.

'What do you think, Phil? Aren't we the perfect couple?' she says.

'You'd never know that your boyfriend used to be on the run and escaped the shooting squad less than a week ago!'

'That's settled, let's go for a saunter,' Nell says, and starts to lead Christopher away.

'You're a good man, Christopher Flinter. And we need good men. Talk to me when you're ready!' Shanahan calls after them.

It is a beautiful May day for a walk. Nell leads them down towards Amiens Street train station to avoid the ruin that is Sackville Street. They turn right and skirt the Custom House. The gunboat *Helga*, long and narrow and dangerous-looking, is tied up to the quay wall. The gunboat's target the previous week, Liberty Hall, is pocked with holes but is still standing. The Loop Line railway bridge, which the gunboat had to lob shells over, looks as if it too, has been hit by artillery fire. They cross Butt Bridge and walk up the quays of the Liffey, past Merchants Quay as far as Parliament Street.

Nell turns to Christopher. 'We can wait here — it'll probably come this way.'

'No, I've come this far. I want to make certain that I say my goodbyes, Nell — they could turn up to Christ's Church,' he replies and turns up the street towards the entrance.

The wide metal gates of Dublin Castle have been left open and there is a lot of military activity coming and going. Christopher looks at his watch: quarter to twelve.

On Dame Street nobody pays the young couple any heed and the soldiers, complacent after their victory over the rebels, loll around, their tunics unbuttoned, enjoying the sunshine.

Christopher and Nell find a good spot in the doorway of a building and wait.

At noon precisely an army lorry lumbers out through the gates and turns down Dame Street. As it slows to make a turn down towards the Liffey, Christopher blesses himself. Now he has a view into the back. Four soldiers are sitting on a bench with their back to the sides of the lorry, their legs resting on a plain wooden box: Byatt's coffin. They turn when they see Nell and shout out something that's lost in the noise coming from the lorry's straining engine. It's not difficult to make out that it is something lewd and Christopher begins to make a move towards the truck but is held back by Nell, much to the amusement of the soldiers.

As the lorry pulls away further into the distance, he remembers Byatt's advice: living well is the best revenge.

He turns to Nell. 'How would you like to see where I grew up?'

Nell stands back and studies his face. 'Is that not where all this started? In the Liberties?'

'It is. And that's where it's all going to end. Have you anything better to do?'

'Well, I was going to say we could go somewhere for a cup of tea. There're a few important things I have to talk to you about.'

'More dark secrets?' Christopher smiles. 'I thought you'd told me everything.'

'A girl always keeps certain things back,' Nell says, 'but I suppose it can wait. Why do you want to go back there?'

'I want to make my peace with Tommy Sherry, maybe press a few pounds on him, if he'll take it. Lying in the bed in the hotel, I've had time to think. He was only doing what any man would have done, I suppose, looking after his family. Afterwards we can go and have that talk you want.'

Nell clutches his arm again and he leads her up Dame Street towards The Liberties, past Christ's Church and on into Thomas Street. Arm in arm, they walk towards John's Lane church, the tall spires that dominate the entrance pointing up to the heavens.

Mass has just ended and crowds pour out onto the street. Some congregate in small groups around the entrance, swapping gossip or just enjoying a conversation with a neighbour they haven't seen in a while. An old priest walks among them, a hand held out here, a pat on the shoulders there. He approaches a small family, a young couple with two boys who cling to their mother's skirts, and talks to them. Christopher remembers the priest. When he was a boy, around their age, the priest probably would have done the same thing, towering over him and Ned, asking them if they were being good boys for their mother and father. The two boys are nodding to the priest and then bury their faces in their mother's skirts. He can feel Nell fidgeting at his side and he turns away from the scene.

Time for him to move on.

The End